DRAKON'S PROMISE
BLOOD OF THE DRAKON

DRAKON'S PROMISE

BLOOD OF THE DRAKON

N.J. WALTERS

Entangled Publishing, LLC
2614 South Timberline Road
Suite 109
Fort Collins, CO 80525
Visit our website at www.entangledpublishing.com.

Select Otherworld is an imprint of Entangled Publishing, LLC.

Edited by Heidi Shoham
Cover design by Kelly Martin
Cover art from Shutterstock

Manufactured in the United States of America

First Edition December 2016

For all of you who believe the dragon should be the hero of the story.

Chapter One

Music pounded through the giant speakers mounted high on every wall, and multi-colored lights flashed all around the crowded dance floor. From his seat in a dark corner of the nightclub, Darius Varkas watched. Bodies gyrated and hands groped as the dancers lost themselves in the booze, the drugs, and the music.

He was bored.

He spun the half-empty glass on the table in front of him and watched the amber-colored liquid swirl and catch the light. A woman wearing little more than chains for a top and what might pass for a napkin as a skirt sauntered up to him, her ruby lips turned up in a welcoming smile. It always astounded him how women could manage to walk in heels that tall and skinny. "Want some company?"

He didn't move. Didn't say a word. The woman's smile slowly faded, and she skittered away, going as fast as she could manage in her impractical shoes. She might not know why she was afraid of him, but she was right to be so. He wasn't totally human. And at times like these, he was more beast than man.

Emptiness ate at him. The cavern in his soul grew larger each passing day. Money was of little interest to him. He had more than he could ever spend, and it was easy enough to make. His business interests, which absorbed most of his waking hours, no longer held his attention.

It was a sign of his desperation that he'd come to the club tonight, something he rarely did, hoping to drive back his dark thoughts. But it hadn't done any good. The noise, the people, and the smells had only aggravated his already black mood.

The phone in his pocket vibrated. He almost ignored it, but only three people had this number. As much as he might want to, he wouldn't ignore his brothers.

He yanked the offensive piece of technology out of his pocket and thumbed the right button to answer the call. "What?" He didn't shout to be heard over the pounding rhythm of the music, knowing his brother could easily hear him.

"Hurt you to answer, didn't it?"

Darius swallowed his angry retort, knowing it would only encourage Tarrant to goad him more. Why his brother was obsessed with technology, he'd never know. "What do you want?"

"The Knights are back."

Fury replaced his annoyance. Darius stood and strode toward the door, his large strides eating up the distance, the music and his drink forgotten. He didn't pause and barely noticed the people scrambling to get out of his way. All he could think about was his brother's words. They beat at his brain until he wanted to roar his anger to the heavens.

Several people stumbled and fell to the floor in their haste. He simply walked over their prone bodies.

Darius could smell their fear, taste it. He knew what they saw when they looked at him. Clad in jeans and a black leather jacket, and standing almost seven feet tall, he was an intimidating sight. With the scowl on his face, he was something out of their nightmares.

He shoved the door open. The heavy metal panel slammed against the side of the building. The bouncer jumped and turned toward him but swallowed back whatever remark he'd been about to make. The patrons waiting outside the club backed up against the brick wall, many of them looking at the ground to avoid Darius's gaze.

He headed down the alley and out onto the sidewalk, glad to have left the stale atmosphere and noise of the club behind. He breathed in the crisp October air. It was tainted with car exhaust and the garbage that littered the streets of the city, but it was better than the stench of booze, chemicals, and sweat he'd left behind. Some days, he cursed his preternatural senses.

"Are you sure?" Even as he asked, he knew better. Tarrant would never have contacted him unless he was absolutely certain.

"Technology is good for some things, brother. I've picked up chatter while monitoring some very particular online sites."

There were places on the net that most people didn't realize even existed, used mostly by criminals, clandestine groups, and even some governments to keep conversations confidential. Tarrant knew where to find them all. Darius rubbed the back of his neck and started walking home. "Why now? Why after all this time?"

"We knew the Knights wouldn't stay gone forever. They're like cockroaches. Just when you think you've killed them all, another one pops up."

Darius almost smiled at Tarrant's comparison. "Keep me posted."

"You know I will."

"Have you contacted Ezra and Nicodemus?" He had no idea where his other two brothers were at the moment. They could be anywhere in the world.

"I did. I heard back from Ezra, but Nic still hasn't checked in."

That didn't surprise Darius. Nicodemus was probably somewhere warm, surrounded by adoring women. How his brother could stand being around people all the time was beyond him, but Nic seemed to enjoy it.

"Let me know when you hear from him."

"Will do."

"And, Tarrant. Be careful." Darius paused before crossing at the light. "I don't want to lose you."

"You watch your back," his brother warned.

"Always." Darius ended the call and shoved his phone back in his pocket. As he approached the glass and gilt luxury high-rise, the doorman leaped forward and pulled the door open.

"Good evening, Mr. Varkas."

He nodded. "John." He didn't pause and continued past the bank of elevators until he came to the one at the very end. This was his private entrance. He placed his hand on the palm-plate and waited until it verified his identity. He might not be fond of technology, but he damn well took advantage of it. When the doors silently slid open, he stepped inside.

The ride up to the penthouse took only seconds. The steel doors slid open and the lights came on as soon as he stepped inside. He was home. Just being here settled him. His gaze flowed around the room. There were floor-to-ceiling shelves on the far wall, containing treasures and mementos from his various trips around the world. The oversize sectional sofa and giant flat-screen television beckoned, but he bypassed them and headed straight to his office.

This was his personal sanctuary. Shelves lined all four walls, and many were packed with books. Tall, clear vases were filled with beach glass from every corner of the earth. Shards of pottery, much of it ancient, filled two shelves. Chunks of raw ore were scattered about. This was only the tip of the iceberg, his most personal possessions. He had much more housed in various vaults and homes around the world.

He stopped at the ornate wooden cabinet that served as his bar. It was inlaid with gold and had once belonged to an Egyptian pharaoh. It had been a gift from the man almost three thousand years ago. Taharqa had died young, but Darius had liked him. That was back when he'd still made friends with humans, before he'd watched too many of them grow old and die, or meet a violent death.

Darius poured some twenty-year-old Irish whiskey into a glass and tossed it back before pouring another. It was impossible for him to get drunk, but he did enjoy the burn and the taste. He went to the window and peered out over the city of New York. He'd made his home here for more than a decade. It would soon be time to move on.

He'd lived all over the globe, seen all the wonders of the world, including some that humans had never seen. He liked New York, the vibrancy of the place and the variety of people who populated the city. It was just starting to feel like home. He was tired of moving.

He swore and turned away from the lights and went to the nearest bookshelf. He let his fingers walk across the leather spines until he found what he was looking for. The leather binding was old and the pages inside yellow and brittle with age.

Darius sat in the leather chair he'd had custom built to accommodate his size, set his drink on the table beside it, and opened the book to the title page.

"Knights of the Dragon," he read aloud. "Knights of the Dragon, my ass." He guessed that Power-Hungry, Murderous Sorcerers wouldn't read as well to the members of the group or the public. The book had been written by a Catholic monk in the late thirteenth century. There had been many such books written since, but this was the oldest he knew of.

The fools didn't even know the difference between a dragon and a drakon. It had been four thousand years since the last dragon had left the world, leaving their sons behind, not caring enough to take them when they went.

Dragons were cold-blooded, cold-hearted, immensely powerful creatures who'd come through a portal from their home world. They'd temporarily taken the shape of men and mated with human females. Some of those women had borne sons—always sons. When the children had reached their teenage years, it had become evident there was something wrong with all of them. They weren't human, nor were they dragons. They were both.

They were drakons, sons of the dragons.

They had the cunning, strength, preternatural abilities, and instincts of the dragon, along with the intellect and emotions of a human. A deadly combination. And unlike their sires, their base form was that of a human. While their dragon fathers could hold a human form for a short span of time, a drakon could inhabit either human or dragon form indefinitely.

He closed the book and tossed it onto the table. It had been over a century since they'd had any trouble from the Knights, those self-proclaimed protectors of the innocent.

Darius surged to his feet and began to prowl around the room. What he really wanted to do was shapeshift, take to the skies, and fly. But the skies were a dangerous place for a drakon these days. Satellite imaging and radar made evading humans a bitch. There were still remote areas on the earth— hidden canyons, isolated deserts, the skies of the ice-bound poles, and crevices deep in the ocean—where a drakon could still fly, but New York was not one of those places.

His phone vibrated again and he quickly answered.

"What?"

"You really need to work on your manners, brother."

"Don't test me, Tarrant."

His brother sighed. "Nicodemus checked in. He's in Vegas."

Darius cursed under his breath. "Does he know the meaning of low profile?"

Tarrant chuckled. "I doubt it."

Their youngest brother would never change, but you'd think he'd be a little smarter after living for more than four thousand years. "Anything else?"

Darius heard a clicking noise and knew Tarrant was on his laptop, which was practically surgically attached to the man. "Nothing. But be careful. If they catch you—" Tarrant broke off, not speaking the words.

"You, too." He ended the call and stared out the window, seeing none of the beauty of the city at night. The Knights of the Dragon killed drakons, but they preferred to capture and enslave them for all time. The blood of a drakon could cure any illness. It also prolonged a human's life and gave him certain powers and abilities, which varied from human to human. Drakon blood was coveted among these people.

Most drakons who fell into the clutches of the Knights managed to either escape or end their own lives. Anything was better than permanent enslavement. He didn't want to even think about the ones who'd been captured. To imagine decades, even centuries, in captivity was too horrific for him to even consider.

Darius turned his back on the city, left his office, and went into his bedroom. He stripped off his clothing and tossed it onto the bench that sat at the end of his large custom-sized bed. Naked, he padded into the attached bathroom and stepped into the shower stall. He turned on the water and adjusted the stream until it was hot.

The spray beat down on him, washing away the odors from the nightclub that still clung to his skin. Drakons were solitary creatures by nature, preferring their own company — except for Nic, who for some strange reason seemed to enjoy people — but sometimes Darius grew lonely and sought out places where humans congregated. Over the centuries, he'd had sex with more women than he could remember, but none of them had ever satisfied the ache in his heart or filled the emptiness in his soul.

Unlike his father, Darius craved a mate. One of the few things his dragon sire had told him before he'd left was that dragons mated only once, and it was a very rare thing. When it happened, it was permanent. Eternal. Darius assumed the same held for him and his brothers. But they'd all given up hope of finding that one special woman long, long ago. The odds of finding such a woman were astronomical. Even if they did manage to do so, she'd be human, with a lifespan measured in decades, not millennia.

Of course, drakon blood could prolong life. They had no idea for how many years, but it did allow humans to live a much longer time. But Darius had honestly never met a woman he'd consider sharing his blood with. That would mean he trusted her not only with his secret, but with the lives of his brothers as well. And he just couldn't see that happening.

He grabbed the bar of handmade soap from the tiled shelf and rubbed it over his chest and arms, inhaling the soothing scent of sandalwood. The artisan who made the soap handcrafted it to his specifications, and Darius paid her very well to keep him supplied.

He might have fallen prey to what drakons called the Deep Sleep eons ago if not for his brothers. Many drakons couldn't bear the endless years alone and succumbed to the Deep Sleep, settling on mountaintops or beneath the oceans, falling into a deathlike slumber until their bodies finally turned to stone. No one knew if these drakons were even still alive after so long. None of them had ever awakened.

They might have had different mothers, but he and his brothers shared the same dragon sire. That family connection had brought them together when they were young. Over the years, it had forged into an unbreakable bond. It had helped keep them all sane and very much in this world.

He finished washing, turned off the water, and rested his hands against the slate tiles. The faucet dripped twice before stopping. He pushed away from the wall and stepped out of the shower stall. A stack of pristine white towels sat on the nearby shelf. Darius grabbed one and rubbed it over his hair and body before tossing it aside. Still damp, he went to his bedroom and threw himself down on his bed.

Why were the Knights back now? What were they planning? Whatever it was, Darius knew it didn't bode well for him or his brothers.

Chapter Two

Sarah Anderson tugged on the hem of her skirt and smoothed out some nonexistent wrinkles. It wasn't like her to be nervous. She was known for being levelheaded and calm.

"Mr. Temple will see you now." The man's personal assistant, a strikingly beautiful woman, smiled and nodded toward the double door that guarded the inner office.

Sarah stood, hitched her purse over her shoulder, and managed a smile. "Thank you." She strode to the door, trying to convey an air of confidence. She needed this job.

Taking a final deep breath to calm the butterflies in her stomach, she turned the handle and shoved the door open. The man sitting behind the desk motioned her in.

"Come in, Ms. Anderson. Come in."

Her sensible leather flats made no sound on the thick carpet. He gestured toward one of the two dark brown leather chairs that sat opposite him. "Please, have a seat. I'll be right with you." He turned back to his computer screen, giving her time to look around.

The office furniture was solid, like the man himself. From

her research, she knew Herman Temple was sixty years old, had reportedly inherited a fortune when he was in his twenties, and had added to it since, dabbling in everything from oil to technology, but mostly pharmaceuticals.

She wasn't a research librarian for nothing. She knew how to find information on anyone or anything. That was her specialty. Or it had been until downsizing at the New York Public Library had left her scrambling to find a new position.

She still didn't quite understand how that had happened. One day she'd been happily working, and the next she'd been unemployed. Thankfully, she did have outside contracts, so she still had some source of income. And it was one of those contacts that had led her to this job interview.

Mr. Temple closed his laptop and smiled at her. "Forgive me, but I had to get that email off quickly."

"That's fine," she assured him. She fiddled with the strap of her purse. When she realized what she was doing, she carefully set the bag down beside her.

Mr. Temple sat back in his large leather chair and stared across the broad expanse of his antique oak desk. His full head of white hair gave him a distinguished air. "I thought you'd be older."

She frowned. "Sir?"

He waved his hand in front of him. "For someone of your accomplishments, I thought you'd be older. Jeremiah speaks highly of you." Jeremiah Dent was a highly respected dealer in rare and antiquarian books, contracted by museums and wealthy clients to find certain volumes for their collections. He was also the one who'd put her onto this job.

Sarah relaxed slightly. This was one area of her life where she was confident. "I graduated from university when I was sixteen." When Mr. Temple raised an eyebrow, she continued. "I had my doctorate by the time I was twenty-one and went to work for the New York Public Library soon after. I was at the main branch for seven years. I've also done contract work for various museums and book dealers around the city. It's all on my resume," she reminded him.

He rested his elbows on the arms of his chair and steepled his hands in front of him. "Yes, I checked all your references."

Of course he had. She felt her cheeks warm and knew she was probably blushing.

"I've amassed quite a library over the course of my lifetime." His abrupt change of topic made her tense. "And that's added to what my family has collected over generations." He gave her a self-deprecating smile. "We're readers in my family, seekers of knowledge. Always have been."

She nodded, and the nervous butterflies in her stomach became excited ones. "I've heard about your library." Everyone who occupied the world of antiquarian books knew of the Temple library. It was one of, if not the best private collections in the world.

He nodded, as if he'd expected nothing less. "We have thousands of books, tens of thousands, as well as stone tablets, papyrus sheets, and scrolls from around the world. What we don't have is a comprehensive catalogue of what's in the collection. The last full inventory was made decades ago, and even that wasn't complete."

Sarah tried to contain her rising excitement, but her body was practically quivering at the thought of getting close to all those books. Some of them were one of a kind.

Mr. Temple smiled and his blue eyes sharpened. "I can see you're interested."

"Very," she told him honestly.

His gaze turned calculating. "Come with me." He stood, stepped out from behind his desk, and headed toward the door. Sarah grabbed her purse, jumped to her feet, and hurried after him. He moved fluidly, like a man half his age, and she lengthened her stride to keep up. He went down a long, quiet hallway before turning into another room.

She really needed to start working out if she couldn't keep up with a man more than twice her age. She bolted into a room and skidded to a halt just inside the door. The ceiling was slightly vaulted, going up at least fifteen feet. The room was the size of a small house. It had to be twenty-five feet wide and thirty feet long, maybe bigger. It was hard to tell with the bookcases towering around her. They filled the walls from floor to ceiling, and there were dozens of freestanding shelves taking up the floor space.

"This is incredible."

Mr. Temple chuckled. "I'm glad you approve." He headed to an area at the far end that held a desk with a computer and phone. Next to it sat a long, old-fashioned card catalogue. Several tall, thin windows let in the natural sunlight but didn't allow it to penetrate far enough to damage the books.

"This is where you'll work," he told her.

"I'm sorry?" He hadn't offered her the job, had he? Had she been too busy gawking at the books and missed something?

"If you take the job." He leaned against the edge of the desk and crossed his arms over his chest. Once again, she was taken by how much younger he seemed. "You're the best, and I need the best. I want this library catalogued." He picked up a sheet of paper from the desk. "This is how I want them listed. It's all standard with a few exceptions." He offered her another smile. "Some of our treasures are quite rare and defy conventional classification."

"Of course." Her head was spinning. This job was too good to be true. That gave her pause as she remembered what her grandmother had always told her. If something seems too good to be true, it probably is. But Sarah had bills to pay and needed this job.

"I need a curator, a caretaker for all this knowledge. It

will take you years to get through it all." He pushed away from the desk. "I also want you to set aside any books that seem particularly rare or interesting to you. I want to see them before they're shelved." He swept his hand out and gestured to the shelves towering around them. "This is only a start. There are three more floors like this and more books in storage. I need someone who can put their hands on the information I need when I need it." For a moment, his pleasant facade dropped and he narrowed his gaze, reminding her that he'd made money in business, a lot of it, and he hadn't made it because he was kind and unassuming.

"You work here and you work alone," he continued. "This computer is not hooked up to the internet, and your work will be automatically backed up on a separate external hard drive daily. You are never to remove a book or any information from my home. You turn your cell phone, purse, and coat in at security in the morning and get them back when you leave in the evening. The phone on the desk connects with security and my assistant if you need anything."

She frowned. That was a hell of a lot of security.

As if sensing her hesitation, he smiled again. "Many of these books are rare and irreplaceable. You understand?"

"Yes. Absolutely." The man was right to want to protect this amazing collection.

"My security measures may seem extreme, but my family has suffered losses over the years." He glanced around the room. "This is my legacy. Businesses come and go, but the knowledge in here is priceless."

Sarah could certainly relate to that. She understood books better than she did people.

He rattled off a salary and benefits package that was very generous and much more substantial than the one she'd had at the library. "When can you start?"

It annoyed her he didn't ask if she even wanted the job,

but simply assumed she did. That irritation disappeared in the next breath when she thought about spending the next few years of her life, maybe longer, lost among all these amazing books.

"Now. I can start now." She laughed. "Or tomorrow."

Mr. Temple was studying her intently and a cold shiver raced down her spine. "Tomorrow will be soon enough," he told her.

· · ·

A little over a week later, Sarah sat at her desk making another entry into her computer. The task ahead of her was daunting, to say the least. She'd decided to tackle the job one shelf at a time. Any book that was misfiled was set aside on a cart to be shelved when she finally reached that section. It was time-consuming to examine each book, match it to the card in the catalogue, and then enter it on the computer. She'd decided to use both the computerized and non-computerized systems. If something ever happened to the electronic version, at least the physical catalogue would be up-to-date as well. She also color-coded the card in the catalogue as she finished with it. When she was finally done with her daunting task, if there were any cards that weren't marked, she would know the books were missing.

As instructed, each day she made a pile of particularly interesting or rare books on the corner of her desk. In the morning, if the books were still there, she shelved them and moved on. Mr. Temple always left a note on top of the pile to let her know he'd examined them.

She closed the book she'd just entered into the system and rolled her shoulders. The problem with this kind of work was that she got so focused she forgot to take breaks. She'd have to start setting an alarm to remind herself to get up and walk around and have a drink.

Victoria Marshall, Mr. Temple's personal assistant, poked her head into the room. "I'm going out to pick up something for lunch. Can I get you anything?"

Sarah smiled and shook her head. "No, I'm good, thanks."

Victoria sauntered up to the desk and perched on the corner. The other woman was always stylishly dressed in the latest fashions and footwear, and her makeup was flawless whether it was eight in the morning or quitting time. Today, she was wearing a fitted pearl-gray suit with a hint of pink peeking out from between the lapels. Her shoes were also gray, and the height of the heels made Sarah wince.

In contrast, Sarah wore plain black slacks and a long-sleeved white blouse topped with a charcoal-gray cardigan. Comfortable black leather flats covered her feet. She'd applied a pale pink lip-gloss this morning but it was probably long gone by now. Yet, despite their obvious differences, Victoria had been welcoming and kind to her.

"I don't know how you do it." She peered over Sarah's shoulder. "Alone here with all these books. I'd be bored out of my mind in less than a day."

Sarah laughed, not taking offense. Victoria wasn't the first person at a loss to understand her chosen profession. "And if I had to answer phones, deal with people and the million details you attend to in the run of a day, I'd go mad."

Victoria grinned. "I'll never have to worry about you trying to steal my job."

Sarah shuddered. "Never."

"And your job is safe from me." Victoria pushed off the desk. "The boss wants lunch from his favorite restaurant, and they don't deliver."

"He really keeps you busy." Mr. Temple seemed nice enough, but there was no denying the man made her nervous. Thankfully, she only saw him in passing. He was always at work in his office when she arrived and still at it when she left for the day.

"That he does." Victoria straightened her jacket. "Sure you don't want me to bring you back anything?"

"Positive, but thanks. I appreciate it."

"No problem." If I don't see you before you leave for the day, have a good weekend."

"You, too." She'd almost forgotten it was Friday. She'd worked last Saturday, mostly just familiarizing herself with the setup and her new position. She'd started in earnest on Monday and was completing her first full week.

She went back to work, losing herself in it until her stomach grumbled. She saved her work and glanced at her watch, surprised to discover that Victoria has left her almost an hour ago.

Sarah stood and stretched. Coffee—she desperately needed coffee. The cup sitting next to her had gone cold hours ago. She was always careful about having a drink around the books, making sure it was in a covered thermal mug. If by some fluke it tipped over, it wouldn't damage the books or her computer.

And food. She needed to eat something. Her friends at the library had always complained she was too thin because she forgot to eat when she was working.

Sarah grabbed her mug, left her work behind, and headed toward the staff kitchen. It was down the hallway, close to Mr. Temple's office. She admired the tall, narrow windows, deep alcoves, intricate crown molding, and the countless small details that marked the building as historic. The stately old building was not only Mr. Temple's workplace, but also his home. It had belonged to his family for several generations. The first two floors were devoted purely to business, and Victoria had told her the third story was his personal home and completely off-limits to staff, which made sense. The separation between home and work was no doubt important to the man.

The staff kitchen was empty when she entered. As far as she knew, only she and Victoria used this one. It only took her seconds to brew a fresh cup of Belgian chocolate coffee—the single-cup brewer and assortment of coffees was a perk of the job that she enjoyed.

She pulled the ham and cheese sandwich she'd brought with her this morning out of the refrigerator and sat at the table. It was quiet. She was used to the steady murmur of voices at the public library. There was an empty quality to this silence that was slightly unnerving. She quickly finished her sandwich and cleaned up her mess. Time to get back to work. A quick glance at her watch reminded her she only had two more hours until quitting time.

Mr. Temple was quite strict about his employees leaving on time. Sarah worked from eight to four, and if she didn't show up at the main door by the appointed time, security would come to remind her. The first evening it happened, she'd been surprised, but when she'd asked Victoria about it, the woman had simply shrugged and told her to count her lucky stars her employer didn't expect her to put in unpaid overtime.

Sarah assumed it had to do with the fact that the building was also Mr. Temple's private residence. The man probably wanted the space to himself at the end of a long day. She could understand that.

She grabbed her mug and left the break room to head back to the library. The sound of loud voices broke the silence and startled her so badly she fumbled her coffee and just managed to catch her mug before she dropped it. She immediately recognized Mr. Temple's voice but not the other man's. His office door must be open.

Not wanting to eavesdrop, she turned in the direction of

the library but couldn't help overhearing their conversation.

"Don't give me excuses. I want Darius Varkas, and I want him now. I've spent years and millions of dollars tracking down one of his kind." Mr. Temple was angry, and the voices were getting closer. There was no way she could make it back to the library before they saw her.

Sarah ducked into an alcove and held her breath, hoping they wouldn't discover her. She hated confrontation of any kind.

"I need the book." The other man's tone was calmer. "The quicker the better."

"We'd still have the book if you hadn't told your friend Rames about it." Mr. Temple was obviously very unhappy. "Don't bother denying it. There's no other way he could have known about it. That no longer matters. What matters is finding the book. It has to be here. There is no way it could have left the house. Security is too tight."

"But you also have so many damn books it's like looking for a needle in a haystack. Are you sure this librarian is any good?"

Sarah tightened her fingers around her mug. They were searching for a specific book. Why hadn't Mr. Temple told her that? And it sounded to her like someone had purposely taken it. But why? Just what book were they referring to?

"Jeremiah Dent told me there are rumors about Ms. Anderson. According to him, she has a very special knack when it comes to books."

Her stomach tightened. She hadn't told anyone about her ability. How had Jeremiah Dent discovered it? Only her grandmother had known about her gift, and she'd passed away several years ago.

Psychometry was the official name. All Sarah knew was that from the time she was young, if she touched a particular item and focused on it, she could pick up information about the people who'd used it. She had a special affinity for books, which was why she always wore thin latex gloves when touching the very old ones. It was easy enough to do. When dealing with old and rare books, it was to protect them from the oils from her skin, which could damage the fragile paper and binding.

She didn't wear them when she was working with more modern books. The newer the book, the less energy attached to it, and the easier it was for her to naturally block any vibes she might pick up. She didn't think Victoria or Mr. Temple had actually seen her wearing her protective gloves.

Now that she thought about it, Jeremiah Dent had always been particularly interested in her work when she researched and dated books for him. Had he seen her touch one of his rare books and go into a trance? Well, she wouldn't quite call it a trance. She didn't know what it was. The world simply fell away, and she saw scenes of the people and places that had touched the object. It helped her date an item, sometimes pointing her in the right direction to find the necessary documentation she needed. She was always careful, but there was no way of knowing what Mr. Dent had seen, and he'd obviously seen something. Enough to suspect she was using more than just her education and research skills to authenticate artifacts.

"She'd better work fast. If not, you'll have to persuade her," the unknown man said.

That didn't sound good at all. In fact, it sounded rather threatening. She'd known this job was too good to be true. The voices were getting closer. She backed deeper into the alcove and tried to make herself smaller.

"I want Varkas. Our contact in the military is getting impatient, and our scientists are waiting to get their hands on a blood sample. Once we have him, we'll have an endless supply of it." Mr. Temple's laugh made her own blood run cold. They were talking about kidnapping a man and using him for experiments.

Surely she couldn't have heard him right. But Mr. Temple had mentioned spending a lot of money trying to find one of Varkas's kind. What exactly did he mean by that?

"The last subject self-terminated. I didn't think the old boy had it in him after so many years."

"And that was your mistake, Christian. You underestimated him and got lax. Not only that, it was your unfortunate choice of companions that led to the loss of the book. If you weren't my son, you'd be dead."

Sarah slapped her free hand over her mouth and struggled not to hyperventilate. The sandwich she'd just eaten curdled in her stomach and threatened to come back up.

"Fortunately, I am your son. Don't worry, find the book, and I'll get Varkas for you. I've got people watching him. He's not going anywhere without our knowing. We can't move until we're 100 percent ready to take him down. There can be no mistakes. We'll only get one shot at him. And the last thing we want to do is attract any unwanted attention." The voices drifted away, and Sarah's knees went weak. Her skin was clammy, and she felt faint.

She sucked in a breath, gathered the tattered remnants of her courage, and carefully peeked around the corner of the alcove. Seeing no one, she hurried as fast as her legs could carry her back to the library. Her hand was shaking when she set her mug on the desk and fell into her seat.

She leaned forward and put her head between her legs. "Oh God. Oh God. Oh God," she muttered under her breath. What had she gotten herself into? She forced herself to breathe in and out. Once she was sure she wasn't going to puke, she sat back in her chair. A bead of sweat rolled down her forehead in spite of the coolness of the room.

She ignored the coffee and reached for the bottle of water she'd brought with her this morning. The liquid was warm, but her fingers weren't trembling quite as hard by the time she'd had a few sips. She screwed the cap back on and tried to gather her thoughts.

Okay, Mr. Temple and his son wanted her to find a specific book. One someone else had hidden or misplaced. A book that sought after would have to be very important. That meant it would have a lot of energy surrounding it.

Sarah stood and walked around to stand in front of her desk. The task ahead of her was daunting. She had to find that book, whatever it was. She also had to find and contact this Darius Varkas, whoever he was, and warn him before it was too late.

For the first time since she'd walked into this building, she concentrated on intentionally lowering the walls she'd built in her mind to protect herself from the constant bombardment of unwanted images and information. Because of her affinity with books, she didn't always have to touch them in order to see the energy emanating from them. Her grandmother, who'd also had the talent, had taught her how to protect herself. Because, really, who wanted to go through life seeing auras shining from almost everything they encountered?

She'd often wondered why she was more attuned to books instead of jewelry or art. Her grandmother had speculated that books were incredibly personal, especially in the case of ancient handwritten texts and diaries. But even those who only read the books and touched each page left emotional traces behind.

The books around her began to radiate the energy that had been left behind by the countless people who'd handled them over the years. Most gave off a soft glow, but a small few were surrounded by a darkness that frightened her. She'd encountered these kinds of vibes rarely over the years, and it never boded well when she did.

"You can do this." The pep talk didn't help. If she thought

it would work, she'd quit her job and move away. But Herman Temple had the money, power, and contacts to find her. She was no spy, able to cover her tracks. She was a normal person, a librarian with a little extra gift. No, if she was going to get out of this situation alive, she needed leverage, and maybe an ally or two.

Mr. Temple and his son seemed to think nothing of breaking the law. Just remembering how easily they'd discussed killing someone and kidnapping another left her queasy again. They were evil, pure and simple.

She'd just started to head down an aisle when she sensed she wasn't alone. She turned and found Mr. Temple standing in the doorway watching her.

Chapter Three

Sarah tried to act natural, but that was beyond her. "Mr. Temple. I didn't hear you come in." She was grateful she always acted nervous around the man. Hopefully, he wouldn't notice the terror making her tremble inside.

"No, you seemed absorbed in your work." He came toward her, and it took everything in her not to break and run. "It's going well?"

She nodded and swallowed. "Yes. I've made a good start, but it's a huge job."

He nodded, his smile seeming more sly than friendly, his blue eyes piercing rather than kind. "Seen any books in particular that interest you?"

She shook her head and then nodded. "None in particular, but all of the books are interesting, if you know what I mean?" She had to get a grip on herself. "I'm doing the computer cataloguing of the books but decided to update the card catalogue as well. That way, if something happens to the electronic data, you still have hard files to fall back on."

Mr. Temple nodded. "That's actually a very good idea."

He stood only a few feet away now and seemed to loom over her. "I started at the first shelf next to the desk and decided I'd systematically work my way around the room."

He turned away from her and ran his fingers over the spines of the books. His movements were ordinary, but she sensed a controlled violence in him that made her shiver. "You should take a few hours and wander around the room— the other two rooms as well, and see if you find anything particularly interesting."

Her throat tightened and her knees went weak. She forced her legs to stiffen and prayed her voice would work. "I'll do that." She rubbed her moist palms on her pants legs. "Was there something specific you wanted?" After all, this was the first time he'd ventured into the library since she'd started work.

He turned around, and she tried to look normal. He shook his head. "No. I just want to make sure everything is moving forward without a hitch."

"It's going really well."

Mr. Temple canted his head to one side and studied her. His eyes missed nothing. She hoped there weren't any beads of sweat on her forehead. "I can see that." He turned away to leave the room. "Spend the rest of the day looking around the library to familiarize yourself with where everything is. I may have a list of books I want you to find on Monday."

"Absolutely, sir. Whatever you need, I can find."

He paused by the doorway and pinned her in place with his gaze. "Good. That's very good."

He left, but she didn't believe for a moment he'd gone far. She forced herself to go back to her desk and take a sip of her coffee. Struggling to act normal, she began to stroll around the cavernous room, pausing here and there to pick up a volume.

Finally, after what seemed like forever, she heard the faint tread of footsteps as he moved away. She slumped against one of the shelves and closed her eyes for a brief moment. Her blouse was stuck to her skin, and she shivered even though she was wearing a cardigan over it. She was cold to her bones.

Whatever book Mr. Temple and his son wanted her to find was valuable enough for them to kill. The information in it must be very special, and very dangerous. Most people thought it was money that ruled the world. Sarah knew better. It was information, pure and simple. And she was the best when it came to ferreting out information.

Which was why she was in this mess in the first place. If she weren't the best, she would never have been contacted for this job.

She couldn't go back in time and change things. She had to deal with the situation at hand. It was time to use her brain and, thankfully, she had a very good one.

Leverage. If she was going to survive, she needed something that would give her an edge. She needed a better understanding of Herman Temple and his son, needed to know what drove them to do what they did. The first step toward that end was finding the book they were searching for.

She opened her senses and peered around the room with fresh eyes. The section with religious texts caught her eyes. Many of the books pulsed with light, but there was one book that emitted a strange combination of both light and dark energy.

She slowly worked her way around the room, careful not to hurry. Paranoia was setting in, and she wondered if the room might be wired with cameras. The thought of someone watching her while she worked gave her the creeps.

She finally stood in front of the shelf with the unusual book. It was a Bible. She drew out the large volume and stroked the old leather binding. The title, which was in Latin, was etched in gold leaf. She opened the cover, careful to use just the tips of her fingers, and turned to the first page. It had been published in the seventeen hundreds in France. She turned the pages and was caught by the beautiful hand-drawn illustrations. This was obviously a specially commissioned book and would have cost a small fortune to produce.

Focus, she reminded herself. It was all too easy to lose herself in the books, but that was dangerous. She needed to be sharp. She was just about to close and reshelf the leather-bound Bible when she realized there was something stuck between the pages near the middle of the large volume.

She struggled to balance the big book and turn the pages. Her heart almost stopped when the pages fell back to reveal a slender volume covered in soft leather. Pure darkness enveloped the small text.

Sarah dropped the Bible, desperate not to touch the tainted volume hidden inside it. Horrified at what she'd done, she fell to her knees, praying she hadn't damaged the fragile religious text. She started to pick up the Bible and the smaller book toppled forward and landed almost in her lap.

The dark energy pulsated, and in spite of her fear and horror, she wanted to touch it, to know what was inside.

"Everything all right, Ms. Anderson?" She recognized the voice of the security guard.

Without thinking about the implications of her actions, she grabbed the smaller volume and shoved it under her cardigan, tucking it into the waistband of her slacks.

"I'm fine," she told him as he drew closer. "Just clumsy. That's what I get for trying to turn the pages of a book this large without putting it on a desk first. I was just so taken with the illustrations." And she was babbling. She shut her mouth.

"What book is it?"

She wasn't imagining the guard's keen interest. Was he part of whatever Mr. Temple was involved in? It stood to reason he might be. Everyone here might be involved, including Victoria.

Sarah thrust the book toward the guard, and he automatically took it. "It's a lovely Bible from the seventeen hundreds with hand-drawn plates. Probably commissioned by a very wealthy man or a member of the aristocracy."

The guard scowled and thrust the book back at her as soon as she stood and dusted off the knees of her pants. "I hope I didn't damage it." She took the volume and ran her hands over the cover and spine.

"It's time for you to go," the guard informed her. Like the rest of the security team that worked here, he was tall and fit and carried a rather scary-looking gun strapped to his belt.

"Already?" She shelved the book and headed to her desk. "I do get lost in my work."

The guard followed her back to her desk and waited as she shut down her computer. The small leather-bound volume was practically burning a hole through her clothes. She was going to steal a book. She almost hesitated. She could run to the bathroom and hide the manuscript in there until Monday and then return it.

Then she thought about the man Mr. Temple and his son wanted to abduct and run experiments on. Whatever was going on might be tied to this book. If it weren't, she'd find a way to anonymously return it at some point in the future.

"Ms. Anderson?"

"Sorry." She flashed the guard a smile. "It's hard for me to transition from work. My mind is still on that gorgeous old Bible."

The guard frowned but nodded as he escorted her from the library to the entrance. She paused at the security booth just inside the front door, and the other guard passed out her belongings.

She pulled on her warm wool coat, shoved her phone into her purse, and then hooked the leather strap over her shoulder. With every passing second, she expected the guards to grab her and accuse her of stealing. She wasn't cut out for this kind of subterfuge.

"Have a good weekend." She waved at both men and felt their gaze on her as she walked down the steps to the sidewalk.

Evening was closing in fast, and she hurried to the subway station. The cool air brushed over her face, making her shiver. She shoved her hands into the pockets of her coat and pressed them against her stomach, feeling the outline of the book.

She wanted to look over her shoulder but didn't dare. She melded with the sea of humanity and waited on the platform. A short five minutes later, she was on the subway, hurtling along the tracks toward home. She got off at the right stop and made the trek to her apartment building. She didn't mind the commute. It gave her time to think. Plus, owning a car didn't make much sense when she lived in the heart of the city. It was too expensive to justify when there was public transportation readily available.

By the time she stumbled through her front door, she was shaking with fear. She was also totally paranoid. She went straight into her bedroom, not bothering to turn on any lights. Outside her third-story window, she saw a dark SUV slowly drive by. Whether it had anything to do with her or not, she had no idea, but she wasn't taking any chances.

She grabbed her leather knapsack and set it on the bed. She transferred the contents of her purse into the larger bag. Then she unbuttoned her coat and drew out the book from beneath her sweater. It pulsed in her hands, the dark energy creeping up her fingers. She quickly dumped it into her knapsack and added a notebook and pen.

She wanted a shower in the worst way but knew time was of the essence. She quickly changed into jeans, a warm sweater, and boots before pulling on her coat once again.

At the last second, she turned on the light in the living

room and pulled her drapes. The soft glow would hopefully make anyone watching think she was home for the evening. She slung the knapsack over her shoulders and left her apartment, going all the way to the basement and out the back door.

She headed for the one place in the city she felt safe—the New York Public Library.

• • •

Someone was following him. Darius didn't look behind, didn't have to. He'd known for several days now that someone was tracking his every move. He'd counted at least four different men keeping a close eye on him every time he left his home.

The Knights of the Dragon had found him. What he didn't understand was why they hadn't made a move to apprehend him? What were they waiting for? Perhaps they weren't 100 percent sure he was a drakon and were watching to see if they could confirm. He'd learned years ago not to try to understand the reasoning or motivation behind any of their actions.

It was time for him to take measures to protect everything he'd built over his long lifetime. He kept his gait normal. His mind, however, was working fast and furious, cataloguing everything he needed to do.

By the time he entered his company headquarters fifteen minutes later, he knew what had to be done. "I want Carl in my office five minutes ago," he told his assistant.

"I'm on it, sir," the young man replied.

Darius removed his wool coat and tossed it over the back of his chair. He wouldn't be here long. He'd dressed for business, not battle. All the better to lull the men watching him into thinking he had no idea they were there. Imbeciles.

He reached into his desk and pulled out a disposable phone and punched in Tarrant's number. His brother answered on the second ring. "Yes."

"I've got men watching me." He peered out his window at the Manhattan skyline. He liked the view, but it was time for a change.

"Shit. You need to get out of there."

"Not yet. I need to know who's behind this. There has to be a money source. I need to find it and plug it." He turned away from the window, ambled over to his desk chair, and sat.

"That's too dangerous, Darius," his brother objected. "What if they're government?"

"If they were, they wouldn't be waiting. It has to be the Knights. They're either waiting for someone or something, or they're not 100 percent certain I'm a drakon. They can't exactly kidnap a prominent businessman and not expect it to go unnoticed. They'd want to be very sure before they took me. And they'd wait for the best time and location. I don't exactly live in an isolated area, and I wouldn't go down without a hell of a fight. The more information I have, the better for all of us," he reminded Tarrant.

"I don't like this."

Of course he didn't. Tarrant lived like a true dragon in a lair in the Cascade Mountains in Washington State. His home was anything but primitive, though. He had every modern comfort and the latest in electronic equipment. Hell, Tarrant even had his own satellite in space, or rather the communications empire he'd built did. Tarrant tapped into it whenever he needed to.

"I'm selling my company."

Tarrant whistled. "That's a big step."

"But a necessary one. If I go missing for months or years, my business would flounder. I have things set up so my investments can practically run themselves and continue to make money." He employed a very old and respected firm that had handled his affairs for several hundreds of years, even if they didn't realize they'd been working for the same man for all that time.

It was better for all concerned if it stayed that way.

"I need to have all my attention on the Knights. I can't afford to split my time. We don't know anything about this particular group, but Knights in the past weren't worried about killing bystanders." And Darius didn't want more innocent blood on his hands.

"I understand."

Darius knew his brother did indeed understand. They'd all lost human friends over the centuries to members of this dark cult. "If I'm gone for too long, see to my investments and have my belongings stored."

"Of course." Darius could hear the familiar tapping in the background as Tarrant continued to work on his computer while they talked. "You're not afraid I'll steal them from you?"

Darius laughed, as his brother meant him to. Drakons were notorious for hoarding their wealth. He would trust no one else with his life's earnings. "I'm more afraid of what you'll invest my money in if I disappear."

"All the more incentive to escape if that happens." Tarrant grew serious. "Do you want me to come to New York? I can be there in a matter of hours." They all had private jets, so there would be no delay while he waited for a commercial flight.

"Thank you, but I'd rather you didn't. If the Knights don't know about you, let's keep it that way."

A knock on his office door made him pause. "Enter." Carl Green, his senior lawyer, strode in. Darius motioned him to take a seat. "I've got to go," he told his brother. "But I'll keep you up to date."

"Fuck. Be careful."

"I will. I'll call again soon," he promised.

"Every six hours," Tarrant demanded. They might not see

each other as much as they once had, but they were still close.

"I'll talk to you then." He ended the call and set the phone on his desk. He'd dispose of it later.

"What can I do for you, boss? Jeremy seemed to think it was urgent."

"I'm selling off our assets, Carl, and shutting down the office."

The other man's mouth dropped open, and he paled. "You can't be serious?"

Darius steepled his fingers and simply stared at his lawyer.

"Okay, so you are serious. Why?"

"Because it's time." He made it a habit never to explain himself. The less people knew about him, the better. "I want job security included in the sale for anyone who wants it. For those who wish to look elsewhere for work, there will be a generous severance package."

Carl pulled a small pad out of his pocket and began jotting notes.

"Contact Kade Ellis at Ellis Explorations and Gideon Westmont at Westmont Mines. Both men will jump at the chance to buy our mines and exploration rights."

"What do I tell them when they ask why you're selling?" Carl held his hands up in mock surrender when Darius frowned. "You know they're going to ask."

Darius sighed and nodded. "Tell them I'm having health problems." That wasn't exactly a lie. If the Knights of the Dragon captured him, his life and continued health would definitely be in jeopardy.

"Damn. I'm sorry to hear that, Darius. Is there anything I can do?" Carl asked, his concern genuine.

Darius shook his head. "Just handle this as quietly and quickly as possible. Tell no one and speak only to Kade and Gideon directly. I don't want this getting out into the media until it's a done deal."

"Got it." Carl jumped to his feet. "I'll contact them immediately." He paused by the door. "I'm really sorry, Darius. Are you sure you want to do this?"

"I have to." He let the other man draw his own conclusions. Faulty ones to be sure, but it was better than telling him the truth. The less Carl knew the better.

When Carl closed the door behind him, Darius picked up his phone and called his youngest brother. It rang four times before being dumped to voicemail.

He hung up and punched in another number. It was answered on the first ring. "Hey, Ezra."

"What's wrong?" Darius couldn't help but smile. Ezra was the most intense of his brothers, and that was saying something, all things considered. He was also as reclusive as Tarrant, maybe more so. He lived on a private island off the coast of Maine, near his beloved ocean. Ezra was a water drakon.

"Just wanted to hear your voice."

"Tarrant told me what was going on. You need to get out of the city now. Come out to the coast with me. Better yet, head to the desert or the mountains somewhere. Hell, go hang out with Tarrant in his Batcave." The reference to the lair of the fictional superhero made Darius smile in spite of the gravity of the situation.

"I'll be sure to let our brother know how you referred to his beloved fortress. You know he's not fond of the Dark Knight." Tarrant disliked anything to do with knights of any kind, even if it was only a nickname for a fictional character. He'd been known to bid on priceless suits of armor only to destroy them in the most inventive ways before melting them down into globs of metal. And they all knew not to get him started on the Knights of the Round Table.

"The Knights of the Dragon aren't a joke, Darius," Ezra reminded him. "They've killed too many of our kind since their inception."

Darius could hear waves crashing in the background and knew his brother was outside, probably needing the water to calm him. "I know, believe me. The last thing I want is to be captured by those lunatics and bled dry. But I have to know who they are and how much they know." He had to protect his brothers at all cost.

"Just be careful. Promise me you'll leave if you even think they're going to make a move on you."

"I'll be careful." He had billions of dollars in savings, vaults full of precious metals and priceless jewels, but they weren't his greatest treasure. That title belonged to his brothers. And like any drakon, he'd do whatever it took to protect his treasure.

Darius tossed the phone onto his desk, took a deep breath, and rolled up his sleeves. He had a lot of work to do and not a lot of time to do it in.

Chapter Four

The library had already closed, but Sarah had connections. All the security guards knew her, as she'd often worked after hours over the years. She'd bypassed her former boss and contacted one of the senior staff instead, citing her need to do research for a client. Her former colleague had hesitated, but Sarah had pushed, telling the other woman she was on a deadline. In the end, she'd left word with security to allow Sarah inside.

It had taken her more time to make the arrangements than she'd hoped. She'd spent the time drinking way too much coffee at a small shop a few streets away and worrying about the situation she'd inadvertently found herself in.

Now that she was here in the library, she wound her way through the stacks and found a quiet corner. Only then did she sit on the floor and open her knapsack. The book she'd stolen from Mr. Temple pulsed with dark energy. She really didn't want to touch it, but knew she had no choice. Maybe this book had nothing to do with what was going on with Mr. Temple and his son. It was all speculation at this point.

But the fact that it had been hidden inside a book of such power and light was suspicious. Someone had known this book was dangerous and had tried to hide it, hoping the pure energy from the Bible would dampen the dark emanations from the smaller book.

From the argument she'd overheard this afternoon, Mr. Temple wanted her to find a specific book, one that would somehow help him kidnap a man. She guessed such an object would have very dark energy, and this book certainly fit the bill. How it could help Mr. Temple and his son carry out their nasty plan, she had no idea.

Sarah took a deep breath, centered herself, and wrapped her hands around the faded leather binding. She lowered her protective shields, and the blast of psychic energy whipped her head back. She gritted her teeth and tried to control it. The darkness swirled around her wrists, as if trying to find purchase.

She did what her grandmother had taught her and surrounded herself with white light. The dark energy recoiled and wrapped itself around the book once again. She heaved a sigh of relief but didn't relax, not for one second.

The intensity of the memories radiating from this volume was unlike anything she'd ever come across. It was—dare she say it—alive. The slender, leather-bound manuscript felt more like a sentient thing than an inanimate object. Still, that didn't mean this particular book had anything to do with Mr. Temple's quest. A book this old was certain to have memories trapped in the pages.

There was nothing on the cover of the book, so she opened it. "*Knights of the Dragon: Necessary Incantations and Spells.*" Not what she'd been expecting. She flipped through the pages, which were all handwritten in what looked to be a combination of Latin, Spanish, and French. She'd have to do some translating. Her language skills were a little rusty, although she'd taken both Latin and French in university because many old books were written in those languages.

"You're procrastinating," she muttered. She leaned against the bookshelf and closed her eyes. She focused on the book, the supple leather binding faded from many years and much handling. The pages were yellowed but undamaged, the writing masculine and bold. She dropped her shields just a little, and images began to bombard her.

Men in brown robes who made her think of medieval monks stood in a dank stone room that reminded her of an ancient castle. She could smell the damp and mildew, feel the chill in the air.

Her eyes popped open, and she took a deep breath. Her visions had never been this vivid before. Usually, they were like photographs from the past in black and white and shades of gray. This felt all too real.

Still, she was committed to uncovering the book's secrets. There was no turning back.

She closed her eyes again and concentrated. She was immediately swept back to the stone room. The men, thirteen in all—the ominous number sent a shiver down her spine— were in a circle. She assumed they were all men. It was difficult to tell, given the robes they were wearing, but considering the age of the book it made sense to assume they were mostly, if not all, men. Only two torches lit the room, keeping most of it in shadow. They were chanting something in a language she didn't immediately recognize.

She caught a few words and realized it seemed to be a combination of languages, like the text in the book itself. She caught some Latin, French, English, and what she thought might be Spanish. Their voices were low but gained volume as they continued.

Sarah moved closer. There was something in the center of the circle. She could sense it, but the darkness of the room kept it hidden. Suddenly, more torches sprang to life, though none of the men had moved to light them.

Even though she wasn't really there, and this was simply part of the past, Sarah was freaked out. It was like a scene out of a horror movie. She expected to see something gruesome in the center of the men.

She angled to the left to get a better view. "Oh my God," she whispered. She'd been expecting a human sacrifice of some kind, most likely a woman, but this was beyond anything she could have imagined.

Heavy chains wrapped around a creature's legs and neck, and giant steel stakes had been pounded into the stone floor to secure them. More chains strapped down his giant tail and body. The beast raised his head as high as he was able and gave a roar that shook the entire room. Sarah jumped back, but the men surrounding the creature were unfazed.

This had to be a dream. It couldn't be a true memory. The flat, triangular head, the folded wings, and leathery scales belonged to something out of myth and legend—a dragon. But dragons weren't real. They were nothing more than a work of fiction.

But the book had been in this place with these men, otherwise she wouldn't be seeing it.

Her gift never lied.

One of the men lifted his arms and began to chant again. The large sword he held gleamed in the torchlight. He brought the thick blade down and sliced into the dragon's flesh. The creature jerked back at the last second, and the sword hit the thick armor-like skin and not the more vulnerable neck.

The man yelled instructions to his cohorts. They grabbed the chains and began to pull on them, yanking the dragon lower until he was helpless to stop them. Why didn't he breathe fire on them? Why didn't he fight?

As though he'd heard her thoughts, the dragon turned his

head and stared at her. *"I am weak. I have been captive for many years."* The voice in her head startled her. It couldn't be real, yet she'd heard it all the same.

The man with the sword managed to drive the blade into the dragon's neck. Sarah gasped, and tears filled her eyes as blood poured from the wound. The leader of the group thrust a large silver bowl beneath the flow.

"I am a drakon, not a dragon," the voice calmly told her. *"I need fire. Help me."*

Sarah didn't hesitate. She knew exactly what the creature needed. It didn't matter that this was nothing more than a glimpse of a memory from the past. She needed to help the dragon. No, he'd called himself a drakon.

Empathy for the creature welled up inside her, and she rushed to one of the torches, pulled it from its metal holder, and tossed it toward the drakon. The beast opened his mouth and caught the torch, swallowing it whole.

The men cried out and scattered, trying to get out of the way. The fire seemed to build inside the drakon, consuming him from the inside out. It burst through his skin, burning him alive.

Sarah slapped her hand over her mouth to keep from screaming aloud. What had she done? The beast looked at her and smiled. Then his entire body exploded like a nuclear bomb.

She was jerked back to reality, but not before the hood of the robed leader fell back. His eyes burned into her as he looked in her direction.

Sarah dropped the book and scuttled away. It lay on the floor looking totally harmless, but she knew better. What had just happened had shaken her to her very core. The man who'd glared at her, who'd seemed to see her at the last second, was Mr. Temple. But that was impossible. Wasn't it?

Was the scene she'd viewed more recent than she'd

thought? It had seemed much older.

She was totally confused. What she did know for sure was that the men who owned and used this book were evil. She didn't believe the creature was real. Maybe her own beliefs and fantasies were playing a part in what she'd seen. She ignored the fact that nothing like that had ever happened before.

Because if what she'd seen was real, dragons existed. And that was another thing—why would the creature call itself a drakon if he were conjured from her own subconscious mind? She'd never even heard the word before.

But blood had been deliberately spilled in the presence of the book. And Herman Temple and his son were searching for a man named Darius Varkas. For whatever reason, they wanted his blood. She couldn't let that happen.

Now that she knew the truth about them, she was as guilty as they were if something happened to Mr. Varkas.

Sarah pulled her shields back in place, gingerly picked up the book by its edge, and shoved it into her knapsack.

She leaned against the bookshelf and took several minutes to compose herself. There was no way she was going to work on Monday. That gave her the weekend to find Darius Varkas, warn him, and figure out a way to save herself. Because once Herman Temple discovered what she'd done, he would come looking for her.

She thumped her head against the shelf and groaned. *Yeah, no problem.*

She was totally screwed.

Chapter Five

It was surprisingly easy to find Darius Varkas. So easy, in fact, it was almost anticlimactic. She envisioned hours of searching, of using her skills as a researcher to delve into various records to find him. Instead, one quick Google search had netted her pages about the reclusive businessman.

Not what she'd been expecting. She scrolled down the screen and clicked on an article. "Mining," she muttered. The man had made a fortune in gold and silver mines around the world. He also owned mines that dealt in rare metals and was fanatical about preserving the environment, even if it meant lower profits. Conveniently enough, his headquarters and home were right here in Manhattan.

Sarah checked her watch and winced. It was almost midnight. Time for her to head home. Problem was she didn't want to go home. Now that she knew the truth about her employer, she was totally paranoid. He knew things about her that most people didn't. The fact that he knew about her gift, and had intentionally sought her out, gave her the creeps.

What would he do if he knew she'd found this book? She

wasn't even certain it was the book Mr. Temple was looking for, but it was damning all the same.

Darius Varkas had an unlisted number, but it didn't take her long to find the building where he lived. She had to speak to him in person. Over the phone it would be too easy for him to ignore her.

Sarah pushed off the floor, gathered her belongs, and made her way to the front door.

She hurried down the steps and headed down the sidewalk. It might be late, but this was New York and there were always people out and about.

First thing she had to do was warn Darius Varkas. Once she'd talked to the man, her conscience would be free and clear whether he believed her or not. Then she'd have to get out of town. She'd send the book to Mr. Temple by courier and then disappear off the grid for a while. She could do that. All she needed was cash, which she could get tomorrow.

Feeling better now that she had a plan, Sarah slowed as Darius Varkas's building came into sight. At the last second, she ducked into a doorway. She wasn't being smart. If Mr. Temple was interested in the man, he probably had people watching him.

She wasn't used to all this cloak-and-dagger stuff. She didn't like cop shows or spy dramas, so she didn't even have that dubious knowledge to fall back on.

She pulled out her phone, went online and searched for the phone number for the apartment building. A place this swanky had a doorman and that meant they probably had a front desk or an office as well. She searched, but all she could find was a number for the property management company. That wouldn't do her any good until morning.

Okay, what next?

The doorman.

Sarah had passed an all-night diner a block or so ago.

She detoured back. It was almost empty except for two other patrons. She went inside and headed for a table at the far end. The waitress strolled up just as Sarah was pulling out her laptop.

"What will it be?" the waitress asked her. She was young, maybe early twenties, with red-streaked black hair and a bored expression.

"Coffee." Sarah needed the hit. "Do you have pie?" She hadn't eaten this evening and was starving.

"Apple, lemon meringue, and pecan."

"I'll take a slice of the lemon meringue."

The waitress nodded and went to fill Sarah's order. She set up her laptop, linked into the wifi and began a search. It took some doing but she found several articles about the building and several quotes from a doorman. She prayed he still worked there.

The waitress returned with coffee and a slice of pie, setting them on the table. "Anything else?"

Sarah shook her head. "No, thanks. I'm good."

As soon as the waitress left, Sarah added sugar to her coffee and had a sip. It was hot and strong, exactly what she needed. She dug around online until she found six men in the immediate area with the same name as the doorman. Grabbing her phone, she started calling them one by one. She got yelled at three times, one call went to voicemail, and another number was no longer in service. She hit pay dirt on the final number.

"Yeah, this is John Barrington."

"Do you work at Darius Varkas's building?" She held her breath and prayed.

"Who wants to know?" His belligerent tone told her she'd gotten the right man.

"It's important I speak to Mr. Varkas," she began. "Tell him it's about the Knights." She rattled off her phone number.

"Just give him the message and my number."

The call was abruptly disconnected. All Sarah could do was wait and hope for the best.

• • •

Darius sat back in his chair and stared at the phone number he'd jotted down. His doorman had just delivered the strangest message from an unknown woman claiming to have information for him about the Knights.

Was this some kind of test? A threat? Either way, he had to know. He dialed the number and waited patiently as it rang twice before a woman answered.

"Yes."

His entire body clenched at the soft sound of her voice. "You were looking for me?" He went on the offensive.

"Darius Varkas?"

"Yes."

She hesitated, and he realized he was holding his breath, waiting for her to speak again. He turned his desk chair so he was facing the window. She was out there somewhere.

"You don't know me." He could hear the nervousness in her voice. "You might even think I'm crazy, but I had to warn you."

"About what?"

"Do you...do you know about the Knights of the Dragon?"

His entire body was tense. It would only take the tiniest spark for him to explode in anger. "What do you know about them?" he countered.

"Not much. I overheard my new employer talking to another man about kidnapping you. I had to warn you."

He frowned. "How do you know about the Knights?" he asked again.

"A book. I found a book in his library. I had to warn you."
He heard the murmur of voices in the background.

"Where are you?" he demanded.

"A diner. I thought about coming to your building, but it
occurred to me Mr. Temple might have people watching you."

"Mr. Temple?"

"Yes. Herman Temple. He's the man who hired me to
catalogue his extensive private library."

"Tell me where you are exactly?" he ordered. "We need
to speak in person. Better yet, come to my home."

"I can't." He could hear the fear in her voice. He didn't
like it one bit. "I'm afraid they're watching you. I know they're
watching me, but I managed to sneak out of my apartment
earlier tonight."

"I can get you into my building unseen. Just tell me where
you are."

She hesitated so long he was afraid she was simply going
to hang up. Then she told him the name of the diner. He knew
it well, had passed by it many, many times. "Wait for me. I'll
be right there."

"Okay."

"What's your name?" Darius realized he didn't know
who she was and hadn't asked.

"Sarah. Sarah Anderson."

"Sit tight, Sarah Anderson. I'm on my way." He ended
the call, pushed out of his chair and headed for his private
elevator, stopping long enough to grab his leather jacket. It
seemed to take forever for the elevator to reach the basement.

He exited the back of the building and paused to look
around. He couldn't sense anyone watching him, but he kept
to the shadows until he reached the end of the block. It took
him only minutes to reach the diner.

He peered through the window and quickly discounted
the male patrons and the waitress. There was only one other

woman in the diner this time of night. She was sitting in the far corner playing with a fork. While he watched, she set the utensil down and shoved aside an empty plate.

Her hair was brown and cut short, with bangs spiking down her forehead. Her face was heart-shaped. There was nothing extraordinary about her appearance, but Darius found himself enthralled. He watched for several minutes, until he was sure the men seated at the counter weren't with her. Then he pulled the door open and walked inside.

She looked up, and their gazes caught. Her skin was smooth, like fine porcelain. And when he got a good look at her eyes, it was like a kick in the gut. They were deep brown, like the finest chocolate. There was no guile there, only genuine concern and worry.

"Mr. Varkas?"

He slid into the empty seat across from her. "Darius. Call me Darius."

She smiled at him, and he noticed one of her bottom teeth overlapped another. He found the tiny flaw utterly adorable. He shook himself. What the hell was wrong with him? He was almost waxing poetic about a woman he'd just met. His brothers would laugh their asses off if they could see him.

"Sarah Anderson." She held out her hand, and he took it. The jolt was like being hit with a live wire. Energy shot up his arm to his shoulder before exploding through his body.

When Sarah gasped and her eyes widened, he knew she'd felt it, too.

What the fuck?

He released her hand, and she rubbed hers against her other arm. Whatever was happening between them was unusual, and therefore dangerous. Darius had no way of knowing if she was involved with the Knights. Just because she looked innocent didn't mean she was.

What better way to trap him than to lure him with a

seemingly guileless woman? The Knights of the Dragon were smart enough to plan something like this.

Darius felt exposed. He stood and motioned to the door. "We need to get out of here and go somewhere we can talk in private."

She licked her lips, and his cock sprang to life. Shit, he did not need this attraction, not now. His suspicions grew when she hesitated.

"Maybe you're waiting for your employer to arrive." He tossed out the accusation to see how she would react.

Her skin paled and her eyes sparked with anger. She began to shove her belongings into her knapsack. "I shouldn't have bothered to warn you," she snapped. Then she paused and rubbed her forehead. "No, I had to warn you. Now that I have, we're done."

She dug into her knapsack and pulled out her wallet. Before she could get out her money, he dropped a twenty on the table. "Will that cover it?"

"More than enough. I only had pie and coffee." She pulled on her coat and slung her knapsack over her shoulder.

He took her arm, braced for the shock this time, but touching her through her coat wasn't the same as touching her bare skin. He caught a whiff of vanilla and knew it was coming from her. "Come on. We need to get out of here."

She let him lead her out the door, but then she pulled her arm away from him. "We're done, Mr. Varkas." She turned and started walking away.

He walked beside her and waited until they were out of sight of the diner before he wrapped his arm around her shoulders and guided her down an alley. "It's Darius," he reminded her.

"What are you doing?" She tried to pull away from him, but he tightened his grip.

"I need to know more, Sarah. I need to know everything."

He stopped and stared down at her. She was tall for a woman, but tiny when compared to him. He pulled on the one string he thought might convince her to come with him if she was as innocent as she seemed to be. "I'm not the only one at risk. There are others."

She stared up at him. He felt himself being judged. Whatever she saw in his face must have convinced her he was earnest.

"Okay, I'll give you an hour or so, but then I'm gone. I've got to get out of town." She shivered, and he wrapped his arm around her again, this time to offer warmth and comfort rather than to coerce her into going with him.

What she didn't know was he had no intention of letting her get away from him. Not until he discovered what it was about her that attracted him on such a primal level. He still wasn't completely convinced she was as innocent as she seemed. It was too much of a coincidence that she'd shown up in his life with information just when he needed it.

It was more likely she'd been sent by the Knights of the Dragon to learn about him, to weaken him in order to make him easier to capture.

It would be smarter for him to say good-bye to her and leave the city.

But there was no way he could let her go, not if there was the tiniest chance she was telling him the truth. If she was truly an innocent in this war, she was in danger from the Knights. The thought of her being harmed in any way made him want to roar with fury.

It took his thousands of years of control to keep the beast inside him in check. Sarah Anderson belonged to him, at least for the foreseeable future. And a drakon always protected what was his.

Chapter Six

Sarah hurried to keep up with the giant of a man beside her. She'd obviously lost her mind. There was no other logical reason why she'd left a public location and agreed to go with Darius Varkas. Yes, he might be in trouble, but he was also a total stranger. Everything she knew about him came from the articles she'd read online, and even they'd been vague regarding his personal life. They all agreed he was ruthless when it came to business. She'd done her part by warning him of the threat. She didn't owe him anything else.

Except, if there were more people at risk, and she could help but didn't, could she live with herself? She nibbled on her bottom lip and shivered against the cold.

His arm tightened around her. "Almost there."

She had no idea where they were going, but his big body certainly gave off enough heat to drive back the chill. Darius was well over six and a half feet tall, maybe even closer to seven, and that was no exaggeration. He was tall and heavily muscled, with broad shoulders. The clothes he wore fit him perfectly, tailored to his size and build. His leather jacket was soft and supple. His clothes might look normal, but on closer examination, they screamed money.

She glanced up and then away before he caught her staring. The grainy pictures in the news article she'd read didn't do him justice. His features were blunt and strong. His eyes were green. Not hazel, but a true green. His straight, black hair hung like a silky curtain around his shoulders. He looked more like a pirate than a businessman. Although these days, there probably wasn't much difference between the two.

"This way." He guided her down a back alley, keeping to the shadows. The skittering of tiny feet next to a dumpster made her shudder. She hated rats.

He reached around her and jammed a key into the lock on a heavy metal door. He yanked it open and all but shoved her inside. She couldn't see a damn thing. The door clanged shut behind her.

She jumped when he grabbed her hand again and started towing her through the darkness. Enough was enough. She dug in her heels. "Wait. Stop."

Darius slowed and finally stopped when she tugged her hand from his. "It's not safe here. We need to go up to my apartment."

She wiped her hand on her jeans, still able to feel the heat from his skin. "Yeah, well I don't know that it's any safer there than it is here."

"You're afraid." He sounded surprised, as though such a thing had never occurred to him.

Sarah adjusted the strap of her knapsack and shrugged, even though she was pretty certain he couldn't see her any better than she could him. He was a vague outline, a darker shadow in the unlit gloom of the basement they were standing in.

"I'm cautious," she corrected. "And after everything I learned today, I have a right to be."

She blinked when she saw something shining in the dark, but the light quickly disappeared. She was probably mistaken. Maybe it had been a reflection off something down here. Yeah, that had to be it. Because the only alternative was that Darius's eyes had glowed.

Sarah was beginning to feel like she was in the middle of a nightmare that wouldn't end. She wrapped her arms around her body and shivered in spite of the fact that she was wearing a sweater under her heavy coat and was no longer out in the chilly night air.

Heavy hands clamped down on her shoulders. "You have nothing to fear from me."

God, she loved his voice. It was so deep and a little rough. She shivered again, and this time it wasn't all because of fear, which was a sure sign she was losing her mind. This was neither the time nor the place for her libido to kick in, even if she had been in a sexual dry spell for more than a year.

"No offense, but I only have your word for that."

He sighed, grabbed her hand, and began to lead her through the dark room. She went with him because, really, where else was she going to go? Home? She was afraid to go back to her apartment. She was exhausted from dealing with all the stress. Hungry, too. The pie she'd eaten had been the first thing she'd had since her sandwich at lunch.

Darius seemed to have no trouble seeing, because he led her straight to an elevator in the corner of the room. The button gave off a small light when he pushed it, and the doors slid open. She blinked when the light hit her eyes.

Darius pulled her into the elevator behind him and pushed the button for the penthouse. She tugged her hand from his and wrapped it around the strap of her bag. *God, he's big.* At five-eight, she'd always considered herself tall for a woman. Next to him, she felt positively tiny.

He was watching her with those gorgeous green eyes. His

mouth was firm, not quite a scowl, but nowhere near a smile. She glanced away, but her gaze was quickly drawn back to Darius Varkas. There was something untamed about the man, probably due to his size and the sense of barely restrained energy that seemed to pulse all around him.

There were no numbers to show what floor they were on, but the lift finally stopped and the metal panels silently opened. Darius stepped out of the elevator and kept his hand positioned so it didn't close.

"Welcome to my home."

Sarah pulled together the remnants of her courage and stepped forward. He released the doors, and they closed. She was beginning to feel like a gazelle being herded to slaughter by a massive lion. No…more like a tiger, or maybe a leopard. But some wild beast.

She made her feet move forward on the gleaming hardwood floor. Off to her right was a sitting area with shelves displaying art and artifacts. There was also the requisite large flat-screen television and a cabinet below, which she assumed housed his other electronic equipment.

The space was huge and very open. About thirty feet in front of her, the city skyline gleamed through the wide windows. "Wow." She passed an antique dining table as she moved closer to the incredible view.

"Are you hungry? Thirsty?" He shucked his coat, tossed it over one of the dining room chairs, and headed toward the open kitchen off to her left. A granite counter separated it from the dining area. Stainless steel appliances gleamed against the dark cupboards.

Darius didn't wait for her to reply and began making coffee. Sarah glanced at her watch. It was well past midnight, but what the hell, wasn't like she was going to be getting some sleep anytime soon. "Sure. Coffee would be great."

For a big man, he moved with grace and speed. She stood

there, swaying on her feet, her gaze glued to his hands as he set the pot brewing. When he glanced in her direction, she looked away, chagrined to be caught staring.

"Why don't we sit down in the living room and you can tell me what you know."

Yeah, that would probably be smart. She needed to sit down before she fell down. The adrenaline that had carried her for hours was pretty much spent, leaving her feeling empty and exhausted.

"Probably a good idea." The sofa seemed a long way away, but she concentrated on putting one foot in front of the other. She practically fell onto the cushions made of buttery soft brown leather.

"Give me your coat." He held out his hand, but she shook her head, reluctant to release any of her belongings. His mouth tightened in disapproval, but he didn't press her.

He perched on the rather large and heavy coffee table in front of her and rested his elbows on his knees. "What do you know about the Knights of the Dragon?"

She marshaled her thoughts. After all, this was the sole reason she was here. She ignored the lock of hair that fell across his forehead, and the narrowing of his beautiful eyes. Really, the man was too good-looking for her peace of mind.

He clasped his large hands together, giving her a glimpse of his thick wrists and muscled forearms.

Sarah shook her head. She had to get a grip on herself. "Okay, let me start at the beginning." She told him how she'd lost her job but had been steered toward the interview with Herman Temple. "It seemed like a dream job," she told him. She scrubbed her hands over her face. "That should have been my first clue that something wasn't right."

One corner of his mouth kicked up. It wasn't quite a smile, but it still made her heart flutter.

"Not an optimist, I take it?"

She shook her head but then thought better of it. "I generally am pretty optimistic about life, but this seemed too good, too perfect, if you know what I mean?"

He looked straight at her and nodded. "I understand perfectly."

It took her a moment to catch the undercurrents in his statement. "You think I'm involved with the Knights, don't you?" She waved off any reply he might make. "You're entitled to your opinion. Do you want the rest of the story?"

"I'll get coffee first. You look like you could use it." He stood and strode to the kitchen. Sarah forced herself not to watch him leave. Honestly, she needed to get her act together. This was no time to be attracted to a man, no matter how gorgeous he was.

He wasn't classically handsome. His features were too rough and blunt, his size too massive. But he was compelling and possessed an animal magnetism that would draw female gazes wherever he went. He certainly revved her engine.

She closed her eyes for a moment and was drifting off when she heard her name being called. She forced her eyes open to find Darius holding out a mug of coffee for her. "Here, you need this."

She blinked several times before taking the offering. "Thanks."

He motioned to the thick wooden tray in front of her on the coffee table. "Sugar. I didn't think you take milk."

"How did you know?" Her heart skipped a beat before it picked up speed.

He shrugged. "There wasn't any in your mug at the diner."

Sarah was surprised he'd noticed. The man was certainly observant. "You're right." She sat forward and added sugar to her coffee, then stirred before taking her first sip. It warmed her insides, and the delicious flavor made her taste buds come alive. "This is amazing." She took another sip, careful not to burn her mouth on the hot brew.

"I get it shipped in special from an organic farmer in Colombia." He sat in the chair across from her, and she was grateful not to have him so close. Not as distracting. Although maybe it was worse. He slumped in the oversize chair with his mug resting against his flat stomach and his long legs kicked out in front of him.

She had another mouthful of coffee and then picked up her story. "Everything was going along fine until today."

"What changed?"

The intensity of his stare was making it hard for her to concentrate, so she looked down at the mug in her hands instead. "I was late having lunch. I lost track of time." She rubbed her thumb around the rim of the heavy ceramic. "That happens when I get into my work." And he didn't care about that. She needed to get to the point.

"I went to the break room to eat, and I heard voices on my way back." She glanced at Darius. He leaned forward and placed his mug on the table.

"What happened then?"

"I hid in an alcove." Her tone was defensive, but she couldn't help it. She hated coming across as a coward. "I don't like confrontation or arguments."

"Okay," he easily agreed. "Then what?"

"I realized it was Mr. Temple and another man. They were arguing about you. Mr. Temple wants to abduct you and use your blood for experiments. He said something about a military contact, too." That was the part she didn't want to believe, but she wasn't naive enough to think the government wasn't involved in a lot of shady projects.

Darius nodded, not seeming the least bit surprised by her outrageous accusations. "Why you?" he asked. "What's so special about you that this Mr. Temple hired you?"

This was the tricky part. She licked her lips and set her cup down on the table. "I…uh, I have certain skills," she began.

He narrowed his eyes. "What skills?" She shivered at the deadly tone in his voice. This was not a man she wanted as an enemy.

What if he didn't believe her? A lot of people didn't. She glanced at the custom shelves lining the wall and stood. She wiped her damp palms on her jeans and walked toward them. Darius watched her.

Her knapsack thumped against her stomach, so she readjusted her hold on it. A bead of sweat rolled down her temple. She was wearing her coat inside, but she still felt chilled in spite of the fact she was sweating.

She chose an object, picking one she thought had some age. The small piece of pottery was perfectly shaped and surprisingly whole. She wrapped her hands around the small pot, closed her eyes, and dropped her shields.

Immediately, she was sucked back in time. Unlike with the book in her knapsack, this time her gift worked as it usually did. Grainy images, like photos or an old movie, flipped through her mind.

"You acquired this piece from a dealer in Peru." She frowned. "That can't be right." Her eyes popped open. "You couldn't have bought this piece off him one hundred years ago."

• • •

Darius was shocked by Sarah's declaration. She was dead-on. He had purchased that particular pot a hundred years ago from a rather shady dealer while he was in Peru. He plucked the pot from her hands and returned it to the shelf.

She glanced away from him, her face pale. He knew she was sweating but wouldn't remove her coat, knew she was afraid, but she hadn't backed down from him. She had courage, whether she realized it or not.

Still, he needed proof this wasn't just a fluke. Maybe the Knights had been researching him longer than he'd thought, and she'd gotten lucky.

He took a small, unsigned painting from the shelf. The frame was original to the piece as well. He handed it to her.

She took a deep breath and wrapped her hands around the aged wood, letting her fingertips barely graze the oil paint. She closed her eyes, and he could almost feel all her attention turning inward. She opened her eyes and stared at the piece. "This is by Leonardo da Vinci." She shook her head. "He couldn't have given it to you. That would make you—" She broke off and sat down hard on the coffee table. Darius gently took the priceless masterpiece from her and set it carefully back on the shelf.

"What did you see?" he asked her.

"Something impossible." She rubbed her forehead. "Maybe something has happened to my gift. That would certainly explain what I saw earlier today."

He could see the hope in her eyes and hated to dampen it, but he needed the truth. "You have a gift for psychometry?"

She nodded. "Since I was a child." She straightened her shoulders and practically glared at him. "Most people don't believe in it."

"I'm not most people," he reminded her. His easy agreement seemed to take the wind out of her sails, and she slumped a little.

"Tell me the rest of it." The clock was ticking. He needed all the facts, and he needed them now.

Sarah pushed off the table and stumbled back to the sofa. She tilted her head back against the cushions and sighed. "I do freelance work for museums and some private collectors. I research and help authenticate and date artifacts."

"And you use your gift." He sat back in his chair. He

wanted to get closer to her but didn't want to unsettle her. He had the sense she'd been pushed almost to her limits and was barely holding it together.

She nodded. "Sometimes." She lifted her head and blinked several times. "I've also done work with several prominent rare-book dealers. I think Jeremiah Dent suspected I was using more than just education and research to help authenticate his books. He must have guessed what my gift is, but he never said anything to me." She sighed. "My gift works with most old things, but I have a special affinity for books."

Her brow wrinkled, and Darius wanted to smooth away her concerns and worries. He fisted his hands on his thighs to keep from reaching for her.

"He must have told Mr. Temple." She shook her head. "I think he got me fired. Or had my boss give me the impression I was being laid off. When I thought about it today, I realized he never told me I was being fired, just that there were cutbacks. Then he jumped right in and told me to contact Jeremiah Dent about an available position in a private library."

"They led you to the job with Herman Temple." The Knights had always been clever.

"Yes. That's exactly it, and I didn't stop to question it."

He heard the disgust in her voice and knew she was feeling at fault about her decision. "If you hadn't left on your own, they would probably have had you fired for real." Or worse, but he wasn't going to tell her that.

"I figured as much."

"And the conversation you overheard?" he prompted.

"Yeah, they wanted me to find a particular book. The other man seemed to think they needed it in order to kidnap you." She frowned. "But that can't be right."

Darius didn't correct her. "Did the other man have a name?"

"Christian Temple. He's Mr. Temple's son." Sarah

unzipped her coat but still didn't remove it or her knapsack. "Mr. Temple showed up at the library a few minutes after I overheard their conversation. I was cataloguing the library systematically, but he told me to look around the room and bring anything I found particularly interesting to him."

Sarah shivered, and he couldn't stay put any longer. He stood and went to sit beside her. She nervously scooted to the corner of the sofa, but he followed her. He took her hand in his. It was small and dainty, her skin pale next to his tanned flesh.

"Did you do as he asked?"

"I knew I didn't have a choice. I got the feeling from their conversation that my work environment is going to get a lot more hostile on Monday, which is why I need to get out of town."

He felt her hand tremble in his, and his beast roared inside him. No one would hurt her and live. Darius knew his reaction to her was totally out of character, but there was no denying the connection he felt with her.

He had to pull back and examine it. As much as it pained him to think it, this didn't change the fact that Sarah could be working with the Knights. He was almost certain she wasn't, but there was also a chance she was an unwitting pawn in their game. She might be under their control and not know it.

Darius knew most humans would scoff at the idea, but he'd lived far longer than they had. He knew there were potions and drugs that could be given to a person to change them. Some of the Knights were particularly skilled at mind control, one of many seemingly supernatural gifts the drakon blood they ingested gave them.

She might honestly believe every word she was telling him, and it might be nothing but lies imparted to her by one of the Knights. The leaders were usually powerful alchemists. In days gone by, they would have been called sorcerers.

Nowadays, they were called scientists. Whatever their name, they were self-serving and willing to sacrifice innocent people for their cause.

"What did you find?" he demanded.

"I looked around, but all objects give off a glow of energy or memories. The older the object the more potent it is."

He nodded his understanding. That made perfect sense.

"In a library that extensive, there are many powerful books. But there was one that caught my eye. It was a combination of brilliant light and an all-consuming darkness." She shuddered, and he could see the fear in her eyes. "Anything with that kind of dark power is never good."

Darius wanted to shake her to get her to finish her tale, but he held his peace, instinctively knowing if he did such a thing, she'd totally withdraw from him. She needed to trust him if he was to learn everything he needed.

"It was a Bible from the seventeen hundreds, one with beautiful illustrations." She rubbed her free hand up and down her thigh. "I was about to put it back when I realized there was a much smaller, thinner book hidden within the pages."

A sense of dread filled him. "That was the dark energy."

Sarah nodded. "I didn't want to touch it at first." She licked her lips. "I didn't know if it was the book they were looking for, but then the security guard came, and I had to get out of there. Mr. Temple is very strict about staff leaving on time. I even have to leave my coat, purse, and phone with security every morning and pick them up when I leave." She hesitated, but then plowed onward. "The book is titled *Knights of the Dragon: Necessary Incantations and Spells*."

"Fuck." Sarah jolted when Darius jumped to his feet and began to pace. "You're right. That book is incredibly dangerous, especially in the wrong hands." He quickly formed and rejected plans in his mind. He had to get that book.

Darius turned back to her. "You need to tell me everything you know about their security layout."

She canted her head. "Why?"

He scowled at her. "Didn't you hear me? It's dangerous, and not only to me, but to others."

"Others?"

"You don't need to know." No way would he trust her or anyone else with the fact that he had three brothers. "Believe me when I tell you people have been killed because of that book." The irony wasn't lost on him. He was asking her to trust him while he couldn't afford to do the same in return.

He rubbed the back of his neck and forced himself to calm down. That book was rumored to have been destroyed several centuries ago. To know that it, or a copy of it, still existed was enough to make his blood run cold.

It was said that inside those pages were recipes for potions that could render a dragon weak, even unconscious in rare cases, and enable the Knights to easily capture them. The ingredients were very rare and costly, but the Knights had ways to get what they needed. No wonder they were so frantic to find the book. He wondered how the hell they'd lost it in the first place.

He shoved the table out of the way, ignoring the coffee that sloshed over the rims of the mugs and spilled onto the floor. Darius crouched in front of Sarah, this delicate human woman who held the fate of many drakons in her small hands. He put his palms on either side of her and was pleased when she didn't move away from him.

"Sarah, it's vitally important I get that book. I need you to think about the security at work. Cameras, guards, alarms, everything." He'd need to get schematics of the building and more. But he'd start here, with his best inside source. Of course, if she was working with the Knights, this might be nothing more than an elaborate plot to capture him.

It was a risk he had to take.

"You don't need to know that," she began.

Darius caught her face in his hands and cradled her cheeks in his palms. "I do, Sarah, I really do. I'm not worried about my life, but those of people close to me." That was the most he could give her.

"No, you don't."

Disappointment seeped into him, and he released her and straightened to his full height. "How much?"

"What?" She sounded bewildered, but he wasn't buying it. If she wasn't willing to give him the information he needed, it was because she wanted something. In his vast experience with humans, that meant money in one form or another. It used to be gold and jewels. Nowadays, it was more likely to be a simple bank transfer.

He put his hands on his hips and simply stared at her, trying not to get lost in her chocolate-brown eyes. They appeared so innocent. "How much for the information?"

She jumped to her feet and glared at him. "You son of a bitch. I'm risking a lot to warn you about the book and everything else."

"That doesn't answer my question." No way could he let her go until he had the information he needed. "The quicker you give it to me, the faster I can pay you. Then you can leave."

She fisted her hands at her sides. "I ought to let you pay for it." Then she fumbled with her knapsack and yanked open the zipper. He wondered if she had a weapon of some kind, and cursed himself for not searching her earlier. Not that it would do her much good. Most conventional weapons, at least any that could fit in her bag, wouldn't do much damage to him. But it would piss him off.

She reached inside the bag and, instead of a weapon, pulled out an old, leather-bound book. She thrust it against his stomach, and he caught it before it dropped to the floor.

"Here's your damn book. I smuggled it out of work at great personal risk. You're welcome." She stepped around him and strode to the elevator. Sarah slapped her palm against the panel, but nothing happened. Only he could make it work.

Darius stared at the book and then back at the very angry woman waiting for an elevator that would never come.

An unusual sensation enveloped him, one he'd rarely felt in the thousands of years he'd been alive. It was shame with a hint of bewilderment.

He might have just made the biggest mistake of his life.

Chapter Seven

Sarah was practically vibrating with anger as she waited for the elevator to appear. The arrogant jerk was still standing there holding the book she'd all but thrown at him. How dare he? After everything she'd been through today, all the fear she'd experienced, his accusing her of being mercenary at best, or a blackmailer at worst, was the last straw.

"Come on." She smacked the pad by the door and a red light scanned her palm, but still nothing happened. Damn it. She was going to have to face Darius again.

She took a deep breath to settle herself and turned, hoping the anger she felt wasn't visible on her face. "You want to open this for me?"

"No." He shook his head as he came toward her. "It's not safe for you out there." He set the book he was still holding on an ornate table just inside the foyer.

"It's not safe for me in here, either," she retorted. She might be physically safer with him, but that didn't mean he hadn't hurt her.

He winced and rubbed his free hand over his face. "Yeah,

I'm sorry about that. I'm just used to expecting the worst from people. Less chance of disappointment that way."

As apologies went, it was pretty darn weak, but she'd take what she could get. "So you're sorry. Fine. Now let me go."

He cocked his head to one side and studied her. She tried not to fidget, but it wasn't easy. There was something incredibly personal in the way his gaze traveled over her from head to toe. She was suddenly very hot in her coat and boots. She was dressed for the outside while the temperature in the apartment had skyrocketed in the past few seconds.

He might be a jerk, but he was a darn good-looking one. There was something so strong and vital about him. He really was a pleasure to look at. Too bad he had to go and open his mouth and ruin it.

Maybe that wasn't fair. He'd had a lot thrown at him in the past hour. She couldn't imagine what it must feel like to find out someone wanted to kidnap you and run experiments. He also didn't know her from Adam. As much as she hated to admit it, there were a lot of people who would have tried to extort money from him for information.

Darn her sense of fairness. It was draining the mad right out of her.

She raked a hand through her hair, brushing the fringed bangs out of her face. "Look, I get that you're upset. You have every right to be." Calm and methodical, that was the way she always approached a problem, and this wasn't any different from any research dilemma she'd ever dealt with. "But it's time for me to leave." She had plans to make if she was going to evade Mr. Temple.

"Please come sit down. I have questions."

He looked earnest, but she wasn't buying it. Oh, she didn't doubt that he had questions he wanted answered, but she knew she wasn't getting out of here until he let her go.

"Kidnapping is illegal," she reminded him.

He flashed a brief smile that made her breath catch. She'd found him attractive enough before, but when he smiled, her entire body tingled. He shouldn't smile. Frowning was much better for her peace of mind.

"You came here of your own free will," he reminded her.

"Not exactly." She shifted her weight from one foot to the other. "I really didn't feel like I had any choice."

His smile disappeared. Irrationally, she missed it now that it was gone.

"I'm sorry for that," he told her. "I would really appreciate it if you would answer my questions. Maybe we can help each other." He held up one hand to forestall her objections. "I'm not suggesting you expect a payoff, but I do owe you any help I can give you. I'm not without resources, and you said you need to get out of town."

That was an argument she couldn't dispute. Having pride was one thing. Being stupid was another. She couldn't afford to be stupid with Herman Temple and the group he belonged to watching her.

Decision made, Sarah walked back to the sofa. She dropped her knapsack on the plush leather and removed her jacket. Darius's expression didn't change, but she sensed his satisfaction. Lucky for him he didn't gloat, or she might have been tempted to find a crowbar and go to work on his fancy elevator.

As she sat, her stomach growled. She put her hand over it, but there was no smothering the sound.

"You're hungry. When did you last eat?"

"Except for the piece of pie at the diner? Lunchtime." That seemed like a lifetime ago.

"What do you want? I can order something." He pulled his phone out of his pocket. "Steak, sandwich, pizza, Chinese, anything you'd like."

"Pizza sounds good. No olives or anchovies." She'd eat

just about anything, but she drew the line at some things.

She could tell he was trying to hide a smile as he made his call. "John, I need two pizzas with everything but olives or anchovies." He paused a moment, and she knew he was listening to the man on the other end of the line. She assumed it was John Barrington, the doorman she'd spoken to earlier to get her message to Darius. "Thanks." He hung up the phone and tucked it away. "Shouldn't be long."

He'd surprised her by thanking the doorman. You could tell a lot about a man by the way he treated others, especially those in a lower economic bracket. He'd left a big tip for the waitress at the diner, too.

"Tell me about the Knights of the Dragon." He wasn't the only one with questions. "I get the feeling they've been around a long time."

Darius sat in the chair across from her and leaned back, getting comfortable. She wished she could relax. She forced herself to shift from the edge of the sofa and settle against the cushions.

"You'd be right about that. Short history is that the Knights of the Dragon came into existence around two thousand years ago, but they didn't take that name until around the thirteenth century. Their main goal is to gain power, wealth, and longevity through the ingestion of drakon's blood."

It sounded like something out of a fantasy novel to Sarah. Certainly not something sane, rational men would believe. "You said drakon's blood, but they call themselves Knights of the Dragon. Why?"

Darius sat forward, his expression fierce. "Who the hell knows? Maybe it allows them to ignore the human side of a drakon. Maybe they sleep better at night believing the people they kill and torture are animals and not men. They don't care to understand the difference between a dragon and a drakon."

"But you do?" This conversation was quickly going down

the rabbit hole.

He nodded. "A drakon is the son of a full-blooded dragon and a human woman. Dragons no longer exist in this world."

"But they did?"

She started getting nervous when he nodded. What had she gotten herself into? It seemed Darius and Mr. Temple were both a sandwich short of a picnic. "Ah, if dragons did exist, why don't we have fossilized evidence?" Someone had to be rational.

"Two reasons. First, they returned to their own dimension around four thousand years ago. Second, both dragons and drakons burn when they die, destroying all evidence of their existence."

Sure they did. She didn't know what in the hell she'd gotten involved in, but Sarah wanted out. Darius's phone rang and he answered it, giving her a moment to catch her breath. This day was getting crazier by the second.

"Send it up." Darius shut his phone and walked to the elevator. This was her chance.

She stood quietly, gathered her coat and knapsack, and tiptoed behind him. When the elevator doors opened, she planned to jump inside.

The doors made no sound as they suddenly slid open. When Darius reached in to lift out the two pizza boxes that were sitting on the floor, she slipped around him, and bolted into the elevator. He slapped his large hand on the doors, keeping them from closing.

"I thought we were eating pizza." He raised one eyebrow and angled his head to one side to study her.

"I decided it's best I leave." She fiddled with the strap of her bag, wishing she had a weapon of some kind inside. Not that she'd actually use it, but she could at least threaten to.

"It was the dragon thing, wasn't it?" He shook his head as though she'd disappointed him somehow.

"It's crazy." She was done being accommodating. "I'm hungry and tired, and I want to go home but can't." The reality of the situation hit her like a ton of bricks. She might never go home again. All her books, the small treasures she'd gathered over the course of her lifetime, might be lost to her forever.

There wasn't anyone she could turn to for help, either. Her parents were both dead, and they'd been only children, so there were no aunts, uncles, or cousins. Being bookish and solitary as a child, she'd also never made friends easily. That had carried over into adulthood. Even if she had some friends, she wouldn't endanger anyone else by bringing them into this situation.

Her eyes welled with tears and a single drop rolled down her cheeks. She brushed it impatiently away. She wasn't a crier. It changed nothing, and all it did was make her face blotchy.

"Hey." He reached in, scooped her up with one arm while balancing the pizzas in his other hand, and pulled her out of the elevator. The doors slid shut, leaving her locked in the apartment with a gorgeous man who believed in dragons and was being hunted by another rich, crazy man who also believed in dragons.

It was official. Her life was a total mess.

"Don't cry." He lifted her feet right off the ground and carried her back to the living room as though she weighed nothing. He set the pizzas down, tugged her coat and bag away from her, and sat on the sofa with her curled on his lap.

He gently brushed her hair away from her face. The concern in his eyes was her undoing. Sarah burst into tears.

• • •

Darius was at a loss as to what to do. Which was really frigging funny when he thought about it. He'd lived thousands of years, had seen the entire world, dealt with all manner of men, made a vast fortune, and yet he didn't know what to do with one crying female. It seemed it didn't matter how long a man lived, women were a mystery.

Not that she didn't deserve to cry. Considering everything she'd been through, it was a wonder she hadn't had a meltdown earlier. She was a librarian, not a warrior.

And she felt way too good in his arms. She was tall for a woman, but slight of build. Still, she had enough curves that no one would ever doubt her femininity. When she threw her arm around him and buried her face in the curve of his neck, he knew it was over for him.

Warmth pooled in the center of his chest and expanded outward. The creature inside him stilled for a long second before roaring in triumph. The sensation that rocketed through him was one he recognized well. It was the same feeling he got whenever he found treasure. But this time it was more intense. It went all the way to his very soul.

He didn't know what it meant, but it scared the crap out of him. After four thousand years of living, he was wary of anything unknown, especially when it came to women. Was this some kind of spell? He didn't think so. Sarah carried none of the trappings of a sorceress. Nor had he eaten or drank anything she'd given him.

It was a mystery.

He should send her away, but the thought of her leaving him was enough to send him into a complete panic. He couldn't lose her. There was nothing irrational about that. She had information he needed. He also should protect her considering she'd put her life on the line for him.

Yes, that was it. What he was feeling for her was no more than an inflated sense of obligation.

She nuzzled his neck, and his dick, which had been at half-mast since he'd laid eyes on her, sprang to life. His chest constricted, and he sucked in a deep breath. He cradled Sarah gently in his arms, careful not to do her any harm. With his vast strength, he had to be cautious and aware at all times, otherwise he might accidentally damage her.

He had no idea how long they sat there. The longer it went on, the more Darius relaxed. In spite of the urgency of the situation, he was in no rush for her to leave her current position. He liked her weight on his thighs, her slender arm banded across his chest, and the warmth of her breath against his neck.

When she sniffed, he rubbed his hand up and down her spine, enjoying the way she snuggled closer to him. After a while, she lifted her head. He immediately felt cold without her there.

"Good grief." She scrubbed at her eyes and scrambled out of his lap. He had to force himself not to pull her back. "I'm sorry about that. I didn't mean to cry all over you."

"I don't mind." At least he hadn't after the initial shock. It had been rather nice to hold her. What he hadn't liked was her tears.

"I must be a mess." She swiped at her blotchy cheeks, and her smile quivered.

"You look beautiful." That was the honest truth. He wanted to kiss her puffy eyes and reddened cheeks, slide his fingers through her short, tousled hair. Most of all, he wanted to know what she looked like beneath the jeans and sweater she wore.

She gave a broken laugh. "Thanks for trying to make me feel better. Do you have a bathroom I can use?"

She didn't believe him, but he didn't belabor the issue. There was no point. "Certainly." He stood and prayed she didn't notice his hard-on, because that certainly wouldn't put her at ease. "This way."

She grabbed her knapsack and followed him to the powder room just down the hallway. She gave him another small smile and shut the door in his face.

He couldn't stand outside and wait for her, even though he wanted to. That would only freak her out. And it wasn't as though she could leave his home, not without his palm print to open the elevator door.

He strode back to the living room, grabbed the pizza boxes, and took them into the kitchen. She needed to eat something.

He got down a couple of plates and popped several slices of the pizza into the microwave to reheat. While it was doing its thing, he opened a bottle of red wine and poured two glasses. Then he dug out several napkins.

The microwave dinged just as he heard the bathroom door open. He was just putting the plates on the counter when she joined him. Her face was still blotchy and her eyes red, but she appeared composed once again. Her bangs were damp, and he figured she'd splashed water on her face. She didn't seem to be wearing much makeup, but she was still beautiful.

And he knew she wouldn't believe him if he told her.

"Eat." He pushed one of the wineglasses toward her plate.

She slid onto one of the stools, picked up the pizza, and took a bite. She gave a little moan of pleasure, which had his cock jumping to life again. He wondered if she'd make that same sound in bed. It was a good thing he'd stayed on this side of the counter, otherwise she'd get an eyeful.

To distract himself, he grabbed his slice of pizza and devoured it and four more. He felt her gaze on him and wiped his mouth on his napkin. "What?"

"You were hungry."

He realized she was just finishing her first piece. "I need a lot of fuel." More than any human his size would. He had a fast metabolism that needed to be fed if he wanted to be at his peak power. "You should have more."

She smiled and took another piece. "It's good."

It was nice sharing a meal with her. He ate another three slices while she polished off her second one. He loved the way she enjoyed the simple meal, the way she caught the strand of cheese with her tongue and licked her lips. His pants grew tighter, and he had to look away, when what he wanted to do was feed her a piece of the pizza and bask in her obvious pleasure.

When she was done, she wiped her hands and took another swallow of her wine. He watched her throat ripple and wanted to kiss her long, slender neck.

"That was delicious. Thank you." She was so polite. He was learning quite a bit about her. She was a sensual creature even though he knew she'd probably deny it. The sweater she wore was soft and warm, her boots built for comfort instead of style. And she ate with gusto, with none of the picking at food that so many women nowadays seemed to do. She'd enjoyed every single bite, moaning several times.

It was quite a turn-on to watch her enjoy herself so much.

"So," she began.

"So," he echoed.

"You said that dragons don't exist in this world any longer, but that drakons do. I'm not saying I believe you, but what exactly is a drakon?"

The words were out of his mouth before he had time to think. "I am. I'm a drakon."

Chapter Eight

"You're what?" She shook her head in disbelief, certain she must have misheard him.

But he looked as shocked as she felt. She got the feeling he hadn't meant to say what he had. Then he shook his head and met her gaze. "I'm a drakon. The son of a dragon and a human female."

Could her day get any worse? Yes, yes, it could, because Darius obviously believed what he was saying. She was trapped in a luxury penthouse apartment with a man who thought he was part dragon and part human.

"And how did this happen if dragons haven't existed on the earth for more than four thousand years?" Time to inject a little reason into the conversation. He couldn't be totally crazy, not if he'd built a business empire. Or at least that's what she was banking on.

Maybe he'd played too many of those fantasy role-playing games as a teenager. Maybe he'd never stopped.

He raked his fingers through his thick black hair. "I'm just a little over four thousand years old, Sarah."

"You don't look a day over two thousand," she quipped. When he didn't laugh at her joke, she hopped off the stool and backed away from him. He sighed and came around the counter. She held out her hands to ward him off. Not that it would do much good considering how much larger he was than her. "Stay back."

"I didn't mean to frighten you." He did seem sorry, but that didn't change the situation.

"And you didn't think telling me that you're a drakon and you've been around for thousands of years would freak me out?" Because she was honestly finding it hard to breathe. Her chest tightened and her throat constricted.

"Calm down, Sarah. No one is going to hurt you."

"And I'm supposed to take your word for that?" The fierce expression on his face made her wish she'd kept her mouth shut. He'd been concerned before. Now he was angry.

She took another step back and stumbled. Darius lunged forward and caught her before her butt hit the floor. He pulled her tightly against him with his arms banded around her.

God, he smelled good. She'd noticed earlier, when she'd cried all over him, but had been too upset to enjoy it. It was a combination of man and a woodsy scent that was both stimulating and relaxing at the same time.

She was attracted to a crazy man. It had been that kind of a day. "You can let me go now," she told him.

"No." He scooped her into his arms. "No, I really can't."

She grabbed his shoulders and gave an undignified squeak. He lifted her as easily as he would a child. She got a fluttering in the pit of her stomach that had nothing to do with the pizza she'd just eaten, and her heart beat faster.

Darius carried her away from the kitchen and living area and down the hallway. She was starting to get worried when he walked into what had to be his office or study. That it wasn't his bedroom both relieved and disappointed her. Then she got a look at the tall bookshelves lining the room. They were packed with books and artifacts from around the world.

"This is amazing." She tapped his arm. "Put me down. Put me down." Surprisingly enough, he lowered her legs until her feet hit the floor.

"Wait here," he told her. He left her alone in the room. She could call the police, but she didn't think there was much they could do to help her. Besides, a part of her didn't want to get Darius in trouble with the authorities. And of course, her phone was in her knapsack in the living room. "Stupid," she muttered.

"Who is stupid?" he asked as he strode back into the study, looking larger than life.

"Obviously, I am." She resisted the urge to check out the library and slumped into a wingback leather chair. She scrubbed her hand over her face. "How did I get into this mess?"

It was a rhetorical question, but he knelt in front of her and held out the small leather book that was at the center of this entire situation. "You got into this mess because you have a unique gift. I'm sorry the Knights found you, but I'm not sorry I met you."

And what was she supposed to think about that? A part of her was charmed, and another part of her thought the entire situation was crazy.

"I need to know what you see when you touch this book."

She'd known he was going to ask her that and had been dreading it. Sarah clung to the arms of the chair, not wanting to touch the book again.

"I know I'm asking a lot," he began.

"You have no idea." No one did.

"Then tell me what it's like for you."

Even kneeling in front of her, he loomed over her. He was the largest man she'd ever met, and there wasn't an ounce of fat on him. It was all muscle, but not the over-blown kind that many body builders had.

"Sarah?"

Crap, he'd caught her looking. His gaze narrowed, and his green eyes seemed to glint in the light.

"I see pictures, like photographs from the past. Black and white and gray." She stared at the small volume he held in his hand and shuddered. "But not with that book. That one is different."

"You saw something, didn't you?"

She nodded, unwilling to lie to him about that. "Yeah, and it was like watching a motion picture in 3D." It had been way too real. The pizza she'd eaten churned in her gut, and she rested her hand on her stomach.

"How bad was it?" His voice was grim. Some intuition told her he wouldn't be surprised by what she told him.

"Bad. There was a room made of stone, and it was damp and dark. Cold, too. I have no idea where it was." She tried to remember as many details as she could. "There was a group of men, all in robes, like monks." But there'd been nothing holy about them.

Darius stayed kneeling in front of her, waiting patiently. She got the feeling he could be very patient when he wanted something. He didn't fidget and appeared outwardly calm. She'd bet her savings that he was hell on wheels in the boardroom.

"They were chanting. A weird combination of languages. I couldn't see what they were surrounding at first. Then the torches flared to life, and I saw a dragon. No, I mean a drakon." Shocked filled her. "He told me that."

"Who? Who told you what?"

"The dragon told me he was a drakon. He didn't speak out loud, but I heard him in my head. I'd forgotten that." How had she forgotten that? No matter, she was remembering it now.

"I take it that's not normal for your visions."

"There was nothing normal about this vision at all." She bit her bottom lip and shivered. "He was chained. Thick, nasty chains. And they tried to kill him with a sword, but he fought. He was weak, but he fought. They cut his neck and collected some of his blood."

As much as she wanted to deny it, she knew the vision had been real, like a recording trapped in the vellum pages of the book, one only she—and maybe a few others in the world—could read.

"I knew what he wanted me to do." Darius was watching her, his intensity unnerving. "I've never been part of the vision before. Never."

"What did you do?" he asked. His voice had dropped in timbre and was so incredibly deep it was almost a growl.

"I grabbed one of the torches and tossed it to him. He caught it in his mouth and then burst into flames. All the men scattered." She looked directly at Darius. "I saw one of them before I dropped the book and broke contact. I saw his face and I recognized him.

"Who was it? Who did you see?" he demanded.

"Mr. Temple. But that's impossible, isn't it? I mean, the vision seemed older, but Herman Temple looked the same. And how could I be a part of the vision? I wasn't there."

"Maybe you viewed the scene through the perspective of someone who was there."

She nodded. That made as much sense as any of this.

Darius stood, went to his desk, and tossed the book down. He pulled his laptop in front of him and began tapping the keys. A few seconds later, he turned the machine so it was facing her. "This Herman Temple?"

Sarah pushed out of the chair and came to stand beside him. "Yes. That's the man who hired me. The same one who was in the vision."

Darius reached into his desk and pulled out a phone. Damn, there'd been a phone in the room she could have used to call for help. He caught her gaze, and one corner of his mouth kicked up as he punched in a number.

"Herman Temple. I want to know everything you can find out about him. Businessman here in New York." He glanced at the laptop screen and rattled off his address. "He's one of the Knights." He paused, listening to what the person on the other end of the line was saying. Then he nodded. "Don't call this number. It won't be in operation any longer. I'll call you."

"Don't forget about his son," she reminded him. "Christian."

"Christian Temple as well," Darius added. "He's the son." He ended the call and then closed his fist around the plastic casing. It cracked. As she watched, the phone was crushed to pieces. He opened his hand and let the remains fall onto the desk.

Her mouth went dry, making it difficult to swallow. She'd known he was strong, but that was downright scary.

"I'm sorry, Sarah, I can't risk anyone using this phone to find the person I called."

She leaned against the desk for support and summoned the courage to speak. "He's important to you."

"Very." He said nothing more, and she realized that was all he was going to tell her. For some inexplicable reason, she felt hurt by his refusal to include her, which made no sense. They were virtual strangers who'd just met tonight. Yes, they'd been thrown together by a very unusual situation, but that didn't make them best buds or confidants.

It was time for her to leave. "I've done what I came to do. You know about the people who are after you and you have the book. I need to get out of here." She turned her back on him and headed for the door. Her role in this drama was over.

She wasn't part of this fight. All she wanted to do was hide so she didn't become collateral damage.

She didn't think it was going to be easy to get off the grid, which was what she was going to have to do with people like Darius and Mr. Temple involved. They had way too much power and money, and Mr. Temple apparently had government contacts as well.

She was well and truly screwed.

She made it as far as the door before a long, muscled arm snaked around her waist. "I can't let you go. It's not safe for you out there."

The husky murmur in her ear made her entire body clench. This was so not appropriate, but there was no stopping her reaction to Darius. Her nipples puckered and her panties dampened. Frustration ate at her, so she went on the attack.

"What are you going to do? Protect me from Herman Temple, his son, and his military contact?"

He tightened his arm around her, drawing her back against his large body. "Yes. That's exactly what I plan to do."

• • •

The situation with Sarah was quickly spinning out of his control. Darius knew he should put her on one of his private planes and send her to one of the many secluded islands he owned around the world. No one would find her, at least not anytime soon. She'd be safe while he dealt with this newest threat from the Knights of the Dragon.

But he simply couldn't let her go.

Every time she tried to walk away from him, the beast inside him roared to life. Instincts honed over thousands of years screamed at him to keep her near, to protect her.

Unable to stop himself, he nuzzled her hair and the curve of her neck, drinking in her unique feminine scent. Every cell in his body reacted to her presence, his muscles clenching, his blood thickening.

He wanted her.

There was no denying the attraction even if he didn't quite trust it. He no longer believed she was working for the Knights, but he was wary of feeling so much for a woman so quickly. That didn't mean he was going to let her go. No way was that happening until he'd had her in his bed.

Patience, he counseled himself. Now was neither the time nor the place. His apartment was being watched, which meant Sarah was in danger.

He forced his arms to release her and was surprised when she continued to lean against him. She turned and peered up at him. "You have enough to worry about with protecting yourself. Why would you concern yourself with me?"

He could tell she was honestly bewildered. That made two of them. Other than his brothers, Darius had worried only about himself for thousands of years. What made this slip of a woman different?

Yes, he'd had human friends over the years, even some who'd known his secret. But the last one of those had died several hundred years ago. The world had changed too much, and money meant more than honor to the vast majority of people.

Maybe that's why he was attracted to Sarah. She was risking her life and her livelihood to warn him of the threat, even turning down money when he'd offered it. She'd been downright insulted when he'd suggested such a thing.

She was brave and honorable and beautiful, a very deadly combination to someone like him who valued all three traits. The human side of him valued the bravery and honesty. The dragon side of him admired her beauty.

"Because you risked your safety and freedom to take that book." He hooked a short strand of hair over her ear. "It took honor to contact me." He cupped the entire side of her face with his large hand. "And it took incredibly bravery to come here with me and share what you know."

He knew he was making a mistake, but Darius couldn't stop from lowering his head, touching his lips to hers. Sweet... she tasted sweet like the wine and slightly spicy from the pizza. Delicious. He licked her bottom lip and groaned when she gasped.

He slid his tongue into her warmth and tasted heaven.

She braced her hands on his shoulders but didn't push him away. As he explored the cavern of her mouth, she curled her fingers inward, clinging to him. Then her tongue tentatively touched his, and he lost it.

He was vaguely aware of lifting her off her feet, of her sliding her hands around his neck. He stroked her tongue and sucked on it when she ventured into his mouth. Her breasts were plastered against his chest, and he wished they were both naked so he could feel her skin to skin.

He was so lost in the sheer delight of her that it took him several moments to realize she was no longer clinging to him but pushing him away. He stopped kissing her, but it wasn't easy. All he wanted to do was strip her naked and devour her from head to toe, tasting every smooth inch of her skin.

She was panting as heavily as he was. Her chocolate-brown eyes were glazed over, her lips swollen and damp. When she licked them, his cock swelled, although he didn't know how that was possible since he was already so aroused.

"That—" She broke off, swallowed, and tried again. "That got out of hand."

"Should I apologize?"

"Are you sorry?"

He shook his head. "No." How could he be sorry for such an incredible experience?

"You can put me down."

He didn't want to, but he knew it was for the best. He had to start thinking with the head on his shoulders and not the smaller one in his pants, or they'd be in big trouble. The Knights were not to be taken lightly. They'd captured and killed many drakons over the centuries.

He set Sarah on her feet, but she gripped his arm, not moving away immediately. She took several deep breaths and finally took a step back. "So, what do we do next?"

Darius had to bite back his first thought, which was to suggest they go to his bedroom and continue what they'd started. Not smart on so many levels. Not only were the Knights watching his apartment building and him, but he didn't think Sarah was ready for them to get naked together, which was really too bad.

She was never going to have sex with him if she thought he was crazy. From her perspective, what he was telling her didn't make any sense. People didn't go around claiming to be the son of a dragon and a human. She also had to trust him if he was going to be able to protect her. Otherwise, she might run off if given the opportunity. She'd already proved herself resourceful, or she would never have been able to smuggle that book away from Temple.

The thought of her running around the city on her own was intolerable. The Knights were not opposed to using torture to get what they wanted. They were ruthless when it came to the pursuit of wealth, power, and eternal life.

"The next thing we have to do is convince you I'm not out of my mind."

She started to object but quickly shut her mouth again. Damn, he hated knowing she thought he wasn't quite sane.

"I'm not dangerous," he said, but he had to rethink his statement when she snorted in obvious disbelief. He blew out a breath. "Okay, I am dangerous, but not to you." He pinned her with his gaze. "Never to you." It was important she understand that.

He held out his hand to her. "Come with me." He held his breath and waited. There was so much riding on this next moment. She could come with him willingly, or he could force her. He wanted her to come of her own free will.

Exaltation filled him when she put her small hand in his. He detoured back to the desk long enough to grab the book. Darius wasn't about to let it out of his sight. It seemed heavier than it had before, and a low hum of energy emanated from the leather binding.

He led her out of the office and down to the end of the hallway. A floor-to-ceiling painting filled the narrow space. Even though the painting and the frame looked old, the subject matter would be at home in any video gamer's room. A large dragon filled the sky while the people below shot arrows at the beast. Several flaming arrows were embedded in the creature's body while a hooded man stood nearby reading from a book.

She squinted, and he could tell she was trying to see the writing on the book, but it was impossible to make it out. Darius reached up and pressed a hidden lever at the top of the frame. The painting swung back to reveal a doorway.

Sarah gasped and tugged her hand away. His stomach dropped, and a deep sadness filled him.

"What's that? Where are we going?"

"I need to show you something." He could explain, but it was better to show her. "Trust me."

She studied his face and finally nodded. Then she stepped onto the staircase behind the painting, and started downward.

• • •

Herman Temple took a sip of the fine cognac in his glass, savoring the rich flavor before swallowing. Flames danced in the fireplace, the only illumination in his study. This was his favorite place in the world. He was surrounded by art and books, and able to relax and forget his worries, if only for a short time. He swirled the amber liquid in the crystal goblet and admired the deep color.

A knock came on the door, and he frowned. His staff knew better than to disturb him while he was in his study. This was his time, and he coveted it greatly. Whoever was there was either stupid, or something was very wrong. And since he didn't hire stupid people…

He sat forward and set his glass on the oak table next to his chair. "Come."

Matthew Riggs, the head of his personal security team, stepped into the room. "I'm sorry to bother you, sir, but we have a problem."

Herman waved the man forward. Riggs had been with him for two years now and wasn't one to exaggerate. "What is it?"

The former military man strode across the room and came to a halt in front of him. He stood at attention as he gave his report. "I spot-checked the security footage from today, as per usual."

Herman knew that Riggs liked to do that to make sure his team didn't miss anything. Then the security footage was filed away or deleted, depending on whether Riggs thought it might be useful down the road.

"And?" Herman was getting a bad feeling in the pit of his stomach.

"One of the security team had to go remind Ms. Anderson when it was time to leave for the day."

Herman didn't see why that was a problem. It wasn't the first time it had happened, and he didn't expect it to be the last.

"The man monitoring the security feeds chose that

moment to step away and go to the bathroom." There were no visible signs of emotion on Riggs's face, but Herman could tell he wasn't pleased. Neither was Herman.

"What happened?"

"Maybe nothing, but it seems she was studying a particular book when Martin went to inform her it was time to go. It was a rather old Bible," Riggs told him before he could ask.

"That's of no consequence." Herman began to relax slightly. There'd been a breach in the security surveillance, but nothing that couldn't be fixed.

"That's what I thought at first, sir, but I viewed the footage several times."

The knot was back in Herman's stomach. He didn't need any more problems or delays. He needed Sarah Anderson to find the book so he could capture and contain Darius Varkas.

The book should never have been lost in the first place. He blamed his son for that. Christian was lax with security. It was only after the book had gone missing that Herman had instituted extra security precautions inside his home. He'd never bothered before, because only the most trusted Knights were allowed entry into his private library. His son hadn't been as prudent. As much as Christian denied it, Herman didn't doubt that he was lying to save his own hide.

After all Herman had taught his son, Christian had still trusted the wrong man. It was a weakness, his son's need for validation from his lovers and close confidants. Usually that validation was bought with money or favors. This was the first time the repercussions had been so dire.

And there was no denying that Gervais Rames had known exactly where to find the book. The only bright spot was the alarm on the vault had been triggered, and he'd been unable to escape the building. Rames hadn't gotten away, but he'd managed to hide the damn book in one of the libraries before he was caught, and no amount of torture had been able to get the location out of him before he'd died.

Time was running out, and Herman was under pressure from the head of the order of the Knights of the Dragon to capture Varkas. And the book was key. Herman might be a man of science, but there was no denying that certain inanimate objects contained power. The book was one such item.

"Well, what is it?" Herman demanded.

"I can't be 100 percent sure because the lighting is poor between the bookshelves, but when Martin came upon her, he startled her and she dropped the book." He took a deep breath and continued. "Sir, I think she picked something up and hid it on her person when she bent down to retrieve the Bible."

"Show me." Herman pushed out of his chair and motioned to his laptop, which sat on his desk.

Riggs quickly brought up the footage from the day's security and found the right spot. "Here it is."

Herman joined Riggs and watched the scene on the laptop unfold. He knew it was just after he'd spoken to her. Like Riggs's had said, it was hard to see if she had indeed taken anything, but she did seem nervous. Of course, she always seemed nervous around him.

"And that's not the worst of it, sir."

Herman stared into Riggs's glacial-blue eyes. "What is the worst?"

"This." Riggs tapped the keys several times and brought up footage from earlier in the afternoon. "Because of the lapse when Ms. Anderson was leaving for the day, I went back to review the rest of the footage."

Herman couldn't imagine what could be worse than Sarah possibly stealing from him. If she'd found the book he was looking for, she wouldn't understand the significance of it, so why would she steal it? He didn't speak, knowing Riggs would tell him the rest.

"It was just after lunch. It seems Ms. Anderson missed hers and went to the break room later than usual."

Herman knew what Riggs was going to say next. "She was in the hallway when you and Christian were talking. And from the look on her face, she overheard plenty." His head of security tapped the button to play the footage, and Herman watched and listened to his conversation with his son. Sure enough, there was Sarah walking down the hallway and ducking into an alcove. There was no way she hadn't heard most of their conversation.

He made himself watch it all. Long minutes after he and Christian had left, Sarah left the alcove and scurried back to the library. Her face was pale and she was shaking.

"Who was the guard on duty?"

"Simms, sir."

"How did this happen, Riggs?"

"I reviewed the footage from the security room, and Simms was texting, sir." Riggs didn't shift or fidget under Herman's scrutiny.

"Texting?" Their entire mission might be jeopardized by some idiot texting. "Deal with him and find Sarah Anderson. Even if she didn't take anything from me, she knows too much to be running around free. I need her here to find that bloody missing book."

"Right away, sir." Riggs turned and strode toward the door.

"And, Riggs."

"Yes, sir."

"Before you arrange for Simms to have an accident, make sure he wasn't texting anything he shouldn't have been. I don't want to discover another potential problem down the road."

"Yes, sir." Riggs nodded and reached for the handle.

"One more thing." His head of security met his gaze. "I

don't have to tell you this had better never happen again."

"It won't, sir," he promised.

"See that it doesn't." The door closed silently behind Riggs.

He drew his phone out of his pocket. He dialed the first number in his contacts list, and when his son answered, Herman glanced down at the security feed, with the picture of Sarah Anderson frozen on the screen. "We have a problem."

Chapter Nine

Sarah's lips still tingled, and her body was alive with sensation. She'd actually kissed Darius. Now she was letting him take her down a secret staircase to God only knew where. Probably not the smartest thing she'd ever done.

How many people had a secret staircase in their home? Probably only eccentric billionaires.

Her mind whirled with thoughts of secret societies, conspiracies, kidnapping, murder, that particularly nasty book, and drakons. The sexual attraction was the cherry on top of this already out-of-control situation.

The most insane part of all was that she trusted Darius. He'd meant it when he said he'd protect her. In spite of the danger surrounding them, that had made her feel safe.

She put one hand on the wall to keep her balance. The stairs were narrow, and there was no railing. She glanced over her shoulder. Darius was right behind her. He had to duck slightly so he wouldn't hit his head. It was a tight squeeze for a man of his size. The only light came from the opening above — and then the secret door shut, leaving them in darkness.

She gasped and froze in place, not daring to move. "I can't see a thing."

"Give it a moment," he told her. Sure enough, dim lights illuminated the stairs, but not much else. All sorts of scenarios popped into her head, none of them good. What could he possible show her that would change her mind?

"Keep going," he told her.

There was no turning back. She certainly couldn't get around him on this tight staircase. And even if she could, where would she go? The elevator was inaccessible.

There had to be some kind of fire exit. Didn't there? Maybe she could find that.

Sarah put one foot in front of the other until she reached the base of the stairs. Darkness loomed before her. There didn't even seem to be a window.

Darius reached around her and must have hit a switch, because suddenly, bright light filled the room, making her blink. The space was gigantic, probably an entire floor of the building. And it was empty. On closer inspection, she noticed there did seem to be windows, but they were covered with heavy metal shutters.

"I don't understand. What is this place?" It reminded her of an empty parking garage with huge metal supports and a concrete floor. She took a step back up one of the stairs.

Darius left her and walked to the center of the space. The ceiling was way above him. "I own the building and have the top three floors for myself."

Since his living space seemed to occupy only the highest level, that meant that this space was actually the equivalent of two stories, which explained the crazy high ceiling. "Why?" Curiosity had the better of her. "Why have all this empty space?"

Darius set the book carefully on the floor and began to unbutton his shirt. Sarah took another step back up the stairs but couldn't tear her gaze away from the swatch of deeply tanned skin he exposed.

"What are you doing?" She winced at the husky sound of her voice.

"Showing you I'm not crazy," he reminded her.

"Ah, yeah." She momentarily lost her train of thought when he tossed his shirt aside and then bent to remove his shoes. "Not sure that's working." The man was stripping in front of her and she couldn't take her eyes off him.

When fully dressed, he was impressive. Naked from the waist up, he was breathtaking. The stark lighting hid nothing from her. From his broad shoulders and washboard abs to his tapered waist, he was the most flawless male specimen she'd ever seen. Nothing in a magazine or movie could touch the sheer masculine perfection of Darius Varkas.

And then there was the tattoo that covered the left side of his body—thick lines of rich bronze, outlined in the same green shade as his eyes, swirled over his chest and arm and disappeared into the waistband of his pants. There was no recognizable design, but it was stunning all the same.

His biceps rippled when he shoved his hair away from his face. He was watching her intently as he unbuckled his belt, unzipped his pants, and pushed them down. His boxer briefs went at the same time and, when he straightened, he was totally naked.

Sarah sat down hard on the stairs. She knew she was staring but couldn't help herself. His eyes seemed to be glowing, which had to be a trick of the light. But it wasn't his eyes that had captured her attention. No, it was the thick erection spearing upward from the thatch of hair on his groin. Darius was built to scale, which meant he was bigger than any man she'd been with. His tattoo also continued down the left side of his body all the way to his ankle.

She fanned her hand in front of her face until she realized

what she was doing and made herself stop. Darius, the devil, grinned at her.

If he made one move in her direction, she wasn't sure if she'd race back up the stairs or jump him. At this point, it could go either way. "You're naked." Way to state the obvious.

"I know." He held his arms out by his sides and slowly turned so she could see every inch of him. The tattoo bisected his back into two planes. The design wrapped around the entire left side of his body with the exception of his hand and foot. His face was also unmarked by the spectacular design.

Sarah rubbed her damp palms against her jeans. "Why are you naked?"

"Watch, Sarah." The way he said her name made her insides melt. "And don't be afraid."

With that ominous warning, she watched and waited. Darius seemed to blur in front of her, and she blinked several times. Her breath caught in her throat, as he seemed to transform before her very eyes. His tanned skin thickened, becoming plate-like armor that shimmered a deep metallic bronze and covered a massive body. His head changed shape, flattening on the top and becoming almost wedge-like, with an elongated jaw. Claws that had to be at least eight inches long tipped his front and back feet.

Sarah was breathing fast, coming close to hyperventilating, but she couldn't help herself. This was impossible. His spine made a cracking sound and an enormous pair of wings emerged. When he spread them, they spanned about thirty feet. The space that had seemed so cavernous only seconds before now seemed way too small to contain such a creature.

When the metamorphosis was complete, the beast leaned his head down and stared at her. The eyes were eerily familiar. They were Darius's green eyes.

"I have to be dreaming." That was the only logical explanation.

"You're not dreaming." The voice was lower and gruffer, but she recognized it.

If she hadn't already been sitting down, she would have been flat on her ass. "This isn't possible." She shook her head as if to deny the image in front of her.

His gaze narrowed and smoke rolled from his nostrils. "Come and touch me."

This had to be some kind of trick, even though it didn't seem like it. Determined to put an end to Darius's games, she pushed herself upright and carefully went down the two steps. Her entire body was shaking, and there was no way she could stop it. She reached out her hand and touched one of the armor-like plates that covered his body. They were like scales but larger and tougher. She stroked her hand over his thick forearm, amazed by how warm he felt. She'd expected him to be cold to the touch, but he wasn't the slightest bit cool.

He huffed out a breath and another plume of smoke floated to the ceiling before dissipating. He had to be fifteen feet long, and that didn't include his tail, which doubled his size.

"I don't understand." There was no way for her mind to process what was before her. Dragons were myth. But he wasn't a dragon, was he? He was a drakon—the son of a dragon and a human.

A scream built inside her, but she swallowed it back. What good would it do? There was no one to hear her. She had no doubt this entire place was soundproofed. As it was, she was having a hard time getting enough air into her lungs to breathe normally.

She was actually touching something from myth and legend. Then she had another thought and withdrew her hand to stare up into his intelligent eyes. "There are more of you, aren't there?"

. . .

Darius wasn't sure what he'd expected from Sarah. She seemed emotionally calm, but her own body betrayed that as a lie. Her hand trembled when she touched him, and her breathing was quick and shallow.

He wanted to stay in his drakon form but decided she'd deal better with the shock if he were human once again. When he began to shift, Sarah jumped back and wrapped her arms around herself. As his body reshaped and reformed, he was reminded just how much this woman had been through in such a short period of time. Her beliefs about the world around her had been completely and utterly shattered.

When he was a man once again, he got dressed, taking his time pulling his clothing back on. When he was fully covered once again, he grabbed the book and walked toward her. She didn't withdraw or flinch from his touch. He'd take that as a good sign. "Let's go upstairs, and I'll answer as many of your questions as I can."

She nodded and led the way back up the narrow staircase. He walked close behind her, ready to catch her if she faltered, but she needed no help. When they reached the top of the stairs, he deactivated the locking mechanism and the tall painting swung open.

Sarah didn't wait for him, but headed straight to the study. She dropped into one of the large wingback chairs and closed her eyes. Not surprisingly, she looked extremely pale.

Darius set the book on his desk before he detoured to his liquor cabinet and poured some brandy into a goblet. "Here, drink this. It will help." She was dealing with quite a shock, whether she realized it or not.

"Thank you." She wrapped both hands around the glass and took a small sip. "It's all real, isn't it? I can't bury my head in the sand and pretend it's all a bad dream or just a bunch of crazy people."

"No, you can't." He put his hands on the arms of the chair to keep from touching her. What he really wanted to do was hug her and promise her everything would be okay.

She took another sip of the amber liquid and nodded. "Okay, tell me more."

He snagged the leather book off his desk, and held it up. "This is dangerous." He flipped open the pages and studied them one by one, drawn to them in a way he didn't quite understand. There was no denying the energy pulsing from the book was growing stronger. "Recipes for potions that weaken us, making it easier for them to capture and enslave us. Incantations as well, but I don't know if those actually work."

"Incantations? Like sorcerers and wizards?" She dropped her head back against the cushion of the chair. "It sounds crazy when you say it, but this entire situation is like something out of a fantasy novel." Then she laughed. "And I'm no heroine."

Darius knew she was wrong. Sarah had already proven her bravery this day. Most people would have taken care of themselves, either by running or extorting money. She'd done neither.

"No. They're more alchemists and scientists than sorcerers." These men were smart and ruthless, willing to use whatever was at their disposal to gain their prize.

"Why do they want you?"

Darius shook his head. "Ingesting drakon's blood cures disease and prolongs the life of the human who drinks it. It also grants some people extra powers. That varies from human to human, but it can be more strength, greater intelligence, keener instincts, and more."

"Really?" Her eyes widened and she took another sip of the brandy. "Wow. Okay, so they want to study your blood to make some sort of super drug or something?"

Darius straightened and took the chair across from her. "Our blood starts to deteriorate the moment it leaves our body. The Knights of the Dragon drink from the source."

She swallowed and put her glass on the table beside her chair. "That's what they were doing in the vision I got from the book, isn't it? They were making the drakon bleed so they could drink his blood."

"Yes. It's what they've been doing for century upon century, ever since the first human discovered what our blood could do."

"But that's terrible."

Darius lowered his head in contemplation. So many drakons had died for the lusts of men.

"Mr. Temple and his son mentioned scientists and experiments and a military contact."

He raised his head and studied Sarah. "That is not new. Such men have been trying for years to duplicate our essence to create more of us. They want to build a private army of drakons, or at least super soldiers, men who will do their bidding and fight their wars. Some of them would sell that knowledge to the military for even more money and power. Many wish to become drakons, to be powerful and live for eternity."

"Eternity?" She grabbed the glass and swallowed the rest of the brandy in one gulp. She wheezed and then began to cough. He was by her side in a heartbeat, carefully tapping her back as she choked on the liquor. When she finally stopped, her cheeks were flushed. "Eternity?" she asked again.

Darius shrugged. "By human standards. Dragons live for a hundred thousand years. We have no idea how long we drakons will live. The only ones of us who have died so far have been those killed by the Knights." He didn't tell her about the Deep Sleep that overtook some drakons.

She leaned forward, the empty glass still clutched in her

hands. "These men will stop at nothing."

It wasn't a question, but he answered her anyway. "No, they will not stop. They'll use whatever power and influence they have to capture us. And they won't hesitate to kill anyone who gets in their way.

"Then there's only one thing we can do." She pointed at the book. "We need to destroy that."

Chapter Ten

As much as it hurt her librarian's soul to even consider destroying a book that old and rare and with such knowledge in it, some things were better left unknown. And any knowledge that could be used to enslave another species should be consigned to a black hole, never to be found again.

It was difficult to believe that drinking a drakon's blood cured disease and prolonged life. It was much less difficult to believe that humans would covet that power for themselves and destroy every drakon in their lust to obtain their goal— eternal life.

As much as she believed in the goodness of mankind, she also knew they could be a greedy, grasping species. You only had to look at the state of the world or read a newspaper to know that. As for the military, she respected the men and women who protected the country, but she knew there were a handful of men at higher ranks both in the military and in the government who would stop at nothing to gain this kind of power for themselves.

Darius pried the empty glass from her hand and set it

aside. The liquor she'd swallowed warmed her stomach, but she was still cold. Sarah didn't think she'd ever be warm again. Her worldview had been forever shattered.

"We have to leave the country." There was no way around it. "If the military is after you, they have unlimited resources at their fingertips—surveillance cameras, electronic records, and heaven only knows what else." She jumped to her feet and began to pace. "They probably already know I'm here." It was a terrifying proposition.

Darius caught her by the shoulders. "I don't think so. I don't believe this Herman Temple would be so quick to give up his leverage to any government department. His contact probably believes he's manufacturing some drug that will make soldiers stronger, faster, and more able to withstand injury."

That made sense and calmed her somewhat. Mr. Temple was rich and powerful in his own right, and he owned one of the largest pharmaceutical companies in the world.

The more she thought about it, the more she believed Darius was right. Mr. Temple's military contact might not even know anything about drakons. It was likely Mr. Temple had promised them some kind of drug to make their soldiers stronger. That kept all the power, and the drakon, firmly in his grasp.

"You're right. The Knights wouldn't risk alerting his contact until they had you. Maybe not even then. Mr. Temple has made a lot of his money in pharmaceuticals. It's more likely he has his people experimenting on drakon blood." That made more sense than allowing the military control over a drakon. He might give the military a sample of drakon blood to experiment with, but he'd never explain where it came from. Mr. Temple would probably tell them it was something his lab developed.

Darius inclined his head. He seemed so composed and

steady. Of course, this probably wasn't the first time he'd been targeted by the Knights of the Dragon. She narrowed her gaze and studied him. For the first time in her life, she wished her gift worked on people and not just inanimate objects.

"What now?" she asked.

Darius reached into his desk drawer and drew out yet another phone. He seemed to have a supply of them. "Now I call my contact and see what he's discovered." He turned away and dialed the number, the action as natural to him as breathing. She wondered what it must be like to live with such secrecy every day of your life. She wasn't sure she could handle it.

Not that he had much choice with Herman Temple and his ilk hunting him.

"What have you got?" Darius asked the person who answered his call. She strained her ears but couldn't hear anything useful. Darius turned toward her, and she leaned back in her chair and looked casually around the room. Not that he was fooled by her display. The man winked at her. Winked at her.

He made several noncommittal noises and then seemed to listen intently. "I'm going to put you on speaker. Sarah needs to hear this."

She sat forward and rested her elbows on her knees. Exhaustion was pulling at her, but there was no way she was going to miss this conversation.

"Who the hell is Sarah?" The voice was deep, male, and angry.

"I'll explain later. What do you know?" Darius asked his friend or colleague or whoever this person was.

"Herman Temple has a history that goes back about sixty years or so. He inherited family money and grew the fortune. That's all public knowledge."

Sarah nodded. There was nothing new there. She'd known

all that and more before she'd stepped foot into his office.

"On paper, he's a businessman and a philanthropist. Dig deeper and it gets interesting."

"I don't have all night." Darius was getting impatient with the speaker.

"You have no appreciation for my intellectual prowess," the unknown man complained.

"Don't make me come out there." Darius voice had grown deeper, his tone clipped. He was glaring at the phone, and Sarah had to bite her lip to keep from laughing. She might not know the man on the line, but she already liked him.

"Very well. Although, you and your friend are welcome here any time." There was a pause. "Now where was I? Oh, yes, my skill as a researcher." His tone turned serious. "I dug up a few photos of Herman Temple's grandfather and his great grandfather. And let me tell you that wasn't easy. I called in a few favors I would have rather not had to."

"And?" She couldn't stand the suspense. "What did you find?" she asked.

"It's the same man. Or his twin. I think that the man in the photos is Temple, and every so often, he reinvents himself as his own son or grandson."

"That's not possible." She rubbed her aching head and thought about her vision from the book. It had seemed old, but the man she'd seen had definitely been Mr. Temple.

"Oh, it's very possible, sweetheart," the unknown man said.

Darius growled at the phone. His nostrils flared and actual smoke flowed from them. He wasn't happy with the speaker, and she had no idea why.

"What he means to say"—Darius took over the conversation—"is that if the man had a ready supply of drakon blood, he could easily extend his life for several centuries, maybe longer."

Sarah thought about the poor drakon from her vision. If he'd died a long time ago, how had Mr. Temple gotten more drakon's blood? There was only one answer—he'd captured another drakon. Either that or the scene in her vision was much more recent than she'd thought. The thought of the poor creature being tortured and bled for years made her heart ache. It was inhuman, barbaric, and downright evil.

She glared at the book sitting on the desk. Only leather and paper, yet it had caused so much harm. She pushed out of her chair, went to the desk, and stared down at the plain leather cover. She pulled up all her shields before she touched it.

The vision swept her in, overwhelming her as though her shield wasn't even there. She heard male voices chanting. One voice rose over all of them. It spoke softly and seductively, promising her all kinds of power and longevity if she'd return the book to the Knights of the Dragon.

Sarah tried to release it and was horrified to discover she couldn't. It was then she understood this object was unlike any she'd ever encountered. The holiness of the Bible had kept the evil at bay, but now that it was free, the volume seemed to be growing in power.

Almost like it was a living entity.

Black tendrils rose from the leather binding. They encircled her wrists and twined around her lower arms. She opened her mouth but no sound came out. Inwardly, she was screaming. She'd never encountered anything this dangerous before. The book seemed intent on consuming her will, bending it to its own wishes.

She thought she heard someone calling her name, but it seemed so distant. She tried to turn toward the sound, but the blackness wouldn't allow her to move.

Sarah knew she was going to either die or become an instrument of evil.

· · ·

Darius took his brother off speaker and watched as Sarah strode to the desk and glared down at the book. He started to ask his brother a question but changed his mind and hung up on Tarrant when Sarah reached for the leather-bound journal. He started to warn her off, but it was too late.

Her entire body stiffened, and her eyes lost focus the second she wrapped her hands around the faded covering. He knew she was being sucked into one of her visions. She'd probably done this kind of thing dozens of times, but he was uneasy.

He tossed the phone onto the desk. "Sarah?" She didn't react to his voice at all. He was hesitant to touch her, not sure what kind of effect, if any, it would have on her.

Her breathing sped up and her mouth opened on a silent scream.

Darius called her name but got no response. He grabbed her shoulders and shook her, trying to jolt her out of her vision. Her body was stiff and unyielding. Sweat beaded on her forehead.

A fear unlike any he'd ever known slammed into him. He was losing her. He didn't question the knowledge or ignore his instincts. He yelled her name and thought he saw a flicker of recognition, but it was quickly gone.

The book was doing this to her.

He reached for the offending item and tried to yank it out of her hands, but she held on tightly. He didn't want to hurt Sarah but knew he had to get the book away from her. He wrapped one arm around her waist and grabbed the leather volume with his free hand. Then he pulled.

It was as though they were both magnetized, the attraction was so great. The pulse in her neck fluttered wildly. Her skin took on a waxy cast and dark circles formed beneath her eyes.

The book was killing her.

With one great pull, he yanked it from her hands and tossed it onto the floor. Even though there could be knowledge in there to help him and his brothers, Darius thrust Sarah aside and let his body shift. There wasn't enough room, and furniture was pushed back or toppled as he grew in size. He reached for his drakon's fire as soon as the shift was complete. Flames shot out of his mouth and surrounded the book. He'd burn it to a crisp so it could never endanger Sarah again.

The fire raced over the leather cover and danced along its edges, but the damn thing didn't burn. Darius stopped and studied the smoldering book and the scorched hardwood floors. The edge of the carpet was on fire, so he breathed out a plume of smoke, smothering the blaze.

"Oh my God."

He turned to Sarah, belatedly wondering if he'd hurt her when he'd tossed her aside. Thankfully, his aim had been true and she'd landed in a chair and not on the floor. "It won't burn." She wrapped her arms around herself and rocked slightly back and forth. "It was like it was alive."

The fear in her eyes had him shifting to his human form. Since he hadn't removed his clothing before he'd embraced his dragon, the garments had been ripped apart, leaving him naked. "You're safe," he promised her. He'd damn well make her safe, no matter what he had to do to achieve his goal.

"You're naked," she countered. The small smile playing at the corners of her mouth eased some of his tension.

"So I am." He crouched by her side and took her icy hand in his. "What happened?"

She shivered and glanced toward the book lying unharmed on the floor. "I wanted to destroy it. I had my mental shields up but got sucked into a vision as soon as I touched it." Her eyes were bleak when she looked back at him. "Voices. There were voices offering me power and wealth, and then one voice rose over the others."

Darius's wanted to torch the book more than ever for what it had done to her. He rubbed her smaller hands in his, but they remained icy cold.

"It was the book." She looked horrified by her words. "The book is alive, and it's evil. It wants to be returned to the Knights."

"There may be some sort of charm or spell to help keep the book in the Knights' hands." At this point, he didn't know what the hell it was. This was going to take research, because if drakon fire couldn't destroy it, he was out of ideas.

"Most likely it was devised to keep drakons from burning it since it was probably used around your kind."

That made a perfect kind of sense to him. "You're probably right."

She shuddered. "That doesn't make me feel better. I can't get warm." The last was said on a plaintive cry.

Darius stood and lifted Sarah into his arms. He turned his back on the book and carried her out of the study and into his bedroom. He ignored his throbbing erection and his sexual needs. Nothing was more important than taking care of Sarah.

His huge bed mocked him as he passed by, daring him to toss her onto the firm mattress and strip her clothing from her body. He kept going into the adjoining bathroom. A huge soaker tub that could fit three normal-sized people occupied one corner of the room. "A bath will help warm you. You've had a shock." That was putting it mildly.

He deposited her on top of the vanity and started the water running into the tub. He was very aware of her eyes on him as he rummaged through a cabinet and found a bottle of sea salt that Ezra had sent him. He opened it and dumped half of it into the tub.

"What is that?" she asked.

He held up the bottle. "Sea salt. It will help cleanse away

any lingering negative energy from the book."

He wasn't sure how she'd take that bit of information and was reassured when she smiled. "That's what my grandmother always said."

Darius tucked the bottle back in the cabinet. "Wise woman, your grandmother."

Sarah nodded. "She was." She dragged her hands through her hair, tousling the thick locks. "I don't have anything else to wear."

"I'll get you a shirt." The thought of her wearing his clothes made him hard all over.

"Ah, you might want to get something for yourself, too."

Shit. He'd gotten so caught up in taking care of Sarah, he'd forgotten he was bare-ass naked. "I'll be back." He hurried from the room and quickly donned socks, jeans, and a black T-shirt. He detoured into his large closet and plucked out a dress shirt. It fit him perfectly so it would easily cover Sarah.

The light splash of water caught his attention, and he hurried back into the bathroom. His fingers strangled the silk and cotton fabric in his hand when he caught sight of her curled up in the corner of his tub. Her slender arms were wrapped around her knees and her head was bent forward. She was wet and naked and shaking.

The last kicked aside all other thoughts. He tossed the shirt onto the counter and knelt by the side of the tub. Water lapped up near the top of the porcelain, so he turned off the taps.

She turned her head and looked at him. Her chocolate-brown eyes were the only color in her otherwise pale face. Even her lips weren't as rosy as they normally were.

"The darkness, the evil from the book was trying to get inside me."

Fury at the Knights, at their power-hungry, grasping souls, bubbled up inside him, but he allowed none of that to show.

Sarah needed calm, not anger. "How?"

She tightened her arms around her knees. "It was like black tendrils wrapping around my wrists and climbing up my arms. I tried to drop the book, tried to yell for help, but I couldn't do anything. I was helpless." Her lips quivered, but she didn't cry.

Darius shook his head. He wanted to banish the fear and the defeated look from her eyes. "Not helpless. You held the evil at bay until I was able to free you."

Steam rose around them. He reached out and brushed aside several strands of hair that were stuck to her forehead. She shivered and seemed to lean into his touch. He did his best to ignore the swell of her breasts and the curve of her hip, but at the same time he wished she'd uncurl from the tight ball she had herself in so he could see all of her.

"Soak until you feel better." He wanted to stay with her, but there were things he needed to do. Plus, he wasn't certain if his presence was a comfort or if he was only making her more nervous. "I'll be back to check on you, but stay as long as you want."

Sarah grabbed his wrist as he stood. "Don't touch it. Don't touch the book, not unless I'm with you." Her fear was palpable, and he found himself nodding just to calm her.

"I won't," he promised.

She relaxed slightly and slowly released him. He wanted to strip off his clothes and climb into the tub with her. Instead, he made himself leave and head back to the study. The book was still on the floor. He ignored it and reached for the phone he'd tossed aside.

His brother answered on the first ring. "What the hell is going on?" Tarrant demanded. "And just who the hell is that woman with you?"

"The woman is Sarah Anderson." He could hear Tarrant's fingers clicking on his keyboard and knew his brother was already gathering information about her. Tarrant horded information like some men did gold. He used that information to take other men's money.

"She's a research librarian with a unique talent." He told Tarrant about her call earlier this evening, how she'd gotten involved with the Knights, her special skill, and about the book. He told Tarrant everything.

"You're sure she's not with the Knights?" he demanded. Darius couldn't be mad at his brother's accusations since he'd asked himself the same damn question.

"I'm sure. She's in shock about everything, and I saw what the book did to her." He heard a splash and then someone moving around and knew Sarah was getting out of the tub. Water would be streaming over her smooth skin, her slender arms, and her plump breasts. He didn't have a visual of her breasts, but he had a mighty good imagination.

"Are you still there?" his brother demanded.

"Yeah. Sorry."

"Keep your focus, Darius. You can't afford to get distracted by some female."

Darius swallowed back a growl. He hated that his brother was right. "I don't know how to destroy the book. Fire has no effect whatsoever."

That gave Tarrant pause. "Let me do some research."

"I imagine Sarah will want to do some as well." It would be interesting to see who found out the most, Sarah or his brother.

"Keep her off the internet. Temple probably has hackers on staff, people who monitor certain sites and take note of the people who visit."

"They can do that?" Darius was continually surprised at how invasive technology was. A man's life and secrets were no longer his own.

"Of course they can. I do it all the time." Tarrant took a

deep breath. Darius could easily imagine his brother rolling his eyes at him. "Just keep her offline. I'll handle the searches."

"And they won't find you?"

Tarrant snorted. "All my signals bounce around the world before eventually ending at a remote military site in the middle of a desert. No one has ever gotten anywhere near to tracking it that far."

"How is that even possible?" Darius was no expert when it came to technology, but even he knew that should be difficult, if not downright impossible.

Tarrant snorted again. "Don't ask."

Darius knew his brother took precautions, but this struck him as just a little obsessive. "Let me know when you find something."

"Do you need more phones?" Tarrant asked. His brother supplied him with disposable phones that were heavily encrypted and when in use also emitted some signal that would block anyone trying to listen in on the conversation. Darius didn't even pretend to understand how it worked. He left that to his brother.

"I have a half dozen or so."

"I'd send you more if you need them, but you need to get out of the city. Tonight."

As much as he hated to admit it, he knew Tarrant was right. "I'll call my people and have them put the plane on standby."

"You need to come to the mountains."

"I don't want to bring trouble your way." No way did he want to lead Temple to his brother.

"If Temple has found you, none of us are truly safe. We'll take precautions and can brainstorm together."

"You just want to meet Sarah."

Tarrant laughed. "That, too."

"I shifted for her." He hadn't shifted in front of a human

for well over a hundred years.

"You just met her." He could hear the disbelief in his brother's voice.

"I know." He couldn't explain why he'd found it necessary to show her all sides of him. It just was.

"That's worrisome. Are you sure she's not with the Knights?"

Darius heard a rustling by the door. Sarah was fully dressed, but instead of her sweater, she was wearing his shirt. The sleeves had been rolled back several times and still hit her wrists. The tail of the shirt almost reached her knees.

"I'm sure," he told Tarrant. "I'll call you when we're in the air." He hung up the phone and closed his fingers around it, crushing it into little pieces and letting them fall on his desk.

"How do you feel about the mountains?" he asked her.

. . .

Herman Temple answered his phone on the first ring. He'd been expecting the call. "Do you have her?"

Riggs paused. "No, sir. I'm in her apartment, and she's not at home."

"Damn it. Where the hell is she?"

"I don't know, sir, but I'll find her. It doesn't appear as though she's fled. All her things are here. The only thing missing seems to be a coat and purse. She changed after she got home from work. Maybe she's out on a date that turned into an overnighter."

That was unlikely. His men hadn't found any evidence of a boyfriend when they'd investigated her, but after this security breach, he realized his intel wasn't infallible. "Keep someone there. I want her the moment she surfaces." He paused and thought for a moment. "What about her phone? Can we track her phone?"

"I've got someone on it."

Herman ended the call and tossed his phone down on his desk. He'd come too far to lose now, and certainly not because of some librarian. He stood and his knees ached. He stilled and sweat broke out on his brow. The last of the dragon's blood was gone, and he was noticing small signs of aging. If he went too long without a new infusion, he'd begin aging and eventually die.

All the money and power he'd amassed over his long life meant nothing if he wasn't alive to enjoy them.

He needed Darius Varkas, and he would have him at any cost.

Chapter Eleven

"The mountains?" Sarah had come to the office to find Darius, only to discover him on the phone.

She was feeling much better after her bath. The biting cold that had enveloped her hands and arms had been replaced with much-needed warmth. She was wearing one of Darius's shirts instead of her sweater. It was huge, but it carried a hint of his woodsy scent and felt like being wrapped in his arms. But from the sound of things, she might need a sweater.

"The mountains?" she repeated, not sure she'd heard him correctly.

He reached into his desk, pulled out a small plastic bag, and filled it with plastic and metal pieces from the phones he kept destroying. They weren't the latest touch-screen models. They looked like something from about a decade ago, used strictly as a phone. He swept the most recent pieces into the bag.

"Yes. We need to get out of the city tonight. I thought I'd hang around a few days to see what I could discover about the Knights, but it's too dangerous now. We don't know how long it will take them to discover you have the book. I'm surprised they haven't already made a move."

Sarah's stomach knotted. She knew he was right. She'd known when she left her home this evening she might never be going back. Had it only been earlier this evening? Her life had changed so much in such a short time.

Darius walked over to her and pulled her into his arms. She knew she shouldn't lean on him for strength, couldn't depend on him for the long haul. After all, she was a virtual stranger, and he had friends and people close to him that he needed to protect. She was under no illusions as to what would happen if it came down to a choice between them and her.

She was human and nothing more than a pawn in this game between the Knights and the drakons.

"Which mountains?" She forced herself to push out of his embrace.

"Cascades in Washington State." He released her but only let her retreat to the length of his arms.

"It's as good as anywhere, I guess." She gestured to the book. "What about that?"

Darius walked to the bookcases and plucked a wooden box from one of the shelves. "This should do the trick. The symbols carved on the sides should help contain the emanations from the book. At least for a while."

It was a heavily carved piece and looked old. "Where did you get it?"

Darius removed the cover and set the box on the desk. Then he picked up a metal letter opener and used the tip of the blade to push the book into the wooden container. She held her breath until it was safely inside. She finally took a breath when he retrieved the cover and secured it. The book was contained.

"This was a gift from a holy man from Persia." He tucked

the box under his arm. "It was a long time ago." Just another reminder of how old he was. "Get your things. We need to go."

She went back to his room long enough to collect her sweater. She yanked it on over the borrowed shirt and pulled her coat on over it. By the time she grabbed her bag, Darius was waiting by the elevator door. Like her, he had a knapsack. She knew the book was inside.

He placed his hand on the security pad and the elevator door slid open. She glanced back at the luxury apartment and wondered if she'd ever see it again. Not that there was any reason she should. She and Darius were allies in this strange war, nothing more.

"How are we getting out of here?"

"I've got a plan." He seemed sure of himself, but she wasn't convinced. They'd been lucky so far. She didn't expect it to last.

"And that plan is?" The man was huge and seemed to take up most of the space in the small elevator, but she must be getting used to him, because it made her feel safe instead of claustrophobic.

The elevator stopped and the door silently slid open. He poked his head out and looked around before he ushered her out. They were in the basement. She recognized it from their trek earlier this evening. His hand was big and warm against her lower back. Even through the layers of clothing, she could feel his heat.

He leaned down and murmured in her ear. "Stay quiet. I don't know how many men the Knights have watching me. Stay right behind me."

"You still haven't told me your plan," she whispered.

"Trust me."

She didn't have much choice. The man was infuriating. She was used to being in charge of her own life and didn't like the idea of leaving all the decisions in someone else's hands.

He must have sensed her hesitation, because he sighed, his hot breath wafting over her ear and neck. Goose bumps raced down her arms. "I'm going to get us out of here and to a vehicle. Satisfied?"

Not nearly enough, but it would have to do. She nodded as she glanced up at him. His mouth was only a few inches from hers. Their breath mingled. He narrowed his eyes and they glowed green in the dim light. For a brief second, she thought he might kiss her, but then he drew himself upright and nudged her toward a dark corner of the basement.

Embarrassment swamped her, and she could feel her face heating. What was she thinking? This was no time to indulge in any attraction—not that he seemed to be having any trouble controlling himself.

She followed close behind Darius, keeping within reach of him. She was trusting him with her life. The only leverage she had to save herself from Herman Temple and the Knights was in the knapsack on his shoulder. Darius could easily dump her, take the book and run, and leave her to take the fall alone.

Sarah sucked in a breath and tried to banish the dreadful thought. He wouldn't abandon her. Would he?

Darius paused by the door tucked in a poorly lit corner of the room. "When I open the door, we're going to move quickly and quietly. If I tell you to stop, you stop. If I tell you to run, you run like your life depends on it, because it likely does. Understand?"

She nodded. "Yes," she added, not sure if he could see her or not.

His large palm covered the entire side of her face. "I'll keep you safe." He used the edge of his thumb to tip her chin upward. Then his mouth was on hers, and it was just as glorious as the first time they'd kissed. Maybe better, because this time she knew what to expect.

• • •

Darius knew it was stupid to give in to his carnal urges at a time like this, but he was unable to stop himself. Her worry and hesitation bothered him deeply. He knew she didn't fully trust him. And while that made perfect sense, it also made him want to roar his displeasure at the heavens.

He wanted her to trust him completely, to know he'd protect her at any cost.

And there was nothing logical about those feelings.

She made a tiny sound of pleasure as she parted her lips beneath his. He smothered the sound and deepened the kiss, pulling her fully into the shadows with him. Her tongue met his in a dance as old as time. She ran her hands over his chest and wrapped her arms them around his neck.

Caution, he reminded himself. She was human and therefore fragile. He usually had no problem tempering his strength with his lovers, but Sarah made him forget everything but the sweet heat of her mouth.

He finally pulled back, not because he wanted to, but because this wasn't safe. They had enemies out there who would stop at nothing to get her and this book, not to mention what they'd do to him if he were captured.

The hands that had been holding him close only seconds before were now pushing him away. He reluctantly released her, but he didn't apologize. He damn well wasn't sorry he'd kissed her, but his timing sucked.

She stared up at him, her lips moist and her breath coming hard and fast. Then she seemed to shake herself and narrow her gaze. Before she could reprimand him for his actions, he leaned down and whispered in her ear. "Later. We need to move."

Her lips pulled together in a firm line, and she gave him a curt nod. Idiot that he was, he was looking forward to verbally sparing with her once they were safely aboard his plane.

He grabbed her hand and kept her close as he led her out the door and maneuvered through the shadows. He noted several men who looked suspicious, but he kept moving through the back alleys that had existed since he'd purchased the surrounding buildings more than a century ago. Even then he'd recognized their strategic value and had made certain they'd remained intact.

He could hear Sarah breathing and knew she was struggling to contain her fear. He knew how scared she must be, but she kept up, never once distracting him from the job at hand. Okay, so her simply being there was a distraction, but that was his problem. She was holding up her end of the deal by following close behind and remaining quiet.

Sarah gave a sigh of relief when they finally stepped out onto the busy sidewalk. Even this late, there were people out and about. He leaned down so no one around them would overhear. "We're not out of the woods yet."

She nodded her understanding and kept her eyes facing forward, even though he knew she probably wanted to look around for potential threats. "How much farther?"

"Parking garage in the next block." He kept her smaller hand locked inside his. No way was he going to allow them to become accidentally separated.

When they reached the garage, he walked right by the main entrance. Sarah asked him no questions and kept pace with his long strides. He should slow down, but the urge to get her away from here was pushing him to hurry.

He ducked in through a small door all but hidden around the back of the building. A large SUV was parked off by itself. Darius narrowed his gaze and studied the vehicle. "Wait here," he ordered.

He cautiously approached the car even though he wanted to toss Sarah aboard and take off out of here. He didn't think it had been tampered with, but he wasn't taking any chances.

· · ·

This was getting ridiculous. Follow me. Stay here. Do that. Honestly, she was getting sick and tired of the orders. She knew he was obviously much better at this kind of subterfuge than she was, but she wasn't stupid. She wanted to live, but she wasn't about to take a backseat in regard to her own safety and depend totally on Darius.

She kept to the shadows and moved closer to the vehicle he was approaching. He turned his head and glared at her, but thankfully he didn't say anything about her blatant disregard for his orders.

While she appreciated his skill and expertise, she wasn't about to blindly follow anyone. It wasn't in her nature. The events of the day had shaken her, but she wasn't going to allow anyone to run roughshod over her. She was an equal partner in this venture.

Darius walked around the large black vehicle and studied it intently. He lifted his head and sniffed the air. She wondered what he could smell that she couldn't. Lastly, he set his knapsack down on the pavement, went down on his knees, rolled to his back and pulled himself beneath the SUV.

He had to be looking for signs of tampering, maybe even bugging. That kind of thing happened in movies and books, and she'd never expected to have to be worried about such things in her everyday life. She was a librarian for crying out loud, not James Bond.

The longer he took, the more her nerves stretched to the breaking point. She bit her bottom lip to keep from asking questions. He didn't need the distraction, and she didn't want to alert anyone to their presence.

She scanned the area but didn't see a single person. That

didn't mean they weren't out there. She sighed and rubbed her forehead. Now she was as paranoid as he was.

Darius finally pulled himself out from beneath the vehicle and rolled to his feet in one lithe motion. In spite of his enormous size, he moved like a dancer, quick and easy. He held out his hand and curled his fingers in a come-here gesture.

It was harder than she thought it would be to leave the dubious protection of the shadows, but she made herself cross the open area to where Darius waited. He had a set of keys in his hand—she wasn't sure if he'd had them with him or if they'd been hidden on the vehicle—had grabbed his knapsack, and now opened the passenger door.

Sarah slid in, and the smell of rich leather tickled her nostrils. Darius got behind the wheel and set his bag down between the seats.

She clicked her seat belt into place. She could put her knapsack on the floor, but she held it in her lap instead. All her identification, banking information, and money were in that bag, along with her laptop. It was all she had to start over if it came to that. A part of her still couldn't believe this was happening to her.

The powerful engine roared to life, but Darius didn't pull away. When she glanced at him, he was watching her intently. "Put your head down and stay there until I tell you."

"Why?" She was tired of simply following his orders.

"The windows aren't tinted, and I don't want anyone to see you."

That made perfect sense. "What about you? If the Knights are watching, they'll certainly recognize you."

Darius reached around to the back seat and grabbed a hat. It was baseball style with a logo for a local security firm on the front. He pulled it down low, hiding most of his face. Then he sat lower in the seat, making himself look smaller.

Sarah leaned forward and rested her head on her knapsack, but turned so she could watch Darius. He gave her a nod of approval and then put the vehicle in gear. They rolled through the parking garage. It seemed to take forever for them to turn onto the street. She could tell the difference from the sounds. The blare of car horns from impatient drivers was much louder.

Neither of them spoke as Darius drove through the city. "Is it safe yet?" She didn't like not being able to see what was going on around them. Plus, with her head in her lap and turned toward him, she had a perfect view of him from the waist down. It was impossible not to notice the impressive bulge filling out the front of his jeans and the way the material pulled taut over his muscular thighs.

She was in danger, not dead.

"Yeah, it's safe, but be ready to duck again if I tell you." His rough voice sent tingles skittering over her skin.

She ignored the physical sensation as she sat up and peered out the window. "Where are we going?"

"Teterboro Airport." He reached out and gave her hand a reassuring pat. "My plane is there."

Sarah briefly closed her eyes. This was really happening. They were fleeing the city with minimal belongings and an ancient book that was frankly evil. She didn't know how else to put it. The book was dangerous, and they had to find a way to destroy it.

She hadn't realized she'd spoken her thoughts out loud until Darius answered her.

"We'll find a way. If it can be created, it can be destroyed." While she appreciated his confidence, she wasn't quite as certain.

"I hope so," she muttered.

"I'll have more resources at my fingertips once we're safely away from here." He stopped at a red light and peered over at her, his green eyes shimmering in the dimly lit space between them. The city lights poured through the windows, but it was still night. The atmosphere was intimate. The light changed, and he looked away, once again focused on the traffic around them.

Sarah released the breath she'd been holding and turned to stare out the window, watching the city pass before her eyes. She had to remember that Darius had lived a very long time—she couldn't quite wrap her head around the four-thousand-year thing—and had seen and experienced more than anyone else on the planet, with the exception of other drakons.

She closed her eyes and tried to relax. Her mind wouldn't shut down, though, and scenes from the past twenty-four hours played out in her head over and over. Exhaustion pulled at her, and she struggled to stay awake.

It seemed ludicrous that she'd be able to sleep at a time like this, but the body could only take so much before it shut down. She covered her mouth when she yawned and forced her eyes open. She could rest once they were onboard Darius's plane.

The man actually owned his own plane. Yet another clue that she was no longer living her normal, mundane life. She took the subway to work. She didn't just roll up to a private plane and climb on board.

Her eyes popped open just as they started to shut again. "Flight plans. You have to file them. They'll leave a path for the Knights to follow."

"Don't worry about that. If anyone cares to search, they'll find one that said we went to Miami."

"You've got it all figured out." Why she was so disgruntled by that fact, she wasn't sure. She was glad he knew what he was doing. She just didn't like feeling useless, like she had nothing to contribute to their safety.

"I always have an escape route. Several, in fact." He tightened his fingers around the wheel. "This is not the first time over the course of my life I've had to evade the Knights."

And he was used to going on the attack, not running. That thought struck her like a lightning bolt. "If I weren't with you, you'd have stayed in your apartment, wouldn't you?"

She didn't need to see the hesitation before his curt nod to know she was right. Now she really felt like an albatross around his neck. "You don't have to go with me. You have the book. You can put me on a plane and I'll disappear. Maybe go up into Canada before the Knights realize I'm gone."

He growled at her. The low, menacing sound raised all the tiny hairs on her arms and the back of her neck. "No. You stay with me."

She'd half expected him to be relieved by her offer. After all, they'd only met this evening. But she also knew that Darius had a huge streak of honor in him. Maybe it was his age, or maybe it was because he was more than human, but she'd risked her life to warn him about the Knights, so he probably felt he owed her.

She didn't want to question why that made her stomach heavy and her chest ache. But another part of her was grateful they were going to be sticking together for the foreseeable future.

The rest of the drive passed in silence, both of them lost in their own thoughts. When he finally turned off the road, it was onto a short drive that led to a private parking lot near an airfield. A security checkpoint loomed ahead.

"Look away," he told her. She did as he asked while he rolled down his window and dealt with the security guard.

"Evening, Mr. Varkas. I didn't know you'd planned to fly out this evening. It's not on my list." The guard was pleasant enough, but Sarah's stomach churned.

"Last-minute business."

"You have yourself a good flight." The guard tapped the vehicle with his hand and the sound made her flinch. And then Darius was moving forward. They were inside the chain-link fence.

"Almost there," he told her. Darius drove the vehicle right up to a small jet waiting on the tarmac. He put the vehicle in park and turned to her.

"I know. I know." She held up her hands in mock surrender. "Wait here." She pitched her voice low and gruff in a poor imitation of his.

He stared at her, and then a smile broke across his face. He chuckled, shook his head, and climbed out of the vehicle, leaving her alone with her thoughts once again.

A man approached Darius as he strode toward the plane. They spoke for several seconds and then Darius came back to the vehicle. He opened her door and helped her out before he reached across the seat and grabbed his knapsack. "Let's go."

Her bag held tightly in her arms, she headed toward the short staircase leading up the plane. The man Darius had spoken with waited with another man at the base of the steps. They both nodded at her but didn't speak. Then they went to the SUV, climbed in, and drove off.

Darius exerted light pressure on her lower back, urging her up. They were exposed and vulnerable out here in the open. Sarah hurried up the metal stairs and stepped onto the luxury airliner. As soon as they were inside, Darius pulled up the steps and closed the door, locking them inside.

There was a small, built-in galley right in front of them. To her right was the seating area. The leather chairs were more like luxury recliners. There were four in total—two of them facing each other on either side of the narrow walkway. Beyond them was a long sofa.

"Where's the crew?" There was no one in sight. Not that she'd expected a flight attendant, but she'd figured the captain or copilot would greet him.

Darius smiled at her, and her stomach dropped. "No. Oh, no. Tell me what I'm thinking isn't true."

"And what are you thinking?" he asked as he placed his knapsack in a storage compartment.

He tried to take her bag, but she clung to it, not willing to relinquish any more than she already had. "You're not flying this machine, are you?"

"Of course I am. I just dismissed the pilot and copilot. That way no one but us knows where we're really going." He carefully pried her bag from her hands. "Don't worry, Sarah. I helped the Wright brothers fix the flaws in their original design. I've been flying planes since the dawn of human flight."

Her fingers lost all strength at that little tidbit of information. He plucked her bag out of her hands and stored it alongside his.

"And if something happens to the plane, I can shift and fly us to safety," he reminded her. "This is the safest flight you'll ever take."

She put out her hand to steady herself as her knees went weak. She knew he was telling her the truth, but it was a truth that was difficult to truly comprehend.

"Want to join me?" He motioned to the cockpit.

Sarah squared her shoulders. Why not? What was one more crazy experience in a day filled with them? "I'd like that."

• • •

A knock came on the door of Herman's study, and he motioned his head of security inside. "Our man has managed to track her phone," Riggs told him.

"She's had it turned on all this time." That surprised him somewhat. Sarah Anderson had struck him as an intelligent woman, not someone who would make that kind of mistake if she suspected she might be in danger.

Riggs didn't smile, but he did look pleased with himself. "She's probably not thinking clearly. My guy managed to pinpoint her location briefly before he lost it."

Herman scowled. "Then we don't know where she is."

"Her last location was a small airport, and guess whose plane took off moments later."

"Darius Varkas." Herman began to pace. "So she went to him with what she overheard." He wasn't surprised Varkas had taken Sarah with him. She was a valuable asset and could be used as a pawn in their little game of cat and mouse. It was what he would have done. She must have stolen the spell book. There was no other reason for them to leave the city. Varkas would have used the woman to find the book if it was still lost.

That meant that Varkas now had the book and knew the Knights were after him. It was the confirmation he needed. If Varkas weren't a dragon, he wouldn't have run. And he certainly wouldn't have taken the woman with him. Excitement roared through Herman. Varkas truly was a dragon. All his years of searching for one, and all the money he'd spent, had finally paid off.

Herman stopped and considered what might come from the book being around Varkas. The spells in the book were powerful. Would being around the book have an effect on Varkas? Only time would tell, but it would be fascinating to find out. Too many people believed inanimate objects had no energy, no power. They were all fools. Some very special objects, such as the book, were imbued with great power if one knew how to wield it.

"Where are they going?" Before Riggs could answer, Herman waved off any reply. "Whatever flight plan he filed will probably be false, but we have to check just in case." He turned back to his head of security. "Someone has to know where that plane was going. Find out."

"Yes, sir. We're trying to locate her phone again, but there's some interference, like it is being blocked. If we can get past that, we'll have her position."

Riggs left as quietly as he'd come. Herman rubbed his hand over his face. He was tired after being awake all night. Another sign that he was weakening. What he needed was a shower and some breakfast. He had confidence that his people would find Varkas and the woman sooner rather than later, and he wanted to be ready.

Herman could feel it in his bones. They were closing in on Varkas, Sarah Anderson, and the book. It was only a matter of time.

Chapter Twelve

Tarrant's voice crackled over his headset. "Eagle's nest to baby bird. Eagle's nest to baby bird."

Darius smiled in spite of himself. "Hello, eagle's nest," he spoke into the attached microphone. "Are you the mama bird now?"

"I might as well be. How are things?"

Darius glanced over at Sarah who was snoozing away in the copilot's seat. She'd missed the sunrise, not stirring as the sky lightened. She really was exhausted. Even now, he could see the dark circles under her eyes.

"We got away with no problems." Which had actually surprised him.

"You haven't let Sarah go online, have you?" his brother asked.

"No. Both her computer and her phone are in her knapsack." When Tarrant began to swear, Darius got worried. "What is it?"

"The GPS in the phone. You need to destroy her phone and the laptop. Temple might have had people put a tracking device on either one or both. Even if he hasn't, he can still trace your location through her phone. He probably knows she's with you, and if they've been monitoring her, they know where you are. Fuck. Are you sure she's not with the Knights?"

"Shut up, Tarrant."

Beside him, Sarah stirred. She blinked several times and yawned. "I didn't mean to fall asleep," she said as she looked at him. Her hair was slightly tousled and her eyes were only half open. "What is it? What's wrong?" She sat up straighter, all exhaustion leaving her as worry replaced sleepiness in her gaze.

"Your phone and laptop. Temple and his men might have put a tracker on them. Even if they didn't, they might be able to use GPS to trace you."

Her mouth fell open but she quickly closed it. "Stupid. How could I have been so stupid? I have to turn in my phone every morning at work—they've had plenty of chances to tamper with it." She undid her seat belt and climbed out of her chair. Darius glanced over his shoulder and watched as she shoved open the door to the cockpit and went straight for her knapsack. She pulled out her phone first, opened the back, and took out the SIM card. Then she reached back into her bag and got her laptop.

"What should I do with it?" she asked. "Remove the battery? Or will simply smashing it do the trick?"

Darius relayed her question to Tarrant. "I'd like her to remove the battery and then destroy the unit. I don't trust Temple and his men. I'd really like to have both phone and laptop smashed to bits and tossed off the plane."

"How about if I burn them to a crisp," Darius offered. "That would fry any circuits and melt the plastic."

"That would work," Tarrant told him. "Just don't blow up the damn plane in the process." Darius was glad Sarah couldn't hear that side of the conversation.

"Oh ye of little faith," he retorted. He pushed out of his chair and exited the cockpit.

Sarah's brown eyes widened as he approached. "What are you doing here? Go back. Who's flying the plane?" Her face lost all color.

"Don't worry," he told her. "We're on autopilot. An alarm will ring if there's a problem, and this won't take long."

"No one is flying the plane," she muttered. "Of course everything will be fine." She laughed, and he was concerned by the slightly hysterical sound of it. She rubbed her hands over her face and squared her shoulders. "What are you going to do?"

"Burn it." He opened a cupboard in the galley and rummaged around until he found a metal ice bucket. Not ideal, but it would have to do. "Remove the battery."

Darius placed the ice bucket on the table beside her. "Put your phone in here." She took out the battery, then dumped the phone and the SIM card into the bucket.

Darius took a deep breath and concentrated on building the fire within him. It wasn't easy. His entire body wanted to embrace his dragon form. Sarah gasped and moved back as he directed his fiery breath into the container. The plastic and wires melted together. Before the fire alarms could sound onboard the plane, he slammed the cover onto the container, smothering the blaze.

"Holy crap." Sarah stared at him and back at the container. "You blew fire."

His body had wanted to shift, but he'd managed to keep that from happening. Not a good idea to let the creature out on a small jet. It had taken effort, and the seams of his shirt had split. Could have been worse.

"I had to destroy the phone. I'll make sure you get a new one," he told her. Tarrant seemed to have an unlimited supply of them, although Sarah's phone had been much newer and more sophisticated than the ones he usually used.

"It's not the phone." She waved her hand as some smoke escaped around the edges of the ice bucket. "Why didn't you just use a match or something?"

Darius shook his head. "Drakon fire is much hotter than a normal flame. It's a faster and cleaner burn." He opened the bucket and there was only a small glob of plastic at the bottom. "I need to destroy your laptop.

Sarah hugged it to her chest for a moment before handing it over. Darius cracked the computer in half and then broke each half into smaller pieces. Sarah watched and dodged a flying piece of plastic. It landed on the seat beside her, and she retrieved it, holding it clutched tightly in her hand.

Darius removed the battery and yanked out the circuitry. He put the pieces into the ice bucket and fried them with his drakon fire. "That should do it."

Sarah swallowed heavily but didn't comment. She was still pale and was clinging hard to the small piece of plastic she was holding.

"Why don't you get something to drink or eat? There's plenty in the galley." He carefully removed the small piece of plastic from her hand, relieved she hadn't cut herself on the sharp edges. Once he checked it to make sure there was no tracking device attached to it, he tossed it into the garbage.

Sarah gathered herself and nodded. "I could use some coffee." She motioned to the ice bucket. "What about that?"

Darius picked up the hot container and carried it into the galley kitchen. He placed it safely in the metal sink, pulled off the cover and turned on the water. Smoke rose, and what little remained of the electronic guts from the computer sizzled. He shoved the cover back on but left it in the sink. "That should be fine now." He motioned to the cockpit door. "I need to get back."

"Oh God, there's no one flying the plane." She shoved

him toward the door. "Go fly. I'll make coffee."

Darius was reluctant to leave her, but he didn't have much choice. He did detour long enough to grab another T-shirt from the clothes he left onboard and quickly changed. Then he made his way back to the pilot's chair and checked to make sure everything was as it should be before he spoke to Tarrant, who he knew was waiting.

"I fried the phone and the electronic guts of the computer," he told his brother.

Sure enough, Tarrant immediately answered. "That should do the trick, but you need to change your landing destination, just in case."

Darius thought about it for a few seconds and reviewed his options. "I can fly into Oregon and then drive up to Washington."

"That means you have to rent a vehicle, and it puts you on the road a long time. We don't know what kind of resources the Knights have, but we have to assume they're the best."

"What do you suggest?" He trusted Tarrant's judgment.

His brother heaved out a breath. "I have a private airstrip up here. It's off the grid and not visible from the air. You have to dip down and fly into a canyon." He rattled off the coordinates. "It will be a tight squeeze for your jet. It was meant for a slightly smaller plane."

"I can handle it," he assured Tarrant.

"If you can't, you're going to be out one expensive plane."

"It's not the plane I'm worried about." It was Sarah. He could easily survive a crash, but she couldn't. Still, it was the best option they had. Tarrant was right about one thing. Landing at another airport and renting a vehicle left them more vulnerable.

"Contact me again when you're close so I can hit the lights on the field. They'll help guide you in."

"Roger that." Darius heard Tarrant disconnect their call.

He leaned his head back and went over his options again and again until he was satisfied what he was picking was the best one. Then he took a deep breath and adjusted his coordinates. When the time came, he'd drop down below any radar before making his approach to Tarrant's secret airfield.

• • •

Sarah opened the ice bucket and stared at what was left of her phone and the inner workings of her laptop. It wasn't much. She put the lid back on. It didn't smell as bad as she thought it would, but it certainly wasn't pleasant.

"Coffee," she reminded herself. She needed it badly. She'd gone from being asleep one minute, to watching her only electronic links to her former life literally go up in smoke the next.

She shook off the remnants of her fatigue. She hadn't slept long enough to totally recharge and was surprised she'd actually managed to sleep at all.

The galley kitchen wasn't large, but it was efficient and very well stocked. It didn't take her long to find everything she needed to brew a pot of coffee. She rummaged around some more and found some small packages of cookies. It might not be the best thing for breakfast, but the sugar would help give her a boost.

Darius glanced her way and smiled when she handed him a coffee. "I didn't know how you take your coffee. It's black. I can go back for sugar or cream if you want it."

"Black is fine," he assured her. He took a sip before setting it in a cup holder. Why it surprised her that the plane had cup holders, she didn't know. It was only logical. Everything had cup holders these days.

Sarah secured her own cup, sat back in her seat, and held out one of the packs of cookies. "You want some? They look good."

"Thanks." He took the package from her, ripped it open, and devoured all four cookies in no time. She handed him another before opening her own. By the time she'd finished one pack and about half her coffee, Darius had downed two more and was draining the last of his coffee.

"Do you want more?" she asked, fascinated by how much food he seemed to consume. Of course, he was a big man and needed the fuel.

"Just coffee, if you don't mind. I'd get it myself, but I think you'd rather I stay and fly the plane."

She shuddered and stood. "You stay right where you are." She gathered all the garbage and headed back to the galley, where she dumped the cookie packages and refilled both their coffee cups.

Darius waited until she was back in her seat before adjusting their direction slightly, his large hands competent at the controls.

"Where are we going? I know you said Washington State, but where exactly?" She could see white puffy clouds in the distance. Below was a long stretch of flat land, dotted with trees and rocks and the occasional house.

"There's been a slight change of plans." He glanced in her direction to see how she was taking his news.

"Why does that not surprise me?" She had a sip of her coffee and held the cup between her hands, letting the heat warm them. She looked away from the scenery outside the window and gave all her attention to the man sitting beside her. "Why the change? No, don't answer that. It's obviously because of my phone and laptop. You think Temple may have been tracking us."

Darius nodded. "It's best to assume he was."

That was the smartest course of action. "Okay, what are our options?" She wasn't about to blithely go along with just any plan.

"We could land in another state, rent a vehicle, and drive."

She mulled that over and shook her head. "That leaves a pretty big trail, doesn't it?"

He nodded. "It does. There are people at the airport, the car rental company, and all along the route. Someone will remember us. At this point, we have no idea who is working with the Knights or how big their operation is. As it is, there's always someone ready to give information if there's money involved, and they will offer a reward as an incentive."

"So what's the best option?" Because she knew he'd already decided what course of action he wanted to take.

"Private airfield close to our destination."

It sounded too good to be true. "What's the catch?"

One corner of his mouth kicked up. "Why so suspicious?"

She snorted. "You really have to ask?"

He shook his head. "No. I know none of this has been easy for you." He paused and she could almost see him considering just how much to tell her. That made her angry.

"Listen. My life is on the line here, too. Don't you think it's time you told me everything?"

"No."

Just that. No. He said nothing more. Wow, his reaction really hurt her more than it should have. They were in this thing together, or at least she'd thought they were. It was a harsh reminder that she was nothing to him. A pawn in a game she hadn't asked to play.

"Sarah," he began.

She shook her head. "I'm going to go stretch out on that sofa in the back for a while."

"Don't go." She could hear remorse in his voice, but it wasn't enough for him to be sorry.

"When you're ready to share more with me, I'll come back. In the meantime, I need to be by myself and remind myself of what my options are." She grabbed her coffee and pushed out of her chair and headed to the door of the cockpit.

"They're not just my secrets, Sarah."

She knew that, but it didn't make it any easier to swallow. She left Darius and walked back to the seating area. The jet wasn't overly large, but it seemed cavernous and empty. She made her way to the sofa at the far end and slumped down on it. She put her coffee in the cup holder and closed her eyes.

What was she going to do when they landed? She had no idea where they were really going. It could be anywhere. Just because Darius had told her they were going to the Cascade Mountains, didn't mean they were actually going there. And now she had no computer or phone.

"How did you get yourself into this mess?" she muttered.

She yawned and gave in to the exhaustion pulling at her. The sofa was comfy, so she curled up and settled her head on the leather seat cushion. She wasn't going anywhere until the plane landed, so she might as well take advantage of the downtime. She could always make plans after she was rested. And if her mind kept coming back to the stubborn, gorgeous, infuriating male piloting the plane, well, that was understandable. Their fates were tied together whether they wanted them to be or not.

• • •

Darius wanted to stop Sarah from leaving but knew it was better to let her go, to give her some space. It wasn't as though she could leave him while they were in the air.

He'd hurt her. That hadn't been his intention. Too many years of secrecy, of protecting his brothers, made it hard for him to even consider sharing information with someone who was both an outsider and a human.

But Sarah was special. If he didn't start opening up to her, she was going to find a way to leave him. Then she would be out in the world alone with Herman Temple and the Knights searching for her.

He growled and tightened his hands on the controls. That wasn't happening. Sarah was his to protect.

He had to start thinking logically. He'd impress upon her how vulnerable she was on her own, and how he could protect her.

No, that wouldn't work with Sarah. As pissed off and hurt as she was, she'd probably walk away from him, just as she'd tried to do last evening when he'd accused her of trying to extort money for information on the book and its whereabouts.

Yeah, not one of his finest moments.

He might have lived a long time, but he'd never had a serious relationship with a woman. He enjoyed women, was generous with his lovers, but he'd always kept his secrets in order to guard not only himself, but also his brothers.

He didn't know if he could lower his protective barriers enough to let Sarah completely into his world. She already knew what he was. In a moment completely out of character, he'd shifted and shown her he was a drakon.

And if they were going to Tarrant's home, she'd meet him. She didn't have to know he was a drakon or his brother. He could tell her Tarrant was simply a friend or a paid employee. Yeah, his brother would like that description. Not.

Tarrant was fanatical when it came to security, and it surprised Darius that he wanted to meet Sarah. He swore, grabbed the headset, and put it back on. "Come in, eagle's nest."

"What is it, baby bird? You're not close yet."

"You can't hurt her. You have to promise me." No way was he landing with Sarah if he didn't have Tarrant's promise. If Tarrant thought for one minute Sarah was a threat to Darius's safety, he would kill her. He might feel sorry about it, but he'd do it and worry about the consequences after it was done.

"You're a suspicious man, brother."

"Realistic. And I know you, Tarrant." Then he relented. "Because I'd probably do the same damn thing." It wasn't easy to admit, but it was the truth. They'd protected one another for millennia. It was as much an instinct as breathing.

"She's got you wrapped around her little finger and you barely know her," Tarrant pointed out.

"No, she doesn't. Not really. I can't explain what I'm feeling," he admitted. "I only know she's important to me." He took a deep breath and slowly exhaled. "I'm not sure I could control my beast if you hurt her."

Tarrant was silent for several seconds. Darius could easily imagine the expression of sheer disbelief on his brother's face.

"Your dragon side is that protective of her?"

"Yes."

"That makes her twice as dangerous."

"Tarrant, am I still coming your way, or am I heading out of the country?" He'd do whatever he had to do to protect Sarah.

"Fuck. Bring her here. I promise I won't kill her. At least not until I get to know her. But if it turns out she's with the Knights—" He broke off, not finishing his sentence.

"She's not. Trust me, Tarrant."

"Shit. If I end up dead or captured because of her, I won't be happy," Tarrant bitched.

"If any of us end up dead or captured, it won't be because of Sarah. That will all be on the Knights, and you can kill as many of them as you want."

"That's something." His brother's wry tone made Darius smile.

"I'll contact you again in an hour," he promised. "I should be getting pretty close by then."

"I'll be standing by," Tarrant promised.

Darius ended the call and looked at the empty seat beside him. He missed Sarah's presence, the slow up and down of her chest as she breathed, the way her hair fringed across her forehead, and the little noises she made as she slept.

He glanced over his shoulder at the closed door. He hated being separated from her, but it was probably for the best. They both needed time to think. He hoped she was getting some rest. He didn't like the dark shadows under her eyes.

Chapter Thirteen

Sarah woke as the plane began to dip downward. Crap. She'd slept longer than she'd intended. They leveled off again, and she rose and went to the bathroom at the rear of the cabin. When she shut the door behind her, the light came on and she peered at her reflection in the mirror.

There were still dark circles under her eyes, but at least she didn't feel as tired as she had before. She turned on the cold water, leaned down, and splashed some on her face. She grabbed a towel—thick cotton, no paper towels here—and blotted her face dry. Then she finger combed her hair.

"Face it. Only a ton of makeup would help." She ignored her appearance and used the bathroom. Her neck was stiff from the way she'd slept, and she rolled it a few times as she washed her hands.

She straightened her sweater and the shirt under it. Darius's shirt. It felt strange to be wearing a man's clothes. She could take it off, but shrugged and left it on.

Now that she was more fully awake, she was thirsty. She'd like more coffee, but she really needed something with a bit more nutrition first. A search of the galley turned up a small refrigerator with several cartons of orange juice. She grabbed one of the disposable cups and filled it. The juice was cool and fresh and tasted delicious.

Sarah glanced toward the cockpit. Darius had to be tired. Then she frowned as she wondered how much sleep he actually needed. He wasn't exactly normal.

Going on instinct, she poured a second glass of juice and fixed a lid on top. She took a deep breath, picked up both cups, and carried them into the cockpit. Darius studied her intently. "Did you sleep well?" He took the juice when she offered it and tucked the cup into the holder. His coffee from before was gone, which meant at some point he'd left the cockpit while she'd been sleeping. She tried not to think about that.

She shrugged. "Well enough."

He stood and eased around her, their bodies brushing in the tight confines. "I'll be right back," he assured her. Then he left her alone.

"Oh God." There was no one flying the plane again. "Why does he do this to me?" she muttered. She eased into the copilot's chair, careful not to accidentally touch any of the controls. The last thing she wanted to do was crash the plane. There were all sorts of dials and levers and knobs. She had no idea what any of them did.

She wanted to close her eyes but didn't dare. Instead, she began to count. By the time she reached one hundred and twenty-six, Darius was back. He slid into his chair, picked up the cup she'd brought him, and drank.

"No coffee?" he asked her.

She shook her head. "I needed something cold."

"How are you feeling?" He studied her intently. "You look more rested."

"Yeah, I slept. How long was I out?" She'd lost all track of time.

"Not quite an hour this time."

"Not very long?" Not nearly as much as she needed, but more than she'd expected to get. She was surprised she'd slept at all. As exhausted as she was, she was also wound up. "How are you doing? You must be tired."

"Don't worry. I'm awake enough to fly the plane. I'll get us down safely."

She glanced out the window, remembering why she was mad at him. It wasn't easy. Looks aside, there was a rock-solid stability about Darius that was very compelling. He was the kind of man you could depend on in a crisis. He'd dealt with everything that had been thrown his way without flinching. Of course, he'd known who the Knights were before she'd told him about them. This was all new to her.

"We'll be landing in a few minutes."

She nodded and continued to admire the scenery. They were much lower now than they'd been. Mountains loomed in the distance and thick forest sprang up all around. There wasn't a house in sight. "It's very isolated."

"That's the way he likes it."

"Who?"

"Tarrant."

Intrigued by the fact that he'd actually answered her, she swiveled in her seat to face him. It wasn't fair. She looked and felt tired in spite of her nap, but Darius looked alert and too handsome for her peace of mind.

"Who is Tarrant? Is he the one you've been in touch with? The one doing the research?"

"Yes. He's the one I've been in touch with." He leaned forward and flicked a switch before continuing. "You two have a lot in common. He's a great researcher and can find out whatever we need to know about anything or anyone."

Now she was intrigued. "How did you meet?" What she really wanted to know was if he was a drakon, but she figured

Darius wouldn't tell her. On one hand, she could understand that. On the other, she was sick to death of not having all the information she needed to assess the situation.

"We've known each other a long time." She noticed how he didn't mention if Tarrant was human or not, which led her to believe he wasn't.

Her stomach was fluttering like a kaleidoscope of butterflies was battering around inside. She'd read that somewhere—that a group of butterflies was called a kaleidoscope or a rabble. Because of her job, she knew all kinds of strange facts. And she was using them now to distract herself from the situation at hand.

She finished her juice, hoping to settle her nerves, but it was an impossible task. There was no way she was going to calm down anytime soon.

"Do you think the Knights know where we are?" It was always in the back of her mind that Herman Temple would find them. She had visions of their plane landing and being swarmed by men in black with high-powered weapons.

"If I thought that, I wouldn't be going anywhere near Tarrant." So he was protective of this other man. Now Sarah was really curious to meet him. "Buckle up," he told her. "We're almost there."

Sarah fastened her seat belt and peered out the window, searching for a runway, but all she could see was forest and mountain.

"Come in, eagle's nest."

Sarah wished she could hear the other side of the conversation. As if Darius sensed her concern, he motioned to the other headset. She quickly pulled it on.

"You're right on course, baby bird." Sarah recognized the voice as the man Darius had talked with last night. He rattled off coordinates, and Darius adjusted their flight pattern. She still couldn't see anywhere to land.

The mountains seemed to loom in the distance, ominous and dangerous. "Uh, Darius? Are you sure this is right?"

"I know what I'm doing, sugar." It wasn't Darius who spoke, but Tarrant. He continued to give Darius instructions, which he immediately followed.

She tightened her fingers around the arms of her chair. Oh God, she was going to die in a fiery crash. There was nowhere to land. There was nowhere to fly.

A huge peak rose in front of them. She bit her bottom lip to keep from screaming. The last thing she wanted to do was distract Darius. Although, maybe she should distract him. His current plan seemed to have a huge flaw.

"We're going to crash," she yelled just before she bent over and buried her face in her knees. If she survived this, she might never fly again.

Several seconds later, when nothing had exploded, she cautiously lifted her head. Tarrant was still rattling off instructions to Darius, but she didn't understand most of them. The engines revved and the plane went lower.

Darius guided the jet through a small opening between two high mountain peaks. She wanted to bury her face again but couldn't make herself look away. They barely made it through. If there was six inches to spare on either wingtip, that was all there was.

Her shirt was stuck to her back and her mouth went dry as a short runway came into view, lit by only about half a dozen lights. There wasn't enough room to land. She hadn't flown a lot in her lifetime, but enough to know that a jet, even a small one, needed a lot of space in order to stop.

"Hold on," Darius told her.

She didn't need to hold on as she hadn't yet let go. Her fingers were white as they strangled the arms of her seat. The jet dropped quickly, barely clearing the tops of the trees. Several times she heard the tall pines scraping against the bottom of the plane.

Then they were on the ground. The wheels hit, and Darius reversed the engine thrust. Sarah began to pray. They raced down the short airstrip. Beyond it were more trees and a damn mountain.

Through it all, Darius seemed calm and collected. Of course he was. He probably wouldn't die if they did crash. She, on the other hand, was a lot more fragile.

The wheels screeched and the plane shimmied. The muscles in Darius's arms bunched as he used all his strength to control the runaway machine. She held her breath as a crash seemed imminent. Parts of her life flashed before her eyes. She thought of her parents, both gone several years now, of friends from childhood, of her dog, Max, a rambunctious Labrador who'd been hit by a car when she was only ten.

Then the plane came to an abrupt halt, the nose about two inches from the trunk of a large pine. She wasn't dead. They hadn't crashed. She sucked in a breath and then another.

Relief was quickly followed by anger. "What in the hell were you trying to do? Kill us?" Male laughter came over the headset she was still wearing, so she ripped it off and flung it aside. "You're crazy."

Darius was flicking switches, and things powered down. He hadn't even broken a sweat. "I got us down in one piece, didn't I?"

She tried to get out of her chair but was shaking too badly. She ended up sitting back down in a hurry.

"Hey." Darius reached over and dragged her out of her seat and onto his lap. It was a very tight fit as there wasn't a whole lot of room. "I told you, I've been flying for years." He closed his muscular arms around her, anchoring her to his lap.

"Flying is one thing. Landing on a practically nonexistent runway is another." Her voice rose with each word until she was yelling by the end. She wanted to lean against him but didn't dare.

"You were really worried." His brows knit and he frowned.

"What gave it away? My fervent prayers? The way I assumed the crash position? I can tell you my life flashed before my eyes." With each breath she took, she grew less shaky.

"I'm sorry you were concerned. There was really no need to be."

She closed her eyes and prayed for patience. "Let me up." She pushed at him until he relented. It galled her that she needed his help to stand. It was a small blessing when her knees didn't buckle and she remained upright. "There was every need for me to be worried. We're virtually strangers, pushed together due to circumstances. I don't really know you."

She didn't need to see Darius to know her words annoyed him. The atmosphere in the cockpit changed in a heartbeat, becoming fraught with anger.

"You know more about me than most people do." His words were almost an accusation.

"I didn't ask for any of this." And it wasn't his fault she was in this situation. She took a breath to calm herself. "I'm sorry. That was uncalled for. You didn't ask for this, either." She stepped out of the cockpit into the main part of the plane.

Darius was right behind her, his big body taking up most of the space. He caught her by the arm and turned her around. "I said I'd take care of you."

Now she was getting angry. "I didn't ask you to. I don't need a man to take care of me. I need someone who will share information with me so we can figure this situation out together." She strove for calm. "I'm grateful for all that you've done to protect me. I truly am. But this is my life, too. There are people out there who want to harm me, maybe even kill me. I can't blindly follow you and hope for the best. If that doesn't work for you, we need to part ways."

• • •

Darius was both bewildered and angry. It had never been his intention to frighten Sarah, and certainly not this badly. He would never have attempted the landing if he'd thought he couldn't do it safely. Yes, there'd been a second or two of concern, but he'd known what both he and the plane were capable of.

But she hadn't.

Disheveled, angry, and tired, she was still the most beautiful woman he'd ever known. His irritation bled away but rolled back in when she mentioned she was grateful to him. It became an inferno when she dared to speak of parting ways.

His nostrils flared, and he was surprised there wasn't steam coming out of them. "You're not leaving."

She'd opened the storage bin and was reaching for her knapsack, but stopped and turned to face him. "We don't owe each other anything. I warned you, and you got me out of New York. We're even."

He moved toward her, crowding her against the wall of the plane. "We're not nearly even." He planted his hands on the wall, leaned down, and kissed her. She made a small sound, and he couldn't tell if it came from distress or arousal. He was about to pull back when she went up on her toes and deepened the kiss.

He nibbled on her bottom lip and then swept his tongue inside. She tasted like orange juice—sweet and tangy. He wanted to touch her but was afraid if he did he wouldn't stop until he had her naked.

His need for Sarah was a fire in his gut. His blood burned for her. His balls ached and his cock was hard as stone.

"We probably shouldn't be doing this." Her eyes smoldered with passion and her lips were damp from his kiss.

"Why not?" He strung a row of little kisses down her jaw and nuzzled her neck.

She sighed and leaned into his caress. "I don't know," she moaned. "We barely know each other," she reminded him.

"After everything we've been through, we know each other better than many people do after years together. You're brave and beautiful." He ran his thumb along the curve of her cheek. "And I want you."

"It's not smart, not logical, but I want you, too."

Inside him, his beast roared his pleasure. *Mine. Mine. Mine*, the creature gleefully chanted. Darius exerted every ounce of control he had to keep from shifting.

Sarah was watching him closely, her pretty chocolate-brown eyes starting to fill with worry. Darius growled and kissed her again. Before he'd realized his intentions, he had her in his arms, her breasts pressed against his chest. They were both fully dressed, but that didn't make the moment any less intimate.

She stroked her hands over his shoulders and down his arms. He wanted to feel her touch over his entire body. After hours of tension, he was finally able to relax. Now he wanted to claim the unexpected treasure that had shown up in his life.

Because that's what Sarah was—a treasure.

He ran his hand down her spine and cupped her behind, lifting her slightly before pulling her closer. It didn't matter that the position was awkward given the low ceilings in the plane. When his erection nestled into the notch of her thighs, Darius knew he'd found heaven. He hiked her higher, and she clasped her thighs around his hips.

Even through the layers of her jeans and his, he could feel her heat. He knew how to pleasure a woman and wanted to spend hours touching Sarah, kissing her, stroking her most secret places. He wanted to hear her moan his name as she orgasmed.

"Hey. You coming out sometime today?" A heavy fist thudded against the side of the plane. Darius wondered if his brother would go away if he just ignored him. "Open the damn door." Tarrant hit it again. Sarah jerked at the sudden noise and quickly released her hold on him. Darius knew the moment was lost.

"Who is that?" She tugged on her sweater and then rubbed her hands over her face. He could have told her there was no hiding the fact she'd just been thoroughly kissed. And even if she'd looked perfectly fine, Tarrant would still be able to smell her arousal.

"Come on, Darius. I don't have all day."

"That"—he glared at the exit—"is Tarrant." He raked his fingers through his hair and went to the door. There was no hiding his arousal, so he didn't bother trying. He unlocked the hatch and shoved it open. The stairs unfolded, and Tarrant was waiting at the bottom.

His brother's face was grim. "You cut it a little close on the landing."

He shrugged. "I wasn't worried." It had been close, but he'd done it, and that was all that mattered. If he'd thought he was about to hit the trees, he would have put the plane into a spin so they would have hit them side on.

Tarrant tried to see around him into the plane. "Where is she?"

"Wait here." He gave his brother a warning glare before he went back inside.

Sarah had her coat on and her knapsack slung over her shoulder. Her lips were slightly swollen and her cheeks were pink, but she looked otherwise composed. "Don't forget the book," she reminded him.

He opened the overhead compartment and retrieved his

bag. There was a low hum from inside that was a lot like static. He could almost hear a voice if he concentrated. He didn't like that one bit. The book was gaining strength.

"You must be Sarah."

Darius whirled at the sound of Tarrant's voice. His brother was standing in the entrance and was staring at Sarah. Darius knew Tarrant was searching for any weaknesses, which he'd exploit if he could.

He growled and wrapped his arm around Sarah from behind. "I thought I told you to wait outside."

Tarrant snorted. "Since when do I ever listen to you?"

Sarah looked at Tarrant and then at Darius and then at Tarrant again. There was wonder in her eyes and a slight smile on her face. "You're brothers, aren't you?"

Chapter Fourteen

Sarah knew she probably should have kept her suspicions to herself when Tarrant's gaze narrowed and he frowned. He was almost as large as Darius, and while Darius intimidated her, Tarrant downright scared the crap out of her.

"Or not." She tried to backtrack. "Maybe you're just friends." When Tarrant continued to frown, she took a step back. "For all I know, you're complete strangers."

One corner of Tarrant's mouth twitched and he turned to Darius. "I think I like her." Then a puzzled expression crossed his face and he took a deep breath, then another. "And you obviously really like her."

"Tarrant." There was a warning note in Darius's voice that she didn't understand. Obviously, she hadn't done a good job pulling herself back together after their kiss, and Tarrant was commenting on it.

Tarrant rolled his eyes and pinned her with his vibrant blue gaze. "Welcome to my home. Betray me to the Knights, and I'll end you."

"Jesus, Tarrant. Knock it off." Darius rocked her slightly

in his arms. "Don't worry. He won't hurt you."

Sarah wasn't as sure of that as Darius seemed to be. "If you don't want me here, I can leave."

Darius tightened his grip on her. "Not that again. You're not striking out on your own."

"You two can finish this discussion in the truck. I want to get out of here." Tarrant turned and hurried down the stairs.

Sarah heaved a sigh of relief now that he was gone. She wasn't ashamed to admit she was afraid of him. Only an idiot wouldn't be. He had the same kind of animal magnetism that Darius did. He was almost as big, with short black hair and amazing blue eyes. His features were more refined, not quite as rugged as Darius's were. Even wearing jeans and a long-sleeved thermal shirt, he looked more like a cover model than a woodsman. There was no denying he was one hot guy, but she felt zero attraction toward him.

"You okay?" Darius turned her around so she was facing him and rubbed his hands up and down her arms.

"Yeah." She blew out a breath. "I'm as okay as it gets, given the circumstances."

His mouth firmed into a thin line and he gave her a curt nod. "Let's get out of here before Tarrant bursts a blood vessel."

That startled a laugh out of her. "He's really intense."

"You have no idea." Darius released her, went to the opening, and waited for her. She wondered where exactly they were going. She hadn't noticed any buildings around. Of course, she'd been in complete terror, fearing for her life during their landing, so she easily could have missed something.

She squeezed past Darius, biting back a moan when her right breast brushed against his chest. Gripping the strap of her bag tighter, she paused at the top of the stairs. Wind gusted past her, but it wasn't as cold as she'd imagined it would be considering their elevation. There was nothing but thick forest and mountains as far as the eye could see.

It was magnificent.

Tarrant waited at the bottom of the steps, arms crossed over his massive chest and the toe of his boot tapping with impatience. Sarah grabbed the railing and went down the stairs with Darius right behind her.

Tarrant reached into his pocket and pulled out a small electronic gadget. "I need to scan you before we go any farther." He didn't wait for her agreement and simply started running the mini scanner over her.

"What exactly are you looking for?"

"Tracking devices on your belongings." He crouched down and ran the small device over her legs. "Implanted in you."

Just the idea of that made her shudder. "We destroyed my electronics. There can't be anything else."

"You'll have to forgive me if I don't take your word." Tarrant continued the scan until he was satisfied. She consoled herself with the knowledge that at least he hadn't asked for a strip search.

Darius, on the other hand, seemed to take it all in stride and even held his arms out by his sides while Tarrant scanned him as well. She watched as he moved the device over Darius's thick arms and broad chest. Darius glanced at her and winked. She'd been caught staring at him. Heat warmed her face, but she didn't look away.

When Tarrant was done, he pocketed the scanner. "Let's go." He swung around and started walking toward a truck that had seen better days at least twenty years ago. It was black with pockets of rust on the body. Dust and mud covered it, and the passenger door was held shut with a bungee cord. She wasn't one to judge people by their belongings, but she'd feel a little better if the truck didn't look like it would fall apart the first time they hit a bump.

"Where are we going?" She needed information. Knowledge was the one thing that always helped center her during times of crisis.

"Home." There was such emotion in that one word that she was struck silent.

She'd never had a place that meant that much to her. Not since her parents had passed away. And even then, she'd always felt like an intruder. Her parents had been so close, and she'd been an unexpected surprise when her mother was in her late forties. They'd loved her in their way but had never understood her. She liked her apartment, but surprisingly, the thought of leaving it behind for good didn't bother her as much as she'd thought it would.

Tarrant unhooked the bungee cord and the door swung open. Sarah peered inside. She'd anticipated the interior would be as bad as the outside and was pleasantly surprised when it wasn't. At least the seats were clean and free from debris, even though there was a small hole on the passenger side where the floor had rusted away.

"In you go." Darius put his hand on the small of her back to get her to move. She climbed in and slid to the center of the bench seat.

Darius got in beside her, and Tarrant shut the door and secured the cord once again. She watched as Tarrant strode around the front of the vehicle and slid in on the driver's side. His door shut with no problem.

The engine roared to life as soon as he turned the key. He obviously kept it in good shape.

Tarrant grabbed a black box off the dashboard, pressed a button, and the few lights on the runway went out. He tucked the remote in his pocket, put the truck in gear, and started down a narrow dirt road. The man did seem to love his gadgets. Maybe that's where all his money went. It certainly wasn't spent on his vehicle.

Even though it was light out, the shadows grew darker the deeper they went into the forest. Tree branches dipped onto the road in places and brushed against the vehicle. The scraping sound was very reminiscent of those final moments of the plane landing and made her shudder.

"You cold?" Darius asked. He didn't wait for her to answer and put his arm around her and pulled her against his side.

"Not cold. Just remembering those final seconds of the landing when I thought my life would end in a fiery crash into the trees."

Tarrant snorted, and Darius sighed. "You're never going to let me forget that, are you?"

"Maybe I'll have forgotten it by my one hundredth birthday," she retorted. She looked out the window but there were no landmarks for her to memorize, no indication of exactly where they were. It was endless trees and a dirt road that really couldn't be considered a road in some places.

The truck bounced around, and she was glad to have Darius's arm anchoring her or she might have ended up on the floor. At least the suspension was good.

The ride was short. A mere fifteen minutes later, they turned off the road and parked in front of a small log cabin. Even though it was cold, no smoke rose from the stone chimney. A porch ran the entire length of the front, but there were no chairs to sit on.

Not exactly the most welcoming place.

Tarrant got out and came around to release the bungee cord. Darius slid out and waited for her to do the same.

"Welcome to my home." Tarrant spread his arms wide. "What do you think?"

She wasn't sure what he was after, so she shrugged and answered truthfully. "It's rustic. Could use some chairs or a nice bench on the front. And a fire wouldn't hurt, either." She shivered as a gust of cold air struck her.

"Stop it, Tarrant." Darius was frowning at the man who may or may not be his brother. They'd neither confirmed nor denied it. But the longer she was around them, the more alike they seemed. It was in the way they tilted their heads when they were thinking, in their builds, and in the stubborn set of their jaws.

"He wants to know more about me." She understood Tarrant more than he probably thought she did. "He thinks I'm with the Knights." She'd rather have it all out in the open than play games.

"It's not the questioning. I expect that from him."

Tarrant slapped his hand on his chest. "I'm wounded."

"I doubt that." Darius wrapped his arm around her shoulders again. "It's the wind. He's the one making it colder around you."

"He can do that?" It was mind-blowing to think that anyone could control the wind. "Is it all the weather or just the wind?" she asked. Her curious mind wanted to know everything.

"Fuck, Darius. Why'd you tell her that?"

"Don't blame me. You're the one who's blowing cold air."

Sarah couldn't stop the smile that spread across her face at their bickering. Yup, they were definitely brothers.

Tarrant threw his hands in the air and stomped up the two steps to the porch. He pushed the front door open and went inside. She was surprised it wasn't locked, but then again, he was so isolated, who was going to break in? She definitely wasn't in the city any longer. She'd never dream of leaving home without securing her three locks.

"Let's go." Darius led the way into the house. The interior was as rustic as the exterior. An old sofa in an unfortunate shade of green was matched in ugliness by the flower-covered chair that sat across from it. The stone fireplace could have been lovely if the soot had been washed from it and a cheerful fire had been burning.

It was an open concept, so she could see the kitchen as well. Mismatched cupboards, a woodstove, and a refrigerator that looked like something from the nineteen-fifties outfitted the room. A small table served as a dining area. The floors were wide hardwood boards that would look gorgeous if refinished.

She assumed the closed doors off to the left were the bedroom and bathroom. At least, she hoped there was a bathroom. The thought of having to use the great outdoors did not appeal to her.

"Well?" Tarrant asked.

"It has good bones." No way was she going to act like a prima donna. She could make do with whatever they had.

"Enough, Tarrant." Darius shut the door to the cabin. The air was cool, and she shivered in spite of her layers of clothing. She was tired, hungry, and wanted a shower and a cup of coffee, not necessarily in that order. At this moment, she'd take the coffee and be grateful.

Determined to go forward in a positive manner, she dropped her knapsack on the ugly couch and went to the kitchen. "Do you have a coffee maker of some kind? A percolator? Even instant coffee will do." She lifted the kettle off the stove and went to the pitted metal faucet, praying it actually worked.

"What are you doing?" Darius asked.

"I thought it was kind of obvious. I desperately need a cup of coffee before we discuss whatever it is we need to discuss."

Tarrant came toward her, his movements graceful for such a large man. Once again, he reminded her of Darius. He took the kettle from her hand and set it back on the cold stove.

"Do you have any wood for the stove?" she asked.

"Follow me," he told her. Tarrant went to the corner of the kitchen and reached beneath one of the cupboards.

Follow him? Where? There was nothing but a wall... which silently slid back to reveal a set of stairs. "You guys really like your hidden staircases, don't you?"

Darius grabbed her knapsack before he joined her. "You'll get used to it."

That implied she was going to be around for a while. In spite of her resolve to stand on her own two feet, it warmed her that Darius seemed to want her around. It would have been easy for him to leave her behind or deposit her at an airport anywhere in the country.

A little voice in the back of her head reminded her that maybe he'd brought her here so they could interrogate her without anyone hearing her scream. Then logic kicked in. Darius could have done that in his secret room in his apartment and no one would have known, either.

Tarrant disappeared down the staircase. "Come on. I have coffee down here."

There was really no other choice. That, and the offer of coffee, did it for her. She stepped onto the stairs and headed downward. It couldn't be any worse than the house above them. Or at least she hoped it couldn't. For all she knew, he literally lived in a cave beneath the ground. Darius followed close behind, carrying both of their bags. Having him there made her feel safer.

Lights illuminated the stairs, as they had at Darius's place. Another light shone at the bottom, luring her with its promise of warmth and coffee.

At best, she'd been expecting something similar to Darius's secret hideaway—a large, cavernous, basically empty room. Never in a million years would she have expected what she walked into.

It was warm for one thing, and bright, in spite of the

fact they had to be underground. Water trickled down one exposed rock wall into a fountain below. There wasn't one, but two large sectional leather sofas dominating one end of the space, situated so they both faced a large flat-screen television. A dark cabinet sat beneath the television and most likely housed other electronic equipment.

All of it was fairly new and none of it set off a warning with her talent. With her mental walls firmly in place, she was safe from accidentally touching the wrong thing and falling into a psychic vision.

Then she saw the kitchen. Like the log cabin above, the floor plan was open concept, but that's where the similarities ended. This kitchen was a chef's dream. A large island separated the space. There was an eating bar on one side of the island with four stools. The counter was natural stone in tones of brown. The cupboards were white shaker-style and the floors were gleaming hardwood.

Best of all, there was a state-of-the-art coffee maker on the counter.

Like a sleepwalker in a dream, Sarah stumbled toward the kitchen and the promise of coffee. Tarrant filled a cup and slid it onto the counter. She sat on one of the stools, pulled the cup closer, and lifted it to her lips.

"Do you need sugar?" Tarrant asked.

"Don't talk to me yet." She took a sip and exhaled with relief when the hot brew slid down her throat.

"Yes, she needs sugar," Darius told his brother. "And food." Seeming very much at home, Darius dumped their bags on the end of the counter, went to one of the cupboards, and took down a sugar bowl. He put it in front of her before digging out a spoon.

"Does this look like a restaurant?" When Darius continued to stare at him, Tarrant relented and opened his massive stainless steel refrigerator. "How about omelets?

They're quick."

"Anything. Thank you," she added. Now that she'd had her first taste of coffee and knew she could have more, she added sugar to it and took another sip. *Perfect.* "I can help. With breakfast or lunch or whatever this is." They'd passed through several zones, and she wasn't quite sure what time it was anymore.

"It's fine," Tarrant told her. "You look like you're ready to drop."

"Yeah, I've only had a few hours sleep in the past twenty-four hours." And it was beginning to really catch up with her now that she finally felt relatively safe.

Taking him at his word, Sarah continued to sip coffee while she watched Darius and Tarrant make omelets. All in all, not a bad way to unwind after the tension of the past day. There was no denying they were both man-candy of the highest caliber. Honestly, there was so much testosterone in the room she began to get hot.

Or it might be because she was still wearing her coat. She took it off and set it on the stool next to her as she watched Darius chop mushrooms and peppers. The room got hotter still, so she pulled off her sweater as well.

"How do you heat this place?" She still couldn't see any kind of radiator.

"Geothermal." Tarrant put a large skillet on the six-burner gas range. "Floor ducts."

She fell silent and continued to watch both men, but mostly Darius. Once he'd finished chopping, Tarrant added the vegetables to the eggs he'd cracked and beaten and started making omelets.

Darius came around the counter and sat beside her. He cupped her face in his large palm, and she wanted to close her eyes and lean into it. Instead, she lifted her mug and had another shot of coffee.

"How you holding up?" he asked.

"I'm fine." In spite of the fact her life was destroyed and she had a crazy bunch of people searching for her, she was feeling better than she had since she'd left work. She and Darius had done it. They'd escaped from the Knights, at least for now.

When Darius leaned inward, so did she. Their lips had barely met when Tarrant slapped two plates on the counter. Sarah jerked back and met Tarrant's glare.

"Breakfast is ready."

• • •

Herman Temple was working at his desk when his assistant buzzed him. "What is it, Victoria?"

"Your son to see you, sir."

He wasn't surprised Christian had shown up. "Send him in."

"Yes, sir."

The door to his office opened and Christian strode in, looking as fit as ever. Herman narrowed his gaze. Christian wasn't showing the effects of the loss of dragon's blood as much as he was. Did his son have a secret stash of it somewhere? Although by now, the potency would be gone. The sad fact was that dragon's blood was only good when it was fresh. It had a very short shelf life.

"Any word?" No hello, no nothing. Straight to business. Sometimes his son was too much like him for comfort.

Herman leaned back in his chair. "Not yet." He waited until Christian was seated before he continued. "We lost the signal for Sarah's phone. We assume it was destroyed."

"Damn." Christian began tapping his fingers on his knee. No, not tapping. Shaking. So his son wasn't as healthy as he pretended. That was a reassurance.

"They have to surface at some point. I have people monitoring all the major airports, train stations, and bus terminals across the country, every car rental, and every car dealership. If they get transportation of any kind, we'll find them."

"We need to bring in the military." Christian jumped to his feet and began to pace. "We need Varkas, and we need him now."

"No military. Not yet, at any rate."

Christian swung around to face him. "Why not? They can find a needle in a haystack with the resources at their disposal."

"*She* doesn't want them involved." That shut his son up. "Karina called earlier this morning and was not pleased we'd let Varkas slip through our fingers." Herman stood and walked around to the front of his desk. "She wants Varkas found and contained, and she wants to be here when it happens."

Karina Azarov was the current leader of the Knights of the Dragon. A member of her family had founded the Knights centuries ago, and there had always been a female from her family at the helm. They had more knowledge about dragons than any other family in the world, and they guarded it with a zealousness that was unnerving. He might be ruthless, but Karina Azarov scared even him.

Christian paled and headed for the door. "Let me know if you hear anything."

Herman waited until his son was gone before retaking his seat and picking up his pen. He tapped it against the pad of paper that sat on his desk His son was becoming a bit too ambitious for Herman's peace of mind. It might be time to do something about that.

He put pen to paper and began to compose a letter to the leader of the Knights.

Chapter Fifteen

Darius offhandedly wondered if he could recapture the mood between him and Sarah if he killed his brother. One look at her told him that opportunity had passed. Resigned to eating breakfast instead of carrying her to one of the bedrooms, he picked up his fork and dug into the omelet. He was starving.

He emptied his plate in short order. Beside him, Sarah did the same. The more she ate, the better her color got. That was good. She was going to need all the strength she could get in the coming days and weeks.

"So where is it?" Tarrant asked.

Darius canted his head toward his knapsack. He knew his brother was curious about the book. Darius was surprised he'd held off asking about it this long.

Tarrant opened the knapsack and pulled out the carved wooden box that contained the book. Darius could feel the power humming from inside.

"Ah, should he be doing that?" There was real concern in Sarah's voice. "That thing is dangerous."

"It will be fine," he promised her. "Won't it, Tarrant?" The warning was there, and his brother had better heed it.

Tarrant carefully set the box on the counter and slowly opened the lid. "I'm not stupid, Darius." Both annoyance and excitement tinged his voice.

"I'm not stupid when it comes to my talent, and it almost overwhelmed me," she reminded him.

She pushed aside her plate and slid off her stool. The skin beneath her eyes looked almost bruised with fatigue, but she was alert and ready to fight, all her attention on that damn book. The worry in her gaze almost brought him to his knees.

"Caution," he reminded his brother when Tarrant reached for the book.

"Right." Tarrant stopped reaching for the manuscript and inhaled sharply before blowing out a deep breath. The air fluttered the pages. He did it again and again until the air built around the object. Then he waved his hands like he was conducting a symphony. The book rose out of the box and floated to the counter.

"Wow." When Sarah instinctively moved toward Tarrant, Darius wrapped his arms around her and pulled her back against his chest.

"No." He didn't want her anywhere near that damn book after the last time.

His brother waved his hand again, and the pages of the manuscript fluttered open. Tarrant studied a page before waving his hand over the book. The page quivered and then slowly turned.

"You must be a wind drakon."

Darius didn't like the admiration in Sarah's voice or the way she was watching Tarrant. "Air drakon," he corrected.

"My brother the earth drakon gets jealous of my abilities." It was an old joke, but Darius wasn't laughing. Not today.

Sarah seemed startled for a moment, and then she smiled. Darius realized that Tarrant had confirmed they were brothers. That meant he'd decided to trust Sarah.

"In your dreams, Tarrant. I'm much stronger." He shut his mouth before he said something even more stupid. He was acting like a child, which was extremely lowering, considering his age.

Tarrant, as always, decided to poke at him. "I fear he lacks finesse and is a more blundering sort of drakon."

Mine. Mine. Mine.

Rage started to build inside Darius, and he had to remind himself that he loved his brother and would never knowingly harm him. Although, right now he wanted to tear him limb from limb for daring to flirt with his Sarah.

Darius was getting hotter, the fire building deep inside. Sarah covered his hands where they were locked around her waist. "Are you okay?" That simple question, along with her touch, allowed him to gain control.

"I'm just worried about my idiot brother."

Tarrant wasn't paying him any attention. All his concentration was on the book. "There is so much here," he murmured. "So much blood spilled for the secrets hidden on these pages."

He knew what his brother must be feeling. The same fury lived in him. To think of the other drakons, possibly even friends, who'd suffered at the hands of the Knights in order for them to obtain some of that information was enough to make Darius want to set the world aflame.

When friends disappeared, Darius was never sure if it was because they'd chosen to go into the Deep Sleep, if they'd simply dropped off the grid, or if the Knights had captured or killed them.

"Fire won't destroy it," he reminded Tarrant. "I've tried."

"No, this thing is pure evil and is protected by the drakon blood that has been spilled on it." Tarrant's eyes were tortured when he looked up. "That isn't ink."

Sarah gasped and swayed. "No."

Tarrant nodded. "It's drakon blood."

Every muscle in Darius's body turned to stone. He clenched his jaw so hard it was a wonder the bone didn't snap under the pressure.

Sarah sucked in a breath and pushed at his hands. He was holding her too tightly. He was hurting her. He released her and whirled her around so she was facing him. Her skin was pale, but her gaze was steady.

"Did I hurt you?" He didn't wait for an answer and tugged up the shirt she was wearing. She batted at his hands and tried to cover her bare stomach, but he would not be denied. "I don't see any bruises."

"You didn't hurt me." She grabbed his wrists and pulled them away. The shirt, his shirt, fell, covering her once again. "You just started to squeeze me a little hard there for a second. You were upset, and rightfully so."

Sarah turned her attention to the book. "What do we do with it? How do we destroy it?"

Darius looked into his brother's eyes and knew Tarrant was as stumped as he was. "It's the drakon blood that protects the book," Darius told her. "Only a drakon's own fire can destroy his blood, which is why the drakon you saw in your vision was able to burn from the inside out and incinerate himself."

Tarrant used air currents once again to lift the book up and return it to the wooden box. Once it was safely inside, he floated the cover back into place. "It's some sort of evolutionary protection." Tarrant leaned on the counter and smiled at Sarah. "Drakons can't harm other drakons with their fire."

"But they can beat the hell out of one another," Darius reminded his brother.

Tarrant's smile only deepened. "I need to do some

research to try to figure this out." He picked up his plate and carried it to the sink. "In the meantime, why don't you two get some rest?"

"You won't try to do anything on your own, will you?" Sarah nibbled on her bottom lip. Darius wanted to lick the small hurt she inflicted.

Tarrant put his hand over his heart. The action seemed flippant, but his promise was solemn. "I won't. I'm going to do some research and see if I can get some idea what we're going to do about the book."

Sarah frowned. "Why does he get to research while I'm not allowed on my computer?"

Darius thought she was adorable when she frowned. Come to think of it, he thought she was adorable when she smiled. He'd lost all perspective when it came to Sarah. "Tarrant knows how to hide his presence online."

Her gaze whipped back to his brother. "How?" she demanded.

Tarrant studied her for a long time, but she didn't fidget or back down. She just stared right back at him. It was a huge turn-on to watch her stand up to his brother. Sarah was a strong woman with a backbone of steel. And he wanted her.

He shifted position as his pants became very uncomfortable, and he prayed Sarah didn't notice his hard-on. Tarrant glanced at him and rolled his eyes before returning his attention to Sarah. "Come with me."

His brother grabbed the wooden box with the manuscript, stuffed it back into the knapsack, and hooked the strap over his shoulder before he left the kitchen and headed down a long hallway. They passed several bedrooms and a study before reaching a heavy, metal door at the end. Tarrant put his palms on scanners mounted on the walls on either side of the door. They were spaced far apart, and only someone of Tarrant's size and arm-span could reach them simultaneously.

The locks on the door clicked. Then Tarrant punched a twenty-four-digit code into the keypad located directly on the door. When those locks clicked, the door slid open.

He motioned them both inside before following them. The heavy door slammed shut behind them. They were in a small elevator.

"Why aren't we moving?" Sarah asked.

"Down," Tarrant said, and the elevator went downward. "Voice activated," he told them.

"This place is more secure than Fort Knox," she whispered. Darius couldn't disagree. Tarrant had always been paranoid, but this took it to an entirely new level.

The elevator stopped and the doors slid open. Another heavy door, this one Darius recognized as titanium, waited directly in front of them. There was no way off the elevator if they couldn't open that door.

Tarrant stepped up to the retinal scanners and positioned his eyes over both. Another click and his brother shoved the door open. "Welcome to my computer lab."

Sarah gasped and stepped forward. "This is amazing."

Tarrant seemed pleased by her reaction. "State of the art. Most are one-of-a-kind prototypes I built myself."

"Holy crap." Sarah put her hands behind her back but moved closer to the long desk-height counters that ran all the way around the room.

Darius thought it was all just a bunch of machines. He didn't understand them, but he knew Tarrant loved them.

Tarrant stowed the knapsack safely in a metal cabinet. Then he sat in a comfortable leather chair on wheels and pulled himself up in front of one of the many computers. "Let's see what your friend Herman Temple is up to." His brother's fingers flew on the keyboard. "It will take me a moment. Ah, here we go."

The New York City street where Herman Temple lived

came up on the screen. Tarrant zoomed in just in time to see someone leaving the building.

"That's Christian Temple." Sarah took a step back before she stopped herself. Darius put his hand on her shoulder and squeezed. "How did you do that? That's not Google Earth. That's real time."

"Satellite," Tarrant told her.

. . .

"You have a satellite?" Sarah knew for sure she'd gone down the rabbit hole. The amount of security and equipment Tarrant had in his room had to cost hundreds of thousands of dollars, if not more. Not to mention the incredible home he'd built underground. This was a multimillion-dollar facility.

Tarrant ignored her, his fingers a blur on the keyboard. "There we go, all back on track again."

"Who are you?" she asked. Tarrant and Darius were brothers, but they were also very different. Darius was blunt and forthright. She knew where she stood with him because, good or bad, he'd tell her. Tarrant was toying with her. He was a man at home with technology. She had a feeling he enjoyed playing games…and coming out the winner.

Tarrant turned around to face her. "I'm Cooper Communications."

She felt her jaw drop but couldn't help it. Cooper Communications was one of the biggest, most powerful communications companies in the world. They had television and radio stations. They sold cell phones and computers. They also built satellites and, if she wasn't mistaken, even had military contracts. If it had to do with communications of any kind, they had a hand in it.

"Holy shit." She was impressed in spite of everything. They might actually have a chance to get out of this situation alive. "Do you know what this means?" she asked Darius, who was hovering behind her.

"It means he likes to play with toys." He glared at his brother. Sarah wondered why Darius seemed angry with him.

"No, it means we have leverage." She turned back to Tarrant. "You have military contracts, don't you?" Her head was whirling with the possibilities.

"Sweetheart," Tarrant drawled. "I can control every satellite circling the planet. And there's not a military system I haven't been able to hack. I can ghost in and out of anywhere without being detected."

That much power in the hands of one man was downright terrifying.

As though he knew what she was thinking, he winked at her. "Don't worry, I'm not planning on destroying the earth. At least not today."

"You need to rest." Darius ran his fingers over her cheek. "You're pale and exhausted."

"It's been a rough day, or two, or whatever it's been. I've lost total track of time." She must look like a wreck after everything she'd been through. *Not that it matters in the grand scheme of things*, she reminded herself.

"Tarrant," Darius snapped out.

His brother tapped some computer keys and the elevator door slid soundlessly open. She hesitated before stepping inside.

"Don't worry, I'll let you out." She couldn't tell if Tarrant was mocking her or not.

"And if he doesn't, I'll bring the whole damn mountain crashing down on his precious equipment," Darius assured her as the elevator doors closed.

"You can do that?" She wasn't sure why that shocked her. "Tarrant called you an earth drakon. That makes sense considering you're in the mining and exploration business."

And she was babbling to keep her mind off the fact that she was locked in a small elevator with a really big and sexy guy, and this elevator may or may not open when it got to the top.

She held her breath until the door slid back and she stepped into the hallway. She put one hand out to steady herself against the wall.

"Sarah." Darius wrapped one arm around her shoulders and the other behind her legs and lifted her into his arms.

"I'm fine." She wasn't weak and didn't want to be perceived that way. "Let me down. I can walk."

"But why would you want to do that when I can carry you?" His blunt reply reassured her. She much preferred Darius to his brother. She had the feeling Tarrant was more like a chess master, always ten steps ahead of his opponent, always playing a game that no one else was aware of.

"The book." God, they'd just left it down there with Tarrant.

"It's fine." Darius carried her into a bedroom and deposited her on a rather large bed. A muted light came on as soon as they'd entered. "It's certainly safe enough."

She couldn't dispute that fact. The book was probably in the safest place on earth. "We still need to destroy it," she reminded him.

"We will. Tarrant will figure out a way." Darius crouched in front of her and unlaced her boots before pulling them off. Then he tugged off her socks. She curled her toes against his touch.

She hated leaving everything in Tarrant's hands. "I'll help him as soon as I've rested."

Darius scowled. "You don't need to work with him."

"Why not?"

Darius tugged her until she was standing and then reached for the fastening on her jeans. She tried to bat his hands away, but he was relentless. "Why are you so angry?" she asked.

He lowered the zipper and pulled her jeans down around her knees. He gave her a gentle push and she landed back on her ass. He took the opportunity to pull her jeans all the way off. She was wearing her panties, bra, and Darius's oversize shirt, the one he'd given her to wear. That seemed like days ago, even weeks, rather than hours.

He kicked off his own shoes and yanked off his socks.

"What are you doing?" He wasn't going to strip in front of her, was he? She'd already seen him naked when he'd shifted, but this was different. For one thing, she was sitting on a very big bed.

Then he reached over his shoulder, grabbed a handful of material, and pulled his shirt over his head. Sarah swallowed heavily as his hard, muscled chest came into view. She should be too tired to even notice how built Darius was. And she certainly shouldn't notice the way his abs rippled like corrugated steel, or the way the color of the tattoo seemed deeper, richer than it had before.

"You need to rest." He rubbed his hand over his face and sighed. "And, God's truth, I could do with some myself."

Of course, he had to be exhausted. He'd been up as long as she had, maybe longer. He'd also flown them here while she'd napped. "Do drakons need as much sleep as humans?" There was so much about him she didn't know.

Darius leaned down, wrapped his arm around her waist, and lifted her as effortlessly as if she were a child. He tugged the covers down and deposited her back on the bed. "No, we don't need as much rest as humans do, but I haven't been sleeping much lately. Scoot over."

"Why?" He didn't think he was going to sleep with her, did he? "Surely there are other beds you can sleep in. If not, those sofas looked mighty comfortable."

He all but shoved her over as he crowded his way onto the bed beside her. He flipped up the covers and threw his arm over her. "But, Sarah, none of them have you."

Her heart did a little flip-flop on hearing that. "This isn't smart." She was already way too attached to Darius.

"Would you rather it was Tarrant here with you?"

"What?" She levered herself up on one arm so she could see him. "Why would you say something like that?" The heat in his green eyes almost scorched her, and his lips were set in a thin line. "Are you jealous?" His jaw tightened and his nostrils flared.

"No. I'm not jealous of that idiot."

He was jealous. Sarah was flabbergasted. Why would he even care what she thought about his brother unless he had feelings for her? That traitorous heart of hers did another flip-flop before it began to race.

It might be better if she allowed him to think she wasn't attracted to him, but she simply couldn't do it. She ran her fingers along his stubborn jaw. "Tarrant is handsome and very intelligent," she began. Darius's entire body turned to stone, and his eyes filled with fury, but along with that emotion was hurt. "But he isn't you."

Chapter Sixteen

Darius knew he was being an idiot, but he couldn't seem to stop himself. He knew Tarrant had more in common with Sarah than he did. They were both researchers at heart, both interested in technology. He was more at home in the depths of the earth, discovering her treasures.

He tried to ignore the brush of Sarah's soft hand over his jaw, the unending throbbing of his cock. Her very nearness was driving him to distraction, but he couldn't walk away from her. He didn't want to.

If she was part of some intricate plan of the Knights, then he was shit out of luck, because he belonged to her, heart and soul, and all they'd done was kiss. How much worse would it be if he made love with her?

He desperately wanted to find out.

The words she spoke almost cut out his heart, but then she quickly healed it and made it soar.

Darius groaned and dragged her down on top of him. Her legs tangled with his as she planted her hands on his chest. That simple touch reached deep inside him and made his beast purr with pleasure.

She started to speak, but he didn't give her a chance. He pulled her down and covered her lips with his. He needed her more than he needed air to breath. And when she kissed him back, he felt invincible.

Soft and plump, her lips parted, and he pushed his tongue inside, claiming what belonged to him and only him. He couldn't bear the thought of another man tasting her sweetness.

He slid his hands underneath the shirt she wore and found the supple length of her spine. The strap of her bra was in his way, but he ignored it, knowing she was more relaxed with the garment still on. He'd much rather have her naked. For now, he enjoyed the press of her mouth against his, the tentative touches of her tongue, and the curl of her fingers against his chest.

Her breathing was ragged when she finally broke their kiss, her eyes dark and mysterious as she stared down at him in the dim light. "What are we doing?" she asked.

He ran his hand down her back and cupped one firm mound of her behind. "If you have to ask, I'm obviously doing it wrong."

As he'd hoped, she smiled, but it was fleeting, disappearing almost as fast as it appeared. "You know what I mean."

Unfortunately, he did. Darius sighed, and the lights chose that moment to click off. Before she could ask, he answered the question he knew was on the tip of her tongue. "The lights are linked to pressure gauges buried beneath the floor. If no one walks around the room for a certain span of time, they go off. They can be adjusted manually, but they're preset to react that way.

"Wow, your brother really does love his gadgets."

Darius could still see Sarah easily. As a drakon, he was as at home in the dark as he was in the light. But Sarah was more relaxed with them off. Maybe she thought he couldn't see her as well.

"He does." Right on cue, the baseboards began to emit a low-level glow, much like a nightlight for adults.

Darius trailed his hands down the back of her thighs, and Sarah shivered, her entire body quaking at his touch. "What we are doing"—he went back to her earlier question—"is sharing our bodies with each other. Giving pleasure with touch." He slid his fingers over the silk covering her firm ass. "What is so wrong about that?"

"When you put it like that, it doesn't seem so bad."

He ran his fingers over her hips, dipped in at her waist and around to her back again, getting her used to his touch. He sensed Sarah was not the kind of woman who could or would bed a man if she didn't have feelings for him.

"I also can't think when you touch me like that," she whispered when he coasted his hand over her behind and between her legs.

"Then I need to keep touching you." He rolled until she was lying under him, propping himself up on his forearms so he wouldn't crush her with his weight. The top button of her shirt had come undone and exposed a pale swath of flesh. Darius nuzzled her bare skin, inhaling her scent. "You are a treasure."

He hadn't meant to say that aloud, but he wouldn't take it back. She gave a small, self-conscious laugh. "Hardly that."

Darius sat back on his heels between her spread thighs and stared down at her in disbelief. She had no idea of her appeal, but he was just the man to appreciate such a gem. He flicked the buttons of her shirt open. As much as he liked the idea of her wearing his clothes, he wanted to see her totally naked. The urge was quickly passing from need to obsession. He knew it was his dragon nature, the part of him that was not human, that craved her naked body pressed against his. Of course, the human side of him wanted her almost as much, making him more volatile than he'd been in his entire existence.

In all the centuries he'd taken women to bed, this was the only time his dragon had ever wanted one as much as the human in him did. That was dangerous for both of them. But Darius knew in his heart he'd stop before he'd ever do anything to harm Sarah.

She wrapped her hands around his wrists, and he stilled as quickly and fully as if she'd manacled him with the strongest chains. "What is it?" He wanted to quell any fears or questions she might have so they could continue.

He was just getting started.

• • •

His skin was warm beneath her hands. Sarah knew she was nowhere near strong enough to stop Darius from doing whatever he wanted, just as she knew he'd stop if she asked him to. Where did such faith come from? She'd known him less than a day but felt as though they'd been together for years.

Her skin still tingled where he'd touched her. She felt more alive in his arms than she had at any other time in her life. Maybe it was the mad run for their lives, or the enforced proximity. Such things could cause heightened emotions. She knew that.

Yet, it was somehow more profound, richer than simply living in the moment. Her craving for Darius went bone deep. Was it because he was more than just a man, or in spite of it?

Did it really matter? When it came down to it, she wanted him.

She had no idea what her life expectancy was now that she was involved in an immortal war, one she hadn't even known existed until such a short time ago. Now she was smack-dab in the middle of it.

Life was precious. Fragile. She hadn't understood how much she valued the ordinary until she'd lost it. But the loss had come with compensation. And he was sitting between her spread thighs, watching and waiting.

He was still wearing his pants, but his chest was bare. Even though the light was dim, her eyes were adjusting enough to see his outline. She was grateful for that small illumination. Being underground with no windows or ambient glow from the outside, could make it pitch dark, like being in a cave. She didn't think she'd enjoy that sensation at all.

She had the feeling it wouldn't bother Darius in the least.

"Sarah?" He was waiting on word from her whether to keep going or to stop.

Death was a possibility, and the unknown crouched outside the bedroom door, waiting for them. In here, they were a man and a woman who wanted each other. For now, that was enough.

Sarah used her hold on him to pull herself to a seated position. She shrugged out of the oversize shirt and reached behind to unhook her bra. She had a slight moment of panic when she slid the garment down her arms and tossed it aside.

A low growl rippled through the air, and the fine hair on her arms stood on end. Then he touched her. It was the lightest of strokes, just the pad of his thumb over one distended nipple. She gasped and sucked in a breath when he did the same thing to her other breast.

He leaned over her, slowly driving her back until she fell against the pillows. His lips found hers as one of his hands covered a firm mound. She wrapped her arms around his neck and held on. The entire world might be upended, but Darius was strong enough to anchor her in the storm.

She gave herself up to the passion that had been bubbling

between them since they'd first laid eyes on each other. *No regrets*, she promised herself. This was a gift for both of them, a respite in an otherwise crazy situation.

Sarah raked her nails lightly over his back, and Darius growled again. Instead of frightening her, the sound was a complete turn-on. It meant he wanted her.

Their tongues tangled as his hand continued to shape and mold her breasts. He broke away and peppered her face, jaw, and neck with kisses. He nibbled at her shoulder and lapped at her collarbone.

Her fingernails made half-circles on his back where she dug into it. His jaw was smooth, no stubble to abrade her skin as he nuzzled the valley between her breasts. He hadn't shaved, either. She was about to ask him about it when he dragged his tongue over the pebbled tip of her nipple before capturing it between his lips.

Any thought of asking questions melted under the sensual onslaught. She arched upward, seeking more of his touch, threading her fingers through his silky black hair and dragging him closer. His rumble of pleasure vibrated through her and set every nerve ending in her body on fire.

"Darius." She didn't know what she wanted to say to him, if anything. She just wanted to hear the sound of his name.

He plumped her breast in his large hand and went back and forth between them, licking and sucking, teasing and pleasuring until she was unable to think. Need pooled low in her belly. Her panties were wet with desire, and she ached to feel him inside her.

With Darius sitting between her thighs, she couldn't even close her legs to try to ease the vast pressure growing inside her. She groaned and arched up in vain, unable to rub herself against him.

"What do you want?" he asked.

Sarah licked her lips and gasped as another blast of sexual

heat flowed through her. "You. I want you."

. . .

Darius silently gave thanks to every deity he'd ever heard named over the course of human history. Sarah was warm and willing in his arms. More than that, she wanted him.

He could smell her sweet arousal, could feel the swell of heat rising from her.

He scooted lower on the mattress and let his hands flow down from her breasts and over her slender torso. She was almost too thin, but her hips were curved and her breasts a firm handful. To him, she was perfect because she was Sarah.

He skimmed one finger over the band of her panties, loving the sound of her breath as it caught in her throat. Her hips bucked upward as if seeking his touch.

He wanted to savor the moment and make it last. He wanted to touch and kiss and lick every inch of her creamy skin. That would have to wait for another day. With his cock straining against the zipper of his pants, and his patience hanging by a thread, Darius knew he could hold out no longer.

He hooked his fingers under the waistband of her panties and dragged them down her legs and off. He would have ripped them away if she'd had another pair to wear. He'd buy her dozens of pairs, colorful and silky, just so he could tear them off her.

He lowered his head and buried his nose against her mound. Her sweet and spicy scent filled his nostrils and wrapped around him in a loving embrace. Darius caught her thighs in his hands and pushed her legs open. With his preternatural sight, he could see every delectable pink inch of her.

She gave a strangled sound. Not quite a groan or a gasp, but something in between. He gave an answering growl and lifted her as he lowered his head.

* * *

Oh, God. Sarah grabbed the sheet beneath her, fisting it in her hands as Darius delved between her thighs. Then his lips touched her slick folds and she lost it. She moaned and bucked her hips as he licked and teased the hot flesh between her legs. He tried to hold her legs open, but she fought him until he let go. Then she twined them around his head.

He laughed and sucked on her clit in such a delicious way that stars exploded behind her eyes. He probed her opening with one thick finger, testing her natural resistance before forging inward. Her inner muscles contracted around him, squeezing, but she was so aroused, so wet, there was nothing to stop him until his finger was buried inside.

Sarah arched her neck as he slowly withdrew his finger and plunged it deep. She bit her lip to keep from crying out, but when he did it again, she couldn't hold back her whimper of need. What he was doing felt incredible. She'd had lovers over the years, but no man had ever touched her like this. It went beyond the physical and into another realm entirely. She felt her soul reaching for his.

That scared her, but there was no stopping it. And truthfully, she didn't want to, no matter what the outcome.

He dragged his tongue over her clit before circling the small nub of pleasure. "Come for me," he demanded. And when he caught it between his lips and growled, it was like having a warm vibrator stimulate her.

Sarah cried out as her orgasm exploded. He said something in a language she didn't understand. All she knew was the pleasure rushing through her veins. Her slick channel clutched at his finger. She wanted him to move, to slide it in and out, but he kept it steady.

She slumped back on the bed. Every muscle in her body had turned to mush. She'd climaxed, but she wasn't satisfied, not like she should be. A want, a need grew inside her with each passing second.

"Darius." She couldn't wait for him any longer. She lunged upward and attacked the opening of his pants. He tried to help her, but she slapped his hands away. His cock was large and hard against the zipper, making it difficult to undo.

"Let me." Darius simply yanked on the material, splitting it wide open. His cock fell out into her waiting hand. Like the rest of him, it was big and firm.

Even though she was wet and aroused, and intellectually she knew he should fit, she had concerns. She'd never had a lover quite like Darius before. But her body knew what it wanted. One look at his cock and it spasmed with delight.

"I'll go slow," he promised. Once again, he seemed to know what she was thinking. It was more likely this wasn't the first time he'd had a lover worry about them fitting together.

He wrapped one large palm around the back of her neck, supporting her as he slowly lowered her so her head was resting on the pillow. All the while, he kissed her until there were no worries, no other thought than joining with him.

He continued to kiss her as he reached between their bodies and guided the head of his cock to her opening. The blunt tip nudged inward, momentarily stopped by the hard clutch of her inner muscles.

Darius was patient, not trying to batter down her natural defenses. No, he kissed her senseless, tangling their tongues, pressing lips together in a dance of desperation. Every time she relaxed, he flexed his hips, pushing his hard length deeper into her slick channel.

He teased one of her nipples before covering the entire mound of her breast with his palm. His large body blanketed hers, but she felt cherished, not crushed. He was only partway inside her and she wanted all of him.

She brought her legs up and clamped her thighs around his hips. He grunted and slid in another inch.

"Do it." She couldn't wait any longer. Didn't want to. When he hesitated, she lifted her hips. At the same time, she locked her ankles around his butt and pulled him closer.

The blunt thickness pressed against the inside of her channel, stretching it. Both of them were gasping as though they'd sprinted a mile, but he was completely inside her. He stilled and buried his face in the curve of her neck, not moving a muscle as he gave her body time to adjust, to accept him.

The slight pinch of discomfort dissolved and was replaced by a pleasure so deep she thought she'd drown in it. With her legs wrapped around his flanks and her arms twined around his neck, Sarah held on tightly, sensing he needed that connection as much as she did.

He nuzzled her neck and worked his way up to the sensitive curve of her ear. He licked at the swirls and gently tugged on the lobe. "Promise me you'll tell me if I'm hurting you."

Even now, with his cock throbbing deep in her core, he was worried about her. Her heart softened and her entire body seemed to sigh and relax, trusting him to keep her safe. "I promise," she told him, even though she wasn't the least bit worried. So far, he'd given her nothing but the most exquisite pleasure.

He pushed upward until his forearms were flat on the bed on either side of her. His biceps bulged as his arms supported his weight. Then he slowly withdrew his shaft until only the tip was still inside her. He paused and flexed his hips, pushing inward once again. The rhythm of advance and retreat became more rapid and ragged as he did it again and again.

Sarah gripped his biceps and drove her hips up on his downward stroke. Every time he filled her, the emptiness inside her disappeared only to reappear when he withdrew. Her blood hummed through her veins and sweat beaded on her brow. She was close. So close.

Darius's eyes were wide open, and his gaze never left her face as he took her harder and faster. His lips were pulled back in a snarl of pain as he plunged inward over and over. She rode the wave with him, fearing she might expire before it crested.

Pressure built within her, burning her from the inside out. Darius supported himself with one arm and shoved the other one under her, angling her body so her clit brushed against his pelvis. She moaned and ground her groin against his. He drove deep and her entire body clenched, poised on the precipice for one glorious second before tumbling over. She cried out his name. Her body spasmed and clutched his cock.

Darius roared, and his shaft seemed to grow larger, filling her even more. Warmth flooded her, and she knew he'd found his release. He pumped his hips several more times before collapsing on top of her. Before his weight could crush her, he rolled so she was lying on top of him, their bodies still joined.

She kissed his chest and nestled against him. He wrapped her in his embrace and pulled the covers over them once again. She was sticky and sweaty and promised herself she'd get cleaned up as soon as she got her strength back.

She yawned and snuggled closer to his warmth. Darius was better than an electric blanket. His heat and the solid beat of his heart lulled her. She yawned again and closed her eyes. She'd rest for a minute more.

Chapter Seventeen

Darius knew when Sarah finally dropped off to sleep. Her entire body went boneless against his, and her breath deepened and slowed. He adjusted her position slightly so she wouldn't end up with a crick in her neck and then simply basked in her trust and the afterglow of their lovemaking.

His cock was still buried in her slick warmth. Even now her body gave the occasional jerk, her sheath rippling up and down his length. He should be spent after such a wild ride, but he was hard and ready to go again. As much as it pained him to do so, he eased his shaft from her slick warmth. Sarah needed rest.

He couldn't help but smile as he remembered the insistent way she'd wrapped her legs around him and bucked her hips against him. The way she'd called his name and gasped with pleasure.

She'd enjoyed their joining just as much as he had. He'd made certain of that. He was old enough and smart enough to know that a physical connection could help bind Sarah to him.

He stilled as the idea took form. He wanted to bind Sarah to him forever. Such a thought had never occurred to him. As much as he needed rest and wanted to stay with Sarah, he needed some space to think.

He also knew Tarrant would be waiting for him to return.

It was harder than he expected to ease Sarah down onto the mattress. She moaned and frowned when her body hit the cooler sheet. He bent over her, inhaled deeply, and breathed warm air over and around her. As if comforted by it, she snuggled down, sighed, and drifted back into a deep sleep. He waited several minutes to make sure she was fully asleep before sliding out of bed. Before he stood, he reached over to the bedside table and hit the manual switch to control the lights. The last thing he wanted was the light to come on and wake her.

He left his clothes on the floor and strode naked to the door. It opened with no sound, and he stepped into the hallway and closed it quietly behind him. Tarrant's room was just down the hall. He'd find a shower and clean clothes there. They were close enough in size that his brother's clothes would fit.

Tarrant's bedroom was the same size as the one he'd just left. There were no mementos lying around, no works of art on the walls. There were, however, several electronic gadgets dumped on the dresser and nightstand.

Darius shook his head and opened his brother's closet. He chose a plain black T-shirt and a pair of jeans and then headed to the ensuite. A large tiled shower beckoned. He set the clothes on the vanity and stepped into the enclosure. He cranked the water and it immediately cascaded over him. Once he adjusted the temperature, he grabbed the soap from the built-in shelf.

He frowned as he sniffed the fragrant bar. It didn't smell like the earth and woods, as his soap did, but like the crisp autumn air. It would have to do.

Darius scrubbed from head to toe, doing his best to ignore his hard-on. But try as he might, he couldn't stop his thoughts from wandering back to Sarah, so snug and warm in the bed down the hall. His beast was restless and wanted to go back and guard her. Darius knew the best way to do that was to eliminate the threat stalking them.

He rinsed the remaining soap away and turned off the water. Steam rose around him and quickly dissipated. He grabbed a towel from a nearby stack and quickly dried himself off.

It only took moments for him to dress. He was more eager than ever to find out if Tarrant had discovered anything that would help. He might tease and torment his brother about his fixation on and fascination with the electronic world, but he was damn grateful for his skills.

Leaving the bedroom behind, Darius headed back to the door at the end of the hallway. He glanced up at the camera, knowing Tarrant would be watching. Sure enough, there was a series of clicks, the sound of metal sliding over metal, and then the door opened. He stepped into the elevator and it went down. When he finally stepped into his brother's workspace, he was growing impatient.

"Well?"

"These things take time." Tarrant's fingers flew over the keyboard in front of him. "And I'm dealing with several problems at once. I want to know who is currently running the Knights of the Dragon. And I'm trying to figure out what to do with that damn book."

Darius pulled up a chair next to Tarrant. "Find anything interesting?"

Tarrant swiveled his seat around so he was facing Darius. "Yes and no. Herman Temple is a lot older than the sixty years it states on his birth certificate. I told you about the photos

I dug up." He reached back to the console and hit several buttons. Four pictures popped up onto the screen. "I can't be sure, but I take him to be at least two hundred, maybe older."

Darius studied the images. His brother was right. They were of the same man. "That's what I was afraid of." The older ones were the most dangerous. They were the ones with a taste for drakon's blood and the strength and health it gave them.

"As far as I can tell, his son is around seventy, even though he looks in his thirties." Tarrant paused. "I've actually done business with several companies they hold an interest in."

Darius leaned back and mulled over what his brother had told him. "No escaping the fact that our paths are going to cross with the Knights at some point or another. They're into business and power, and so are we."

The corners of Tarrant's mouth turned up in a sly grin. "Yes, it is inevitable. What's also inevitable is that I am no longer a shareholder in a certain company. As of a few minutes ago, they have satellite problems that only I can fix. Unfortunately, it may take me a long time to get to them."

"Is that so?" He loved the way his brother's mind worked. Darius was more direct when dealing with problems, but Tarrant treated it all like a game of chess. And he was a grand master.

"It is. Sad really. When their shareholders start abandoning ship, I'll scoop up the shares for cheap and bring the company back from the depths."

"Then why did you sell your shares if you only plan to buy them back?"

"I try to teach you about business, but you refuse to learn."

He thought about taking a swipe at his brother. He could use a good fight to work off some of his tension. But this was no place for a brawl. Tarrant would lose his mind if any of his valuable equipment was damaged. "Explain it to me, wise one. I know you make money on the deal, but why would you buy back stock in a company owned by the Knights?"

Tarrant's smile widened. "Shares are at all all-time high right now. I sell. I make a ton of money. Stocks plummet when there are problems. I buy them cheap, fix the problem, and then they're worth a lot once again. I make money on both ends of the deal. But even better, I'll gain control of the company. It will no longer belong to the Knights. It will be mine."

Darius laughed. "I do love the way you think."

One of the many computers made a beeping sound, and Tarrant pushed his chair toward it, the wheels gliding over the floor. "Hmm."

"What is it?" Darius stood and went to look over his brother's shoulder.

"I emailed a certain priest I know about the book."

"You told him about the book?" Darius wasn't sure he approved. "Can he be trusted?"

"Yes." The word was clipped, and there was no mistaking the underlying anger.

"I trust your judgment, but it's not just me involved, Tarrant."

"Ah, the little woman." Tarrant tapped a few keys and the bedroom suddenly appeared on the screen. Sarah was sprawled peacefully across the bed with the covers tucked tightly around her.

"You didn't have that screen on earlier, did you?" Darius didn't want to kill his brother, but might have no choice if he'd seen Sarah naked.

Tarrant snorted. "As if I want to see your bare ass. No thank you. I thought you might like to keep an eye on her."

Darius blew out a breath and raked his fingers through his hair. He knew he was acting slightly irrational but couldn't help it. "I need to work off some steam."

"I can help you with that as soon as I finish here."

"Did your priest have any suggestions?" Somebody had to know how to destroy the damn book.

Tarrant scrolled through the email. "As a matter of fact, he did. He suggests performing an exorcism on the book while burning it with the fire from a sanctified candle and dousing the ashes in holy water."

"Why an exorcism?"

"Because the book seems to be possessed in some manner, almost sentient. We need to drive it out or negate its power."

"And what if that exorcism ends up being a way to trap one of us." Darius prowled around the room, mulling over the logistics and possible outcomes. "I know you trust this priest, but the Knights have a way of persuading people."

Tarrant typed a quick reply before spinning around to face Darius. "Father Simon Babineaux is sixty years old. I saved his life when he was only a boy. I offered him my blood when he was in his forties. He refused. Not because he feared or loathed what I was, but because he values our friendship more."

Darius felt like an idiot. "I'm sorry. I know better than to question your judgment."

Tarrant's mouth fell open for a second and then slammed shut. "Now I'm scared."

"What?" Darius scowled.

"You apologizing has to be a sign of the end of days."

"Shut up, smart-ass."

Tarrant stood and slapped Darius on the back. "Come on, old man. I know what you need."

Darius elbowed his younger brother. "Old man, my ass."

Tarrant merely laughed. "I'm not an expert, but your ass does look old."

He tried not to join in, but he couldn't hold back his laughter. It was a very familiar joke between them. Tarrant often taunted him because he was older by three whole months.

Tarrant tugged on the T-shirt Darius was wearing. "I see you found your way into my closet."

"Yeah, thanks for the loan."

"What do you plan to do about clothing for the little woman?"

"Stop calling her that. Her name is Sarah." He took one last glance at the screen. She was still sleeping deeply. Some of his agitation settled as soon as he saw her.

They went through the security protocols and stepped into the elevator. Tarrant crossed his arms over his chest and leaned against the wall. "You've got it bad. This isn't like you." Teasing time was over and Tarrant was deadly serious.

"I know." He tried to find a way to explain his connection to Sarah, which wasn't easy because he didn't understand it himself. "I feel her here." He touched his chest. "My beast wants to protect her above anything else. The only reason I can be away from her is I know she's safe."

"Shit." Tarrant rubbed his hand over his jaw. "Let me think about this."

Neither of them spoke again until they were back in the hallway with the bedrooms. "Any ideas?" Darius asked.

"Yeah. One."

Darius raised an eyebrow in silent question.

Tarrant led the way to a door just down from his bedroom. Darius smiled and followed his brother.

• • •

Sarah woke suddenly. She bolted upright in bed and tried to calm her ragged breathing. "It was just a dream," she assured herself. No one was lurking in the shadows waiting to kill her, at least not at the moment. She was safe in a drakon's lair.

She was also alone. It was disconcerting to wake up in a strange bed and not even know what time of the day or night it was. She had no idea how long she'd slept.

"Shower first." She slid out of bed, wincing at the slight twinge between her thighs. "That part wasn't a dream." She'd really had sex with Darius. Amazing sex. Unforgettable sex. Unprotected sex. Yes, she was on birth control, but she'd missed her pill this morning.

"Don't borrow trouble." She grabbed the shirt she'd pilfered from Darius's closet back at his apartment and pulled it on. She needed a shower and clean clothes.

The attached bathroom was like something out of a magazine. The stone-tiled walls, heated floor, and granite countertop didn't seem out of place in spite of the fact it was in an underground home.

She dumped the shirt and stepped into the shower, not lingering, even though she wanted to. She had no idea where Darius was, or even if he was still here. The last thought gave her a jolt and made her rush through washing her hair. She ended up with soap in her eyes for her effort and swore at Darius and all men as she thoroughly rinsed.

She dried off and wrapped one towel around her body and used another one to dry her hair. Thankfully, it was short and she didn't need a hair dryer. A few swipes with the towel and some finger combing made it presentable. She didn't have any makeup with her beyond the lipstick in her knapsack, and that was still in the living area as far as she knew.

The discarded shirt lay on the tiles, but she didn't want to put it on again. She didn't have clean underwear, either. Keeping a tight hold on the towel, she padded to the bedroom door and opened it a crack.

No one called out a greeting—or a warning, either, for

that matter. She went down the hallway to the next door. It was open to reveal another bedroom. Even though it was sparse, it had a lived-in feeling about it.

The floor was warm against her feet, but she felt vulnerable wearing only a towel. She ignored the twinge of guilt that assailed her when she opened a dresser drawer. It contained men's socks. She grabbed a pair of white gym socks and pulled them on. The heel went partway up the back of her leg but it was better than bare feet.

The closet beckoned, so she explored there next. Sure enough, it was filled with clothing. She decided on a soft cotton sweater and a pair of sweatpants. The sleeves of the sweater fell well past her hands, and she folded them back until they finally hit her wrists. The sweatpants had a drawstring, which she pulled tight. Then she rolled up the bottoms of the legs until she had thick cuffs on both sides.

She knew she must look ridiculous, but she didn't care. She was warm, but more importantly, she was covered. Darius might have seen her naked—her face heated as she left Tarrant's bedroom—okay, he'd done a whole lot more than see her naked. He'd touched her all over, using his tongue and lips on the most sensitive parts of her body. A shiver raced down her spine and her nipples peaked, rubbing against the sweater.

"Stop thinking about it." Of course, telling herself to do something and actually doing it were two different things altogether. She crossed her arms over her chest and headed toward the kitchen. A cup of coffee would help.

Something made her stop and listen. There was no sound coming from the kitchen area, but she'd heard something. If they were down in Tarrant's computer lab, she was out of luck. No way could she get in there on her own.

But there was another doorway on the opposite side of the corridor. It was rude to go poking around in someone else's home. She ignored the fact that she'd already raided the man's clothes closet. That had been a necessity. This was nothing more than curiosity.

She heard another sound. It was a cross between a grunt and a thump. Had the Knights found them? Sarah hurried to the door and shoved it open. It opened onto a landing and a set of stairs. She hurried down, holding on to the rail so she didn't slip in her stocking feet.

She was almost at the bottom when a huge body went flying by. Literally. She gasped and sat down hard on the stairs. The room was enormous, about four stories high, and the length of several football fields. The walls were rock. It seemed to be a natural cave that had been enlarged. But that wasn't what held her spellbound. No, that was the two magnificent drakons currently facing off against one another.

She recognized Darius immediately by the metallic bronze scales covering his large body. The other drakon was around the same size, his body covered in silver scales. Both had wedge-shaped heads, long tails, and massive wings.

Darius whirled around as soon as she made a sound. That allowed the other drakon to smash into him and send him sprawling. "No." She jumped to her feet, determined to protect Darius, which was totally stupid, because—duh—he was fighting another drakon.

What had happened while she'd been sleeping? Had they fought over the book? Over her being here?

She pounded down the stairs as Darius roared and threw himself at his brother. Tarrant evaded rather than fighting back.

Had they been sparring? Maybe they'd only been playing around, like a sport or something. She couldn't picture them slapping on a pair of skates and playing hockey, but fighting, yeah, she could easily see how that would appeal.

Only Darius seemed a little more serious about the

situation than Tarrant did. Was that because she was there?

"Darius." She called his name, but he ignored her. "Hey, Darius. Over here." She cautiously padded over to where he'd cornered his brother. She needed her head examined getting between two brothers, let alone two drakons, but she'd seen the affection the two had for each other. And as someone who'd never really had one for herself, she knew the value of family.

She slapped his flank. Damn, hitting him was like smacking the side of a tank. He whirled and gave her the most incredulous look. "If you're finished beating up your brother could we talk?"

The air around him shimmered, like a living rainbow, and then Darius was standing there. A very naked, very unhappy Darius.

He caught her by her shoulders and gave her a light shake. "Don't ever get between two drakons that are fighting. Do you have any idea how dangerous that is?"

She shook her head. "It didn't look that serious to me. It looked more like you getting tossed around." When the other drakon snickered, she gave him a pointed glare. "At least he didn't run like you did."

The silver drakon frowned and smoke billowed from his nostrils, but Darius chuckled. "He did run, didn't he?"

The other drakon shimmered, and then a very naked Tarrant was standing next to them. Holy smokes, these guys were built like gods. His tattoo was similar to Darius's, only it was silver and outlined in the same icy-blue color as his eyes. While she could appreciate Tarrant, only Darius made her heart speed up and her insides tingle.

"I didn't want to beat him up and make him look like a loser in front of you. Obviously, that was an error on my part."

Sarah laughed. She couldn't help herself. The entire situation was absurd. "I need coffee." She started back toward the stairs and waited when both men paused to pull on their clothing, which was stacked neatly by the exit.

"Thanks for the loan of the clothes," she told Tarrant.

He finished yanking on his T-shirt before running his gaze over her. "You're welcome." There was a tinge of sarcasm in his voice, a subtle reminder that she'd intruded where she hadn't a right.

"I'm sorry. I shouldn't have entered your room without permission, but there was no one around." She had invaded his private space when he'd opened his home to them. It wasn't well done of her. "Truly, I am sorry."

Tarrant studied her for several long seconds and then nodded. "No harm done." She wasn't so sure about that, but she was grateful he was willing to let it go.

Darius put his hand on the small of her back. His heat penetrated the cotton sweater she wore. "His clothes never looked this good on him."

Tarrant snorted and started up the stairs. She and Darius followed behind. "Were you afraid when you woke? I shouldn't have left you." He rubbed his hand over her spine. He always seemed to be touching her in little ways and, God help her, she loved it. Affection had been sparse in her childhood, and she soaked up every little sign of his caring. She worried she was too needy, too open and vulnerable.

She hurried up the steps, breaking the contact. "I'm fine. I've lost all sense of time, but I'm feeling much better."

Darius picked up his pace and his hand landed on her back once again. "Are you sure you're all right? You seem upset."

Of course she was upset. Her entire life was a mess. Her entire reality was skewed. And she was really attracted to a mythical creature who would be alive long after she was dust. "We had unprotected sex," she blurted out and then groaned. She hadn't meant to be quite that blunt, but the issue had to be dealt with.

Darius pulled her to a stop on the top landing. She was grateful Tarrant was long gone. He did not need to hear this conversation.

"You can't become pregnant."

She frowned. "Why not? Your father and other dragons came to this world and got human females pregnant. Can't you do the same?"

Darius crowded her until her back was against the wall and he was looming over her. "My father and his fellow dragons got women pregnant because they wanted it to happen. A dragon—and therefore a drakon—decides when it wants to procreate. Then, if conditions are right, the female will end up with child."

"You mean you could get me pregnant without my approval." That didn't sound fair at all.

"According to lore, two dragons must agree before such a thing can happen, so it's really up to the female dragon. When only one dragon or drakon is involved with a female of another species, he has only to make the decision. If the woman is fertile, pregnancy will occur.

She glared at him. "You better not decide to be a father any time soon." The last thing she needed was an unplanned pregnancy on top of everything else.

He jerked back as if she'd struck him. "I would not do such a thing. I have no sons." Then the expression in his eyes turned sad. "Would it be such a terrible thing to bear my child?"

Chapter Eighteen

Darius had thought himself hardened, immune to any puny hurt a human could mete out to him. He'd been wrong. Sarah cut him to the core with her demand he not get her with child. And still he wanted her.

Her hair was damp from her shower and her face devoid of makeup. Dressed as she was in Tarrant's oversize clothes, she should have looked ridiculous. Instead, she was adorable, and sexy as all get out. The baggy sweater made him want to slide his hands beneath it to discover if she was wearing a bra.

"No, it's not that," she began and then stopped. "The topic is irrelevant. The last thing we need is to worry about an unplanned pregnancy. I'm fighting for my life here, and so are you."

"Would you bear my child?" He should let it go. That would be the smart thing to do. He'd never cared about having a child before, never trusted a human female enough to even consider sharing his secrets with her. But Sarah already knew he was a drakon, knew the danger surrounding him.

"Darius." Her voice softened slightly. "We've been thrown

together in a dangerous situation. Ours is not what anyone would call a normal relationship." She patted his chest. "We have much bigger problems to handle right now. This is not the time or the place to even be contemplating if we should or shouldn't have a child."

He didn't like what she was saying even though he knew she was right. He wanted her to want to have his child, which made no sense. They barely knew each other and there were perilous days ahead. Maybe that was what made the idea of having a child so appealing. He would be leaving a part of himself behind in case he was captured or killed.

"You didn't answer my question."

"You know, for a man who's lived as long as you have, you're dumb as bricks about some things." Sarah took a deep breath. "If I manage to survive this war I've found myself in the middle of, I'd like to have a child. But since I'm not hopeful of that outcome, the last thing I'm thinking about, or even want right now, is to become pregnant. Is that clear enough?"

"It's very clear." Darius leaned down and nuzzled Sarah's neck where the collar of the sweater dipped down to expose her smooth white skin. He growled when he caught a whiff of Tarrant's soap. Yes, that was the only soap available to her, but that didn't mean he could be rational about it. He wanted his scent on her skin, not his brother's.

He ran his fingertips down the side of her cheek. "Were you trying to protect me from my brother?" His blood ran cold at the thought of Sarah running into the midst of two battling drakons, but another part of him was filled with pride and a smug sense of satisfaction that she cared enough to do such a thing.

"Men." The word was infused with a deep sense of frustration. Darius found himself smiling in spite of himself.

Sarah whirled around and yanked open the door. "We're

done."

He reached out and shoved the door shut before she could step out into the hallway.

"What are you doing?" She put her hands on his chest but didn't push him away.

"I'm kissing you." He rubbed his lips over hers and then dragged his tongue over her plump bottom lip. The fire inside him threatened to overheat and explode. Sarah made a mockery of any sense of self-control he had.

Her breathing quickened to little puffs of air on his skin. He groaned and took her mouth, needing to taste her. Her fingernails dug into his biceps when she grabbed hold of him. He stilled, wondering if she wanted him to stop. Then she went up on her toes and deepened their kiss.

His beast growled with satisfaction. Darius tilted his head to get a better angle. Sarah was tall for a woman, but their height difference was giving him a crick in his neck. He cupped her ass in his hands and lifted. She immediately wrapped her legs around his waist and hung on.

Desire roared through him like an out-of-control freight train. He turned so her back was against the wall and kissed her again and again. He couldn't get enough of the taste of her, the sensual heat. Voracious, he felt like a man who'd been starved for centuries and she was sustenance.

"Are you two planning on joining me anytime soon?" Tarrant's voice came over the intercom system.

Sarah stilled and then pushed against him until he released her luscious lips. "How do you do that to me?" He could tell it was a rhetorical question and wisely kept his mouth shut. "Put me down."

He'd forgotten he was still holding her and reluctantly let her slide down his body until she was standing on her own two feet once again.

She glanced around. "Can he hear us?"

"He can," came Tarrant's reply.

Sarah reached up and dragged Darius's head down until it was close enough for her to whisper in his ear. "Can he see us?"

"I'm not sure." Better to be honest.

Her cheeks reddened. She whirled away and was through the door before he could stop her. He loved his brother, honestly he did, but he was seriously contemplating the joys of being an only child.

His body was humming with pent-up lust and his erection was obvious. He ignored both and followed Sarah to the kitchen where Tarrant waited. The air was redolent with the delicious smell of steak and spices. Tarrant had a huge grill pan on the stove and had large cuts of meat sizzling.

"What can I do to help?" he asked.

"Not much. The potatoes are already baking." He pointed at the microwave.

"What about a salad?" Both men looked at Sarah like she was speaking a foreign language. She rubbed her hand over her forehead. "Let me guess. That's girl food." Both of them nodded in tandem.

Her gurgle of laughter was followed by a groan. "I'm going to starve if we're here long. I'm not much of a meat-eater. I rarely eat red meat."

"What do you eat?" The idea of not eating meat was unthinkable to Darius.

Sarah sat on one of the stools on the far side of the kitchen island and rested her elbows on the top. "Regular food. Fruit and vegetables, whole grains, fish and chicken." She gave him a pointed look. "Yogurt."

Darius curled his lip. "That's not real food."

"You really are a throwback, aren't you?"

Before he could respond, Tarrant jumped into the fray. "There are a few cans of vegetables in the pantry if you want to open one of them."

Sarah slid off the stool and walked to the cupboard Tarrant indicated. She pulled open the door and peered inside. "Green beans, corn, peas." She shifted around several cans. "Carrots." She pulled out the can. "These will do. I'm in the mood for carrots."

Darius was in the mood to drag her back into the bedroom, but that wasn't going to happen. "Carrots it is." He took the can, found the opener, and had the lid off in no time. He located a saucepan, dumped the carrots into it, and placed it on the stove.

"That wasn't so hard, was it?" Back on her stool, Sarah folded her hands and smiled sweetly at him. He simply growled, not bothering to respond.

She straightened and her expression turned serious. "Okay, where are we with the book?" She looked expectantly at Tarrant.

"I've done some checking with some people I know," he began.

"Is that safe?"

"Safe enough," Darius answered before Tarrant could take offense and say something in anger. "We need to trust someone."

She rubbed her forehead. "Yeah. Sorry about that," she told his brother. "I'm more paranoid than usual."

"Understandable." Tarrant flipped the steaks one more time and then forked them onto three separate plates. "My source recommends an exorcism on the book while burning it with the fire from a holy candle and then dousing the ashes in holy water." He set the plates in front of each stool and then got cutlery.

"Wow, that's extreme."

Darius pulled the potatoes out of the microwave and put them in a bowl before depositing them onto the island.

Tarrant dumped the heated carrots into another bowl and shoved them in front of Sarah.

"Do you have any other ideas?" Darius asked. He took a seat beside her and put one of the potatoes on her plate before piling four on his own. Tarrant got butter and sour cream from the refrigerator before joining them. Darius could tell his brother was curious about what Sarah had to say.

"Not at the moment, but I wouldn't mind doing some digging around online. I'm not without resources of my own." She cut a piece of the steak and popped it into her mouth. She chewed several times and then smiled. "It's good."

Tarrant grunted and kept eating, but Darius smiled. "You could set it up so her searches wouldn't be detected, couldn't you?" Darius was curious to see what Sarah could come up with.

Tarrant thought about it a minute. "Yeah, I can do that." Darius knew his brother was more than capable of doing it, he just hadn't been sure he would. "We can go back to the lab after we eat."

"You mean back to Fort Knox," she mumbled.

Tarrant cracked a grin, and Darius couldn't help teasing him. "At least she didn't call it the Batcave." That drew a deep, feral growl from his brother.

Sarah stopped eating and drew back. "Should I ask?"

"Batman," Darius told her. When she still looked confused, he added, "You know, the Dark Knight from the comics and the movies."

"Ah, I get it. You don't like the knight reference." She mimicked zipping her lips. "You'll never hear it from me."

"Good." Tarrant shot him a glare. "Now if only my brother would do the same."

They kept the conversation fairly light while they finished eating. Darius and Tarrant stuck to the meat and potatoes, leaving the carrots for Sarah. There were still a lot of them in the bowl when she was done eating. More than half her steak was still there, too.

"You didn't eat enough." Darius didn't like the idea of her being hungry. He turned on his brother. "We need girl food."

Sarah smiled and rubbed her hand over his arm. "I had more than enough to eat and it was delicious. Thank you, Tarrant."

Darius wasn't convinced. "Are you sure?"

"Absolutely. I can't eat nearly as much as you two can." She pushed her plate toward him. "You can finish it if you'd like."

"You can also clean up while Sarah and I get to work down in the computer lab." Tarrant rose and indicated for Sarah to come with him.

Darius didn't want her out of his sight. No, that wasn't quite true. He didn't want her alone with his brother. He loved and trusted Tarrant, but he honestly wasn't sure what he might do if he thought for one second Sarah was a threat.

"I need coffee first. If that's okay?"

"I'll brew some fresh while I'm cleaning up and bring it straight down." He gave his brother a significant look that warned of immediate and dire retribution if he hurt one hair on Sarah's head. Tarrant smirked and left the kitchen.

Sarah rubbed his arm again. "Don't worry, Darius. I'll be fine."

He wished he could be as certain. "I won't be long," he promised. Then he dropped a kiss on her lips and watched her leave.

• • •

Tarrant was waiting for her by the large steel door at the end of the hallway. It was already open, so she stepped inside the elevator. The door slid soundlessly shut and Tarrant gave the command. She held her breath until he went through the necessary security protocols and the door opened up into his lab. She'd never thought of herself as claustrophobic before, but being trapped in such a small space with Tarrant was nerve-wracking. Not that he threatened her in any overt way, but she could feel the tension rolling off him in waves that were almost suffocating.

"You can breathe now," he told her.

Sarah sucked air into her starving lungs. When she was calm enough, she decided to confront the problem head-on. "Look, I know you don't know me or trust me. I get that. I understand that."

"Good." He crossed his massive arms over his wide chest. "Then you should also know that if you betray us or hurt my brother in any way, I'll kill you."

Every primitive instinct she possessed screamed at her to run, but there was nowhere to go. A part of her was glad Darius had someone in his life who cared about him so deeply. Another part of her was jealous of that obvious love. She'd never had that kind of relationship with her parents, or anyone else, for that matter.

"I understand. Where can I work?"

Tarrant tilted his head and studied her like she was a puzzle he couldn't quite solve. "Over here." He pointed to a computer in the corner. "Be assured, I'll be monitoring everything you do."

"I'd expect nothing less." She slid into the chair and pulled it up to the desk. She jiggled the mouse to wake up the machine.

"My brother likes you, Ms. Anderson." Tarrant was standing right next to her, taking up way too much room. There was menace in his every word that was more than a little scary. "I've never seen him take to a woman as quickly or thoroughly. Use that power wisely."

"Are you asking what my intentions are?" She had no idea what possessed her to ask him such a thing and in such a flippant manner. Honestly, you'd think she had a death wish.

Tarrant growled again. "Be very cautious, Sarah." The softly spoken words had her insides trembling. Since there was nothing else left to say, she gave her attention to the computer. This was the world she understood—books and knowledge.

She sent her fingers flying over the keyboard as she began to search, going deeper and deeper with each keystroke, each click. She reached out to several reliable contacts and asked hypothetical questions under the guise of helping a collector with a particular book. She kept all specifics out of it.

She lost herself in the work and had no idea how much time had passed when she finally surfaced. Her shoulders and neck ached, and she leaned back in her chair and groaned.

"Stiff?" Darius asked. He put his hands on her shoulders and began to rub.

Sarah groaned and leaned forward. "That feels good. How long have you been here?"

"Several hours." He found a particularly tense spot and worked the knot out. "You didn't drink your coffee."

The mug was sitting just beyond the keyboard. She hadn't noticed it there. Even more telling, she hadn't noticed Darius putting it there. "I got lost in my work." She tilted her head back so she could see his face. "I'm sorry."

"Don't be. It's important we find out answers."

"What time is it?"

"It's evening." Tarrant's voice ripped through the circle of intimacy that surrounded her and Darius, reminding her that they weren't alone. "Just past nine."

She yawned and stretched. "My body clock is so screwed up." Tarrant was hunched over another computer. "Have you learned anything more?"

He shook his head. "No. I have some searches going. I still have a business to run in spite of the Knights breathing down our necks."

"Do you still want coffee?" Darius asked. "You need a break."

"Yeah, I wouldn't mind one. Both." She rubbed her eyes and stood. "Yes, I'd like both a coffee and a break." She grabbed the cup and headed to the exit.

Tarrant ignored them as they went to the door that shielded the elevator. As soon as they stepped in front of it, the doors opened. Darius's hand was in its usual position at the small of her back.

The second the elevator doors closed, she gave a sigh of relief. The elevator was no bigger, but she felt much safer sharing it with Darius and not his brother.

"Up," Darius gave the voice command before giving her a questioning look. "Is everything okay?"

"It's fine," she assured him. No way was she going to tell tales on Tarrant. What was said between them stayed between them. When they reached the next level, the door slid open. It closed automatically and relocked as soon as they stepped through it.

The corridor seemed positively huge after being in such close quarters. "It's weird being underground and not seeing the sunshine. Or moonlight for that matter."

She went straight to the kitchen sink, poured out the cold remains of her coffee, and started a new pot brewing. She leaned against the counter while she waited. "What have you been doing for the past few hours?"

Darius prowled around the room, his motions fluid and quick for such a large man. "Not much. You and Tarrant are the research experts."

"We all have our skills. Mine just happen to be in research." She pushed away from the counter. "But fair warning, if the

Knights come for me, I'm hiding behind you."

The frown on his face dissolved and was replaced by a warm smile. "You trust me to protect you."

She knew in her heart that Darius would protect her with his life. That kind of sacrifice and commitment was rare in this world. "Yes, I trust you to protect me." She waved her hand in the air. "I followed you here, didn't I?" She lowered her voice and whispered. "To the Batcave."

He chuckled and looked more relaxed. God, he looked good, whether tense or at ease, with his silky hair hanging to his shoulders, his smoldering green eyes, strong features, and kissable lips. And he'd brought her coffee. She just hadn't been aware enough at the time to acknowledge it.

"Can we go outside?" she blurted. "I need to breathe real air. Feel the breeze on my face." As big and lovely as Tarrant's place was, it was still underground. "We can stay close to the cabin, sit on the porch stairs." There weren't any chairs to use, but she didn't care. She'd sit on the ground at this point.

Darius came to her and rubbed his hands up and down her arms. "We can go outside."

Her shoulders slumped slightly with relief. She'd half expected him to tell her they had to stay inside. It wasn't that she felt like a prisoner. She knew staying inside was safer for security purposes. Still, she needed to feel as though she had some kind of control over her life, her surroundings.

And right now, that meant going outside to breathe in the evening air—something simple that she'd never take for granted again.

The coffeepot gave a final hiss, and she filled two mugs, adding sugar to her own. "Lead the way." She picked up her mug and followed Darius over to the inside door. He pressed his hand to the scanner and the door opened. They went up the stairs with him in the lead.

With each step she took toward the outside world, she

felt the tension in her body dropping away. The old cabin was suddenly beautiful to her eyes as she stepped into the kitchen. Anxious now, she hurried toward the front door, aware of Darius right beside her.

Her free hand fumbled with the door and then the wood panel was open. She turned her face up to the night sky as she stepped out onto the porch and inhaled.

"Beautiful." She set her mug down on the railing and peered up at the stars. Everything inside her settled. Along with it came the awareness that she was exactly where she needed to be.

Chapter Nineteen

Darius was very aware of his surroundings. It wouldn't pay to get careless. They should be safe here, but he didn't underestimate the tenacity and resources of the Knights of the Dragon. Still, leaving the safety of Tarrant's home was worth the payoff.

Sarah had her head tilted back and a look of wonder on her face as she studied the sky. They were far from any major city. This high in the mountains, there were no ambient lights to block the majesty of the stars. The sky was like a dark blanket with diamonds spilled over it.

This was the world at its best. Darius could easily remember a time long before electric lights, long before humans had populated the planet, scurrying over it like locusts destroying everything in their path. But many remote, beautiful places remained, and this was one of them.

"What do you think of Tarrant's suggestion of an exorcism?" Sarah wrapped her arms around herself. "I thought exorcisms were for people, not objects."

He should have realized she'd be cold in the chilly

evening air. It was autumn and they were in the mountains. He stepped behind her and wrapped his arms around her. She leaned back against him, seeking his warmth. "The idea has merit. This is not a normal object. You said yourself it seemed almost alive."

She shivered, and he didn't think it had anything to do with the cold, but rather from her memories of touching the tainted manuscript. "Yeah, you're right about that."

"Tarrant trusts his source, and my brother does not trust easily."

"Yeah, I get that." Something in the tone of her voice made him stiffen.

"What did he say to you?" She hadn't been alone with Tarrant for long, but certainly long enough for him to have threatened her.

"Nothing." She wasn't exactly lying to him. It was more like evading. Sarah wasn't the type to tell tales. If Tarrant said something to her, threatened her, she'd deal with it in her own way.

Which meant he'd have to have a discussion with his brother later.

"Forget about the book and the Knights for now."

"How can I?" she asked. She tipped her head back so she was staring up at him. "It's the reason we're here."

It was, but that didn't mean they couldn't take a few moments to enjoy themselves. If there was one thing Darius had learned, it was that each minute of life was precious. Humans were fragile, and death could come in a flash, taking with it the promise of tomorrow. It was that appreciation, a zest for life and all it offered, that had kept him and his brothers sane and interested in living.

"Both you and Tarrant have sent out queries, haven't you?" When she nodded, he continued. "There is nothing else you can do at this moment to further our cause?" She shook her head. "So, all there is left to do is enjoy the stars and the night."

Sarah sighed and looked up at the sky. "They are pretty. They're so much brighter here than they are in the city. There seem to be so many more of them."

"But the brightest one is right here in my arms."

She stiffened and then sighed. "Our getting involved doesn't make any sense. Not only are the Knights after us, but also, I'm human and you're immortal. Then again, maybe you're only looking for a fling. And that's fine," she added in a hurry, "but that's not the kind of relationships I have."

"I don't want a fling." His voice was a guttural growl. He wasn't happy, and neither was the dragon inside him. "You're important to me, Sarah." He turned her in his arms so she was facing him.

"How is that possible? We've known each other such a short time. Yes, there's no denying the sexual chemistry, but any kind of connection between us is limited."

He hooked a lock of hair behind her ear and ran his fingers down the side of her throat. "Does that mean we ignore it?" She shuddered at his touch, and her eyes grew heavy with desire.

"Yes. No. I don't know."

He leaned down and licked the pulse point in her neck before lightly nipping at it.

"I can't think when you touch me like that," she complained.

"Then I'll simply have to keep touching you, won't I?" He'd said the same thing to her before, and he meant it. He put his hands on her hips and slipped them beneath the hem of the sweater she wore. She moaned, wrapped her arms around his neck, and leaned into him.

"You're a bad influence on me."

"Undoubtedly," he agreed. He enjoyed the softness of

her skin as his fingers inched upward. His knuckles grazed the undersides of her bare breasts. He slid them back and forth. The little sounds of pleasure and frustration she made served to fire his blood and fuel his desire.

He sucked in a breath when she suddenly reached between them and placed her hand over his erection, which was straining against the zipper of his jeans. She molded her hand against his hard length and his balls drew up tight.

"See what happens when you tease me."

"Sarah, sweetheart, I have to tell you that if you meant to discourage me, you failed miserably."

Her laughter spilled out around them. "Hmm, I can see that."

"Let's go inside." He wanted to get her into bed, strip her naked, and love her until she fell into an exhausted sleep.

"No. Here. Now. Under the stars."

It was chilly, especially for her. He was able to regulate his body temperature with little problem. He hesitated, and she took action. She shoved her hands under his borrowed T-shirt and pushed it up.

Seeing he wasn't going to be able to stop her, and didn't really want to, he released her long enough to drag off the shirt and drop it at his feet. An owl hooted in the distance and an opossum waddled along the edge of the trees. He doubted she even noticed.

He stiffened when he thought about Tarrant watching them. His brother would have known the second they stepped outside and would have automatically engaged his security cameras. Darius was as sure of that as he was of his desire for Sarah.

He gazed out over the yard and, sure enough, he found the security camera tucked up high in a tree where most humans would never see it. A red light on the camera flickered on, a sure sign of acknowledgement from his brother. Then the light went out, and Darius knew that Tarrant had switched off that particular camera.

He knew he'd get a security lecture later, but for now, he and Sarah were alone. Tarrant would continue to monitor the area. He wouldn't be able to help himself. But he wouldn't intrude on them.

"Is everything okay?" Sarah started to pull away, but he stopped her.

"Everything is perfect." He slid his hands back under her sweater and found the full mounds of her breasts. They both groaned when he cupped them. "You're perfect."

"The things you say to me." She ran her hands over his pectoral muscles and then down his abs. "I almost don't believe them. I mean, I'm okay with who I am, but I'm far from perfect. I'm perfectly ordinary."

He ran his thumbs over her distended nipples, wishing he could see them as well as touch them, but he didn't want to remove her sweater for fear she'd take a chill.

"It's how I see you." He didn't know how else to explain it to her. "Every cell in my body yearns for you."

"Oh, Darius." He loved the way she sighed his name. It made him feel wild and free, yet he never wanted to leave her side. She'd tamed the beast inside him.

• • •

Sarah knew they should go inside. That was the prudent thing to do. But being around Darius brought out a side of her that she'd never known existed. She wanted to be naked in the moonlight and make love under the stars. It was foolishly romantic and completely impulsive—two words that she would never have associated with herself.

She'd been sensible her entire life. She'd worked hard and used her intellect to get a job she loved. Where she hadn't excelled was in the area of relationships. She'd never formed close friendships with other women and had only had two serious boyfriends—both academics like herself.

Was it any wonder she was drawn to Darius with his rugged good looks, physical strength, and animal magnetism? He was larger than life and, like a moth to a flame, she was drawn to him.

Her breasts ached for more of his touch. His skin was warm beneath her palms and getting hotter by the second. He was so big and strong and, for the moment, hers.

Maybe it wasn't smart, but Sarah was done listening to only the intellectual side of her brain. For the first time in her life, other more primitive instincts were demanding attention, and she was more than ready to let them have their way.

She found the opening of his jeans and managed to undo the button. Darius groaned when she slid the zipper down and found his erection.

He spun her around until they were in the shadows of the porch on the far end. Her back was against the wall, but she could still see the stars and feel the night air lightly caress her skin. She should be cold, but that was impossible with the heat they were generating between them.

Darius bent to kiss her, and she met him halfway. He ate at her lips, his hunger for her evident. Their mouths came together again and again, each time more frantic than the last. Their tongues dueled and their breaths mingled.

"Have to taste you," he muttered as he pulled away. Before she knew what he was about to do, he dropped to his knees. He had the baggy sweatpants around her ankles in the next breath. She wasn't wearing any underwear, and the cool air slid beneath the hem of the sweater to tease her heated flesh.

His low growl reverberated through the trees, and the world around them went silent. She thought he would touch her then. Instead, he rested his head against her stomach and simply held her.

Emotion clogged her throat, and tears threatened to spill from her eyes. Darius wanted her, but he was right when he said there was more than just sex between them.

The wild passion of only moments before had morphed into something much deeper and infinitely more precious.

She threaded her fingers through his thick hair and it slid along them like silk. He stirred and slowly eased away from her. He looked up at her, and his green eyes were literally glowing. Her hands stilled. "Are you okay?"

"I'm better than okay." He pushed the hem of the sweater up and kissed her stomach before circling her navel with his tongue. His tongue was slightly rough, which added an extra element to his caress.

She wanted his tongue on other parts of her body.

As though he understood exactly what she wanted, he leaned back slightly. "Spread your legs." She widened her stance but couldn't go as far as she wanted because of the sweatpants still tangled around her ankles.

Darius gave another one of those low, rumbling growls she was coming to adore. It belatedly occurred to her that he could probably see more of her than she could of him. All his senses seemed to be enhanced.

"You can see all of me, can't you?"

"Oh, yeah." He ran his hands up the insides of her thighs and put his mouth on her. He teased the slick folds of her sex, using his clever tongue to drive her passion higher.

Her eyes practically rolled back in her head. She was peripherally aware of the night air brushing over her exposed skin, of the swish of the branches as they swayed in the light breeze, the starlit night around them, and the rough boards of the cabin at her back. But mostly she was aware of Darius's hands and mouth on her body.

Blood pumped faster through her veins, and her lungs drew in more air. He swiped his tongue over her clit, eliciting a long moan of pleasure.

"Love the sounds you make," he muttered. He stood and lifted her. She tried to wrap her legs around him, but the stupid sweatpants were hindering her. Darius gave a grumble of displeasure, and then held her in one arm as he swiped at the pants with the other. She caught a glimpse of a long, lethal claw, and the material parted.

She immediately wrapped her legs around him, ignoring the fabric still bunched around each ankle. Darius held her weight easily as she reached between them and wrapped her hand around his cock. It was hard and hot, pulsing with life. She wanted him inside her.

She angled his shaft toward her and slowly lowered herself onto him.

• • •

Darius gritted his teeth, waiting in agony for Sarah to complete their joining. He could still taste her on his lips, sweet and salty and warm. He loved the slight weight of her in his arms, the way her thighs clamped around him.

Then she drew him into her body, and he knew he'd found heaven. It was just as good as it had been the first time. Better, because now he knew what to expect. Her hot, moist body closed around his hard shaft, willingly taking him. He was more beast than man, but she still wanted him.

He closed his eyes and committed this moment to memory. It was stored in a special place where only memories of Sarah dwelled. If he lived another four thousand years—no, forty thousand—this night would still be as vivid as it was now.

"Sarah." He said her name and nothing more. She

wrapped her arms around his neck and kissed his neck and jaw.

His cock pulsed inside her, demanding he get on with the pleasurable task at hand. Holding her easily in his arms, he walked to the edge of the porch so she'd have a better view of the world. "Look, Sarah. Look at the night around us and know you're more beautiful than all the stars."

He was a blunt man, not a poet, but there was something about Sarah that made him want to say such things. She tightened her grip on his neck, and he felt one warm tear slide down his skin.

Keeping one hand on her ass, he caught the back of her head with the other and eased her away. Tears swam in her eyes. "Am I hurting you?" That was the last thing he wanted.

She shook her head. "No."

"Then why are you crying?"

She shook her head again, not answering him, so Darius did the only thing he could think of. He kissed her. With their lips melded together, he shifted his hold on her so he could ease her up and down his swollen cock. Her inner muscles rippled around him every time he almost totally withdrew and again when he pushed back into her.

His movements grew jerkier and faster. She tightened her legs around him and raked her nails over his back. He growled and lowered himself to his knees with her still on his lap. Then he eased her down onto the porch and began to fuck her hard and fast.

She moaned and thrashed her head from side to side as he pushed them both higher and higher. He shoved her sweater up, exposing her full breasts to his view. He bent forward and caught one pert nipple carefully between his teeth and flicked it with his tongue.

Sarah went wild. She bucked her hips and tugged on his hair, pulling him closer. He managed to get one hand between them and brushed her clit with the pad of his thumb. She cried out, and her body clamped down hard around his cock.

His orgasm started in his balls and shot out through the top of his shaft. He barely managed to swallow back a roar. He lifted her, wrapping her close to his heart as his body shook and shuddered.

Through it all, she held on to him. Peace enveloped him, along with a certainty that Sarah was his. She belonged to him in a way that no woman ever had or ever would. What he was going to do about that remained to be seen.

She shivered and snuggled closer. He didn't want to leave her but didn't have much choice. She grumbled under her breath when he separated their bodies. "I didn't get to touch you as much as I wanted." Her sleepy complaint had his cock standing at attention even though he'd just come.

"Next time," he promised, and that was one promise he planned to keep. The thought of her mouth on his dick was almost enough to make him come again.

He stood and hitched his jeans up and then lifted Sarah in his arms. He smiled at the remains of Tarrant's sweatpants around each of her ankles. The oversize sweater covered her sufficiently. He'd have to come back for their coffee cups. They couldn't afford to leave any evidence lying around, anything that could prove they'd been here.

"Why am I so tired?" she complained as he carried her through the cabin to the hidden entrance. He loved the way her cheek nestled against his chest. The way she trusted him to carry her down the narrow staircase. It was a tight fit, but he did it.

"Stress," he told her. The door opened at the bottom before he got there, a reminder from Tarrant that he was watching and aware. Darius carried Sarah into the room they were sharing and placed her on the bed. He removed the shredded fabric from around her ankles but left the socks and sweater in place. "You worked for hours and your body is still feeling the strain from everything you've been through." He brushed a finger over her cheek. She sighed and her eyelids fluttered shut.

"Sleep. I'll watch over you."

"Okay." She rolled onto her side, pulled her knees up to curl into a ball, and was almost instantly asleep. Darius watched her for several minutes before finally leaving. He hurried back upstairs and collected their coffee mugs. The night was still and the wildlife the only other creatures around.

When he was back in Tarrant's fortress, he dumped the mugs in the sink and checked on Sarah, who was sound asleep, before heading to the heavy door at the end of the hallway. It was time to have a chat about Sarah with his brother.

· · ·

Karina Azarov reread the letter that had arrived only moments ago by special courier. That Herman Temple would have it hand-delivered by his head of security was telling.

She tossed the heavy vellum paper onto her desk and leaned back in her chair. "Did you read it?"

Matthew Riggs shook his head. "No."

That was it. Just one word. That was one of the things she liked about Riggs. He didn't talk any more than he had to and didn't make excuses when things went wrong.

"What happened?" She wanted it straight and knew he'd give it to her. She listened as he told her about the librarian with the special powers, the missing book, the snafu with the security protocols, and finally about Sarah Anderson going to Darius Varkas.

Fury filled her, but she kept it under control. She was so close to her goal of avenging her family. She wouldn't do anything to jeopardize that objective.

She stood and walked to the window, but even the spectacular garden below couldn't hold her attention. "Herman is blaming Christian for the entire situation, starting with the disappearance of the book." That wasn't surprising. Herman hadn't lived as long as he had by not knowing when to make a strategic retreat or, in this case, offer up a scapegoat for her anger.

And he was right. Someone would have to pay for this fiasco. They'd had a dragon in their sights and let him slip through their fingers. Her own fingers were fisted, and she forced herself to relax. Once she had herself under control again, she turned and caught Riggs staring at her legs.

Well, she did have spectacular ones, and they were showcased in her four-inch Louboutin pumps. She looked damn good and knew it. Her body was just another tool in her arsenal, one she used whenever she needed.

"Looks like I'm leaving Boston and heading back to New York with you." She walked over to Riggs and ran her fingers down his chest, enjoying the way he swallowed heavily. "I can count on you to protect me, can't I?"

"Absolutely."

She patted his firm stomach. "I knew that I could." She picked up the house phone and made arrangements to leave town. "On the way there, you can give me more details about the situation, starting with everything you know about Sarah Anderson." She already knew all there was to know about Darius Varkas. She'd had her own people investigate him when she'd discovered Temple had his people following him.

"Yes, ma'am." The words were polite and deferential, but the tone and the wicked gleam in his eyes were anything but. Yes, she could certainly use Matthew Riggs and planned to, in more ways than one.

"I'll see my sister while I'm in New York." Why her sister insisted on working instead of joining the family business was beyond her. But Valeriya was the baby in the family and they'd all indulged her, even Karina. Valeriya was weak, not strong like Karina was. Her baby sister didn't have the stomach for catching or killing dragons.

"Let's go." She walked toward the exit, confident that Riggs was right behind her. He slipped around her at the last second and opened the door. She went through it and headed toward the car she knew would be waiting out front.

Chapter Twenty

Darius should have been relaxed. He should have been curled around Sarah, holding her as she slept. Instead, he was about to have a chat with his brother. These things never went well. They were both strong-willed and always certain they were right. Of course, in this instance, he *was* right, but Tarrant wouldn't see it that way.

Before he could make his way to the locked door at the end of the hallway, it slid open and Tarrant stepped out. "She asleep?"

Darius nodded. "She's still exhausted."

Tarrant brushed by him and headed toward the kitchen. He followed close behind, his stomach grumbling at the prospect of food. He hadn't eaten nearly enough these past two days. His brother seemed to be of the same mind, because he began pulling out pots and pans.

The two of them had worked this way many times in the past, and it wasn't long before a huge pot of pasta and sauce were bubbling away on the stove and two massive steaks were marinating. They'd start with the pasta and finish with the steaks.

Darius wiped his hands on a kitchen towel and tossed it aside. He pinned Tarrant with a glare and leaned against the counter. "What did you say to Sarah?"

"What did she tell you I said?"

He hated when Tarrant did this, answering a question with another question. "She didn't tell me anything. She didn't have to."

Tarrant nodded and stirred the sauce as the tomatoes and spices began to bubble. "I told her the truth. That if she's with the Knights and does anything to hurt you, I'll end her."

Darius's dragon roared inside him and his body began to shift. He struggled to control the transformation, ruthlessly shoving his body back to his human form. He crossed his arms over his chest to keep from reaching out and strangling his brother.

"Look, I know you don't like it." Big understatement there. "But" — Tarrant set the spoon down on the counter — "I don't care. It had to be said. That way, if I have to kill her, she can't say she wasn't warned."

Darius's fingers were wrapped so tightly around his upper arms he knew he'd have bruises. "You don't touch her." His voice had deepened.

Tarrant dragged his fingers through his hair, the expression in his eyes one of pure exasperation. "Listen to yourself. You barely know this woman, and you're ready to die for her." He put his hands on his hips and glared back. "You might be ready to give your life for her, but I'm not."

"I shouldn't have come here," Darius muttered.

Tarrant got right up in his face. "Fuck you. Yes, you should have come here. I'm your brother."

The fear in Tarrant's eyes drained the anger right out of him. Darius reached out and wrapped his hand around the back of his brother's neck and pulled him in tightly. Their foreheads touched and they stared into each other's eyes.

"I'm sorry, T."

"Yeah, me, too."

They stood there for a long moment. Darius remembered all the times they'd been there for each other. For four thousand years, the four of them had been a unit, but there was no denying he was closer to Tarrant than he was to either Ezra or Nic. Not that he didn't love them all equally—because he did. It was simply that he and Tarrant had known each other since childhood, before they'd realized what they were, that they were different from the other boys in their village.

"Thanks for turning off the camera. I know that had to go against your instincts."

Tarrant raised his head and grinned. "It did, but I didn't want to see your hairy ass. It might have scarred me for life. I might have gone blind."

Nudity was no big deal for them, considering the age they'd been born into. They'd run around half naked their entire childhoods. Then there was the whole shifting thing. Hard to keep your clothes on when you shifted. Tarrant had done it to give Darius and Sarah privacy.

"Thanks anyway."

Tarrant gave him a quick nod. "Pasta is done." He stepped away and grabbed the hot pot off the stove while Darius busied himself putting dinner rolls and butter on the table. The two of them sat on the stools and ate in silence until both plates were half empty. It was only then Tarrant ventured to speak. "There has to be a reason why you're so attracted to Sarah."

Darius twirled spaghetti around his fork but paused before eating it. "That's what I'm afraid of." He ate the mouthful of pasta and chewed, not really enjoying the subtle flavors. "It's more than just attraction." He set his fork down on the side of his platter and thumped his chest with his fist.

"I feel her here. I want her with me all the time. I want to do whatever it takes to make her happy."

Then he added the real shocker. "I don't want to live without her."

Tarrant's mouth fell open, and he pushed his plate aside. "Holy shit." His eyes widened. "Do you think this is—" He broke off and tried again. "That she's—"

Darius nodded and said what his brother hadn't been able. "I think she's the one. The one our sire told us came along very rarely."

"But she's human," Tarrant pointed out. "How can she be your mate?"

"We're not fully dragon," Darius reminded him. "There are no other dragons here and no female drakons. Drakons are all male. That leaves only human females for us to mate with."

"That's fucked up," Tarrant muttered. He sighed and rested his elbows on the counter. "She's human," he repeated. "Her life span is in years, decades, no more.

Darius's chest ached and he rubbed it. "I know."

"Shit. Okay." Tarrant rubbed his hands over his face. "Let me think." His head jerked up. "You can give her your blood to extend her life. The Knights have been doing it for hundreds of years, why shouldn't we do it for someone we actually want to have an extended life."

"That's assuming she feels the same way about me." Darius wasn't sure what Sarah felt for him. He knew she was attracted to him. That didn't mean she loved him.

And he wanted her to love him. That's what he needed to fill the empty void inside, the one that beckoned him to the Deep Sleep of the drakon.

Darius finished his pasta first and pushed away from the counter. He got the steaks out the refrigerator and soon had them sizzling on the big grill pan.

"What are you going to do?" his brother asked.

"Protect her. Destroy the Knights." It was a simple plan, but Darius figured those were the best kind.

Tarrant snorted. "A little light on details, bro. How do you plan to protect her and defeat the Knights?"

Darius flipped the steaks and thought about it. "The book is the first problem. It needs to be destroyed."

Tarrant held out two plates and waited while Darius deposited a steak on each one. "Father Simon is willing to do the exorcism on the book, but you'd have to go to him."

"Where is he?" Darius asked. The thought of taking Sarah away from the safety of Tarrant's fortress was abhorrent to him, but he knew she wouldn't stay behind. Nor could he leave her.

"Right now he's visiting a place called Salvation in North Carolina."

Darius rolled his eyes and picked up his knife and fork. "Why doesn't that surprise me? It couldn't be in the same bloody state. It has to be on the other end of the country."

Tarrant shrugged, popped a piece of meat into his mouth and chewed. "Be thankful. At least he's in the United States. Father Simon has spent his life traveling and researching the occult in order to be able to understand it. He rarely stays in one place for long."

It made sense that a priest might have access to books and knowledge that wouldn't be readily available. The Church and the Knights had crossed paths many times in the past, and depending on the priest, it had gone both very well and very badly for the drakons.

"You're sure we can trust this priest? If he gets his hands on the book and uses it…" The implications were too horrific to even imagine.

Tarrant finished his meal and shoved his plate away. "I saved his life a long time ago. He knows what I am and has kept my secret all these years." There was pain in his brother's eyes as he continued. "I already told you that I offered him my blood, a chance at immortality, or at least prolonged life, but he wouldn't take it. Said it isn't his place to live forever."

Darius knew how hard it was to lose friends, which was why he'd stopped making them centuries ago. He stuck to his own kind, to his brothers, until Sarah.

"Give me another day or two to see what else I can uncover. We need to know as much about the Knights as we can—who their current leader is and who their more prominent members are. We've gotten lax in the past few decades, while they've been lurking in the shadows getting stronger."

Darius couldn't argue with Tarrant about that. They had gotten remiss about keeping an eye on the Knights. Honestly, he'd hoped they'd disbanded after the last major strike against them a century ago. In reality, they'd been regrouping and getting stronger than ever.

Having the military involved could be problematic. Thankfully, the Knights were usually too focused on their own ends to involve outsiders. But that could be changing, which would complicate matters.

"We need to reach out to other drakons and let them know." Darius rose from his chair and began to clean up from their second meal. "I know you have a list of the whereabouts of most of the drakons in the world."

"I do like to keep in touch from time to time."

Darius paused before sliding a plate into the dishwasher. "Like what? Once every hundred years or so?"

"That sounds about right," Tarrant agreed.

Drakons weren't exactly sociable, at least not with each other. It was partly due to their aggressive nature when they were together in a group, and partially a protective measure that had evolved over time. If their enemies found them, they would only find one of them and not more. Even Darius and his brothers were rarely together at the same time, not since technology had evolved. They mostly stayed in contact by phone or video chat.

He missed the old days when they could spend weeks together in some isolated section of the world, shifting and flying through the air, unseen by humans. Thanks to satellites, those times were mostly gone.

It was also the reason Tarrant had gotten into every arm of the communications and technology industries. When the brothers wanted to spend time together, Tarrant would use his expertise to tap into the world's satellites and make sure they had a little glitch wherever the brothers gathered. That was a risk they rarely took. Too many such incidents and someone would notice.

With the kitchen cleared away, Tarrant turned on the dishwasher. It was such a mundane chore that it made Darius smile. None of them could endure a messy space.

Well, that wasn't quite true. Nicodemus was the exception. If he wasn't careful, his younger brother would end up buried alive in his belongings. It wasn't that his home was dirty. It was just filled to capacity with stuff. And it certainly wasn't junk. Nic could outfit several world-class museums from top to bottom with art and antiquities and never notice the dent in his collection.

"Let's go." Tarrant finished cleaning the counter and tossed the dishcloth into the sink. Darius followed his brother back down to his fortress. He wanted to stop and check on Sarah but was afraid if he did, he wouldn't be able to keep himself from going to her.

Wisely, his brother kept his thoughts about Sarah to himself on the elevator ride back down to his computer lab. Tarrant went straight to his chair and rolled it in front of a computer. A few keystrokes later, he opened up a file.

"Here's a list of every drakon I know about." The list was in a long dead language, one that only a drakon would know and understand. It was also in code, one only Tarrant and his brothers knew.

Darius leaned over his brother's shoulder and read through the names. He was impressed. Not that he'd ever tell Tarrant that. He wouldn't want to give Tarrant an even bigger head than he already had.

"How much should we tell them?" Tarrant asked.

"Tell them the Knights are back and they're after me specifically. Give them Temple's name and ask if any of them know anything else."

"What about the book?"

Darius shook his head. "Keep that between us. Last thing we want is a bunch of pissed-off drakons coming here looking for that book. We destroy it and pray there are no other copies out there somewhere."

"That's a pleasant thought," Tarrant muttered as he composed the email. Once the note was finished, Tarrant sent it and then turned his chair around. "What now?"

"Now we wait to see if any of them know anything they're willing to share. You keep digging into the Knights. We need to find out who is calling the shots, because I don't think Herman Temple is their leader."

"And where will you be while I'm doing all that?"

Darius ignored Tarrant's question and headed back toward the elevator. "You know damn well where I'll be."

"I'm going to research mates and see if anyone else has any information."

He paused and then nodded. "That might be best." If Sarah was truly his mate, Darius needed to know what to do about it. She was already a part of him, a piece of his soul. Maybe she even was his soul. Either way, he didn't think he'd survive long without her. Now that he understood what he'd been missing all these long centuries, he didn't think he could go back to living the way he had.

In this case, ignorance truly had been bliss. He stepped into the elevator and rode it up to the main floor. Tarrant opened all the doors for him and they closed once again.

His brother was even more isolated than he was. At least Darius lived out in the world. Tarrant chose to spend most of his time alone in the fortress he called home. Darius worried about his brother but knew there was nothing he could do for him, except be there whenever Tarrant needed him.

Darius gently pushed open the bedroom door. Sarah was curled up in the center of the big bed, one hand on top of the covers and her mouth slightly open. She gave a tiny snore, and it made him smile. He was sure she'd deny any suggestion that she snored.

He stripped off his clothes, carefully peeled back the covers, and slid in next to her. She stirred and he gathered her into his arms. She rooted around several times before settling with her head on his shoulder.

"Sleep," he whispered. "I'll protect you." He had no choice. The delicate human female in his arms was his heart.

• • •

Herman projected a facade of calm. It didn't matter that he was older than the woman walking into his office. There was something lethal about Karina Azarov. She was ruthless in her ambition to destroy or control all dragons and would stop at nothing to reach her goal.

He didn't make the mistake of believing she was weak because she was female. The women in her family line had always ruled the Knights with an iron fist.

"Welcome to New York." He waved her to a seat. "I trust you had a good flight."

"What do you know about the whereabouts of Varkas and the woman?" Karina demanded.

Pleasantries were obviously not welcome, so Herman sat at his desk and rested his hands on the rich mahogany. He knew it projected an image of power. The corners of her lips twitched, as though she knew what he was doing and was trying not to laugh at him. He wanted to wrap his fingers around her scrawny neck and snap it like a twig.

Her two-man security detail was with her, but he had Riggs in the room, and he'd put his man up against her two any day of the week. "Nothing new. We're monitoring all airports, bus stations, highways, and communications from their last known location. With the amount of fuel they had, they could only go so far without setting down. If they move again, we'll have them."

"Good. I want Varkas found." She stood, dismissing him even though they were in his office. "Contact me the second you hear anything." She strode from the room and her security detail fell in behind her.

Herman glanced at Riggs. "Stay with her. I want to know what she does and who she speaks with."

"Sir." Riggs left the room, closing the door behind him.

A secret door swung open, and Christian stepped out.

"You heard everything." It wasn't a question. Herman knew damn well his son had listened to every single word.

"We'll find Varkas."

Herman wasn't quite as sure. He'd been around a lot longer than his son and had seen dragons disappear. They were old and powerful and resourceful, and it wasn't smart to underestimate them.

"Keep monitoring the situation and let me know when you have something." Herman waited until his son was almost out of his office. "And, Christian, don't double-cross me by going to Karina." Christian stiffened but said nothing as he left.

He couldn't count on his son not to turn on him. He could definitely count on Karina turning on him if things went sour. It was time to start protecting himself. It might even be time for a new leader of the Knights of the Dragon. He picked up his phone and dialed the number of another old member of the Knights. "Good afternoon, Jeremiah. We have a situation."

Chapter Twenty-One

Sarah came awake slowly. She was warm and cozy and not alone. She wasn't the least bit surprised that Darius was wrapped around her, his big body practically covering hers. They were both lying on their sides, and he had his massive arm around her and her body tucked up against his.

"Good morning or evening or whatever time of day it is." She'd lost all sense of time. Surprisingly, it didn't bother her as much as it had. Her well-scheduled life was shot to hell, so what did it matter if it was morning or night?

"Good morning," he answered. His lips pressed against her temple. "And it is morning. Five minutes past ten."

"How do you know? Is it some internal clock?" She really needed to learn more about drakons.

He chuckled and rolled her onto her back so she was staring up at him. He raised his right hand and pointed at the nightstand. "External clock."

A burst of laughter left her. "So no mystical connection to the sun or moon?" she asked when she finally regained her composure. For such a serious man, Darius had a wicked sense of humor.

"I knew it was several hours past dawn, but I couldn't have given you an exact time." He leaned down and brushed his mouth over hers.

She kissed him back but didn't linger.

He frowned. "What's wrong?"

Once again, Darius was blunt and straight to the point. She liked that about him most times, but not in embarrassing situations like this. "Morning breath." She really needed to brush her teeth.

He flashed a quick grin. "I don't mind."

"I do." She felt grungy all over. "I need a shower and clean clothes." Then it dawned on her that Darius wasn't wearing a shirt. He couldn't be naked, could he?

Of course he could. The wicked gleam in his eyes told her without a doubt that he wasn't wearing anything but the bed sheet.

"What time did you come to bed?" She really didn't want to think about him being naked, not when she had bed head and stale breath.

"I'm not sure, but it was late." He rolled onto his back and stretched his arms up in the air. She got an eyeful of rippling biceps and rock-hard abs before he dropped them back down.

"I'm glad you got some sleep." He'd been pushing himself hard since this whole situation had begun.

He turned his head so he could see her. "I'm fine. No need to worry about me. I can go days without rest if necessary."

"Good to know, but I'm still glad you slept."

He rolled onto his side, and his eyes took on a familiar gleam. "I'm glad you managed to rest. You needed it." He reached for her, but she scooted back.

"Shower and toothbrush," she reminded him.

He sighed and let his hand fall back to the mattress. "You're really serious about that?"

"Dead serious." She was weak where he was concerned, but there was no way for her to feel sexy with morning breath and feeling this grungy. She was wearing the sweater she'd confiscated from Tarrant's closet, along with the sweat socks she'd purloined. After sleeping in them all night, she felt less than fresh.

Darius shoved back the bedclothes and sat on the edge of the mattress, giving her a prime view of his back. He definitely wasn't wearing any underwear. Her heart began to beat faster, and all the air in the room seemed to disappear.

He stretched his arms again, and the muscles in his back bunched and relaxed. The tattoo covering his left side made him seem even more dangerous and exotic, a visual reminder that he wasn't human. She swallowed heavily and twined her fingers together to keep from reaching for him. Honestly, it wasn't like her to be so drawn to a man.

"Do you give off pheromones?" It would explain her sudden and complete attraction to him.

His head whipped around. "What do you mean?"

She wished she'd kept her mouth shut, but it was too late for that now. "You know." She waved her hand toward him. "Some scent or something that attracts women."

His frown was fierce. "I don't need to emit some scent to attract a woman."

Great, now she'd insulted him. As quickly as his frown appeared, it disappeared. She wasn't sure she liked the speculative gleam in his eyes.

"So you admit you're attracted to me." He swiveled around on the mattress and rested one knee on the bed, giving her a prime view of his erection. Most men woke hard in the morning, but it was still impressive.

"That's hardly a secret." Sarah was proud at how level her voice was. "But it's not like me to feel such a pull to someone, and certainly not so quickly."

"So you figured it must be some drakon trick I used on you?"

She shrugged, only partially ashamed of her accusation. How was she supposed to know what drakons did or didn't do? "Maybe."

Darius shook his head. "As far as I know, I don't give off these mysterious pheromones you spoke of. If it's any consolation, you do the same to me." He cupped her cheek and rubbed his thumb over her bottom lip. "I've never wanted a woman the way I want you."

Her insides quivered. Maybe he was handing her a line. That's what men did when they wanted to get lucky. But Darius wasn't like most men. He was blunt and honest. "Really?"

He kissed her before she realized his intent. "Enough to risk morning breath and your wrath."

She knew she was smiling like an idiot but couldn't seem to stop herself. It felt like high school all over again, and she was telling a hunky guy that she liked him. And lo and behold, he liked her back. She really needed to get a grip.

"Did you learn anything new after I went to bed?"

Darius skimmed his hand down her neck and over the front of the sweater. His palm landed right on her breast, the heat of his skin seeping through the material. "Only that seeing Tarrant's priest about an exorcism seems to be the only possible way we might destroy the book."

It wasn't easy to keep her mind on the conversation with Darius touching her. "And where can we find this priest?"

Darius pulled his hand away and stood. He was turned away from her, but that didn't help matters. He was still naked. "Father Simon is currently in a town called Salvation in North Carolina."

"Salvation?" She sat up and the sheet pooled in her lap. "How are we going to get there undetected?"

Darius grabbed the jeans he'd worn last night and pulled

them on. He zipped them before he turned around, but there was no hiding the heavy bulge or disguising his arousal. "You shouldn't look at me like that unless you mean business," he warned.

Her gaze snapped up to his face. He was dead serious. "North Carolina?" she prompted.

He raked his fingers through his hair. It wasn't fair that he looked sexy and ready to face the day while she felt like a wrung-out dishrag. "We'll get there the same way we got here," he told her. "Plane."

"Won't they track us?"

He shook his head. "We won't exactly be filing a proper flight plan. Tarrant will handle that end for us. We'll land at a small airport nearby and drive from there."

"Renting a car will be dangerous, won't it?" The logistics involved were simple, unless you were dealing with the Knights. She wouldn't underestimate them.

"I've got an idea about that." He grabbed his T-shirt and dragged it over his head. "I'm hoping this Father Simon has someone he trusts who can loan us a truck or car. The longer we stay off the Knight's radar, the better chance we have of destroying that damn book."

She scooted out of bed, making sure the hem of the sweater was pulled down enough to cover her. She wasn't wearing any underwear. "We could get in and out without the Knights of the Dragon ever knowing we were there."

Darius grunted. "That's the plan."

"And Tarrant trusts this priest?"

"He does."

That was it—no trying to convince her, no reasons why she should trust Tarrant. Not that she really had a choice. Darius was not one to sugarcoat anything or to evade the truth. "When do we leave?"

"Not yet." He came to her, wrapped his arms around her,

and held her close. "We need to see if Tarrant's found out any other useful information. Then we formulate our plan and several escape routes. I won't take any more chances with your safety than I have to. I'd leave you here, but I know you wouldn't stay."

"You've got that right. I'm not hiding while you risk your life." The very idea made her sick to her stomach. She needed to be near him to protect him, which was ludicrous, because—hello—he was a drakon. Still, there was no denying the powerful instinct that welled up inside her.

"I didn't think so." He nuzzled the top of her head. "And, truthfully, I'm not sure I could leave you behind." He sounded totally disgruntled with himself, but his confession warmed her soul. He wanted her with him.

"I'll get cleaned up, and we'll go see what Tarrant has discovered, if anything."

"I'll find you something to wear," he promised. "Then we'll eat."

She was hungry. "Sounds like a plan."

He gave her a gentle squeeze. "You go ahead and get your shower. I'll have clothes on the bed for you by the time you're done."

He released her and headed for the door. She almost called him back, not ready for this quiet interlude to be over. There were so many things that could go wrong with their plan. They could make it all the way to Father Simon and he could turn on them and hand them over to the Knights, or try to use the knowledge in the book to enslave Darius. Or he could try to help them but not be able to destroy the book.

She shivered and rubbed her hands over her arms. That book was evil and had to be destroyed. No more hiding. The time had come to take action. She hurried into the adjoining bathroom, stripped off her socks and sweater, and jumped in the shower.

She had no idea what would happen in the days or even weeks ahead. The only thing she did know was that she'd be at Darius's side all the way.

• • •

Darius found Tarrant in the kitchen. The smell of coffee lured him to the pot, where he filled a mug and took a sip.

"About time you dragged your lazy ass out of bed."

"Good morning to you, too." Darius leaned against the counter and took another sip of coffee. "I need clothes for Sarah."

"What am I, the butler?" When Darius didn't bite, Tarrant sighed. "I collected her clothes and ran them through the wash. They're dry and sitting in the utility room."

He wasn't sure how he felt about his brother handling Sarah's panties and bra, but in this situation, he couldn't really quibble. "Thanks."

"You're welcome." The words were polite enough but came out sounding more like a curse.

"I'm going to raid your closet and get a shower."

"Of course you are," Tarrant muttered. "I'll just make breakfast. Or rather, brunch."

Darius ignored his brother's sarcasm, slapped him on the back, and smiled. "Sounds good to me." He left the room with Tarrant's growl following him.

Darius detoured by the utility room long enough to grab Sarah's clothes. When he entered the room they'd shared, he could hear the water running in the bathroom and knew she was naked in the shower. His erection, which had gone down slightly, jumped back to life.

He forced himself to set the clothes on the bed and leave the room. As much as he wanted to spend hours in bed with Sarah, he had to ensure her safety first. That meant destroying the book, and then the Knights, in that order. He didn't want to kill anyone, but he would in order to protect his brothers and Sarah.

The Knights would never stop hunting them. Never leave them alone. The only way to get rid of the threat was to get rid of the Knights permanently. It had never been a priority before. Even though they had primal natures, drakons didn't like to kill unless there was no other choice. They especially didn't want to risk the lives of innocents. But now it wasn't just himself and his brothers he had to protect. He had Sarah to protect as well. She was everything to him, and he'd destroy anyone who stood in the way of her safety.

Darius hurried into Tarrant's room and took a quick shower before redressing in a clean pair of jeans and another T-shirt he helped himself to out of Tarrant's closet. After pulling on socks and a nice pair of leather boots, Darius was ready. He cleaned up the bathroom before he went back to the kitchen.

The other bedroom door was still closed and Sarah was nowhere in sight when he stepped into the kitchen. Tarrant had been busy. Darius could smell bacon and ham warming in the oven. Several skillets were filled with eggs that Tarrant was busy scrambling.

Without bothering to ask what he could do to help, Darius poured juice, filled coffee mugs, and set them on the counter of the island.

He heard the bedroom door open and Sarah appeared seconds later. Everything inside him settled when he laid eyes on her. She was wearing her own clothing—jeans, sweater, and boots—but she was also wearing his shirt beneath the sweater.

"Thanks for washing my clothes." She glanced from man to man, looking unsure who she should be thanking.

"Tarrant took care of it," he told her.

She seemed a little embarrassed but offered Tarrant a small smile. "Thanks, I appreciate it."

Tarrant shrugged. "No problem."

"What can I do to help?" she offered.

Darius pointed her to one of the stools on the opposite side of the counter. "Sit. We're almost done here." Tarrant shot him an irritated look. "Or rather Tarrant is almost done." Darius opened the oven door and pulled out the platter of bacon and ham that was warming there.

"It smells delicious." Sarah slid onto the same stool she'd used before and went straight for the coffee. She added sugar and then took her first sip. "Nothing tastes quite as good as the first sip of the day."

"I beg to differ," he murmured in her ear as he set the platter in front of her. "You taste mighty good first thing in the morning."

"I'm standing right here," Tarrant reminded them. He plunked a huge bowl filled with scrambled eggs down next to the platter. "No sex talk. At least not until after we eat."

Sarah's cheeks turned pink, and Darius couldn't help but grin. He didn't like that he'd embarrassed her, but damn, she was sweet. He motioned to the food. "Help yourself."

He and Tarrant both waited until she'd scooped a small portion of eggs onto her plate and added several slices of bacon and a piece of ham. Then he and his brother divided what was left between them.

Sarah paused with a forkful of fluffy eggs halfway to her mouth. "Wow, you guys really pack away the food."

"Big appetites," Darius reminded her. When she blushed again, he realized that there was a double meaning to his words.

"Again, I'm right here. You want to talk sexy, go back to the bedroom." Tarrant popped a piece of ham into his mouth and chewed.

"Anything new to report?" Darius began to methodically eat his meal.

Tarrant shook his head. "Not really. I dug up a bit more information on Temple and his son, but I'm no closer to finding the head of the Knights. Temple has a lot of business and social connections, and I'm going through all of them. It's likely he does business with other members of the group." He downed half his coffee in one swallow. "I contacted everyone on my list, but no one has gotten back to me with any extra information. I have to assume they're even more in the dark than we are." He paused and emptied his mug. "And Ezra called. He wanted to come, but I told him to stay put."

"Ezra? Who is Ezra?" she asked. "And what list?"

Before Darius could answer her questions, Tarrant surprised him by doing so himself.

"The list is of known drakons. It's written in language the world no longer knows. It's also in code," he added. "Just to be safe."

To give her credit, Sarah didn't seem the least bit perturbed by Tarrant's continued mistrust of her. She seemed to take it as a matter of course. "And Ezra?"

This time Darius didn't wait for Tarrant to answer her. "Ezra is our brother."

She swiveled on her stool until she was facing him. "Just how many brothers do you have?"

"Three." Tarrant swore, but Darius would be nothing less than honest with Sarah. "Different mothers, same dragon sire."

"Wow. Just wow. I'm an only child. I always wanted a brother or sister." As if realizing she might have revealed too much about herself, she grabbed her mug and chugged her coffee. When she was finished, she set the mug on the counter. "So Darius tells me we're headed to North Carolina."

Tarrant studied her for a long moment before slowly nodding. "The sooner the better."

Chapter Twenty-Two

Darius turned to his brother. "Has anything happened?"

Sarah was glad the spotlight was off her. She hated being the center of attention. She especially hated being vulnerable, and she felt that way at the moment. Darius had three brothers. He and Tarrant were tight. That much was obvious. But there were two more men out there somewhere who had Darius's allegiance.

Jealousy was not a pretty emotion. She felt petty and stupid for coveting something she'd never had — unconditional love and acceptance.

"The book. It's getting stronger. Maybe being around us is feeding it somehow." Tarrant calmly picked up a piece of bacon, bit of the end, and chewed thoughtfully. "Hard to tell without having the time to study what's inside. I only had a peek at it before."

"No." Sarah sent Darius a pleading look. "It's too dangerous." That book had tried to destroy her.

"No one is going to handle the book," he promised her. She took him at his word but still glanced at Tarrant.

"I'm inquisitive, not stupid." He ate the rest of the piece of bacon and then picked up his fork. "As much as I'd like to know what the hell is written in it, I'm not stupid enough to risk my freedom for it." He started in on the mound of eggs on his plate.

"Good to know." Sarah began to eat. She knew she needed the fuel, and everything was delicious, even if her appetite wasn't as sharp as it had been. All this talk about the book was enough to put a girl off her food.

Darius had been quiet, which meant he was thinking. As if sensing her gaze on him, he looked her way. "What?" he asked.

"That's my question," she shot back.

"Maybe there's a way we can study the book without having it affect any of us. After all, Tarrant used his talents as an air dragon to open it."

She shook her head. "It's too dangerous." The food she'd eaten started to curdle in her stomach, and she carefully set her fork down on the edge of her plate. "That book tried to take me over. I think it would have consumed me if it could have. Maybe even taken over my will and made me do things I didn't want to."

"It's that powerful?" Tarrant shoved his empty plate aside. The discussion obviously hadn't spoiled his appetite.

"Yes. It felt different the second time I touched it. Like it was gaining power."

"I'd love to see inside it again." Tarrant rubbed his jaw. She could tell he was mulling over the problem. "There's so much knowledge trapped in those pages."

"Think you could read it? It seemed to be a mishmash of ancient languages and symbols." Some of which she'd never encountered. The researcher in her was intrigued by the idea of deciphering the information written on the pages. Then she remembered that it wasn't written in ink. "Do you think the drakon-blood ink is making the book more powerful?" she asked Darius.

"Undoubtedly," Darius told her. "You know from your gift that people and actions leave psychic residue or memories attached to objects. The rituals the Knights have performed over the centuries have added to the power."

Darius reached out and covered her hand with his, giving it a squeeze. "And, yes, if anyone can read what's on the pages of the book, Tarrant can. He has a gift for languages and codes of all kinds."

"That's a handy talent." She could read and understand several languages, but if Tarrant could do what Darius said, it opened up the secrets of the world to him.

He picked up his coffee mug and saluted her. "I do what I can."

"It's probably best the book is destroyed and whatever secrets it holds go with it." Even though Darius was sitting next to her, he seemed lost in thought. "If the rituals exist in any form, they can be used against us."

"Still"—Tarrant sighed—"if I could just decipher the knowledge before the book is destroyed, we'd gain a giant foothold in our war with the Knights. We might even be able to discover how to counter their potions and spells, maybe even defeat them. Whatever power the book holds, it's helped imprison many of our kind. It might also hold the key to releasing them." He stood and began clearing away dishes.

"What do you think?" Darius asked her. "Fear aside, do you think it's possible for Tarrant to get another look inside the book?"

"Anything is possible, but the danger is too great. What if he reads something that imprisons him in some way? We won't be able to read the book to find out how to neutralize it." Just the idea of touching the book again gave her the heebie-jeebies. "I never believed in magic before, but the book scares me. I have no idea just how powerful it is."

"She has a point," Darius told his brother. "If you read something that traps you in any way, you're basically screwed."

She liked that he took her concerns seriously. Considering his age and experience, it wasn't something she'd expected, but he'd treated her opinion with respect since their first meeting.

"Yeah, I'd thought about that, but it might be worth the risk."

Darius shook his head at his brother. "It's not worth your life. We've survived this long without knowing the secrets of the Knights, and we'll continue to survive without them."

Tarrant nodded. "Then you two had better get ready to go. The quicker the book is destroyed, the better." He leaned against the counter, and she'd have sworn she could see flames flickering behind his blue eyes. "And we'd better pray they don't have another copy of it."

She pressed her hand against her stomach. That was a huge concern. "They needed me to find the missing book," she pointed out.

Darius stepped behind her and placed his hands on her shoulders. "They did. That could mean one of two things. Either it's a one-of-a-kind book and they're desperate to get it back, or there are only a few copies and Herman Temple is desperate to find this one before the leader of the Knights discovers it's missing."

Tarrant picked up the theme. "Could be there are a small number of these books, held by the most powerful of the Knights."

Sarah nodded as her understanding grew. "To admit to losing it would jeopardize Temple's standing in the group."

"And put his life in danger," Darius asserted. "It would be seen as a weakness by an organization that does not tolerate mistakes."

She shivered and leaned back against Darius, grateful for

his body heat. "They seem to have no qualms about killing." Not from what she'd overheard.

"If the leader of the Knights finds out, he might pay Temple a visit," Tarrant pointed out. "We might be able to use that to our advantage."

"How?" Darius asked.

Tarrant began to smile. "I'm not king of the satellites for nothing. I've been recording the street view of Temple's home to see who comes and goes. I just need to review it."

"Brilliant." It was also scary and illegal as hell, but since Tarrant was on their side, she wasn't going to worry about the legalities of the situation. Nothing about these circumstances was normal. They called for extraordinary measures.

"Let's get the book and get the hell out of here." Darius stepped back, and she slid off the stool. "The quicker that book is destroyed, the better."

Sarah agreed. She only hoped their plan worked. They didn't have a Plan B if this one failed.

Tarrant led the way back down to his computer lab. Knowing what to expect, she didn't find the security measures as off-putting anymore. Darius stood beside her, a quiet but commanding presence.

Computers hummed and the air seemed charged when they stepped into the room. Tarrant went straight to his desk and scanned the three screens that displayed a multitude of information.

"Anything?" Darius asked.

Tarrant sat in his chair and began typing. "Give me a minute or two." With that, he ignored them, his entire being focused on the keyboard and screens in front of him.

"We should get the book."

"Yeah, we should." She really wasn't looking forward to this, but it had to be done. She took a deep breath and followed Darius to a cabinet at the far end of the room. Even with the metal door between them and the box containing the book, she could feel the pulse of power it emitted.

Darius paused several feet away from the cabinet. "Its pull is stronger."

"You feel it, too?" She was glad it wasn't just her.

"Yes, I do." He turned and caught her shoulders in his hands. "Are you sure you won't stay here with Tarrant?"

He was trying to protect her. While she appreciated it, she couldn't allow him to face the danger by himself. He was in this mess because of that book, and she was the one who'd stolen it and brought it to him.

"I go with you." She was adamant about that.

He kissed her. It was a soft kiss, but it still curled her toes and melted her heart. She kissed him back, tasting promise and possibility. She knew even if they destroyed the book, until the Knights of the Dragon were defeated, she'd never be safe. Her lifespan was extremely limited, but whatever time she had, she wanted to spend it with Darius.

Some might call her foolish, but he made her feel alive in a way she never had. Whatever the outcome, it was worth it.

"If you two are done, you've got a plane to catch," Tarrant reminded them.

Darius slowly lifted his lips from hers. "Don't mind my brother. He's just jealous because he doesn't have a woman of his own." His husky murmur made her tingle from head to toe. She wanted to ask if she really was his woman, but that smacked of neediness. She reminded herself to stay in the moment and take each one as the gift it was.

"He's also right," she reminded him. "We need to destroy the book." She pushed past Darius and pulled open the cabinet door. The knapsack sat on a shelf with the box and book inside it. She took a deep breath and grabbed the leather strap. The hum from the book grew louder. "Let's go."

"Let me take that." Darius reached out and snagged the

knapsack. She held on for a brief second before releasing it.

"I'm not sure who's in the most danger from the book, me or you." Better to be honest with him.

"I can hear it humming, almost make out words but not quite," he admitted.

It was terrifying to her that the book still seemed to be growing in power. "We need to get rid of it. Maybe we could drop it in a volcano or something?"

A smile flickered on Darius's lips even as he shook his head. "The flame from holy candles and holy water, remember?"

"And only after the exorcism," Tarrant reminded them. "I'll contact Father Simon and let him know to expect you. He'll make sure someone meets your plane."

"I pray your trust isn't misplaced." Darius gave his brother a one-armed hug and thumped him on the back. Sarah noted he was careful to keep the knapsack away from Tarrant.

Even so, Tarrant canted his head to one side as if listening to a voice only he could hear. "Are you sure I can't have another peek at the contents of the book?" He started to reach for the bag.

"We need to go. Now." Darius held the bag out of Tarrant's reach. Tarrant's eyes narrowed and he emitted a low growl.

"I want to see the book." His face began to morph, shifting to drakon form.

Sarah stepped between the two men and shoved them apart, or at least tried to. No way was she moving either one of the massive men. It was a supremely stupid move, but not the first time she'd done it. Like the last time, the shock of it drew their attention to her.

"The book is beginning to affect you," she told Tarrant. "You don't want to hurt your brother, do you?" It was a gamble, but one she felt secure taking. The love and respect between the men was as solid as bedrock. She was banking on it.

Tarrant shook his head and dropped fully back into his human form. "Get the hell out of here and fast." He turned away from them and stared at the wall.

Darius started to reach out to his brother, but Sarah grabbed him by the arm and yanked him toward the door guarding the elevator. "The best thing you can do to help him is leave."

"Take the truck," Tarrant told them. "I'll run up later to retrieve it." He reached down and tapped several buttons, and the door swung open, allowing them to step into the elevator.

"I'll call you from the plane," Darius told him.

The door slid shut, trapping them inside. Sarah held her breath until the doors opened and she stepped into the apartment hallway.

"I hate leaving him like this."

Sarah rubbed his arm, wishing there was something more substantial she could do to reassure him. "It's for the best. The sooner the book is gone from here, the better for Tarrant."

"I know you're right." He glanced at the door, but it had already shut and the locks were engaged. They weren't getting back down to the computer lab unless Tarrant let them in. She was guessing nothing short of a major earthquake or nuclear bomb was getting anyone inside.

Darius gripped the leather straps of the knapsack. "Why is it affecting Tarrant more than me?"

Sarah led the way to the living area, knowing instinctively that Darius would follow. Her bag was still on the end of the counter where it had been dumped when they'd arrived. She grabbed it and headed for the door to the secret staircase. The bag didn't contain much, since her laptop and phone had been destroyed, but it did hold her identification and bank card. Not that she could use any of it, at least not for the foreseeable future. Still, it was her last link to her life, and she wasn't willing to let go of it just yet.

She went up the stairs with Darius right behind her. She thought about his question as they left the cabin and made their way to the truck. Darius stowed the knapsack behind his seat and both of them climbed in. She got in through the driver's side so they didn't have to worry about securing the bungee cord on the passenger's side.

"As weird and unlikely as it sounds, I think the book somehow knows he can read it." It was only speculation on her part, but it felt right.

The keys were in the ignition, and Darius started the truck. He put it in gear, swung the vehicle around, and headed back down the dirt road. She caught a glimpse of the dilapidated cabin in her side mirror and realized she was going to miss the place, and Tarrant.

"It makes as much sense as anything about the book does." Darius wrestled with the wheel as they went over several nasty bumps in the road. Sarah grabbed her seat belt and snapped it closed.

"If the book is becoming sentient, as it seems to be, then it wants someone who can read it. You and I can't. Well, I can probably read part of it."

"I know many ancient languages." His voice was stilted.

"I know you do, but you don't know as many as Tarrant does, do you?" She slapped her hand on the dashboard as the truck went down in a nasty rut. "And the two of us might be able to decipher some of the code it's written in, but it would take us a lot longer."

Darius sighed and swung the wheel hard to the left to avoid a large rock. "You're right. Tarrant is much better at languages and communication as a whole."

"It's what fascinates him, like the earth and mining does you, and books do for me. We each have our strengths. Tarrant can't destroy the book. Only you can."

Sarah was glad the landing strip wasn't any farther away. Her insides couldn't take many more jolts. It was only when they pulled up on the edge of the airfield a thought occurred to her. "Oh God, we're going to have to take off on that short runway, aren't we?" The book aside, she didn't want to die in a fiery blaze when the plane crashed into the trees.

Darius just laughed and climbed out of the truck. "You'll have to trust me." She scrambled out on his side and grabbed her bag. Knapsack over his shoulder, Darius headed for the plane.

"I trust you," she muttered. "Just not the shortness of the landing strip and the tin can with wings."

He pulled down the stairs and ushered her inside. Darius went straight to the back of the plane and stowed the knapsack in a cabinet. "I figure the farther away from us the book is, the better."

"Smart."

"I need to refuel."

"I'll come with you." She didn't want to be alone with the book. It wasn't smart to underestimate its power. "Until the book is destroyed, I don't think either one of us should be alone with it. The more time we spend with it, the more it seems to be affecting us."

Darius nodded and took her hand. "You're right."

She dumped her bag on the floor and went with him. Like everything he did, Darius was efficient, and in no time the plane was refueled and they were seated in the cockpit. The engines roared to life.

Darius flicked several switches and turned on the radio, not bothering with the headset. "Baby bird to eagle's nest. Come in, eagle's nest."

Sarah swiveled as far as her seat belt would allow. "Seriously?"

He grinned just as Tarrant's voice came through the

headset. "This is eagle's nest. What's your status?"

"Package is stored and we're readying for takeoff." Darius began to maneuver the plane, turning so it was facing the runway. She clamped her hands around the arms of her seat and held on for dear life.

"Keep in touch. I'll let you know if I find out anything more that might help. Just get where you need to go, do what you need to do, and get the hell out."

"Roger that," Darius told him.

"Just land where I told you to and you'll be fine." Tarrant went silent and Sarah could almost picture him tapping away at his keyboard. "Your contact will send someone to pick you up. Stay safe."

"Ready for takeoff." The engines began to rev, and Sarah gripped the seat until her fingers turned white. "Here we go," he said. The plane began to roll down the runway, gaining speed as it went. The trees in the distance loomed closer and closer.

She wanted to close her eyes but couldn't. If her end was coming, she wanted to meet it head-on. "Oh God."

Darius laughed and pulled back on the controls. The nose of the plane went up and the wheels left the ground. They needed to get higher. The trees were right in front of them. Then just as she thought they'd smash into them, the plane suddenly shot upward several feet in the air.

She let out a yelp as the bottom of the plane scraped over the tips of the trees. An angry squirrel glared at her from its perch in a nearby pine.

Darius laughed. "Tarrant must not have trusted my piloting skills."

"What do you mean?" It was hard to talk and pray at the same time.

"Air drakon. That extra boost to get the plane above the tree line was all Tarrant."

They were in the air, but they still weren't safe. Darius maneuvered between the giant walls of the mountain. Sarah only released the breath she'd been holding when they left the shadows of the mountain and entered the clear sky.

Her top was stuck to her skin, damp with sweat. Darius, on the other hand, was cool and relaxed. "You enjoyed that."

He grinned and fiddled with some buttons on the control panel. "We all have our talents."

She shook her head, unable to be angry with him. He really was skilled when it came to flying. "I'd love to see you fly high in the sky. Not in a plane. Just you in your drakon form." It was like an ache in her soul. To see him free and wild was a yearning in her heart.

"Maybe someday you will."

"Maybe someday." She held on to the hope like a talisman as she settled in for the ride to Salvation, North Carolina.

Chapter Twenty-Three

It was dark when they finally landed. Darius taxied the airplane to the assigned area and shut down the engine. The resulting silence seemed deafening. "We're really going to do this?" A part of her wanted him to restart the plane and get them out of here.

"We have no choice," he reminded her.

"I know." She unbuckled her seat belt and pushed out of her chair. "Do you think Father Simon sent someone to pick us up like he said he would?" She'd silently fretted for hours over the loyalty of this priest that Tarrant trusted.

"Tarrant said there would be someone waiting." He left the cockpit, and she followed close behind. "And there is."

"How do you know?" she demanded. She hadn't seen anyone.

He stopped so suddenly she almost plowed into him. "My vision is as good in the dark as in the day," he reminded her. "There's a man in a truck waiting not far from here. We're on the clock as of now. We don't know who the Knights have working for them or how far their reach is."

"I know." And it was making her nervous as hell. She took a deep breath to calm the jitters plaguing her. "Let's do this and get the hell out of town."

He grinned at her before planting a hard kiss on her lips. "You've got yourself a deal." He headed to the end of the plane to retrieve the backpack while she grabbed her own bag. He was back before she'd settled it on her shoulder.

Something hit the side of the plane, and she gave a slight jump. "The welcoming party?"

"Stay behind me," he ordered. He went to the door, unlocked it, and pushed it open. She peeked around his shoulder, wanting to see. The man standing at the bottom of the stairs was around six feet tall with long brown hair.

"Come with me," the man told them. He turned and headed toward a battered truck waiting just to the side of the runway.

With a sense of déjà vu, Sarah followed Darius down the stairs. She could feel the power of the book. It seemed to be getting stronger. She twined her fingers together to keep from reaching out and snatching it away from Darius.

"Okay?" he asked.

"Yeah." She didn't want to talk until the book was gone. It was taking all her willpower to stay in control around the powerful manuscript.

The man was already behind the wheel of his truck, tapping his fingers on the wheel. The second they were both inside and Darius shut the door, he pulled away. He kept the speed around the limit as he drove them through the darkness toward the town of Salvation.

"Where are we going?" she finally asked, unable to simply be taken wherever this stranger wanted them to go.

He glanced at her and then turned his gaze back to the road. "I'm takin' you to Father Simon. I don't know what this is about, and I don't want to."

She couldn't really blame him for that. The less he knew, the safer he was. They drove for what seemed like forever, even though it was probably around thirty minutes. Nerves were getting the better of her. The area grew more rural, the homes farther apart.

Their driver turned off the main road. A little white church stood in a clearing surrounded by tall trees. With the pale moonlight illuminating it, it looked like something out of a gothic tale. Their driver pulled up at the bottom of the stairs. Darius climbed out and she scooted along the seat and stepped down onto the gravel driveway.

The second the door was shut, the driver peeled out of the parking lot, leaving them alone. "Guess he isn't planning on sticking around." She gave a slow turn and shivered, feeling someone or something watching them.

Darius touched the small of her back. "Let's get inside."

"If this is a trap, I'm going to be very pissed off," she muttered.

"You and me both," he murmured in her ear.

She strode up the walkway toward the front door. It was warmer here than it had been in the mountains, but it was still chilly. Darius reached around her and pulled the door open. She stepped into the small vestibule and paused.

It was so quiet she half expected not to find anyone waiting for them inside. Darius took the lead and stepped into the church. It was a simple building, the floors well worn, pews old and well used. Her gaze went to the altar at the front with a large wooden cross dominating it. The room was ringed in religious statues.

"Welcome." The man who stepped out of the shadows to greet them wasn't anything like she'd expected. He had to be in his mid-sixties, but he was still very fit. He was wearing jeans and a button-down dress shirt instead of ceremonial robes.

Darius strode down the center aisle, and she followed

him. "Father Simon?" he asked.

The man nodded. "Simon Babineaux." That surprised her. She'd thought his last name was Simon, not his first. "We have a mutual friend."

Darius nodded. "We do."

The priest studied Darius through his wire-rimmed glasses. With his shock of white hair and trimmed white beard, he looked like a very trim Santa Claus. "Hello, my dear." He held out his hand to her. "Forgive me for being rude, but we should get straight to the point of your visit."

She took his hand, and he gave hers a brief squeeze before releasing it. Father Simon's gaze went straight to the knapsack on Darius's shoulder. "It's in there, isn't it?"

"You can feel it, too?" That surprised her. She wondered if everyone could sense the book now that it was gaining power.

"Yes. Objects of this sort often give off energy all their own."

She couldn't argue with that. With her talent, she found that the older the object, the greater the vibes coming off it due to the sheer history it had lived. But the book was different. It was tainted. Evil.

"Come." He led them toward the back of the church. "I would have picked you up at the airfield myself, but there were things I had to do here in order to prepare. I'm only a guest at this church for a few weeks, so it took me some time to gather everything I needed." A circle of candles had been set up around a font on a pedestal that she assumed held holy water. It was made of some sort of stone and looked very old—heavy, too. Symbols had been carved around the sides of the vessel. "Everything has been properly sanctified," he assured them. "Light the candles," he told Darius.

She half expected him to simply blow fire to light them. Instead, he picked up the single flickering candle that stood next to the font and used it to light the others. Smart. If Father Simon didn't know Darius was a drakon, he didn't need to.

"Now, step inside the circle. The sacred space will help keep you safe."

Sarah was nervous. What if the priest was trying to trick them, to betray Tarrant and entrap Darius? She didn't need to worry about herself. If this was a trap, she'd end up dead. Darius, on the other hand, could suffer for eternity.

"Are you sure?" she asked Darius. He ran his thumb over the curve of her jaw and nodded. She took a deep breath and stepped into the circle. Darius joined her and set the knapsack on the floor. He crouched in front of the bag and gingerly opened the flap. She wished Tarrant were here right about now. He could use his power over air to lift the damn book out without them having to touch it.

"That is the object?" Father Simon asked when Darius drew out the box.

Darius shook his head. "No." He set the box on the floor and removed the lid. The manuscript was surrounded by shadows, pulsing with an unnatural energy that made her skin crawl.

The priest sucked in a breath and then recited a prayer as he pulled a small book out of his pocket. He opened it to a page he'd marked and began speaking in Latin. She recognized some of the words but couldn't concentrate. Not with the book so near.

Her mouth was dry, and she trembled as she reached for the book.

"Sarah." Darius grabbed her hand, and she jerked away, appalled by her actions.

"I can't seem to help myself," she confessed. "I want to touch it." She felt weak and useless.

"I want to touch it, too," he told her. "It's a powerful draw." He took her hands in his. "Hold on to me, and I'll hold on to you."

The flames flared. They rose to about a foot above the thick pillar candles. Energy crackled and surrounded them like a wild wind. The flames flickered and then steadied. The priest's voice grew deeper, his words more strident as he tried to drive out whatever evil force inhabited the book.

"One of you needs to pick up the book." Father Simon's instructions were almost lost to the whirlwind that was growing stronger with each second. The door to the church blew open and banged against the side of the building. "Do it now."

Darius grabbed the book and held on with both hands. His entire body jerked with the force that shot through him. Sarah felt useless, less than useless, just standing there. Father Simon continued with the exorcism, imploring whatever evil was in the book to leave, banishing it in the name of God.

The floorboards trembled, and she stumbled. She reached out blindly and her hands connected with the book. The room went dark. She lost all sense of self, going blind and deaf to everything around her. Lost in the dark void, she heard a sly voice calling her, imploring her to repeat certain words.

She bit her bottom lip until she tasted blood. Whatever the book wanted her to say couldn't be good. The darkness surrounded her, seeping into her skin, eating at her insides. She wasn't even sure she was breathing. She fought the voice with everything she had. No way would she let the book use her to imprison Darius, because that's what it was trying to do. It wanted her to recite the incantation that would render her lover powerless.

She'd die before she'd let that happen. It was then she realized she loved him.

Pain pounded at her skull and something dripped from her nose. Pressure threatened to make her eardrums explode. The book was killing her.

• • •

An immense power shoved Darius away from the book the second Sarah's hands connected with it. He'd seen the floor buckle, seen her falling, and had been powerless to stop her hands from connecting with the book.

"Leave her," Father Simon yelled over the howling gale inside the church. "Someone has to burn the book while the other holds it. Do it now. It's her only chance."

Darius was torn. He wanted to yank the book from her grasp but knew the old priest was right. If he took it from her, she might die. Blood was already dripping from her nose and ears. Agony was etched on her face, and her breathing was getting shallower with each passing second.

"What do I do?" he shouted. He'd do anything to keep Sarah safe, and instead, she was the one fighting the evil of the book. The drakon inside him roared in displeasure.

"The candle." The priest pointed to the original candle, the one he'd used to light the ones that ringed them.

Darius grabbed the wax pillar from the holder and set the flame to the corner of the book. Father Simon continued to recite his prayers. Darius had no idea if it was helping or not, but they had to see this through to the end. It was their only hope.

His back was turned to the priest, blocking the man's view of Sarah and the book. The flame from the candle was making the edge of the book smolder, but nothing more.

"Open the book," Darius yelled at her. He needed to touch the candle to the paper, not the binding. "Sarah, you have to open the book." He put every ounce of power he had into trying to reach her.

The power of the book engulfed her, wanting to swallow her whole. But Darius would not be denied or defeated. He bellowed her name, ignoring the chill of the air surrounding them as his breath frosted before his very eyes. He clung to the holy candle, which was still lit in spite of the wind whirling around them. Darius reached out and touched Sarah's arm, needing the contact with her.

"You have to open the book. I can't do it. You have to." He called her name again and again. Darius swore he heard laughter in the air. The book was winning.

• • •

Sarah was lost in darkness. It was slowly suffocating her, sucking the life from her body. She wanted to let go of the book but couldn't make her hands work properly.

Then she thought she heard a voice. Not the sly one whispering promises in the dark, but one that was loud — and impatient.

"Open the damn book, Sarah. Do it now. I need to burn the pages."

She recognized that voice, didn't she? It was certainly drowning out the insidious whispers that threatened to drive her mad.

"You need to open the book. Sarah. Open the fucking book. Now."

Something touched her lips and warmth seeped into her, driving back the cold. She sucked in a breath and tasted blood. Her blood? But she tasted something more. Life and hope.

Darius.

The name lit like a beacon in her mind.

"Open the book. Please, Sarah."

The book. She had to open the book. She clamped her jaw shut as the whispers started again, prodding her to speak the words it wanted her to say. Her fingers wouldn't obey her at first. She curled them against the binding and yanked with every ounce of strength she had left.

The pain was excruciating. She felt one finger snap and then another. She screamed as her fragile bones were broken, but she didn't stop. Darius was depending on her. Their lives and freedom depended on her.

She dug deep and found a single spark of light within her. She drew on it, fanning it to life. Her eyes flew open, and she met Darius's worried green gaze. She opened her mouth and gave a primal scream, pouring every ounce of energy she possessed into opening the book. The covers parted—not all the way, but far enough. Darius thrust the candle flame against the pages.

They smoldered and then burst into flames. Every window in the church exploded, blowing shards inward, like tiny missiles. Several stung her skin, but they didn't really hurt. She was beyond pain at this point.

She could hear the priest now, but his voice was muffled. The wind whipped with the fury of a hurricane, but their circle remained strong. The pages burned while the binding remained intact. The flames were perilously close to her hands, but she couldn't let go of the book. Not yet. Not until every last page was ash.

"Hold it over the font," Father Simon ordered.

She couldn't move, but felt Darius lift her right off her feet. He set her down in front of the stone vessel and angled her arms so they were over the holy water. The flames were hot against her skin. She knew she was getting singed but really didn't care.

Strong arms wrapped around her from behind. Darius. He'd changed her life. She didn't mind dying now that she knew he'd be safe from the book.

"Stay with me," he commanded. He was always ordering her around, wasn't he? But she knew it was because he cared.

The last page turned to ash and the binding began to smolder.

"She needs to drop the book," Darius yelled.

"Not yet," Father Simon warned. "The binding needs to go, too."

"It will burn her."

"Better that than dead," the priest pointed out.

She wanted to tell Darius not to worry, but talking was still beyond her. It was as though her entire body was wrapped in thick padding, insulated from the pain and suffering she was enduring.

Darius swore and slid his hands down her arms until his hands were under hers, supporting them. She was grateful, as standing was becoming incredibly difficult.

Flames licked at her fingers. Darius yanked the book out of her hands and held it cupped in one of his. The flames attacked the book with a vengeance, burning quickly and easily.

"Now," Father Simon commanded. Darius tilted his hand and dropped the remaining flaming mass and all the ash into the holy water in the font. He held her hands over the font and wiped them so not a single piece of ash remained. She could feel his touch but not her own hands. She was drifting, somewhere between reality and dreams.

Father Simon continued to pray, and the wind that whipped around them suddenly died as quickly as it had come, leaving all in silence.

As though the wind had been the only thing holding her upright, Sarah's knees gave out and she collapsed. Before she could hit the floor, Darius caught her.

"Is it done?" he asked.

Father Simon nodded. "The holy water and ashes need to be buried in a consecrated grave. "I've already cleared a space. You'll have to lift the font and carry it out back. It all needs to go into the hole."

Darius left the circle. As he did, every flame suddenly died.

For all the violence of the night, the pews were still standing. Broken glass covered every surface, hymnals were strewn everywhere, and several of the holy statues had toppled and broken. But their circle had remained intact.

"Clear off a space for her," Darius commanded. Father Simon used his shirtsleeve to wipe off a corner of one of the pews. Darius set her down carefully. "I'll be right back," he promised. "Keep an eye on her."

She watched him as he went back to the heavy stone font and lifted it right off the floor. He disappeared out the open door with it in his arms. He was safe and the book was destroyed. It almost didn't seem real.

"How are you feeling?" The good father sounded concerned, but she couldn't bring herself to care, nor could she answer him. She was still lost, unable to find her voice.

She felt his hand on her forehead and heard his prayers. She was so tired but didn't dare close her eyes, not until Darius returned. Had they really destroyed the book, or was it all an illusion?

Worry spiked, breaking through the first layer of insulation around her. Her breathing increased and her heart began to race. She had to find Darius.

Then he was back, striding into the room and filling it with his presence. His arms were empty, and he wiped his hands on the legs of his jeans. "I filled the hole in the graveyard back in," he told the priest.

Father Simon nodded. "I'll have sod and gravel laid and a stone erected tomorrow. That grave will look as though it's been here for decades." He looked from Darius to her. "You need to leave. It may no longer be safe for you here."

Darius looked as handsome as ever as he came to her and lifted her into his arms.

"She needs tending," the priest said. She could have told Father Simon not to worry, that Darius would take good care of her, but she didn't have the energy to bother.

"She is mine." Darius statement should have raised her feminist hackles. Instead, it made her feel all warm and tingly inside. Cared for.

Her head lolled on his shoulder and her eyelids fluttered shut. Now that she knew for sure Darius was safe, she let go and tumbled into darkness.

Chapter Twenty-Four

Darius kept his hand wrapped around Sarah's wrist so he could feel her pulse. It was slow but steady, a sure sign she was still alive, still with him. It had been over twenty-four hours since they'd destroyed that damn book, and she'd shown no signs of waking since they'd arrived at the safe house. He'd talked to Tarrant and to Ezra and Nic, but none of them could offer any advice.

He'd cleaned the dried blood from around her nose and ears. Two of her fingers were swollen and bruised. He'd straightened and taped both of them. The burns on her hands were superficial, and he'd used an ointment he'd found in the first-aid kit on the plane to treat them.

It wasn't as though he could take Sarah to a hospital. He could just imagine that scenario. "She was hurt while ridding the world of an evil manuscript." Yeah, that wouldn't exactly go over well. They'd try to admit him to the psych ward.

Then there was the fact that the Knights of the Dragon were still out there. Just because the book was gone didn't mean the Knights were.

He rubbed his fingers up and down her arm, willing her to wake.

When he'd left the church, there'd been no sign of their driver, so he'd taken the priest's car and driven back to the airfield. While he was waiting for the plane to be refueled, he'd contacted Tarrant and told him his plans. Then he'd strapped Sarah into the seat next to him and flown to one of his safe houses in North Dakota. He'd thought about going back to Tarrant's fortress or even to Ezra in Maine—no way in hell would he take her to Las Vegas, which was where Nic still was—but he wanted her to himself.

It was the drakon part of his nature. She was his treasure. His to guard and to protect.

So he'd brought her to one of his many hideaways. He had them scattered all over the world. Some he hadn't visited in decades, but they were all there, just waiting until he needed them. He made certain they were all kept in working order. This was one of his favorites. It was small but well-built and blended almost perfectly with the landscape. Unless someone knew it was here, they wouldn't find it.

Even with the Knights still searching for his plane, he thought they'd be safe enough for a day or two. The private air strip, like the cabin, was remote.

He reluctantly released Sarah's hand and stared out the window. He had a perfect view of mountains, trees, and rocks, lots of rocks. This place usually relaxed him, but not this time.

He stood and stretched his arms over his head. He was stiff and, if he was being truthful, tired. Yes, he could normally go days without sleep, but fighting the evil in the book and destroying it, coupled with all the travel, plus days without adequate sleep, and he had to admit he was exhausted.

Sarah was tucked under the covers. She wasn't totally naked, but close enough. He'd removed her shoes and jeans, along with her sweater, leaving her in her underwear and his shirt. The temptation to strip her bare had almost been too much to resist, but he had.

Swearing, he yanked off his T-shirt and sat on the side of the bed. Sarah didn't move as he unlaced his boots and shucked them. Keeping his jeans in place, he lay down on the bed beside her, staying above the covers.

He wrapped one arm around her waist and pulled her into the curve of his body. She fit perfectly, like she'd been made for him.

He was still in awe of what she'd done back in the church. She'd stood tall and resolute, fighting the evil taint of the book, fighting the compulsion to do as the book commanded. Through it all, she hadn't wavered.

She, who was human, had shown more loyalty, more courage and heart than any paranormal creature or human male he'd ever met. He wouldn't say the last out loud or she'd accuse him of being chauvinistic. And perhaps he was. He'd grown up in a time when women had been strong. They'd worked alongside their men for survival, but they'd also been protected and cherished as the life-givers they were.

He kissed the top of her head. He knew just how strong she was and was in awe. Now he simply wanted to cherish her.

He also wanted to keep her.

"You're thinking too hard. I can hear you," she mumbled. His heart squeezed when she spoke, and he quickly rolled her onto her back.

"You're awake." He ran his fingers over her precious face, relieved that the grayish cast was finally gone from her skin. She was still too pale, but it was an improvement. Better yet, the lines of pain that had etched her face had disappeared. "How are you feeling?"

"Like I fought a tornado and lost." She shifted her head slightly and frowned. "Where are we?"

"North Dakota."

Her eyes widened. "How did we get here?" She suddenly jolted. "The book. Is it gone? Did we destroy it?"

"You don't remember?" He placed his palm on her forehead, concerned by her lack of memory. She didn't have a fever.

She raised her hand and pinched the bridge of her nose. "It's fuzzy. I remember the darkness. It was so cold." She shivered, and he pulled her tighter against his body, sharing his warmth with her.

"You were holding the book."

"That's right." She licked her lips, and he groaned. He wanted to lick her lips for her, but she was in no shape for what he wanted to do to her. She needed rest and care. He ignored the incessant throbbing of his cock and focused on comforting Sarah.

"My fingers." She held up her left hand and stared at the two that were taped. "They're broken, aren't they?"

He nodded. "Broken or dislocated, I'm not sure which. I set them before I taped them. I couldn't risk taking you to a hospital."

She nodded and the cotton pillowcase scrunched beneath her head. "No, a hospital is definitely out." She paused for a moment. "I understood the language of the book."

"What?" He hadn't realized that.

"It was prodding me to say words that would imprison you. It wanted me to trap you."

Darius's blood ran cold. If she'd given in to the compulsion, he might well be a prisoner of the Knights.

"You're sure it's gone? The book was destroyed?" Her fear touched his soul.

"Yes," he assured her. "I watched it burn, watched the ashes disintegrate in the holy water. Then I carried the remains out to the cemetery and buried it, water, font, and all, in a consecrated grave. And that was after I used drakon fire to burn anything that was left." He ran his fingers through her short hair, loving the way the brown strands clung to his skin. "Father Simon promised to have a stone erected and to lay sod. He's probably already done it."

Her chocolate-brown eyes widened. "How long have I been out?"

"More than a day. You didn't stir during the flight. Didn't have to watch me land," he teased.

"Small consolation," she muttered. "An entire day."

"You've been through a lot." He couldn't stop petting her, running the tips of his fingers over her face, needing to reassure himself she was really awake.

"It's like the book wanted to suck me into it, or at least my soul." She shuddered. "I never want to touch anything that tainted and evil again." Her frown deepened. "Do you think there are more books like that out there in the world?"

"Unfortunately, I do." It was a worry they all shared. "It doesn't make sense to have only one, especially since Herman Temple isn't the leader of the Knights. There have to be more, but not many. Maybe three or four. They wouldn't want too many people to have access to such powerful knowledge."

She nodded and sighed. "They'll still be searching for us, won't they?"

He couldn't lie to her. "Yes. But don't worry, Sarah. I'll protect you."

• • •

His words soothed her but were also a knife to her heart. Was she nothing more than an obligation to him? "I can take care of myself." She'd meant the words to come out with more force and conviction, but she was still incredibly weak. Her entire body was trembling, probably partly from hunger if she'd been out as long as Darius had said.

His scowl was dark and fierce. "I'll take care of you."

"Why?" This probably wasn't the time to talk about their relationship. No, scratch that. It definitely wasn't the time. Not when she was feeling so shaky and, yes, fragile.

"Why?" he parroted.

"Yes. Why do you want to take care of me? You don't owe me anything. We did what we set out to do. The book is gone. There's no need for you to be burdened with me any longer."

His eyes narrowed and began to glow. His entire body tensed before he rolled off the bed. He stood there, hands on his hips, looking impossibly handsome and extremely pissed off.

"Do you want to leave?" Before she could attempt to answer, he swiped his hand in the air in front of him. "Forget it. The Knights are still out there, and they'll be searching for you. They'll want to make you pay for what you've done. Even more importantly, they know about your talent and will want to use it to help them find other valuable books. It's safer for you to stay with me."

A muscle twitched in his jaw and every muscle of his naked torso stood out in chiseled perfection. The color of his tattoo seemed deeper, richer. He looked like some pagan warlord, ready to fight. All he was missing was a sword or axe. In a word, he was magnificent.

"Is that the only reason you want me to stay?" she prodded. "Because I'll be safer with you?" She pushed upright and rested her back against the headboard.

Darius began to pace at the end of the bed, back and forth, his long strides eating up the small distance. The bedroom wasn't large, but it was lovely. The floors were hardwood, the furniture rustic. She particularly liked the large picture window off to her left and the fireplace on the far wall. There was no fire crackling there at the moment, but maybe he'd build one later if she asked.

He stopped and crossed his arms over his chest. He certainly wasn't playing fair. How was she supposed to concentrate on the problem at hand when he was half naked? Two could play that game. She let the covers fall to her waist. His gaze followed. She was still wearing his shirt, and her underwear as well. Hardly an ensemble to entice him.

Which was probably just as well. They needed to settle things between them before they muddied the waters with sex again.

"You're staying with me." He said each word slowly, and she heard his underlying anger. More than that, she heard fear. Or maybe she was only hearing what she wanted.

"But why?"

Darius threw back his head and roared. She was surprised flames didn't shoot out of his mouth. His eyes darkened. "Because you are mine."

Her heart softened, and she held out her hand to him. He peered suspiciously at it for a long time before he finally took it. She tugged, and he reluctantly sat on the edge of the bed, next to her.

"You're a drakon and I'm human," she reminded him. "You're immortal, while I only have a few decades to live."

He shook his head. "No. I won't believe that. There has to be a way." He looked determined and ferocious. "You will drink my blood. That will keep you young."

"That's what the Knights do." She shook her head, every cell of her body revolting against the idea of doing the same thing they did.

"You would rather die and leave me?" There was such pain and longing in his voice it tore at her heart.

She threw herself at him and wrapped her arms around his neck. "I never want to leave you, but I don't want to be like them."

He buried his face in her hair and inhaled deeply. "Oh,

Sarah, you could never be like them. They are parasites. You…you are my heart."

She peered up at him and saw the truth in his eyes. "I love you," she told him. She pressed her fingers against his lips before he could speak. "You don't need to say anything back. When I thought I was going to die, when I knew I would die to keep you safe, I knew I loved you. I promised myself if I survived, I'd tell you."

She slid out of his arms and stood on shaky legs. "I need to go to the bathroom and get a shower." She made her way to what she hoped was the door to the bathroom. She reached out and grabbed the doorjamb for support.

When she looked back, Darius was still sitting on the bed watching her, his eyes no longer haunted but filled with male satisfaction. He came to his feet in a hurry. "You are hungry. I'll cook something while you get cleaned up." His gaze narrowed and swept her from head to toe. She knew she must look like a mess, but that didn't stop her entire body from heating at his perusal. "I'll get you another one of my shirts to wear."

He went to the rustic wooden dresser, opened a middle drawer, and pulled out a long-sleeved cotton shirt. It was dark brown and looked comfortable and warm. He dug around the top drawer and came up with a pair of socks. They'd be far too big for her feet, but they'd keep them warm.

"I need clothes," she muttered.

"That's being taken care of. I'll have to drive to the nearest town tomorrow to pick up the package."

"You didn't order it online did you?" The Knights were everywhere. He gave her an offended look that patently said he wasn't an idiot.

"Tarrant ordered it. All I have to do is pick it up."

She nodded, trying not to laugh. He was extremely disgruntled. "I'm sorry." The least she could do was apologize for offending his male sensibilities.

He grunted and brought the clothes to her. "Do you need me to help you?" His voice deepened, and she began to perspire at the mere suggestion of him wet and naked in the shower with her.

She began to tremble, and she hugged the clothes to her body.

Darius began to back away. "Probably not a good idea." He swung around and stomped out of the room, leaving her standing there sweaty and turned on.

"Shower," she reminded herself. She shut the door to the bathroom, set the clean clothes down, and turned on the water in the stall. She longed to get clean. Probably just as well she hadn't taken Darius up on his offer to help her. It would have been a tight fit with both of them.

She groaned and her entire body clenched with need. Oh yeah, it would have been a tight fit all right. She stripped off her dirty clothes and left them in a pile on the floor. It was awkward with two of her fingers taped, but she managed. The water was nice and hot and exactly what she needed. There was soap and shampoo on a ledge, and she set out to use both.

• • •

Darius thought he'd lose his mind as he listened to the sound of the shower. Sarah was naked with water running over her skin. He growled and slammed a pan on the stove. He wanted to soap his hands and run them all over her body.

He bowed his head and simply stood in the middle of the tiny kitchen, breathing in and out as the grilled cheese sandwich began to sizzle. Sarah loved him. He'd hoped but hadn't expected her to say it, not so soon. She'd been willing to die to protect him. She'd fought the evil of the Knight's secret book to keep him safe.

His breathing increased and smoke billowed from his nostrils as his dragon side sought to take control. His beast didn't like the idea of Sarah being in danger any more than he did.

His phone rang, and he shook off the compulsion. "Yeah." He knew it had to be one of his brothers.

"Any change?" Tarrant asked. He'd been calling every few hours to check on Sarah's condition.

"She's awake. She's in the shower, and I'm making her something to eat."

"That's good. I'm glad to hear it." Tarrant paused. "I like her."

"So do I." He knew Tarrant didn't mean anything by it, but his words fanned the flames of jealousy. "I'm keeping her."

"I thought you might." His brother's easy agreement allowed him to settle before he said something totally stupid.

"I'm going to feed her my blood to keep her from aging." No way was he going to lose Sarah if he could do anything to prevent it.

"Hold off on that a bit. She's safe for now, and I want to do some more digging into the whole mate thing. Just because we don't know anything about it, doesn't mean there aren't other drakons out there who do. Maybe their sires told them more than ours did."

"You think that might change things?" It was an intriguing idea, one that appealed to him. The idea that he could keep Sarah forever made his heart sing.

"I have no idea, but it can't hurt to ask."

"Your list?" Tarrant and his famous list. For once, Darius was grateful for his brother's obsessive need to be able to contact as many of their kind as possible.

"I've already contacted them all and asked if any of them have information. I also told them about the book we destroyed so they'll know what to do if they come up against something similar."

"Good." And it was good. For far too long, the Knights of the Dragon had hunted them. Maybe it was time the drakons stopped being so solitary and banded together to fight back.

The shower turned off, reminding him that he was supposed to be cooking something for Sarah to eat. He flipped the sandwich. The bread was dark brown but thankfully not burned. "I've got to go. Call me if you hear anything."

"Will do. And don't forget to head to town tomorrow to pick up your package." Tarrant paused and then continued. "You know you'll have to leave soon after. You won't be safe there once you've been into town."

The sad reality was that they couldn't trust the humans in town not to pass on information to the Knights. And Darius couldn't even blame the townsfolk. The Knights would masquerade as police officers and people would talk. Hell, for all they knew, there were Knights in every level of law enforcement and government.

"We'll leave soon after."

"Where will you go?"

Darius turned the heat off under the pan and picked up a spoon to stir the chicken noodle soup he had simmering on another burner. "I'm not sure yet. I'll let you know when I get there." He ended the call and tucked the phone in his pocket just as Sarah entered the room.

The shirt she was wearing fell to mid-thigh and gaped at the neckline, and the socks were pulled almost to her knees. She hadn't bothered to put on her jeans. She should have looked ridiculous in his shirt and socks. Darius wanted to sweep her into his arms and carry her back to the bedroom.

"Sit. I have soup and sandwiches ready."

Sarah slid onto one of the kitchen chairs and waited as he served up the simple meal. Neither of them spoke as they ate. It was a comfortable silence.

As soon as she was finished, Darius cleared the table and came back to stand next to her. Her hair was damp and her face makeup free. Her clothes were too big and she was still too slender, but to him, she was the most beautiful woman in the world. Her beauty and kindness and courage shone from her eyes.

He went to his knees beside her chair, and she swiveled so she was facing him. "What is it?" she asked. "What's wrong?"

He cupped her precious face. "Nothing. Nothing is wrong. Everything is right." Then he kissed her.

Chapter Twenty-Five

"We've got them."

Herman Temple swiveled around in his chair as Riggs strode into his office. "Where?"

"A private airfield just outside of Salvation, North Carolina." Riggs stopped on the other side of the desk, his eyes gleaming with excitement. "We've had feelers out to every small airfield around the country, offering a small monetary reward for information. A man called in. Seems he picked up two people after their plane landed and took them to see a priest."

"A priest." Herman rubbed his chin and considered the possibilities. "Go. We need to know everything this priest knows."

"I'm on it." Riggs left without a backward glance.

Herman pondered the changes in Riggs over the past few days. Most people wouldn't have noticed, but Herman wasn't just anyone. He hadn't lived for as long and risen as far as he had within the Knights without observing such things. Plus, the dragon's blood he'd ingested over the decades had increased his ability to detect small details, which was very useful when it came to business, and also when dealing with his people.

And Matthew Riggs was different. And different in his world was never good. The change had occurred after he'd sent his man to Boston, to Karina.

His gut tightened as he considered the ramifications. Riggs was either sleeping with the leader of the Knights, working for her, or both. Either way, Riggs's usefulness to him might soon be at an end.

And speaking of endings. He picked up his phone and punched in a number. "Karina, my dear, I just wanted to give you an update." Riggs had probably already informed her, but better to keep up appearances.

"Have you found Varkas?"

Always so brittle, so single-minded. Herman couldn't imagine sleeping with her. Yes, Karina was beautiful, but he'd be too worried about getting a knife in the back to be able to enjoy himself.

"We know where he was last. Riggs is on his way to investigate. We'll have Varkas soon enough."

"Call me when you do." She disconnected the call. Herman took a deep breath, forcing himself to remain calm. He hated the way she treated him like a lackey. He was older than she was, had been a member of the Knights far longer.

But she came from the founding family. Knew all their secrets. Secrets Herman coveted.

He hit another button on his phone. Christian answered on the first ring. "Any news?" his son asked in lieu of a greeting.

"Get to the plane. Fast. Riggs is on his way to an airfield in North Carolina. Varkas and Ms. Anderson were seen there."

"I'm not far from the airport now. I'll probably beat Riggs there."

"Good." His son was like him. Ambitious. "I want

someone there to look out for our interests."

Christian paused, and Herman knew he'd surprised him. "I understand." Christian's voice gave away nothing, but Herman knew he'd keep a close eye on Riggs. And Riggs would keep a close eye on Christian.

Herman thought about joining them, but knew he was better off here. Varkas might have passed through North Carolina, but Herman knew he was long gone. The question was, what did he do while he was there?

• • •

Darius let himself sink into the kiss. Sarah's tongue stroked his and sent pulses of pleasure bursting throughout his body. He slid his hand around her nape and held her as he tasted her sweet lips.

"I was afraid you might never wake up." His voice was husky with arousal and remembered fear. He rested his forehead against hers.

"I'm sorry you were so worried."

"Just don't ever do that again."

A soft gurgle of laughter escaped her. "I don't plan on it." Then she sighed. "But then again, I never planned on any of this. What's our next move?"

He eased back and rested his hands on her thighs. Her skin was warm and smooth. It would take no effort at all to ease the shirt out of his way and have access to her sweet body. His cock throbbed with no relief in sight. Sarah had been through a trauma. She needed care, not for him to jump her and carry her back to bed.

"I'll pick up the parcel Tarrant arranged to have delivered, and then we leave town."

Sarah rubbed her hand over her face. "There's nowhere safe, is there?"

Darius reluctantly shook his head. "Not until we destroy Herman Temple and everyone who knows about us."

Sarah shuddered, her face pale. "That's—" She broke off before she said more.

Darius slowly stood. A sick feeling pervaded his stomach. "It's war, Sarah. Plain and simple. We've left them alone for centuries, hiding and running, but they continue to hunt us." He knew his eyes were probably glowing with barely suppressed anger. "It's time we became the hunters. They won't stop until we're all dead or enslaved. I can't live like that, not anymore."

He turned away, unable to look at Sarah, to see the grief and sadness in her eyes. Darius opened the back door and stepped out onto the porch. The creature inside him wanted to be free. His skin itched and his soul ached.

It wasn't smart to give in to such needs, but he no longer cared. He stripped off his pants just as he heard the soft shuffle of footsteps behind him. Sarah sucked in a breath. "What are you doing?" she asked.

"Reminding myself, and you, of what I really am." He stepped out into the clearing behind the cabin and embraced the dragon that dwelled inside him, that part of himself that was not human.

Thick plate-like armor snapped over his skin as his body changed shape, becoming larger and stronger. His head flattened and his jaw elongated. Claws replaced fingernails and toenails, and wings erupted from either side of his spine.

He stretched, extending his tail and his neck. He felt Sarah's gaze on him and turned his head so he could see her. Her mouth was open, her eyes wide, but not with fear. With wonder.

Darius stayed where he was but extended his neck until his head was practically touching her. She reached out and tentatively touched his face. "I know what you are," she reminded him. "I know who you are." Her hands were soft and tender as they stroked his forehead. "I know you don't want to hurt anyone but that you have no choice. I get that. I do."

Her assurance settled something dangerous bubbling inside him. He wasn't sure what he'd have done if she'd feared him or looked at him like he was nothing more than a killer.

Sarah slid her hand away from his face and sat on the step. She pulled the hem of the cotton shirt over her knees. It was chilly and she wasn't wearing much.

"You should go inside." His voice was deeper and gruffer in this form.

She shook her head. "I want to be with you."

Those six simple words calmed both man and dragon, chaining them more easily than any potion or incantation the Knights had ever created. He was completely and utterly lost and didn't care.

He'd lived alone, except for his brothers, for four thousand years. After knowing Sarah, he couldn't go back to that way any longer. If she left him, he had two choices—death or the Deep Sleep of his kind. He didn't want to live in a world without her.

And that kind of declaration would probably scare her to death. She was human with a limited lifespan. His job was to use his blood to keep her alive, unless he could find another way.

"Darius?" He brought his attention back to Sarah. "What are you thinking about?"

He shook his head. "It doesn't matter."

"I think it does, but that's neither here nor there." She yawned and rubbed her face. "I shouldn't be tired, but I am."

He shifted without thought, going from beast to man in a heartbeat. Her eyes widened and her gaze went straight to his groin. There was no hiding his arousal. He grabbed his jeans and pulled them on.

"Of course you're tired. You've been through an ordeal. You need to rest." He didn't wait for her to stand. He put one arm around her back and the other under her knees and lifted her. He liked the way she automatically wrapped her arms around his neck.

"Will you stay with me?"

He really needed to go to town and get that package. Sarah needed clothes. But that could wait. "Yes, I'll stay with you." No one knew they were here but Tarrant, and Sarah needed to rest and regain her strength.

He pushed the door open with his shoulder and kicked it shut with his foot. He carried her into the bedroom and placed her on the bed. She grabbed his hand and didn't let go. "Stay."

There was no way he could resist her plea, and he didn't want to. He pulled the covers around her and stretched out beside her. "Sleep. I'll watch over you."

She rested her head on his shoulder and placed her hand over his heart. "And I'll watch over you." It only took a few minutes for her to drift off. It worried him that she was so tired after sleeping so long already. She was human, her body much more fragile than his. Whatever she needed, he'd make sure she had.

Even as he closed his eyes, Darius couldn't quite shake the worry that time was running out. They'd have to move soon, even if he had to carry a sleeping Sarah onto the plane.

• • •

The truck rolled to a stop outside a small church, and Riggs studied the building carefully. It was quaint, with its white paint, and looked like it had been here for more than a hundred years. The only exceptional thing about the building was that all the windows seemed to have been smashed.

"This is the place?" he asked the man behind the wheel.

"Yes." The man was sweating. Riggs could practically smell his fear. He should be afraid. He had no idea what he'd involved himself in by making one simple phone call. It was his own greed that had brought him to this point. Like Judas, he was betraying a friend for monetary gain.

"And Father Simon is inside?" Riggs didn't trust anyone but figured the man was too afraid to lie. Christian shifted impatiently in his seat. Riggs had been pissed to find the bastard waiting at the airport for him. He knew right then and there that Herman no longer trusted him, not if he'd sent his son to go with him. Herman didn't trust Christian, which meant he now trusted Riggs even less.

"He should be."

"And you saw Varkas and the woman leave?" Riggs wanted as many facts as he could get before he disposed of the informant. The Knights couldn't afford to leave loose ends.

"I don't know their names, but they left and got back on the plane. I was parked close to the airfield watching for them to come back. I heard the man make a phone call while he was fueling the plane." He drummed his fingers nervously on the steering wheel.

Riggs pinned the driver with a glare. "And I'm only hearing about this now?"

The man rubbed one of his hands over his faded jeans. He stank of cigarette smoke. "I was hiding but could hear some of it."

"Well?"

His eyes took on a sly glint. "It's worth more?"

"Yes." Christian made an impatient sound, but Riggs silenced him with a glare. "It's worth more." It didn't matter how much they offered to pay the man since they had no intentions of ever allowing him to collect.

"He mentioned North Dakota. That's all I heard."

"And the woman?"

He shrugged. "He carried her onto the plane. Like she was sick or passed out or sleeping or something."

"And that's everything you know?"

The informant nodded vigorously.

"Okay, let's go talk with Father Simon." They climbed out of the vehicle, and he and Christian followed the local as he led the way to the church door. Riggs let him go first. He hated having Christian at his back. He didn't trust the bastard.

As he pulled open the door, an idea formed in Riggs's mind. The more he thought about it, the more he liked it. He waved Christian ahead of him. The younger Temple frowned but did as he was told. That was Christian's biggest problem. He was too used to being told what to do and didn't know how to act independently. That would play right into Riggs's hands.

Riggs had been expecting the priest to be a much younger man, not one who looked to be in his sixties. With his white hair and beard and T-shirt, he looked more like an aging hippie.

"William," Father Simon addressed the local man. "What are you doing here? Have you all come to help replace the windows?" The priest shrugged. "Vandals. Even in a small town they can be a problem."

Riggs noticed the priest didn't approach them. The man was smarter than he let on. "I'm looking for someone, Father Simon. Maybe you can help me."

"If I can. Who are you looking for?"

Riggs gave the old man credit. He looked like he didn't have a clue. "A man and a woman," Riggs prompted.

The old man's gaze narrowed and then shot to the informant. "What have you done?"

"I'm sorry, Father," the man babbled. "I needed the

money."

"Shut up." Riggs cuffed the man in the back of the head.

"You should have come to me." Father Simon shook his head. "You won't live long enough to spend your money."

The traitor glanced from Father Simon to Riggs. This was going to get messy faster than he'd hoped. Riggs pulled his gun from his shoulder holster and aimed it at his target. The man turned and ran for the door. Riggs didn't bother telling him he couldn't outrun a bullet. He simply shot him in the back. The body was still falling when he turned his attention back to Father Simon.

"You understand there's more at stake than money." Riggs wouldn't underestimate the priest.

"We can give you anything you want," Christian rashly promised. "Money, power, anything."

And this was why Christian would never be a leader. It was obvious to Riggs that none of those things interested the good priest. "I don't want to hurt you," he told the old man. "I can make your death quick and painless." He paused to let his words sink in. "Or I can make it long and very painful."

The priest laughed. "My son, do you think that frightens me?" He raised his own hand and a knife glinted in his fist.

For the first time, Riggs began to worry. The old man might kill himself before he had a chance to question him. "Isn't suicide a sin?" He didn't know much about Christianity, not being a man of any faith, but he knew that much.

The old man shrugged. "I'm dying anyway. I have cancer." He tilted his head to one side. "And maybe I won't kill myself. Maybe you two will be the ones to die."

The back of Riggs's neck prickled. The priest was seriously creeping him out. He didn't seem scared, just calm and determined.

"We can cure your cancer," Christian promised rashly.

No surprise showed in the priest's eyes. Not a flicker.

"You know, don't you?" Riggs asked.

Father Simon nodded. "Yes, I do. But I'm human, and not meant to live any longer than is natural for me. I'm fine with that. I've had a happy, productive life. I've made good friends. Friends I won't betray." The priest turned his attention to Christian, a shrewd look in his eyes. "Not like your friend here. He'll betray you just as William did me."

Christian's gaze narrowed, and he pulled his own gun. "I don't think so."

Fuck. Riggs turned and fired as Christian uttered his last word. Shock crossed his face as he tumbled back. The shot was straight to the heart, and he was dead before he hit the floor. "I really hadn't wanted to do that yet."

"But you would have eventually," the priest pointed out.

"Yeah, I would have." Riggs had to give the old man credit. He was totally calm in spite of the situation.

"You should walk away while you still have a chance," the priest told him.

"I can't do that." And surprisingly, Riggs wished he could. He liked Father Simon. He reminded him of his grandfather, a tough, uncompromising son of a bitch who'd held honor above anything. His grandfather wouldn't understand the choices Riggs had made, but for better or worse, he'd made them.

"Then you know what you have to do." Father Simon held up his hand. "I won't betray my friend no matter what you do to me. Are you willing to take the risk that I might get lucky and slit your throat before you can finish me?"

Again, prickles raced down Riggs's spine. No matter that he was a priest, this man had a past, and a dark one. The way he held the knife in front of him, and the ease with which he did it, told Riggs he knew how to use it.

"Tell me about the book," he demanded.

The priest's expression remained the same, betraying

nothing. Then he sprang forward, knife slashing out.

Instinctively, Riggs raised his gun and fired. The old priest jerked and seemed to be suspended in midair for a long moment before tumbling to the ground. Riggs swore as he walked to the man. He checked for a pulse, but the priest was dead, and Riggs didn't know any more than he had when he'd walked in the door.

He searched the priest's pockets but found nothing of interest. Then he systematically looked through the church. He checked the office and the computer but found nothing. Father Simon had been damn careful and taken his secrets to the grave with him. It was time for Riggs to leave.

He examined the church. It was old and well-built, but it was also constructed of wood. He tore down banners and used what was at hand to start several small blazes burning. Then he headed for the door, stopping long enough to remove Christian's phone and identification.

He closed the door behind him and didn't look back. Thankfully, the keys were in the ignition of the truck. Riggs slid into the driver's side, started the vehicle, and pulled away. The trip to the airfield went quickly. The pilot said nothing when Riggs climbed on board alone and told him they were heading to North Dakota.

Riggs strapped in and was already calling Karina by the time the plane left the ground.

"Yes," she answered. He loved the sound of her voice, lush and sultry. He wasn't stupid. He knew she was using him, but he was using her, too, and they both knew it. They were a lot alike.

"There was a slight problem." He told her about Christian and what had occurred, leaving nothing out.

"You're on your way to North Dakota."

It wasn't a question, but he answered her anyway. "Yes."

"Check the plane when you find it. We need to know

where Darius Varkas has been."

Riggs had planned to check it, but now he'd have to share his information with her, or at least some of it. Time would tell what he held back and what he told her.

"I need to get my people on this," he reminded her.

While Herman Temple would have been livid at his obvious attempt to get off the phone with her, Karina merely laughed. "You do that. And, Matthew, I'll be waiting."

His body tightened and his cock stirred at the sexual promise in her voice. Having sex with Karina was like sleeping with a venomous snake. She was sleek and beautiful and deadly as hell. Was it any wonder he was infatuated with her?

But he wasn't stupid. He ended the call and contacted his computer guy. "I need a list of every airfield, public and private, in North Dakota. Our plane is somewhere in that state, and we need to find it."

Chapter Twenty-Six

It was light out when Sarah woke. She had no idea what time it was or even what day, and she really didn't care. All that mattered was she was alive and with Darius. His arm was wrapped around her and her head was pillowed on his chest. Even in sleep he kept her close.

Sunshine illuminated the space, giving it a warm, cozy glow. She snuggled beneath the covers, feeling more like herself than she had since they'd destroyed the book.

"How are you feeling?" Darius asked. She wasn't surprised he was awake.

"Good." She remembered waking several times to go to the bathroom, but other than that, she'd slept very well.

He moved his big hand up and down her back, the motion soothing and comforting. "We have to leave today."

She sighed and ran her fingers across his chest, tracing the intricate whorls of his tattoo. How could she resist when it was right there? He was still wearing only his jeans, having slept in them. That couldn't have been comfortable.

He caught her hand and flattened it against his hard chest.

His skin was warm, and she kneaded it with her fingertips.

He gave a gruff laugh. "Keep that up and we won't get out of here anytime soon."

She loved the way he responded to her every touch. "Is it so dangerous to stay here? We're safe, aren't we?"

"For now. But the Knights have more resources than you can imagine. We need to keep moving, stay one step ahead of them."

She tilted her head back and kissed the strong edge of his jaw. Darius really was magnificent, whether in human or dragon form. "Soon. We'll go soon. We can even stop and pick up the package on our way out of town. I can change on the plane."

"Efficient." He shoved the covers away and lifted her like she weighed nothing at all. She found herself lying on top of him, staring down into his deep, slumberous green eyes.

Her grin slid away when he cupped her ass and squeezed. The shirt she was wearing had been pushed up, leaving her lower half bared. She groaned when he dipped his fingers into her moist depths.

"You're mine, Sarah." He kissed her, and she let herself sink into the seductive heat. His lips were firm and supple, his tongue warm and demanding. She gave him everything he wanted and more.

Her entire body thrummed with awareness. He stroked her sensitive folds even as he kissed her almost into oblivion. It was always this way when he touched her. He took her over, made her lose all sense of self.

She wasn't having it. Not this time. It was her turn to send him reeling. She pushed away, and he immediately withdrew. "Is everything okay? Are you feeling sick? I should have kept my hands to myself," he muttered.

Her poor drakon. He was extremely aroused. There was no mistaking the thick bulge pressing against her stomach as anything other than his swollen shaft. She pushed back until she was sitting on top of him, perched on his upper thighs.

"You have entirely too much clothing on." She'd surprised him. She could tell he'd been expecting her to get off him and walk away. Wasn't happening. This time, she was going to have some fun.

She had the button undone and the zipper almost down when he wrapped his hand around her wrist, shackling it. "Are you sure? We don't have to do this."

"Don't you want me?" She knew he did, but she wanted to hear the words.

He swallowed, the sound audible. "If I wanted you any more than I do, I'd explode."

She couldn't help but smile. "Then what's the problem?" She tugged until he released her wrist and she could go back to unzipping his jeans. Having two of her fingers taped made it more difficult, but she managed. She wasn't about to let a minor injury stop her. His cock was hard and ready. She stroked from root to tip, wringing a deep groan from him.

Sarah climbed off him and grabbed the thick denim. She tugged, and he helped her remove his jeans. When he was totally naked, she gave a hum of pleasure. He really was gorgeous. His magnificent body was bisected by the tattoo that covered the left half of him from his neck down. It made him look primitive and dangerous. He certainly was that, but he was so much more.

"Sarah." He reached for her but she scrambled out of reach.

"No. I want to touch you. This time I'm in charge."

The low growl that came from deep in his chest made the fine hair on the back of her neck stir. She wasn't frightened. Oh no, she was turned on.

"You just lie back and enjoy yourself."

The scowl on his face suggested he didn't like that idea.

She hesitated but only for a heartbeat. "Trust me. You'll enjoy this."

Darius lay still on the mattress, but he was by no means relaxed. Tension radiated from every pore in his big body. She scooted up so she was kneeling by his waist. His chest was incredible. Thick bands of muscle roped the lower half. She skated her fingers over them and drew a loud groan from him.

She let her hands drift higher, tracing every hard line. Muscle rippled beneath his skin in response to her touch.

"Take off the shirt." His ragged command made her nipples tighten and her pussy clench. She slowly lifted the garment over her head. It wasn't quite a strip tease, but she did try to make it as provocative as possible.

He moaned her name and reached for her. She held the shirt in front of her and shook her head. "My turn. Remember?"

He grunted but dropped his hands back down onto the mattress with a hard thud. She almost laughed. Her drakon looked so unhappy. She glanced down at his lower half. He might not like not being able to touch her, but he found it arousing.

She tossed aside the shirt.

"Finish it."

Since wearing only a pair of socks wasn't particularly sexy, she pulled them off. When she was totally naked, he skimmed his heated gaze over her.

"You're incredible."

She felt herself blushing beneath his stare. She'd told him she loved him. And while he hadn't given the words back to her, she knew he cared for her. That was enough. He'd taken care of her and put her needs before his own. *Mine.* He'd called her that. She had to remember he wasn't human, but much more. And he wanted her to stay. Hell, he wanted her to drink his blood so she'd stay young and be able to be with him.

His actions said more than words ever could. Now it was her turn to show him how much she cared.

She knelt beside him and wrapped her uninjured hand around his cock. He was thick and pulsed with life. She licked her lips, and he groaned. A quick glance told her he wasn't going to wait much longer.

Sarah lowered her head and stroked her tongue over the mushroom-shaped head, lapping a bead of liquid from the slit. He made a sound that was half pleasure and half pain.

She circled the tip, swirling her tongue around the sensitive ridge before taking the head into her mouth. He yelled her name as she teased him. She released him with a wet pop. "Do you like that?"

He growled, his entire body vibrating. She took that as a yes and went down on him again. She gripped the lower half of his shaft and began to pump her hand up and down. She used her tongue and lips for maximum pleasure. And when she withdrew, she lightly scraped her teeth over his sensitive flesh.

He fisted the bedclothes, tugging at the sheet until it ripped. His hips flexed, jerking upward as she brought her mouth down on him. He tasted salty and warm. She licked her lips and went back for more. His musky smell surrounded her, made her want him even more.

He might not be touching her, but his reaction to her was pushing her close to the edge. She ached for him.

Darius released the abused bed sheet and tangled his fingers in her hair. He gave a gentle tug until she reluctantly released him. "You have to stop." His chest was rising and falling like a bellows at a forge.

"Why?" She wasn't ready to stop.

"Why?" He shook his head. "I'm too close, and I want to be inside you." He dragged her over him, and she moaned when her slick folds rubbed against his erection. He swore, and his fingers dug into her hips. "Guide me home."

It wasn't just the words, but the way he said them that made her heart skip a beat. With him holding her steady, she gripped his cock and placed the thick head against her opening. He waited, the tip poised at the entrance to her body.

"Sarah." Her name came out as a strangled plea.

She pushed down, and his shaft slid inside. She was wet and more than ready to take him. He filled her, stretching the walls of her slick channel, but she didn't stop until she was seated on his pelvis.

Darius released a sigh of pleasure and slid his hands up to cover her breasts. Her pert nipples stabbed at his palms. He massaged the swollen mounds, seeming to know exactly how much pressure to exert to make it the most pleasurable.

Sarah couldn't sit still any longer and began to move. She rose up on her knees until several inches slipped out and then she sat down again. His hands moved from her breasts, down her torso to her hips. He gripped them and guided her in a deep, hard rhythm that grew faster and faster.

"Touch yourself. I want to watch you." His request startled her, but she was so close to coming she didn't care. She touched her fingers to his mouth and he took them inside, licking and sucking on them. When they were nice and wet, she withdrew and delved between her thighs.

She touched her clit and cried out.

"That's it," he encouraged. "Pretend it's my fingers on you." He gripped her hips and kept guiding her up and down his rigid shaft. "Hurry, Sarah."

His urgency spurred hers. She was so very close. She shut her eyes and sank into the passion. She stroked her clit lightly and then with more pressure. Darius pumped his hips, lifting her right off the bed as he pushed into her. It was fast and furious, with little finesse. Raw need engulfed them both.

Her inner muscles clenched and then began to ripple. She cried out as she came, only vaguely aware of Darius's roar of pleasure. His shaft seemed to expand and then she felt the flood of his release. She fell forward and let out another cry as her nipples rubbed against his firm chest.

He banded his arms around her and pressed frantic kisses against the top of her head. "I'll never let you go," he whispered.

It was as good as a declaration of love. Everything inside her settled, and she truly accepted that the life she'd known was over. They had enemies, and who knew how long they'd have to hide or where they'd have to go, but she didn't care. As long as they were together, nothing else mattered.

They lay there a long time, both of them catching their breath. As her heartbeat returned to normal, his thundering pulse also calmed. Darius stroked her back and arms and butt. She wasn't even sure he was aware of the fact he was touching her. He was very tactile, and she enjoyed that part of his nature.

Finally, he sighed, and she knew what was coming. "We have to leave, don't we?"

"Yes."

She was disappointed but didn't want him to know. "Where will we go next?"

He grazed his fingers down the center of her spine. Her inner muscles automatically clenched, and his cock flexed inside her. He might have just come, but he was still hard.

"I'm not sure. Maybe we'll go east again."

"Isn't that dangerous?" She wasn't sure there was anywhere safe.

"Staying in one place is dangerous. We should be fine as long as we keep moving." He was silent for a long time. "We need to dump the plane."

"Why? How will we travel?"

"We've landed in two fairly public places—in North Carolina and here in North Dakota. People have seen us whether we realize it or not. And people talk."

She shivered at the realization of just how exposed they were. In this age of satellite imagining, GPS, and cell phones, there really wasn't anywhere to truly hide.

He tightened his arms around her. "Hey, don't worry. I have a lot of places we can stay, and I know the most remote spots in the country, areas where most people don't dare to venture."

"Do you have a Batcave like Tarrant?" She actually missed the place.

He slowly withdrew, and both of them moaned at the separation. Darius rolled off the bed and then gathered her in his arms. "No one has a place quite like Tarrant."

She laughed as he carried her into the bathroom. "No, I suppose not."

"We'll keep moving and start making plans. We need to get rid of Temple and his people and find out who is in charge of the Knights."

"Offensive, not defensive." It made sense. It wasn't like he could hide anymore.

"Exactly." He set her on the vanity, and she sucked in her breath as her butt hit the cool countertop. "Once we're in the air, I'll make plans to dump the plane and get us a vehicle. I'm thinking it might be time to pay Ezra a visit."

Darius stepped away from her to turn on the shower. As amazing as the view was—and it was spectacular—it was his words that captured her attention. "Your brother?"

"He's got a place in Maine. Almost as isolated as Tarrant's, but we can drive there once we ditch the plane."

She slid off the counter and went to Darius. "Is it safe for us to go to him?" She knew the last thing he wanted to do was put one of his brothers in jeopardy.

"At this point, I'm not sure." He pulled her into the shower, and she stepped beneath the spray, letting the water warm her chilled skin. "I'll talk to Tarrant and Ezra about it. We all have to be careful. No telling what the Knights know about any of us."

She grabbed the soap and began to wash. "The faster we're out of here, the better." She couldn't help but worry. It was as though there was some internal clock ticking down, warning that time was running out.

• • •

Riggs had his seat belt off and was at the door the second the plane landed. He opened the hatch, shoved out the small set of folding stairs, and was on the tarmac in seconds. There it was. The plane they'd been chasing all over the country. It was amazing what you could find out when you offered a monetary reward. Some local aviation buff had remembered seeing the small plane fly overhead not quite two days ago. The timing fit, so Riggs had come to check it out and found the small, private landing strip.

He approached the plane cautiously. Although he didn't think Darius Varkas would have it booby-trapped, it paid to be vigilant. He signaled his men to spread out and wait. They were all well trained and heavily armed. No one was getting on that plane but him.

It didn't take him long to gain access. The interior was what one would expect from an executive jet. The seats were leather and the interior spacious. He ignored it and went straight to the cockpit. He slid into the pilot's seat and accessed the instrumentation. "Damn."

Nothing to show where they'd been, but that was to be expected. Varkas was smart. But was he smart enough?

Riggs knew they'd flown to North Carolina after they left

New York, but where had they been in the time between? He needed the flight data recorder, or the black box, as most people called it, even though it was orange.

Riggs looked around, not really expecting to find anything. He was just about to give up when he noticed the portable aviation GPS mounted on the co-pilot's side. It was turned on and fully functional. "Gotcha."

Riggs smiled. Things were looking up. He accessed the history and noted where the plane had been.

He wanted to use his phone to check the coordinates but didn't dare. He knew the Knights were monitoring him. They kept an eye on everyone's phones, but more so since the security slipup with Sarah Anderson. If the idiot guard hadn't been texting, he would have seen Sarah sneaking around the corridors of Temple's home, and none of this would have happened.

He pulled a notebook out of his pocket and jotted down coordinates. From what he could tell, the plane had been in Washington State, somewhere in the Cascade Mountains. It would be interesting to see who or what was there. It might only be a pit stop like this place, or it could be something more. Either way, he'd find out.

He needed to find Varkas and the book, but there was no way of knowing if Varkas and the woman still had it. All he knew was if it was out there, he wanted it. He'd spent a couple of years now doing Herman Temple's dirty work. The man liked to think he was a big deal, but he was weak. He depended on others to do what needed to be done.

That book was important. It was his ticket to bigger and better things. Riggs didn't need anyone. Not even Karina. All he needed was the book. Capturing Varkas would be the icing on the cake.

Riggs tucked his notebook back in his pocket and then smashed the GPS unit against the floor. He wasn't sure it was totally destroyed so he stamped on it with his boot and pocketed several of the pieces to dispose of later.

He was the only one who knew exactly where Varkas and the librarian had been. He sure as hell wasn't sharing it with Temple. It remained to be seen just how much he revealed to Karina. He'd have to think about that.

With the younger Temple out of the way, if he removed the elder one, he'd move up in the Knights. He wanted the power and the longevity that came from being in the upper echelons of the organization. And he had the skills to get what he wanted.

Riggs left the plane and hurried down the steps. "Have you put a tracker on it?" he asked one of his men. He fully expected to capture Varkas, but better safe than sorry.

"Yes, sir."

He nodded, expecting nothing less. These were all tough, highly-trained operatives. He'd handpicked them himself for this job. "Let's go. We need to follow the road and see where it leads us." And if he found the book and was able to capture Varkas, all the better for him.

He wasn't about to wait for Temple or Karina to call the shots. He wanted Varkas for himself.

Chapter Twenty-Seven

Darius was waiting by the door as Sarah finished putting on her boots. She was dressed again in her jeans and one of his shirts. She hadn't bothered putting on underwear, stating she wasn't wearing them again until they were washed.

Knowing that she was naked under her jeans was making it hard for him to concentrate.

She gathered her bag and slung it over her shoulder. "I'm ready. Do you have everything?"

"Yes." His knapsack had several changes of clothing. Sarah didn't know it, but he had a handgun and extra ammunition tucked in the front pocket as well. He wasn't anticipating trouble, but it paid to be prepared.

He opened the door but shut it just as quickly. "Someone is coming. I can hear footsteps."

Sarah glanced toward the window. "Maybe it's just a hiker."

He shook his head and dropped his knapsack to the floor. "There's more than one set of footsteps. I'd say there's at least a half dozen men, maybe more." He hated to frighten her, but she needed to know the truth. Plus, she'd more than proved she could handle herself in a crisis.

"What do you want me to do?" She set down her bag and clenched her fists by her sides. She was pale, but her shoulders were set with determination. He strode to a cabinet on the far wall. When he opened the door, it was empty. A quick tug on a hidden lever and the wall behind slid out of the way to reveal a weapons locker. "Can you shoot?"

"No. I've never fired a weapon before, but I can aim and pull a trigger."

He passed her a gun, checking to make sure it was loaded first. "Here's the safety. Make sure it's off before you fire, otherwise leave it on."

"Gotcha." She held it in her hand with the barrel pointing down.

"Never aim at anyone you're not willing to kill. Take your time when you squeeze the trigger and remember there will be some recoil." That was as much of a lesson as he had time for. "Hopefully, you won't have to use it." He grabbed a knife with a foot-long blade and tucked it into the waistband of his jeans. A knife was a much quieter way to kill a man than a gun.

There was a large stone fireplace in the middle of the far wall. Darius grabbed her free hand and dragged her toward it. He hadn't bothered lighting a fire, for which he was eternally grateful. Thankfully, the hearth was relatively clean. He kicked the logs out of the way and motioned to her. "Sit or crouch in there. If bullets start flying, it's the safest place for you. The stone is thick enough to stop just about anything."

"Where will you be?" Sarah knelt on the floor and crawled into the small space, getting as comfortable as she possibly could. It was a snug fit, but she sat with her back against one wall with her feet braced against the opposite one.

"Outside." When she started to protest, he leaned down

and kissed her. "I have to. I have to know who's out there. If it's the Knights, I can sneak around behind them and start picking them off one by one."

She grabbed his arm. "Be careful. Promise me you'll be careful."

"I promise." He kissed her again—a hard, quick one that left him wanting more. "I have a lot to live for." He left her curled up in the fireplace with only a single gun for protection, one she didn't really know how to use. No matter. He didn't plan on allowing anyone close enough to touch her.

Darius went into the bedroom, kicked aside the rug, and yanked up a trap door. If he thought he could manage it, he'd have snuck Sarah out this way, but the men outside were too close, and he couldn't risk her being hurt or killed.

He jumped down into the hole and hurried along the path that he'd gouged out of the earth decades ago. It wasn't a long tunnel, and he paused and listened before pushing open the hidden door at the other end. He was about ten yards from the house.

He was about to make his move when he realized his phone was in his pocket. He yanked it out and crushed it in his hand. He had to plan for the worst-case scenario. He couldn't allow the Knights to get their hands on Tarrant's number. Muttering a curse, he closed his hand around the electronic components and smashed his fist into the dirt wall of the tunnel. The earth gave way, and his fist went about three feet back. He opened his palm and released the pieces of the phone. Then he pulled his hand back out. The earth flowed back into the space. No one would be able to know by looking that there'd ever been a hole there.

Satisfied he'd done all he could to hide his phone, he listened. When he was sure there was no one nearby, he hauled himself out of the tunnel and slowly closed the door. No need to advertise the escape route. He might need a way to get back to Sarah.

He sniffed the air and quietly moved off to his right. It was time to go hunting.

• • •

Sarah shifted in the confined space of the fireplace, trying to discover a more comfortable way to sit. She didn't find it. She rested her right arm on her bent knee. The gun felt unnatural in her hand. And heavy, far heavier than she'd ever imagined one would be. She was grateful her injured fingers were on her left hand and not her right, or she'd never be able to use it.

"You can do this," she muttered. She'd never fired a weapon in her life, had never even considered killing another human being, but she'd do it if she had to in order to protect Darius from the Knights. No way was she going to allow them to capture him so they could drink his blood and perform experiments on him. Her vision had showed her what the Knights were capable of, what they'd done to that other poor drakon.

She forced herself to take a deep breath and then another. The cabin was quiet now that she was alone. She wasn't even sure how Darius had left. He hadn't used the front or back doors. He'd disappeared into the bedroom. The window maybe? Or another fancy hidden door? She had no idea and wasn't about to leave her hiding place to find out.

"He can take care of himself." He'd been outwitting the Knights for thousands of years. She, on the other hand, had been in this war for a matter of days. She wished she were tougher, one of those women who knew how to handle a weapon with ease. Darius would have been better off with a woman like that. Instead, he was stuck with a librarian.

If she survived this, she was determined to start working out, maybe take up martial arts or weapons training.

Who was she kidding? She hated exercise, unless it was walking or yoga. But she could learn to shoot. That was something she could do. It was good to have a goal.

Where was Darius? She wished she knew. The not knowing was worse. Time seemed to drag on. How long had he been gone? Realistically, she knew it was probably less than five minutes, instead of the five hours it felt like.

"Sarah Anderson?" The male voice startled her, and she almost answered before she caught herself. "I know you're in there."

He couldn't know. Not unless she gave herself away.

"It's Matthew Riggs. I don't know if you remember me or not."

She did. He was Herman Temple's head of security. She'd always found him cold and a little frightening.

"Mr. Temple is sorry you got caught up in this situation," he continued.

Sarah snorted. Situation. Is that what they called wanting to kidnap, experiment on, and potentially kill Darius? A situation? Her palm grew damp and she transferred the weapon to her other hand long enough to wipe her right one on the leg of her jeans. When this was over, she'd need more than new clothes, she'd need another shower.

"We only want to talk to Darius Varkas. I don't know what tall tales he's spun for you, but he's a danger to national security."

She had to give him props for trying. He was very convincing. If she didn't know better, she might actually believe his lies. She balanced her arm on her knee for support and braced the butt of the gun with her left hand like she'd seen them do on television. The extra support helped steady her aim. Then she thumbed the safety off the gun.

"If you come out, I can get you away from here," Riggs promised. "Take you home. You don't need to be a part of this.

You took something from Mr. Temple, and he wants it back. Return the book, and you can walk away from all of this."

She rested her head against the hard stone of the fireplace. It was too late for that. It was too late the moment she'd come to Herman Temple's attention, too late when she'd found the book. Whether she wanted to be or not, she was a part of this secret war. As strange as it was to admit, she wasn't sorry she was involved. She would never have met Darius otherwise, and she wouldn't change that for all the safety in the world.

When they got away from here and were safe once again, she wanted lasagna. Maybe French fries. And ice cream. Chocolate, too. Eating was her way of dealing with stress, and right now she was ravenous.

"You have ten seconds, Sarah. Then there's no going back."

She kept her lips sealed and started counting. She was at nine when she heard the scream. It was high-pitched but undeniably male. She knew it wasn't Darius.

A fierce gladness welled up inside her. As much as she didn't want anyone to die, it was their choice to be here. All they had to do was walk away and leave her and Darius alone.

Riggs shouted instructions. The front door burst open and a man came in low. He was dressed all in black with some kind of mask or hood covering his face. He was also holding a wicked-looking rifle in his hands. Sarah didn't stop to think. She steadied her arm, aimed the gun, and pulled the trigger.

The man dove to one side and returned fire. The bullets tore into the fireplace and shards of stone flew, gouging her skin in several places. She kept shooting, taking time to aim as best she could. The man was obviously a professional.

A roar shook the foundations of the cabin. Sarah almost smiled. Darius had shifted, and he wasn't happy from the sound of things.

"Parker, get out here," Riggs yelled.

The man who'd broken into the cabin quickly crawled to the door, using the cover of the sofa to block her view. She took another shot but missed, and then he was outside.

She knew she should stay where she was. Knew Darius would be angry with her if she didn't. But she couldn't stay hidden while he was fighting. She might not be the best shot in the world, but she might be able to be of some help.

Her muscles were cramped after being contorted into an unnatural position for so long, but she dragged herself out of the fireplace. Something dripped down her cheek and she swiped at it, not surprised to find blood. Her right arm hurt, too, but there was no time to bother with that now.

She crawled toward the living room window and snuck a look out of the corner of the glass. Five men circled Darius, their faces all showing fear but determination. She wondered how many of them had actually seen a drakon in his animal form before. Not many, if any. The Knights probably wouldn't want to share any knowledge with the men they deemed expendable.

Her brain was her best asset. She knew the leaders of the Knights would protect themselves with money, power, and men like these. They'd keep themselves safe until the dirty work was done and then would step in to claim the spoils.

Darius's tail whipped out and caught one man in the neck. It snapped and he fell to the ground. She'd seen him in his dragon form before, even seen him sparring with Tarrant, but she knew now that she'd never really seen him fight.

Her drakon was a brutally efficient fighting machine.

Gunfire rang out but was deflected off the thick scales that covered his body. Darius opened his mouth and flames roared out. One of the men caught fire and ran screaming into the woods. Sarah slapped her hand over her mouth so she wouldn't make a sound and distract him.

"This isn't working," one of the men yelled. "Why isn't he

running? Aren't they supposed to run?"

"Not anymore." Darius's voice was so low and guttural she almost didn't recognize it. "We left you alone, but no more." He flicked out his powerful tail and caught another man unawares. He cried out as he was thrown about fifty feet away and landed with a solid crack against the trunk of a tree. She knew he was dead before he hit the ground.

"Retreat," Riggs called. "Get back to the plane."

"Do you really think I'm going to let you escape?" Darius asked. His tone was calm, almost conversational. He was downright scary when he was like this.

"It's up to you." Riggs yanked a grenade off his belt and pulled the pin. "You can come after us or you can maybe save Sarah. What's it going to be?" Then he tossed the grenade through the open door.

She screamed and dove to the floor. The grenade rolled across the hardwood and came to a stop just inside the fireplace.

The explosion smashed her against the wall. The windows blew out, sending a shower of glass rocketing through the room. Fire roared, flashing outward from the point of impact. She dropped the gun and buried her face in her arms as the heat blasted over her.

She heard a roar but wasn't sure if it was the fire or Darius.

"Sarah." Strong arms lifted her and hurriedly carried her away. They didn't go out through the front door but toward the bedroom. Then they were somewhere dark and damp. Darius was moving quickly. A tunnel? She couldn't concentrate. Her ears were ringing and everything was a blur. The world whizzed by her at such a fast pace her stomach roiled and she was afraid she might throw up. She closed her eyes and tried to breathe deeply, but it hurt.

"Sarah. Don't close your eyes. Look at me."

She frowned at the fear in his voice. Were the Knights

still here? Was he in danger? It wasn't easy, but she forced her eyes open. Darius's chest gleamed with sweat and was marred with dirt and soot.

"Where?" She wanted to ask where they were going but could only manage one word. She was so weak. It was also hard to hear with her ears ringing.

"Almost to the plane. Stay with me."

He shouldn't be taking her there. Riggs and the others would expect that. "Not safe," she managed. She'd tried to yell, but it was more like a whisper.

"I'll keep you safe." A muscle in his jaw tightened. "I'll do a better job, I promise."

She knew he was blaming himself. "Not your fault," she got out before she started to cough. That quickly turned into a groan of pain. She hurt everywhere. She felt as though her entire body had been beaten.

She heard the roar of an engine and then Darius swore. "They're taking off. I don't know what they've done to our ride."

Darius burst across the runway and up the stairs of his plane. She tried to figure out why the stairs were already down. He took her to the back and gently laid her on the plush leather sofa.

She got her first good look at him. "You're naked." She didn't know why she was so surprised. She knew he'd shifted, which meant he'd either stripped or shredded his clothes.

He didn't smile. If anything he looked more worried. He grabbed a towel from the bathroom and pressed it against her cheek. "You're hurt. I don't know how badly."

Darius tried to be gentle as he checked her arms and legs, but she cried out several times as pain shot through her.

"I think your right arm is broken, but I can't be sure. I know it was grazed by a bullet." He carefully pressed against her stomach, and she gasped. "I don't know about internal injuries. I can't take you to a hospital. The Knights would find you within a couple hours, a day at the most."

She licked her lips and fear shot through her. "Am I going to die?"

"No!" He shook himself. "No, you're not going to die." He stood and strode away. She wished he'd stay with her. The world was getting darker by the second. She knew she might not make it, not without medical intervention, and she didn't want to die alone.

Then Darius was back carrying an empty glass and a knife. She frowned. How would an empty glass help? Her thoughts were totally muddled.

He sat on the floor next to her and set the glass beside him. He lifted the knife and casually cut his arm. Blood flowed. As she watched in shock, he caught the blood in the glass. The wound was already closing, but he managed to fill the glass half full.

Darius's expression was fierce as he eased one arm beneath her head and raised it. "Drink." He brought the glass to her lips. She shook her head and tried to pull away, but he wouldn't let her. "You have to. It's the only way to save you. Please, Sarah."

She stared up into his beloved face and was shocked to see tears in his eyes. Or maybe it was the tears in her own eyes making her see things. There was no way to be sure. "You can't leave me," he told her. "Drink. Please drink," he pleaded.

Even though the thought of drinking blood appalled her, she opened her mouth. He tipped the glass up slowly, and she forced herself to drink. She closed her eyes so she wouldn't have to see the thick red liquid. She swallowed and moaned. It didn't taste bad at all. In fact, it tasted rather good. She drank until there was no more.

She opened her eyes just in time to see him set the glass aside. "Give it a minute. It will help heal you," he promised.

Her body throbbed with pain, and the ringing in her ears hadn't quite stopped. She was afraid Darius was in for a disappointment. His blood didn't seem to be working on her.

Heat flashed through her entire body like a jolt of electricity. Her back involuntarily arched, and she groaned in pain as every internal organ felt as though it was on fire. Tears filled her eyes and spilled down her cheeks.

"Sarah." Darius lifted her onto his lap and leaned against the couch opposite the one she'd been lying on. He touched her face, pushing her hair out of her eyes. "It won't hurt for long. I'm sorry, baby, but you're so injured. So hurt."

Something landed on her face. It seemed wet at first, but then hard as it tumbled off her cheek. She couldn't process what was happening. All she could do was breathe through the pain. The fire inside her gradually eased until the warmth was almost comforting. She relaxed in his arms, only then realizing how tense she'd been.

"That's it," he crooned. "You're doing so well."

She reached up and stroked his cheek. A salty tear hit her thumb and then turned into a hard stone before rolling off and hitting the floor. "What's that?" She frowned as she tried to make sense of things.

A jolt of pure adrenaline surged through her, and she sat upright. "Whoa, that's some kick."

Darius laughed and hugged her tightly. "You'll get used to it."

"I will?"

He kissed her forehead, the tip of her nose and her cheeks. "You'll need my blood every now and again to stay young and healthy. It won't hurt like this again. You were so injured." He pulled back and scowled at her. "Why didn't you stay in the fireplace?"

"If I had I'd be dead. The grenade rolled to a stop just inside it."

He yanked her close and plastered her cheek against the heavy pounding of his heart. "I'm so glad you didn't listen to me."

She laughed. "Remember that in the future."

He eased her away and there was worry in his gaze. "Do we have a future? You saw what I did to those men, didn't you?"

She nodded. There could be nothing but truth between them. "I did. You did what you had to do."

"I killed two more in the woods before I shifted. I gutted them."

She flinched, but her gaze never left his. "I need to take shooting lessons."

His forehead creased and then cleared as he understood the meaning behind her words. "We can do that." He kissed her then, hard and fast. "God, Sarah, I love you."

"You do." She tried to scramble out of his arms so she could face him, but he wouldn't let her go. She was forced to look up at her drakon.

He lifted something off the floor and waited until she held out her hand before dropping it in her palm. She stared at a small piece of glass about the size of a dime. "Is that from where the cabin window was smashed?"

Darius jolted and then started to laugh. She could hear the loud booming noise clearly. Her ears no longer hurt, and the ringing had stopped. In fact, she felt great. Nothing hurt. Even her taped fingers felt normal. His blood had really healed her. She touched her forehead, and while there was dried blood there, the cut was gone. Her skin felt smooth and wasn't tender at all.

It really was a miracle.

As much as she loved to hear him laugh, she wanted to know what the joke was. She poked him in the shoulder. "What?"

Darius set her on the couch and proceeded to pick up about a dozen more pieces of glass. He handed them to her and closed her fingers around them. "They're not glass, love."

Her insides fluttered at the casual use of the endearment. Good God, he'd told her he loved her. "I love you." She had to say the words. She'd come close to losing him.

He kissed her closed hand. "I love you, too. As much as I'd like to stay with you, we need to get out of here. I don't know where the Knights are going or if they have backup nearby." He stood. "Stay here until I see if I can get the plane in the air, and then you can get cleaned up in the bathroom." He motioned to the two bags he'd somehow managed to snag on the way out of the cabin. "You can borrow some of my clothes."

"That's getting to be a habit."

"Don't worry, love, we'll get you some new clothes." He brushed his lips over the top of her head and started down the aisle to the cockpit.

"Darius." He turned and cocked an eyebrow in question. She held out her hand. "If this isn't glass, what is it?"

"Drakon's tears. All drakon tears are different, but one thing they have in common is they're extremely rare. A drakon cries for one reason only—because his heart is breaking. Fire drakons cry rubies, water drakons sapphires, and air drakons emeralds. But an earth drakon"—his voice grew husky—"an earth drakon cries diamonds." He turned and left.

She heard him swear seconds later. "What is it?" she called.

"Someone's been in the cockpit. There's what looks like pieces of a portable GPS on the floor. I didn't know the damn thing was here. I don't think they damaged anything else." The engines roared to life. At least they could get out of here before the Knights came back.

Sarah stared down at the small fortune she held in her

hand. Each rock was the size of a pea—maybe a bean would be a better estimate. No matter, these diamonds were priceless, and not because of their monetary value, but because of what they represented.

Darius loved her.

The plane taxied down the runway, and she hung on as it gained speed. It took off and rose steeply before finally leveling off. She carefully tucked the gems into her pocket. She'd have to get something to put them in, preferably find some way she could wear them.

She had no idea where they were going from here, but she was ready to stand and fight by her man's side. She went to the bathroom and caught a glimpse of her appearance and groaned. She looked like she'd been in an explosion. Her face was covered in dried blood and soot, and her clothes were tattered, burned, and torn.

In short, she was a mess.

But that didn't matter. Darius loved her, and she loved him, and they were safe, at least for the moment. She knew the Knights might have put a tracking device on the plane and knew Darius would have thought of that and would already be making plans.

Time to get cleaned up and go help him. She grabbed a towel, wet it from the tap, and began to scrub.

• • •

Riggs walked to the back of the plane. This conversation wasn't going to go well and he wanted privacy.

Thanks to the copilot's love of gadgets, Riggs had the information he needed. It would be interesting to see who or what was in the Cascade Mountains. But right now, he had a much bigger problem on his hands.

"Well?" The low, well-modulated female voice made his

entire body clench with desire.

"He was here but got away. The woman is either injured or dead."

"What about the book?"

He wished he knew why that book was so damn important. "Negative. Didn't see it. I'm not sure if they still have it."

Silence on the other end. It drew out, but he knew the value of silence too and was pleased when she broke first. "What are you doing now?"

"I lost several men. I've never fought one of them in their dragon form before."

"You saw him? You actually saw him?"

Riggs frowned. She sounded fearful but excited, almost turned on. "Yeah, I saw him. I put a tracker on his plane so we'll know where he lands. We'll get men in place as soon as we determine his location."

One of his men walked back to his seat. Since they knew better than to interrupt his call, it had to be important. "Hold on a second," he told Karina. "What is it?"

"Sir, the tracking device stopped sending a signal."

Riggs silently swore but outwardly gave no sign he was upset. "Work on it," he told his man. He took a deep breath and returned to his call. "You heard?"

"Yes. Varkas is proving to be rather resourceful. What are you going to do about it?"

"I know where he's been. I'm going to see if I can't find any clues to his whereabouts. In the meantime, my men will work on trying to get the tracker back online."

"What aren't you telling me, Matthew?"

He debated the pros and cons in a heartbeat and went with his gut. "They made a stopover in the Cascade Mountains. Probably just a safe house, another cabin like the one we found them in."

"Maybe. What are the coordinates?"

Riggs silently swore and gave them to her.

"I'll send a team to check out the area. As you said, it's probably nothing. You need to keep on Varkas's trail. I want him, Matthew."

"I'll get him for you."

"Do that and Christian's place within the Knights is yours."

"Fuck that, I want Herman's position." Riggs was through screwing around, through playing lackey.

Karina's laughter flowed over him like a drug. "Find Varkas and that can be arranged." She ended the call and Riggs tucked his phone into his pocket.

He strode to the front of the plane where his best tech guy was tapping away at his keyboard. "Anything?"

"Sir, I'm not sure why it's not working." There was frustration but also excitement in the man's voice. Riggs knew he lived for this tech stuff.

"Keep working."

"Yes, sir."

Riggs took one of the leather seats, closed his eyes, and could once again see the creature they'd fought. What must it be like to be one of them, to be invincible?

Not quite invincible, or the Knights would never have been able to capture any. Riggs knew private military suppliers who would wet themselves at the prospect of getting dragon DNA to work with. They'd pay whatever Riggs asked.

They'd want to create a serum that would allow a man to shift into a dragon, the perfect fighting machine.

If they were ever successful, Riggs was determined to be first in line.

Chapter Twenty-Eight

"Are we there yet?" she asked. Darius shot her a look, and she grinned at him. "I've always wanted to say that."

After ditching the plane, they'd travelled the back roads in a battered pickup before switching to a much newer truck in Chicago. They'd stopped long enough to buy a few things, but other than that, they'd kept moving. It was mind-boggling the amount of wealth Darius controlled to be able to have safe houses and vehicles stashed all over the country.

The window was down about two inches on his side, and the wind blew in through the opening, tousling his hair. They were in Maine, and she could smell the sea. With the gleam in his eye and one corner of his mouth kicked up in a half grin, he looked like the quintessential bad boy. And he was all hers.

She still couldn't quite believe he loved her, but the rare and precious diamonds nestled safely in the pocket of her jeans said otherwise.

"We're almost there."

"Is it safe to stay with Ezra?" The last thing she wanted to do was put one of Darius's brothers in danger.

"Ezra has his own island, and Tarrant set up his security system. No one can get on or off the island without him knowing."

"His own island?"

Darius nodded. "Ezra is even more reclusive than Tarrant. I'm a veritable social butterfly compared to those two."

Sarah laughed. She couldn't help herself. Hearing Darius call himself social when he was known as the reclusive billionaire was too funny. "What about your other brother? You called him Nic?"

"Nicodemus. He's not like the rest of us. He craves connection. Right now, he's in Vegas."

"Las Vegas?"

"Yup."

Wow, that brother really didn't fit with the others. "You're all close."

"We decided years ago that the best way to survive was to stick together. It hasn't always been easy. In case you hadn't noticed, we're all a bit opinionated and stubborn."

"No." She feigned surprise. "I never would have guessed."

"Smart-ass." He reached out and brushed his knuckles down her cheek. "We're here." He pulled the truck off the road.

"The Atlantic Ocean," she murmured. It was always a stirring sight to watch the waves crash against the shoreline.

Darius pointed to an island some distance away from the private dock where he'd parked. "That's where we're going."

"And how are we going to get there. There's no boat." She rolled her shoulders and stretched. "Unless you're planning on sprouting wings and flying."

He chuckled. "I could, but that probably wouldn't be wise." Darius put his arm around her and tucked her against his side. "Ezra already knows we're here." He raised his free hand and pointed. "See, here he comes."

A fancy speedboat cut through the waves, heading toward them. Darius gave her a squeeze and went back to the truck to gather their belongings. He set them by her feet before driving the truck into the nearby boathouse. Ezra was just pulling up to the dock when he returned.

His brother jumped out and secured the boat before striding toward him. Ezra threw his arms around Darius and gave him a bone-crushing hug. "Glad you're safe."

"Me, too." He thumped Ezra on the back and then released him. "This is Sarah." He reached out and pulled her against him. "Sarah, this is Ezra."

She stuck out her hand. "Nice to meet you." Ezra took her hand in greeting but didn't linger.

Then Darius narrowed his gaze and studied his brother. "What's wrong?" Darius demanded.

"Let's talk on the way." Ezra grabbed the two shopping bags and led the way back to the boat. Darius helped Sarah into the vessel and stored the rest of their belongings.

"What's going on?" Sarah demanded.

"I don't know but I'm about to find out."

• • •

Ezra released the lines and had them heading out to sea in no time. He stood with his hands on the wheel looking totally relaxed and at home, but there was a fine tension in his shoulders. "What happened?" Darius asked his brother.

"The priest is dead and someone was sniffing around Tarrant's place."

Darius swore, and Sarah gasped. "Is Tarrant okay?" she asked.

"He's physically fine. They didn't find anything beyond the cabin, but he's hurting over Father Simon." Ezra eased the wheel a little to the left and adjusted their course.

"How?" Darius demanded.

"Fire destroyed the church." Ezra spoke loudly to be heard over the wind that was whipping up. "But the priest had been shot. There were two more dead men on the scene as well."

"Fuck. Who?" Darius rubbed the back of his neck. This wasn't good. Sarah snaked her arm around her waist, offering him her support. Having her close helped him in ways she could never imagine.

"A local and an unidentified male. Tarrant hacked into the local police station to have a peek at the crime scene photos. He thinks the other body is Christian Temple."

"This is a total clusterfuck."

"Tell me about it." Ezra maneuvered the small craft into the dock, cut the engine, and quickly tied off the lines. "The local is most likely the man who drove you to see the priest. Tarrant figures he was approached by the Knights and paid to take them wherever you'd gone. We don't know what the priest told them. Tarrant insists the priest wouldn't talk, but they did find his cabin in the mountains."

Darius helped Sarah out of the boat. When she was steady on the dock, he grabbed their belongings. "That's not on the priest, that's on me. There was a portable aviation GPS on the plane. It must have belonged to the copilot. All they had to do was check the history to see where we'd been. I had no idea it was there. I was so worried about getting Sarah to safety, I never thought to warn Tarrant."

And that was unforgivable. He'd never before put the safety of another person above that of his brothers, but Sarah's well-being came before anything else. It had been instinct to do whatever it took to protect her.

"I screwed up."

"Tarrant is always on alert, so no harm done. The news that the priest didn't betray him will help him get through the death of his friend." Ezra stood in the center of the dock and spread his arms wide. "Welcome to my home."

. . .

Valeriya Azarov stopped outside her sister's office. Karina was on the phone…again. Her sister had arrived at her New York home with no notice. Very out of character. Then she'd demanded Valeriya's presence for dinner tonight.

Not for the first time, Valeriya wished she'd been born into another family. Hers had secrets. Lots and lots of secrets. And she wanted no part of them.

"Are you sure?" Karina's voice was brusque and cold, a sure sign she was speaking with someone she considered a subordinate. It was the tone she most often used with Valeriya. "You checked around the coordinates I gave you?" Her sister paused. "Fine. It was a long shot. Call Riggs and see if he needs you. I want Darius Varkas found."

Valeriya sucked in a breath and backed away from the door. A finely honed sense of self-preservation had her tiptoeing back to the top of the stairs. This time when she made her way down, she made sure her shoes clicked on the hardwood.

Karina stepped out her office and barely spared her a glance.

"Wait here." Karina crossed the gleaming floor and started up the staircase.

Valeriya went straight for her sister's office. There was nothing lying around, nothing in the garbage, but there was a small notepad on the corner of the desk.

Valeriya quickly found a pencil and lightly rubbed it over the paper. It wasn't words that formed, but numbers. She returned the pencil to its exact location and then ripped the paper from the pad. She folded it and started to tuck it into her purse.

She stopped, pulled down the neckline of her dress, and tucked the small piece of folded paper in her bra. She hurried back to the foyer, making it just as her sister started down the stairs.

"Come. We have dinner reservations," Karina informed her. "And I hate to be late."

Valeriya obediently followed her sister out of the house and into the waiting car. The security team was already in position. Two of them rode in the car with her and Karina. The other two were in a car following them.

Valeriya couldn't wait to have this family dinner over with so she could go back to her apartment and work. Her sister disapproved of her profession, but writing and illustrating children's books had allowed Valeriya to carve out a life for herself, away from her sister and her expectations. Most of all, she wanted to have a better look at what was on the piece of paper she had tucked in her bra.

"I'm surprised to see you in New York. You rarely leave Boston these days." Which was one of the reasons Valeriya lived here.

"Business," replied Karina. "But you're not interested in family business, are you?" It was a familiar argument, but one that still had the power to make Valeriya's stomach hurt.

"You know I'm not."

Karina nodded. The car stopped in front of a very exclusive and expensive restaurant. Valeriya would much rather have a burger than whatever overpriced gourmet food was served here.

Her sister paused just outside the establishment. "There may soon come a time when you'll have to get involved whether you want to or not. I've indulged your childish whims long enough. It's time to grow up and take your place among the Knights."

"No." She offered no explanations. She didn't owe her sister any. They'd been over this a thousand times in the past decade. "I have a life of my own, and I like it just fine."

"We'll see." Karina nodded to one of her men, and he pulled open the door of the restaurant.

Chapter Twenty-Nine

Ezra's home was simple but beautiful. Standing on about sixty acres, it was constructed of natural stone and thick logs and fit right into the landscape. He didn't have a secret bunker like Tarrant.

Sarah stood on the front veranda and stared out at the water. It was soothing to watch the waves roll in and smash upon the rocks before rolling out.

It was late but she wasn't sleepy. She'd slept for most of the drive here and was now wide awake and worrying.

Darius slid his arms around her waist and kissed the top of her head. "What are you thinking about?"

"The Knights and poor Father Simon. And Tarrant. This has to be hard on him." She leaned back against Darius's chest. He was so strong, reliable, dependable...and hers. "You should call him."

Darius pulled out the new phone that Ezra had given him and punched in the number. "I'll put it on speaker so you can hear."

She half turned in his arms, wanting to be able to see his

expression. His face was stoic, but she knew her man was hurting over the death of the priest.

"What?" Tarrant's voice was flat and curt.

"Father Simon didn't betray you." Leave it to Darius to go straight to the point. He was as delicate as a sledgehammer.

"I know," Tarrant fired back. "I don't know how those bastards found me, but it wasn't because of Father Simon."

Darius dragged his hand over his face. "Portable GPS on the plane, likely belonged to the copilot. He probably turned it on when they were prepping the plane, assuming he was going to be flying. I didn't notice it. That's on me."

"No. I should have told you to look for one. You're not the tech guy. I am."

Darius didn't want his brother taking the blame. "It's on the Knights. They have feelers out all over the country. The guy who drove us to see Father Simon betrayed him. As for North Dakota, it was just bad luck that someone contacted them about seeing the plane land there. I destroyed our phones and computers, but the portable GPS is on me. I didn't pay enough attention. I never imagined they'd find the plane."

Tarrant was silent for a long time. "I'm going to kill the motherfucker who murdered Father Simon."

Sarah shivered at the determination in his voice. This was a man ready to go to war.

"Then I'm going after the rest of the Knights," Tarrant continued. "I don't care if it takes me the remainder of my days. I've got plenty of time. If I can't destroy them, their children and grandchildren will pay for their crimes."

Darius looked as worried as she felt. "Tarrant—"

"No." Tarrant cut him off. "We've stayed out of their way. Tried to avoid them. What has that accomplished? Nothing. If we'd gone to war with them back when they first formed and wiped them all from the map, we wouldn't still be fighting them centuries later. They had their chance to walk away and didn't take it. I'm done."

The line went dead. "Tarrant," Darius shouted. "Damn it." He grabbed the phone and redialed the number, but no one answered.

"I'm sorry." She wished there was more to say, more she could do.

"Yeah, me, too." Tension vibrated from his large body, but he didn't move away from her. If anything, he moved closer.

Ezra pushed open the front door and joined them. Darius turned to his brother with her still in his arms. "You heard." It wasn't a question, but Ezra nodded.

"I did. I'm not sure what he'll do. He's known Father Simon for almost forty years. They were friends, and our brother does not make many friends."

"And you're a social butterfly living out here on your island." Darius heaved a sigh and kissed the top of Sarah's head. "I'm sorry, Ezra. That was uncalled for."

Ezra's turquoise-blue eyes were as turbulent as the sea that surrounded his home. His shoulder-length, dark brown hair was whipped away from his face by the wind. He looked more like Tarrant than Darius did, but all of them were big, strong men with wills of iron and an intellect that appealed to her.

"It's okay, bro. None of us are what you would call sociable, except for Nic." He turned his gaze out to the sea. "The water and her inhabitants are my friends. I understand them much better than I do humans."

Sarah sensed it was a huge deal that he'd opened his home to her. His brothers were always welcome, she knew that all the way to her bones, but having her here couldn't be easy for him. "Thank you for allowing me to stay. It won't be for long," she promised.

Ezra glanced at Darius before reaching out to cup her face in his big hand. "You're welcome here for as long as you wish to stay," he told her. The sincerity of his offer couldn't be denied, and it touched her deeply.

"Thank you."

"Your room is the one to the right at the top of the stairs." Then Ezra walked down the porch stairs and headed for the beach.

"Where are you going?" she asked. She didn't like the idea that her presence here was driving him from his own home.

"Swimming," he called back.

"He's kidding, isn't he?" It was October, and the water had to be freezing.

Darius shook his head. "No, he's not kidding. He swims all winter long." He led her toward the door, but she glanced over her shoulder one final time. "He's not human," Darius reminded her. "He'll be fine. He's more at home in the water than he is on land."

"Right. Water drakon. That makes sense." And that was more than she could wrap her poor beleaguered brain around. She'd been forced to rethink everything she thought she knew about life in the past week.

Darius shut the door behind them and tugged her toward the stairs. "Still not tired," she reminded him.

The smile he gave her was filled with sexual promise. "I know."

"Darius." His name was a breathy whisper on her lips.

"I love you," he told her.

Tears welled in her eyes, and she placed her hand over his heart. "I love you, too."

"Forever."

"For as long as we have."

He growled his displeasure. "Forever," he insisted.

She sighed and nodded. "Forever."

She knew the war wouldn't wait, that the world was just

outside the door, threatening what they'd found between them, but she wouldn't let it intrude. Not on this special moment between them.

"I'm so glad I found you." She smiled and patted his cheek.

"Sarah, I was lost and didn't even know it."

Her heart skipped a beat. Her drakon might be blunt and matter-of-fact most of the time, but there were moments like these when he was so poignant he broke her heart.

"So was I," she assured him. She had no idea what their life would be like, or even how long they'd live, but she'd take whatever she could get.

Epilogue

Valeriya stared at the piece of paper she'd taken from her sister's office. It had been two days since she'd had dinner with Karina, but the paper kept haunting her. The numbers weren't right for a bank account. Nor were they a phone number.

She dropped the paper onto her sofa and wandered over to stare out the window. Manhattan was spectacular at night. She loved it here, but she missed the forest that surrounded the family home in upper New York state. Karina rarely went home, and neither did she. It was too empty without her parents there. Too many memories.

She was lucky to have this apartment. It had belonged to her father's parents and they'd left it to her when they'd passed. She'd spent more time with them than Karina had. She'd always felt her sister didn't like them very much, looked down on them because they were content to live their lives without getting involved with the Knights—unlike her mother's parents, who'd both been active in the Knights until they'd died of carbon monoxide poisoning in their home. An unfortunate accident, the investigation had determined. She wasn't so sure.

Valeriya's office was perfect for her. The tall windows gave her plenty of natural sunlight to work by, and the view was stunning, day or night. The huge desk had belonged to her grandfather, but the bright blue sofa was all her. She had an easel set up in one corner, where she often painted or sketched. When she was working on a book, she used both traditional methods of illustration and her computer.

She was grateful to be able to make a living doing something she loved. She knew she owed that to her grandparents. Along with the apartment, they'd left her a small inheritance, enough for her to get by on as long as she was frugal. She'd run as soon as she was old enough to leave home, coming here and forging a life for herself.

But Karina wasn't going to leave her alone for much longer. Valeriya knew it in her gut.

She went back to the sofa and picked up the piece of paper. She had to know what these numbers were. Maybe it was nothing, but she sensed they were important.

Karina was looking for someone. That was evident from the phone calls Valeriya had overheard in the short time they'd been together. Coordinates maybe. She went to her desk, pulled up a search engine, and plugged the numbers into it.

"Gotcha." A map popped up and she clicked on it. "The Cascade Mountains in Washington State." She'd been thinking about a new children's series set in the forest. If anyone asked about her trip, she'd tell them she was going to do some research.

It didn't take her long to book a flight online and pack her bag. She might live in the city, but she did have a few outdoor skills. She was no experienced hiker, but she could get by, at least enough to check out the coordinates. She'd probably find nothing, but if the person Karina was searching for was still around, Valeriya could at least warn them.

She loved her sister, but she'd never understand her lust for power and vengeance. Valeriya wanted no part of it, but she couldn't sit back and do nothing and allow her sister to hurt an innocent man. And it was a man. What was it Karina had said? "I want him found." She'd said his name, too. Valeriya tried her best to remember. "Varkas. Darius Varkas," she repeated. She wondered who he was and how he was connected to her older sister's mad schemes.

Valeriya slung her purse, which doubled as a laptop case, over her shoulder and grabbed the handle of her suitcase. She had three hours before her flight took off. Time enough to get to the airport, check in, and get through security, as long as traffic wasn't too heavy.

She glanced over her shoulder as she closed the door to her home. The urge to run back inside and lock the door almost overwhelmed her. "It's just a quick jaunt to the West Coast," she assured herself. "I'll be there and back in a couple of days."

Still, a cold shiver snaked down her spine as she locked the door and headed for the elevator. Whoever her sister was searching for was probably long gone. She'd take some pictures, do some research, and come home with a clear conscience and plenty of inspiration for her new children's series.

The elevator door pinged and she stepped inside. The door closed and she hit the button for the lobby. This was a quick trip, nothing more.

Acknowledgments

Thank you to Heidi Moore for encouraging me to submit to Entangled Publishing. I love working with you!

Thank you to Liz Pelletier and everyone at Entangled for making me feel so welcome. I'm looking forward to working with you all for many more years to come.

About the Author

N.J. Walters is a *New York Times* and *USA Today* bestselling author who has always been a voracious reader, and now she spends her days writing novels of her own. Vampires, werewolves, dragons, time-travelers, seductive handymen, and next-door neighbors with smoldering good looks—all vie for her attention. It's a tough life, but someone's got to live it.

www.njwalters.com

Discover more Entangled Select Otherworld titles...

The Werewolf Wears Prada
a *San Francisco Wolf Pack* novel by Kristin Miller

Melina Rosenthal worships at the altar of all things fashion. Her dream is to work for the crème de la crème fashion magazine, *Eclipse*, and she'll do pretty much anything to get there. Even fixing up the image of a gorgeous, sexy public figure who's all playboy, all the time. Even if he's the guy who broke her heart a year ago. And even if Melina has no idea that Hayden Dean is actually a werewolf...

Flying Through Fire
a *Dark Desires* novel by Nina Croft

Thorne's willpower has been honed over ten thousand years. He might want Candy, but the last thing he needs is an infatuation with a young, impetuous werewolf. Candy makes him lose control, and that could have disastrous consequences. As the threat escalates and they become separated by time and space, Candy must find a way back to him, because while Thorne alone has the power to defeat the dragons, only together can they finally bring peace to the universe.

THE HUNT
a *Shifter Origins* novel by Harper A. Brooks

Prince Kael has just lost his father to an assassin, and he's the next target. A murderer is on the loose, the kingdom is in disarray, and Kael is determined to make the person responsible for killing his father pay. But falling for the beautiful Cara, panther-shifter assassin and main suspect his father's murder, wasn't part of the plan. He's not at all sure she did it, and he finds himself going against everything he's ever known just to claim her.

QUANTUM
a novel by Jess Anastasi

Someone wants Captain Admiral Zander Graydon dead. Like yesterday. Zander's convinced his attractive assistant knows more than she's willing to say, and if he can stop running long enough, he'll find out exactly what she's hiding. Lieutenant Marshal Mae Petros is determined to keep her CO safe. Before she tips her hand, however, Mae has to figure out if the alluring man she's protecting is the real Captain Admiral Graydon. Or an alien shape shifting imposter.

Made in the USA
Coppell, TX
22 August 2022

81885400R00204